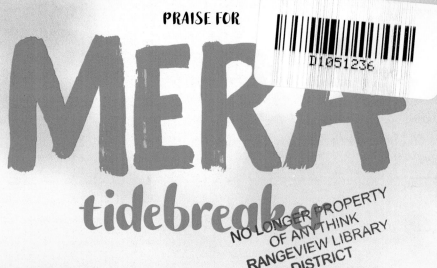

MERA

tidebreaker

"**MERA: TIDEBREAKER** *will pull readers through the waves and down into an immersive world full of intrigue, heroism, and romance. This royally enchanting origin story will captivate you until the very last page and leave you questioning what you'd do if you had to pick between love and duty. A must-read!*"

—Sasha Alsberg, *New York Times* bestselling author of *Zenith*

"**MERA: TIDEBREAKER** *offers a riveting new portrayal of the ocean's fiercest princess. With her passion, strength, and willfulness, Mera is sure to capture the hearts of both long-time readers and those who are discovering Atlantis for the first time.*"

—Marissa Meyer, #1 *New York Times* bestselling author of *The Lunar Chronicles*

•••••••••••••◉•••••••••••••

Mera is teenage royalty and heir to the throne of Xebel, a colony ruled by the other not-so-lost land under the sea, Atlantis. Her father, his court, and the entire kingdom are expecting her to marry and introduce a new king. But Mera is destined to wear a different crown...

When the Xebellian military plots to overthrow Atlantis and break free of its oppressive regime, Mera seizes the opportunity to take control of her own destiny by assassinating Arthur Curry—the long-lost prince and heir to the kingdom of Atlantis. But her mission gets sidetracked when Mera and Arthur unexpectedly fall in love. Will Arthur Curry be the king at Mera's side, or will he die under her blade as she attempts to free her people from persecution?

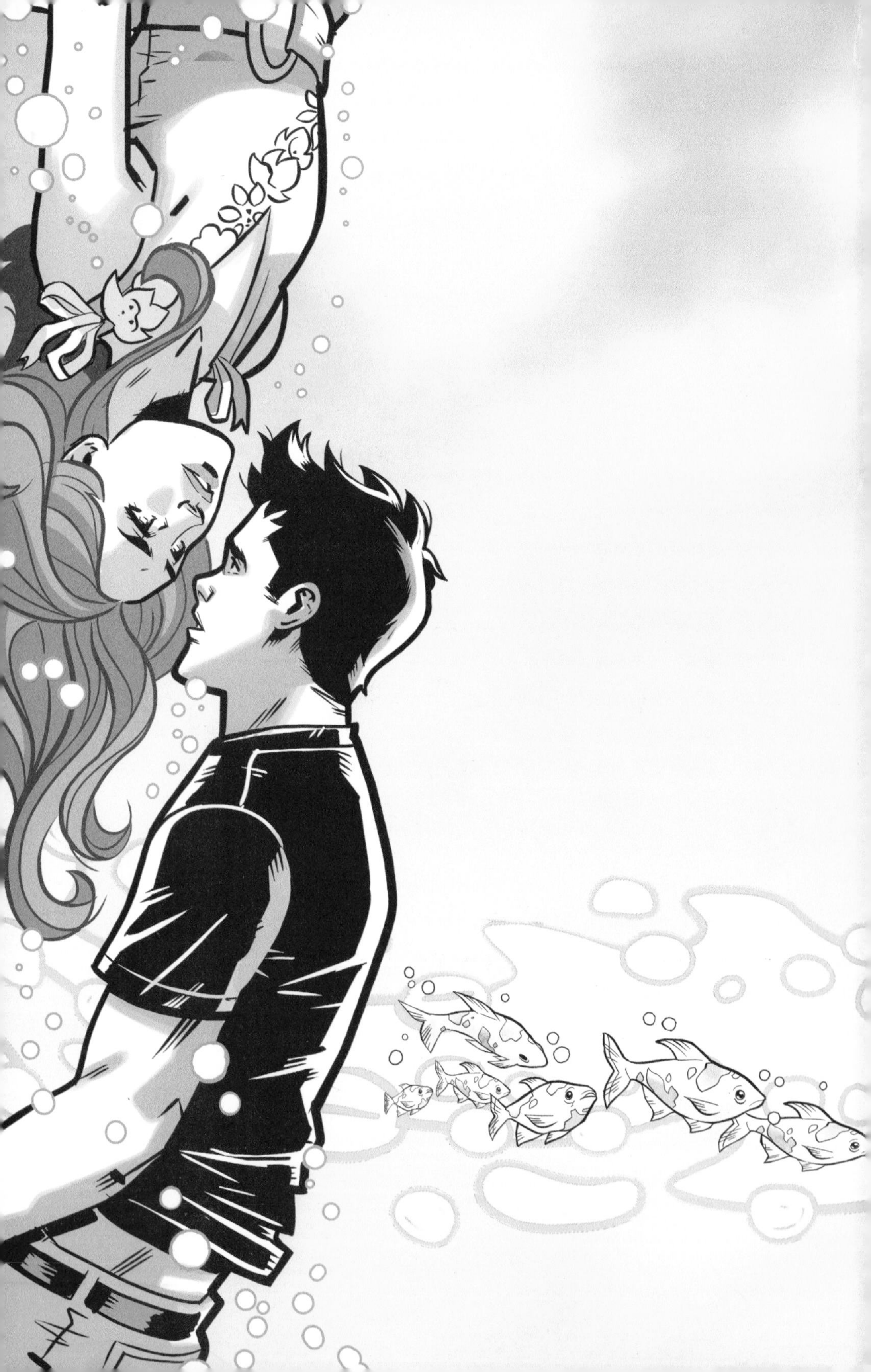

MERA

tidebreaker

WRITTEN BY

danielle paige

ILLUSTRATED BY

stephen byrne

COLORIST

david calderon

LETTERER

joshua reed

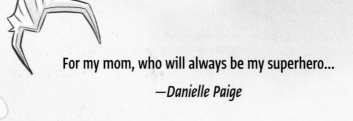

For my mom, who will always be my superhero...
—*Danielle Paige*

For Gaye and Martin, who gave me everything.
—*Stephen Byrne*

When I was young I fell in love with so many superheroes, but even though I wanted to be a writer I never once imagined writing them. They were as iconic as Wonder Woman and as far away as Krypton. They were glorious and immortal and untouchable. I thought my place was happily turning the pages or watching the big or small screen where the Dark Knight rose and fell and Superman soared. I never dreamed of writing a comic or graphic novel; I saw myself as a reader or a watcher. A spectator.

I grew up to write for television and books, writing in other creators' worlds and creating my own. And I watched and fangirled as the DC Universe expanded to become an even larger part of our culture. And when DC asked me to write MERA: TIDEBREAKER for their new young adult line, DC Ink, I was beyond ecstatic. I was getting invited to play in the epic, amazing sandbox I'd watched my whole life.

Before I started writing this book I thought a lot about what it means to be a hero—and what it means to be a teen.

No one, not even Superman, is born a hero—he or she has to figure out how. Finding one's power and what to do with it is at the heart of most comics and at the heart of most stories about young people.

Getting to write the part where Mera is figuring it out—who she is, what and who she wants, what the truth is, and what she is truly capable of (both as a teen and as a potential hero)—is what I hoped to capture when writing MERA: TIDEBREAKER.

I adored writing my version of Mera's story. And I am so thrilled to get to show (for those who don't yet know) that she is so much more than Aquaman's great love. From page one, Mera is a fighter...but she has to figure out what to fight for.

Whether you're 14 or 80, I hope when you read MERA and the other amazing titles in this line, you find your "superpowers." I want you to know what I didn't always know: that you are capable of more than you think. You can be a hero, too.

I am thrilled that MERA: TIDEBREAKER is kicking off DC Ink. And I am so happy to have found a place within the DC family.

Danielle Paige

DANIELLE PAIGE

BEN ABERNATHY &
MICHELE R. WELLS Editors

STEVE COOK Design Director - Books

AMIE BROCKWAY-METCALF Publication Design

BOB HARRAS Senior VP - Editor-in-Chief, DC Comics

BOBBIE CHASE VP & Executive Editor, Young Reader & Talent Development

DAN DiDIO Publisher

JIM LEE Publisher & Chief Creative Officer

AMIT DESAI Executive VP - Business & Marketing Strategy,
Direct to Consumer & Global Franchise Management

MARK CHIARELLO Senior VP - Art, Design & Collected Editions

JOHN CUNNINGHAM Senior VP - Sales & Trade Marketing

BRIAR DARDEN VP - Business Affairs

ANNE DePIES Senior VP - Business Strategy, Finance & Administration

DON FALLETTI VP - Manufacturing Operations

LAWRENCE GANEM VP - Editorial Administration & Talent Relations

ALISON GILL Senior VP - Manufacturing & Operations

JASON GREENBERG VP - Business Strategy & Finance

HANK KANALZ Senior VP - Editorial Strategy & Administration

JAY KOGAN Senior VP - Legal Affairs

NICK J. NAPOLITANO VP - Manufacturing Administration

LISETTE OSTERLOH VP - Digital Marketing & Events

EDDIE SCANNELL VP - Consumer Marketing

COURTNEY SIMMONS Senior VP - Publicity & Communications

JIM (SKI) SOKOLOWSKI VP - Comic Book Specialty Sales & Trade Marketing

NANCY SPEARS VP - Mass, Book, Digital Sales & Trade Marketing

DC Comics, 2900 West Alameda Ave., Burbank, CA 91505
Printed by LSC Communications, Crawfordsville, IN, USA.
2/22/19. First Printing.
ISBN: 978-1-4012-8339-1

PEFC Certified
This product is from sustainably managed forests and controlled sources
PEFC
PEFC/29-31-337   www.pefc.org

Library of Congress Cataloging-in-Publication Data

Names: Paige, Danielle (Novelist), writer. | Byrne, Stephen (Comic book artist), illustrator.
Title: Mera : tidebreaker / written by Danielle Paige ; illustrated by Stephen Byrne.
Description: Burbank, CA : DC Ink, [2019] | Summary: "Princess Mera is teenage royalty and heir to the throne of Xebel, a penal colony ruled by the other no-so-lost land under the sea, Atlantis. Her father, his court and the entire kingdom are expecting her to marry and introduce a new king, but Mera is destined to wear a different crown. When the Xebellian military plots to overthrow Atlantis and break free of its oppressive regime, Mera seizes the opportunity to take control over her own destiny by assassinating Arthur Curry--the long-lost prince and heir to the kingdom of Atlantis. But her mission gets sidetracked when Mera and Arthur unexpectedly fall in love. Will Arthur Curry be the king at Mera's side, or will he die under her blade as she attempts to free her people from persecution?"-- Provided by publisher.
Identifiers: LCCN 2018043960 | ISBN 9781401283391 (paperback)
Subjects: LCSH: Graphic novels. | CYAC: Graphic novels. | BISAC: JUVENILE FICTION / Comics & Graphic Novels / Superheroes. | JUVENILE FICTION / Comics & Graphic Novels / Media Tie-In.
Classification: LCC PZ7.7.P15 Me 2019 | DDC 741.5/973--dc23

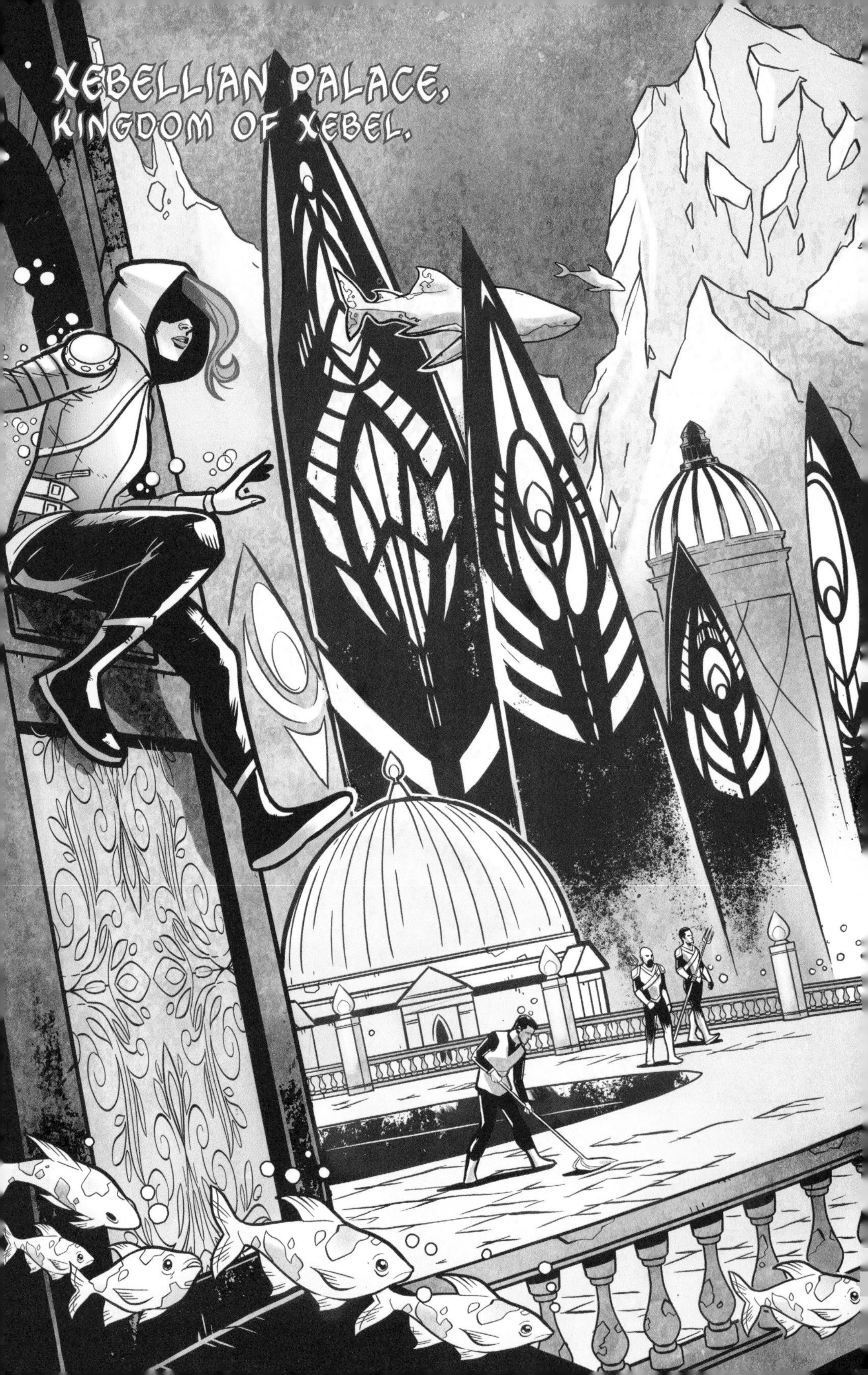
XEBELLIAN PALACE,
KINGDOM OF XEBEL.

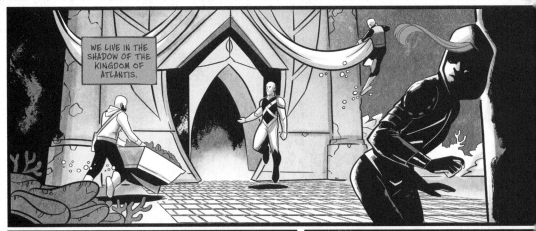

WE LIVE IN THE SHADOW OF THE KINGDOM OF ATLANTIS.

WE LIVE, WE PLAY, WE SURVIVE IN THE DARK.

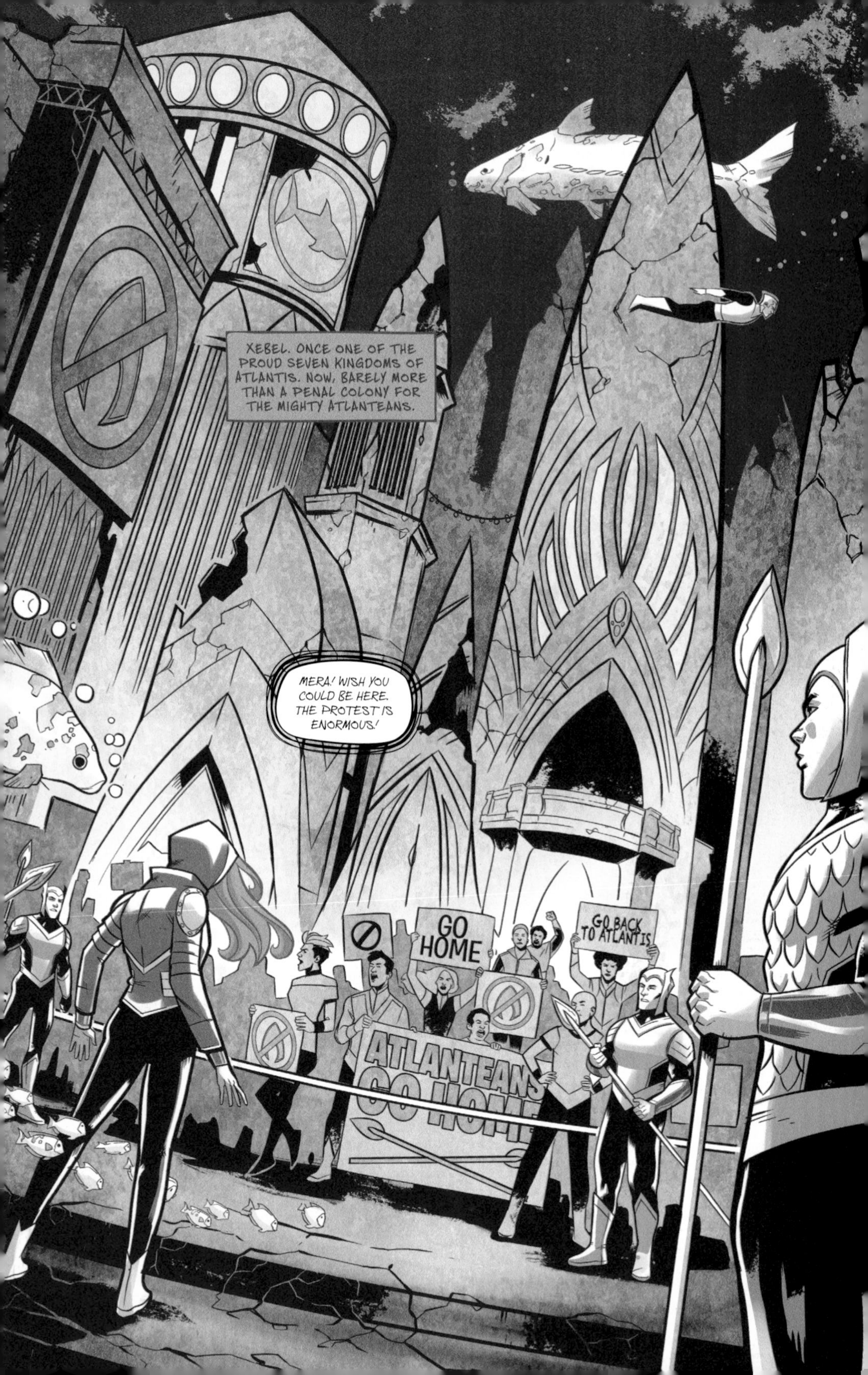
XEBEL. ONCE ONE OF THE PROUD SEVEN KINGDOMS OF ATLANTIS. NOW, BARELY MORE THAN A PENAL COLONY FOR THE MIGHTY ATLANTEANS.
MERA! WISH YOU COULD BE HERE. THE PROTEST IS ENORMOUS!
GO HOME
GO BACK TO ATLANTIS
ATLANTEANS GO HOME

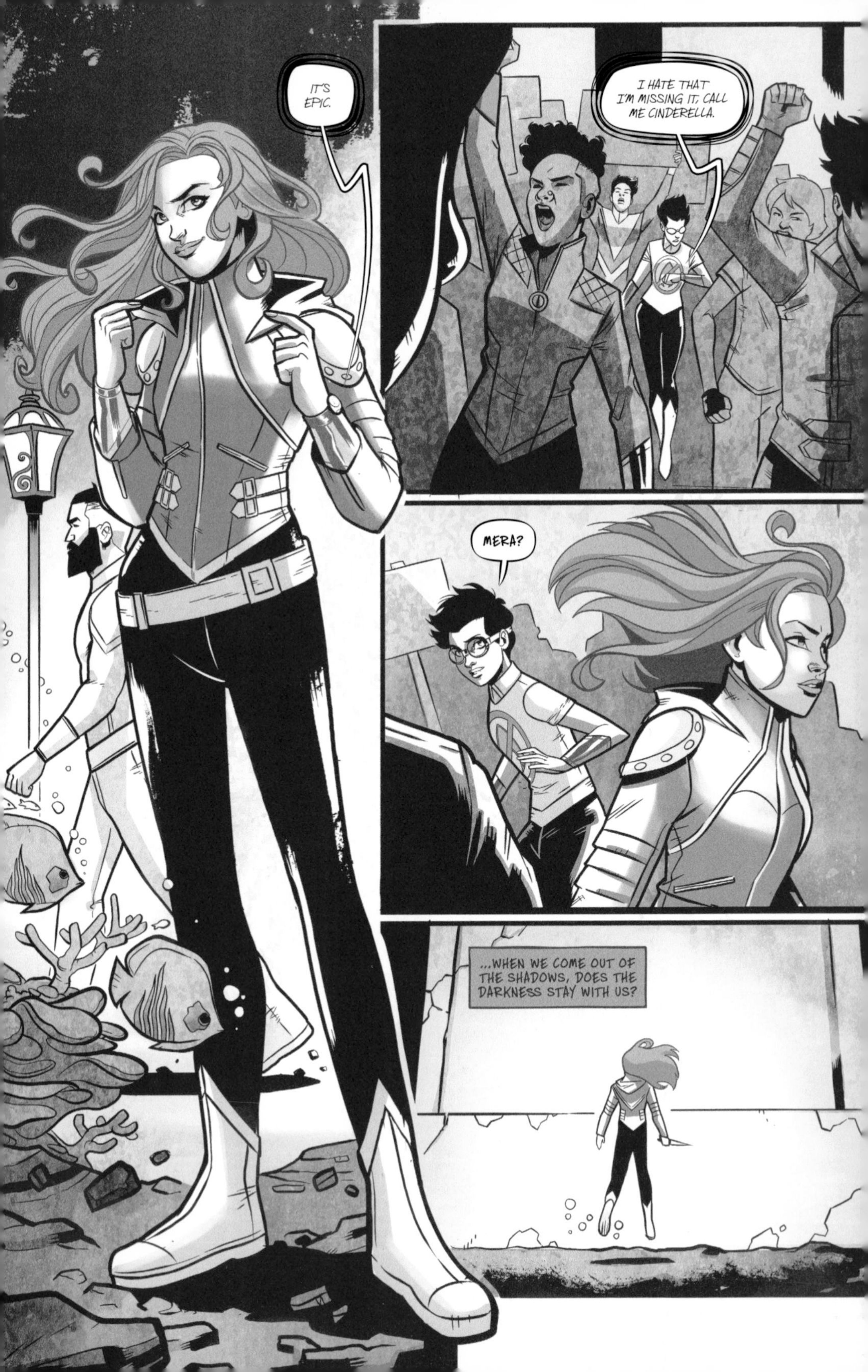
IT'S EPIC.
I HATE THAT I'M MISSING IT, CALL ME CINDERELLA.
MERA?
...WHEN WE COME OUT OF THE SHADOWS, DOES THE DARKNESS STAY WITH US?

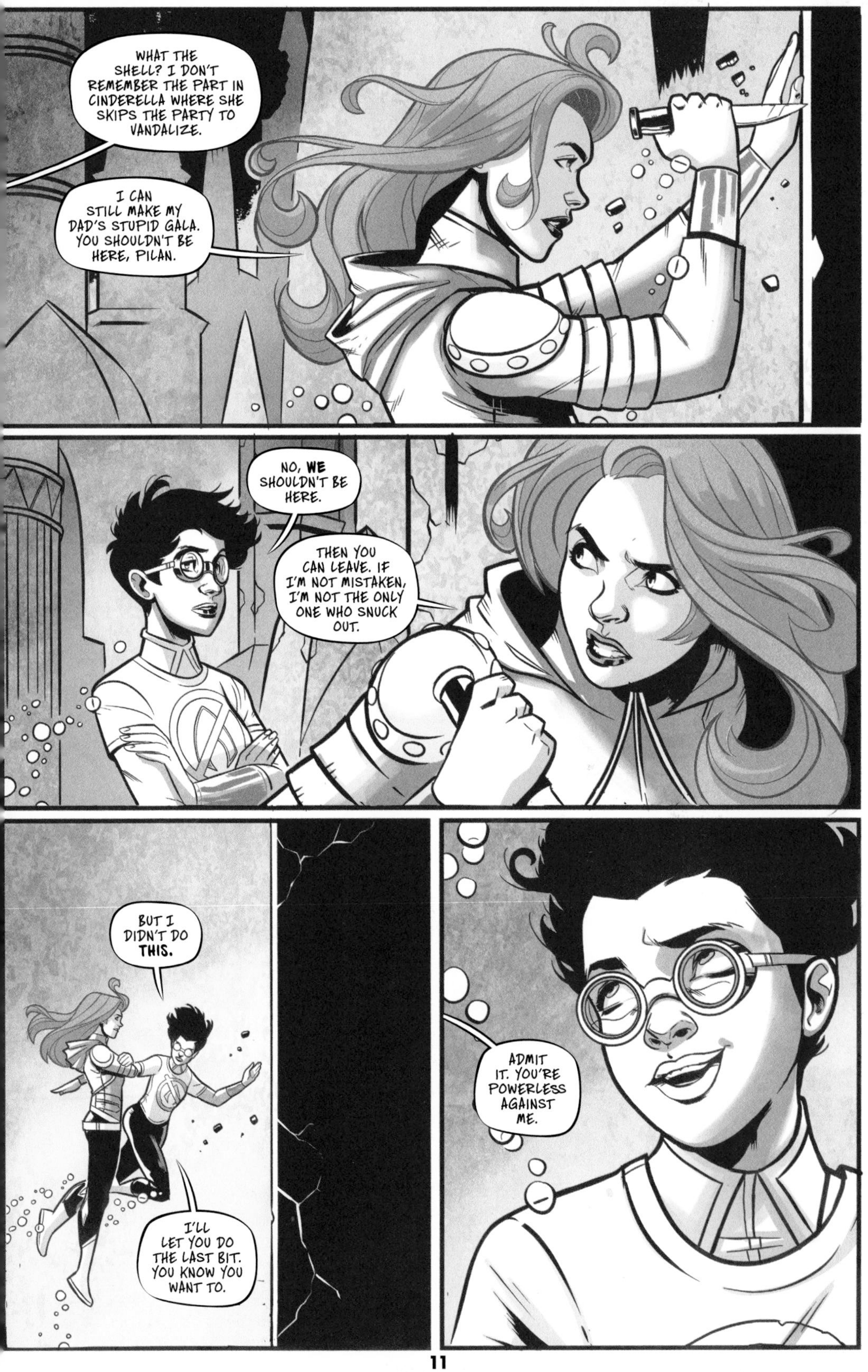
WHAT THE SHELL? I DON'T REMEMBER THE PART IN CINDERELLA WHERE SHE SKIPS THE PARTY TO VANDALIZE.
I CAN STILL MAKE MY DAD'S STUPID GALA. YOU SHOULDN'T BE HERE, PILAN.
NO, WE SHOULDN'T BE HERE.
THEN YOU CAN LEAVE. IF I'M NOT MISTAKEN, I'M NOT THE ONLY ONE WHO SNUCK OUT.
BUT I DIDN'T DO THIS.
I'LL LET YOU DO THE LAST BIT. YOU KNOW YOU WANT TO.
ADMIT IT. YOU'RE POWERLESS AGAINST ME.

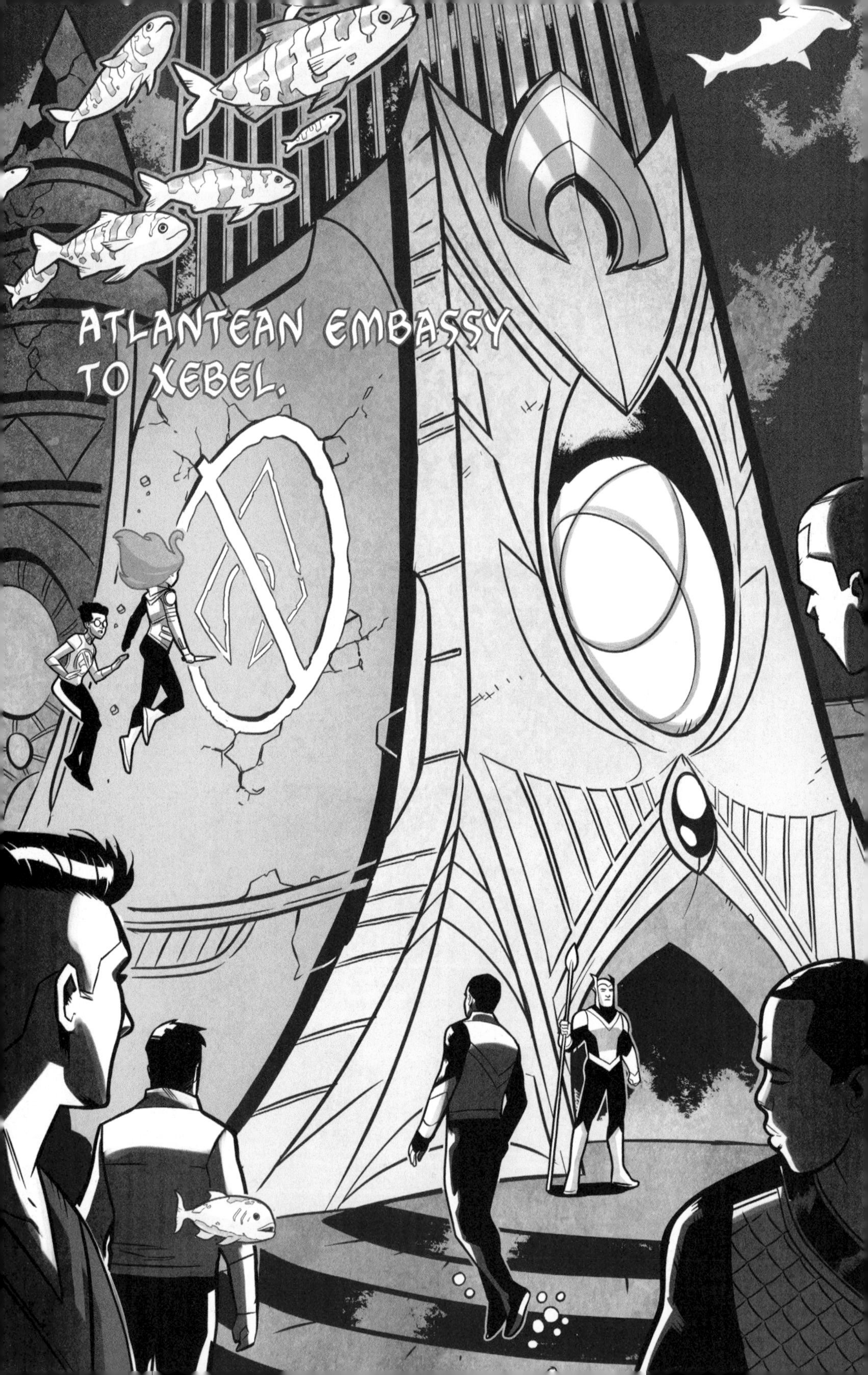
ATLANTEAN EMBASSY TO XEBEL.

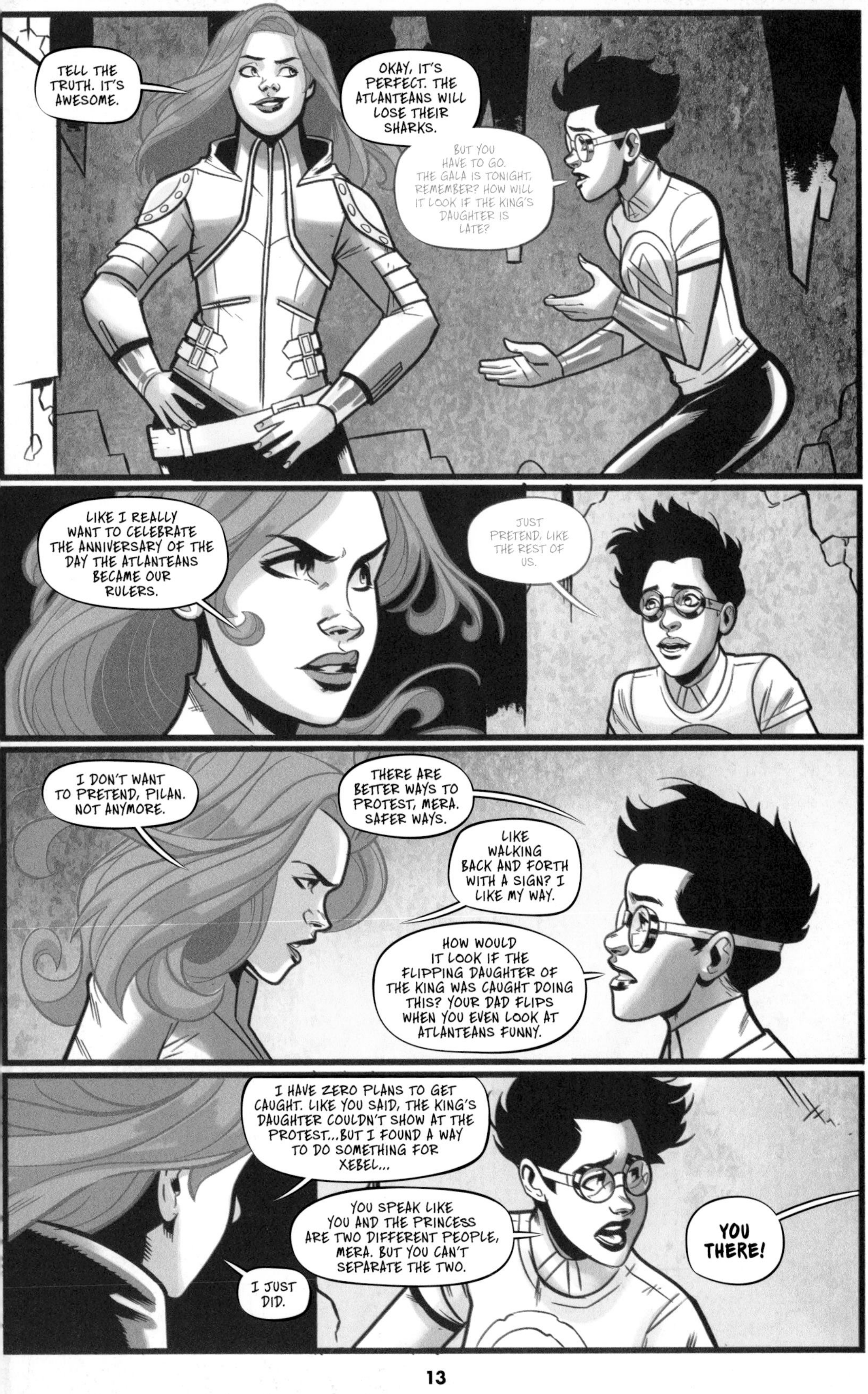
TELL THE TRUTH. IT'S AWESOME.
OKAY, IT'S PERFECT. THE ATLANTEANS WILL LOSE THEIR SHARKS.
BUT YOU HAVE TO GO. THE GALA IS TONIGHT, REMEMBER? HOW WILL IT LOOK IF THE KING'S DAUGHTER IS LATE?
LIKE I REALLY WANT TO CELEBRATE THE ANNIVERSARY OF THE DAY THE ATLANTEANS BECAME OUR RULERS.
JUST PRETEND, LIKE THE REST OF US.
I DON'T WANT TO PRETEND, PILAN. NOT ANYMORE.
THERE ARE BETTER WAYS TO PROTEST, MERA. SAFER WAYS.
LIKE WALKING BACK AND FORTH WITH A SIGN? I LIKE MY WAY.
HOW WOULD IT LOOK IF THE FLIPPING DAUGHTER OF THE KING WAS CAUGHT DOING THIS? YOUR DAD FLIPS WHEN YOU EVEN LOOK AT ATLANTEANS FUNNY.
I HAVE ZERO PLANS TO GET CAUGHT. LIKE YOU SAID, THE KING'S DAUGHTER COULDN'T SHOW AT THE PROTEST...BUT I FOUND A WAY TO DO SOMETHING FOR XEBEL...
YOU SPEAK LIKE YOU AND THE PRINCESS ARE TWO DIFFERENT PEOPLE, MERA. BUT YOU CAN'T SEPARATE THE TWO.
I JUST DID.
YOU THERE!

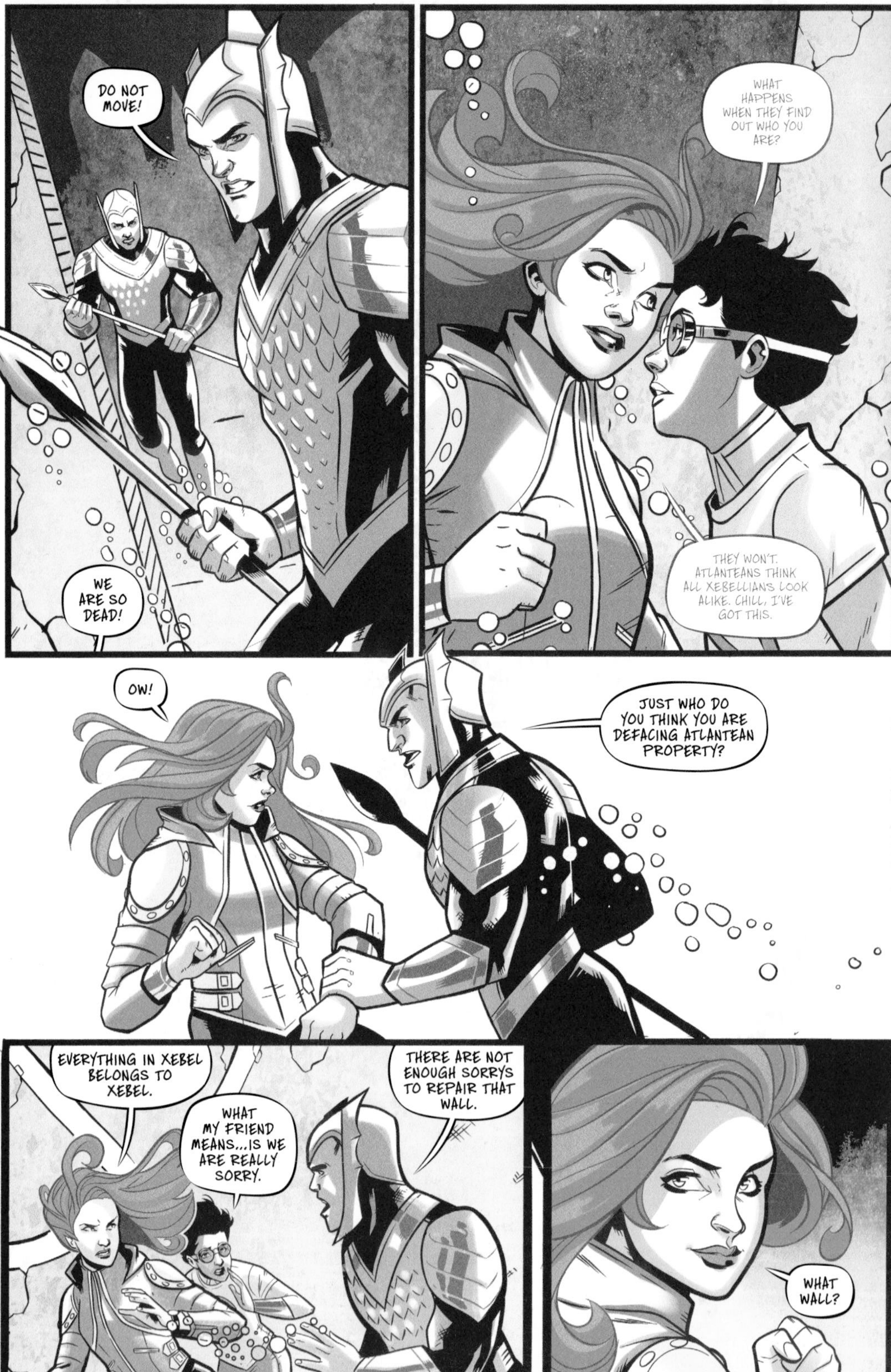

DO NOT MOVE!
WE ARE SO DEAD!
WHAT HAPPENS WHEN THEY FIND OUT WHO YOU ARE?
THEY WON'T. ATLANTEANS THINK ALL XEBELLIANS LOOK ALIKE. CHILL, I'VE GOT THIS.
OW!
JUST WHO DO YOU THINK YOU ARE DEFACING ATLANTEAN PROPERTY?
EVERYTHING IN XEBEL BELONGS TO XEBEL.
WHAT MY FRIEND MEANS...IS WE ARE REALLY SORRY.
THERE ARE NOT ENOUGH SORRYS TO REPAIR THAT WALL.
WHAT WALL?

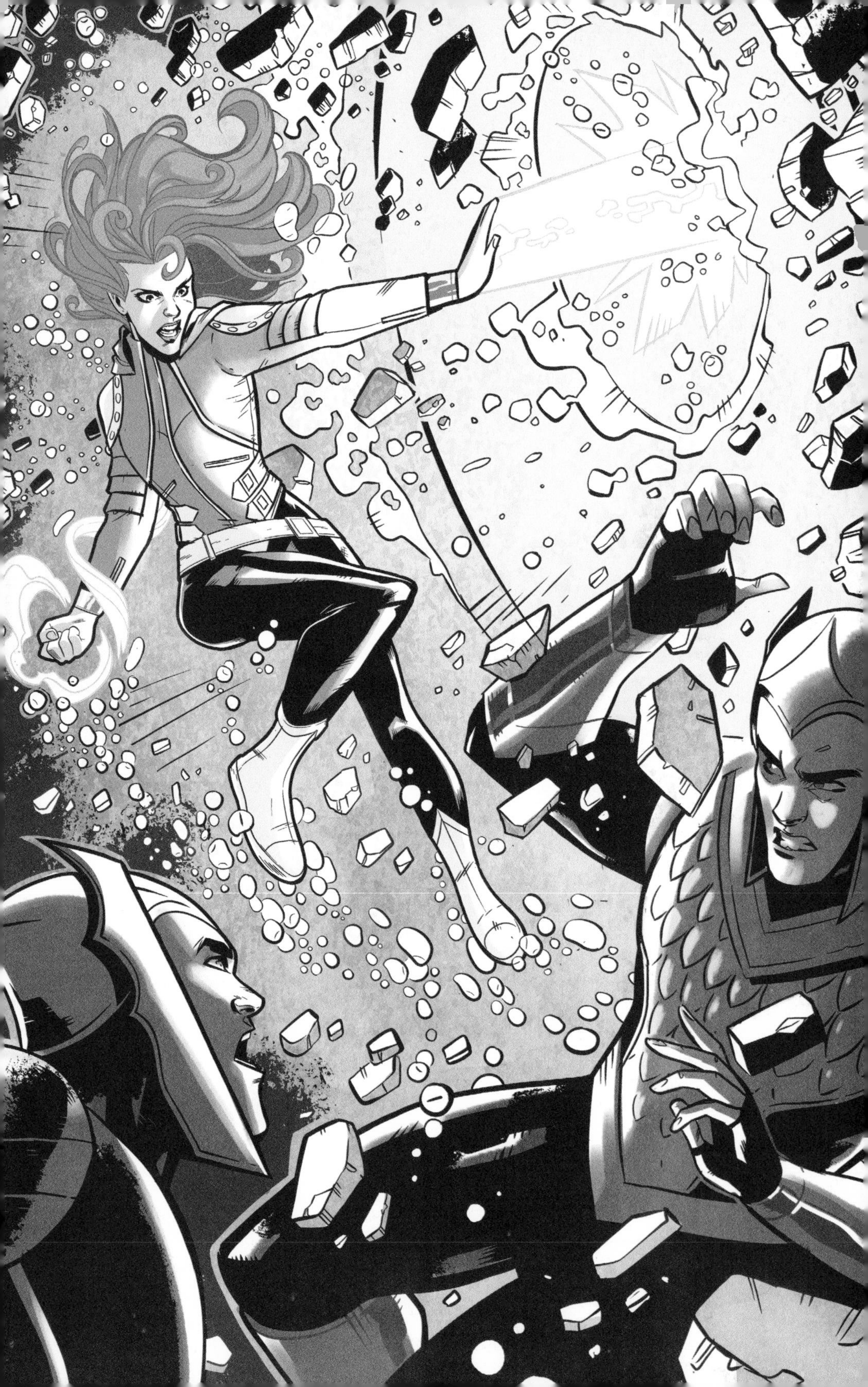

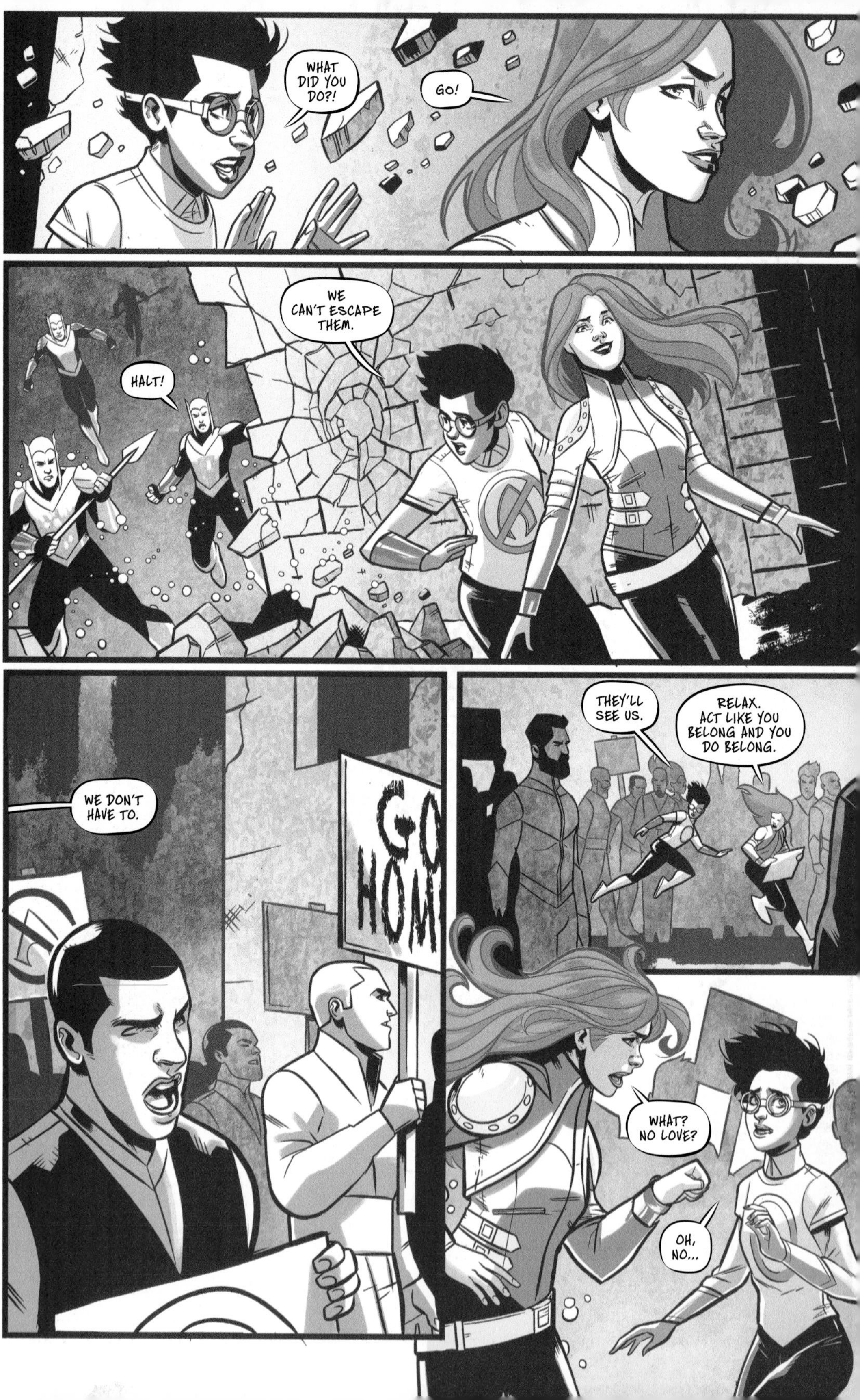
WHAT DID YOU DO?!
GO!
WE CAN'T ESCAPE THEM.
HALT!
WE DON'T HAVE TO.
GO HOM
THEY'LL SEE US.
RELAX. ACT LIKE YOU BELONG AND YOU DO BELONG.
WHAT? NO LOVE?
OH, NO...

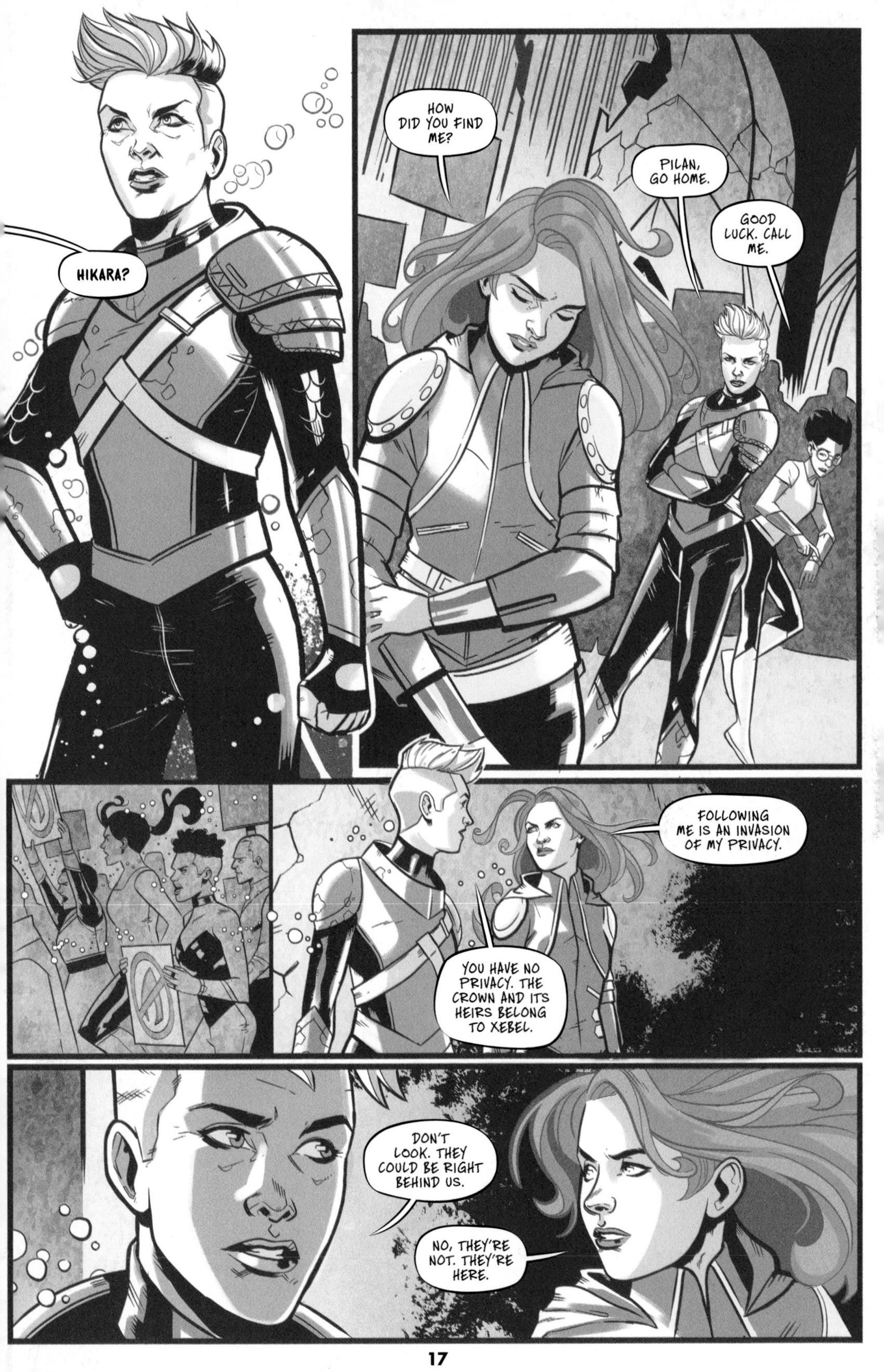
HIKARA?
HOW DID YOU FIND ME?
PILAN, GO HOME.
GOOD LUCK. CALL ME.
FOLLOWING ME IS AN INVASION OF MY PRIVACY.
YOU HAVE NO PRIVACY. THE CROWN AND ITS HEIRS BELONG TO XEBEL.
DON'T LOOK. THEY COULD BE RIGHT BEHIND US.
NO, THEY'RE NOT. THEY'RE HERE.

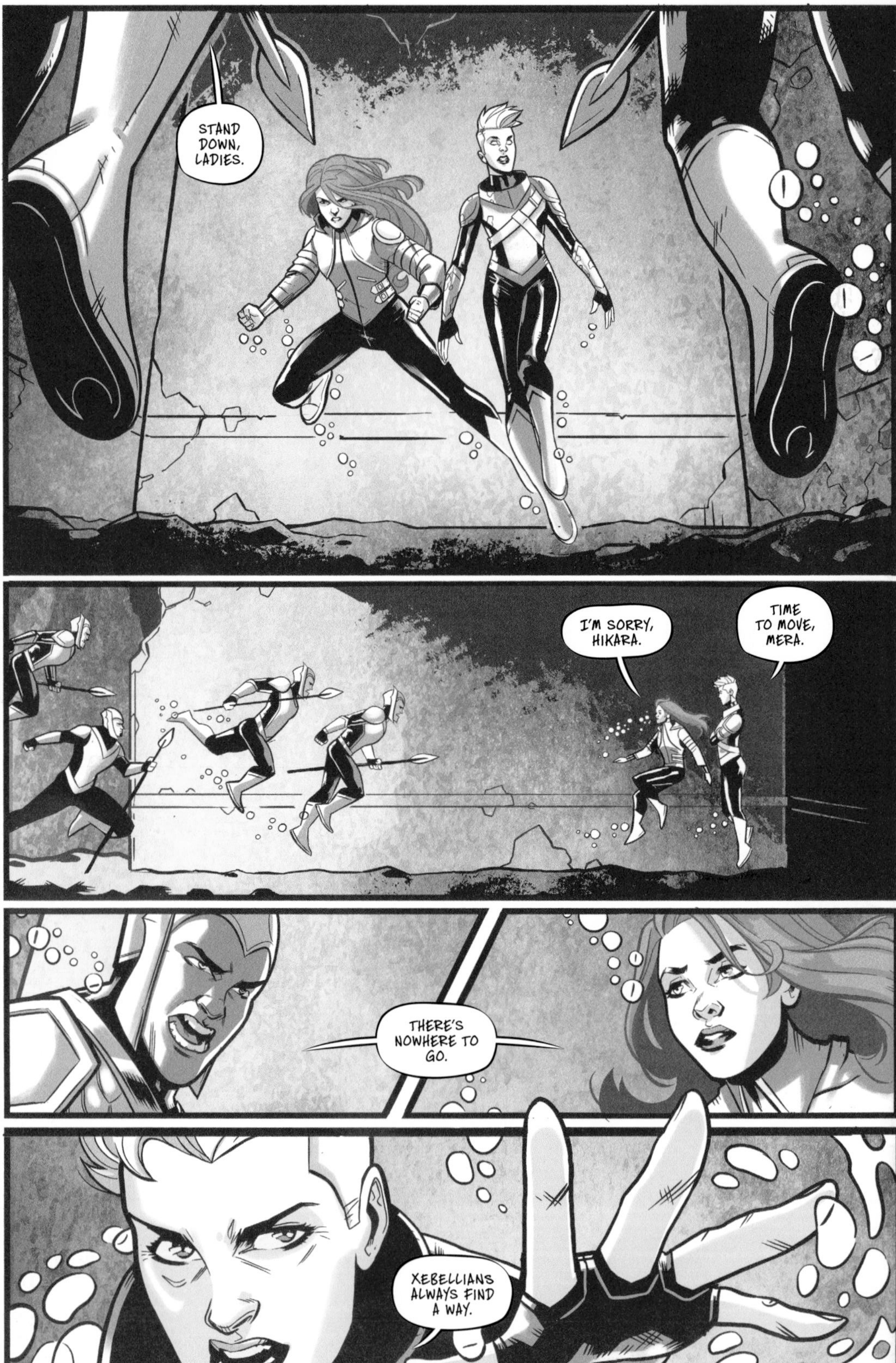
STAND DOWN, LADIES.
I'M SORRY, HIKARA.
TIME TO MOVE, MERA.
THERE'S NOWHERE TO GO.
XEBELLIANS ALWAYS FIND A WAY.

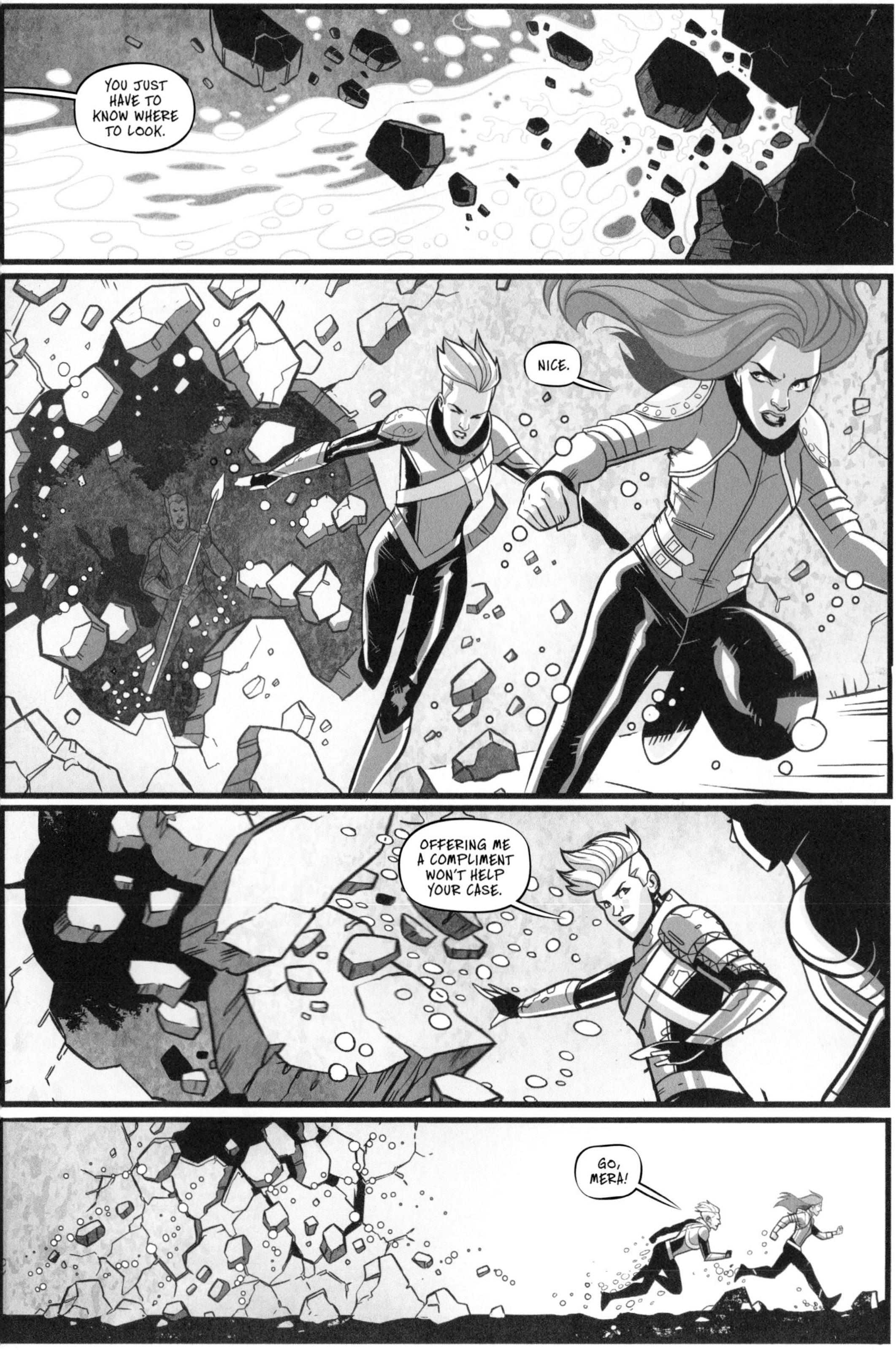
YOU JUST HAVE TO KNOW WHERE TO LOOK.
NICE.
OFFERING ME A COMPLIMENT WON'T HELP YOUR CASE.
GO, MERA!

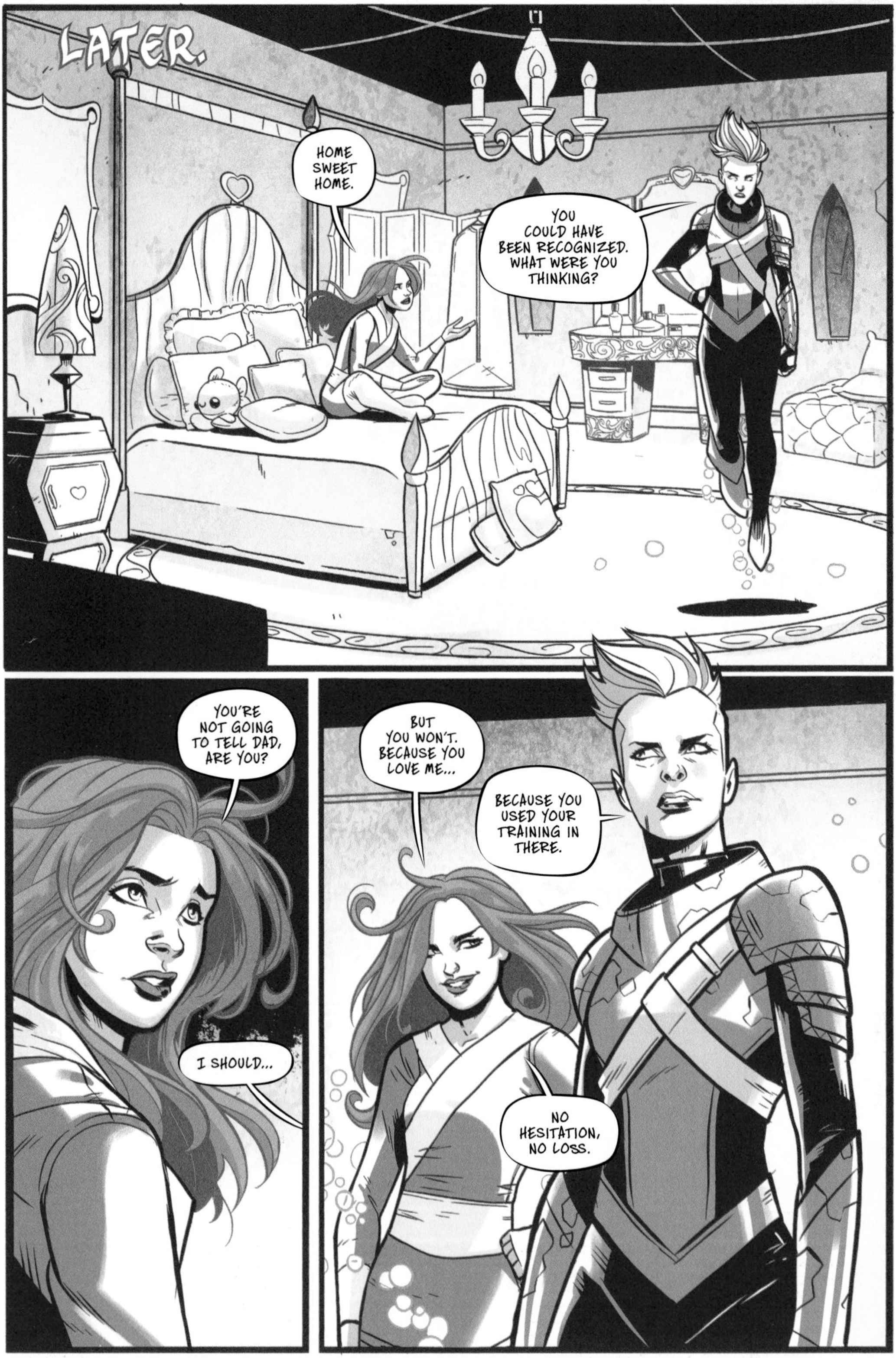
LATER.
HOME SWEET HOME.
YOU COULD HAVE BEEN RECOGNIZED. WHAT WERE YOU THINKING?
YOU'RE NOT GOING TO TELL DAD, ARE YOU?
I SHOULD...
BUT YOU WON'T. BECAUSE YOU LOVE ME...
BECAUSE YOU USED YOUR TRAINING IN THERE.
NO HESITATION, NO LOSS.

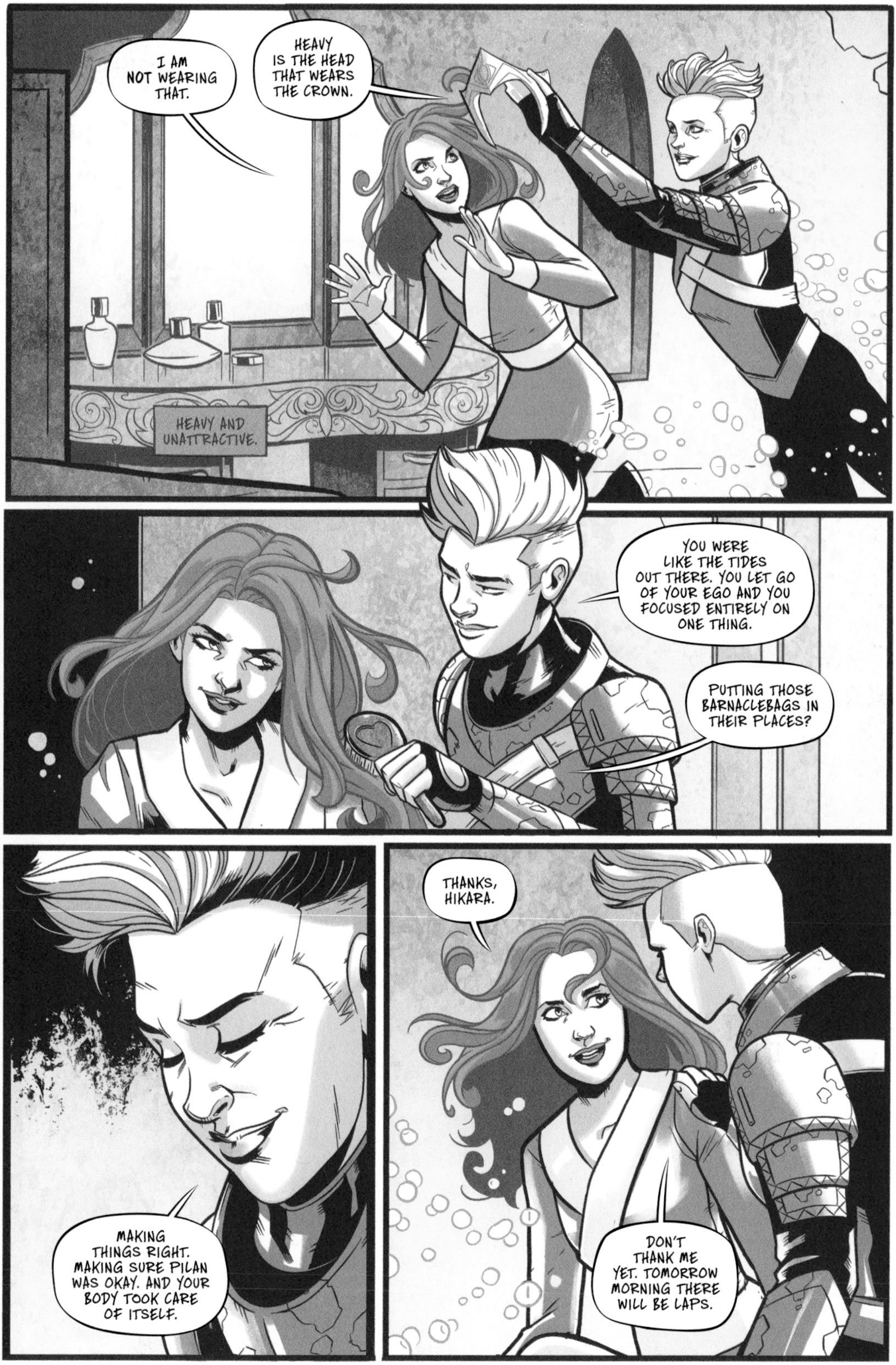
I AM NOT WEARING THAT.
HEAVY IS THE HEAD THAT WEARS THE CROWN.
HEAVY AND UNATTRACTIVE.
YOU WERE LIKE THE TIDES OUT THERE. YOU LET GO OF YOUR EGO AND YOU FOCUSED ENTIRELY ON ONE THING.
PUTTING THOSE BARNACLEBAGS IN THEIR PLACES?
MAKING THINGS RIGHT. MAKING SURE PILAN WAS OKAY. AND YOUR BODY TOOK CARE OF ITSELF.
THANKS, HIKARA.
DON'T THANK ME YET. TOMORROW MORNING THERE WILL BE LAPS.

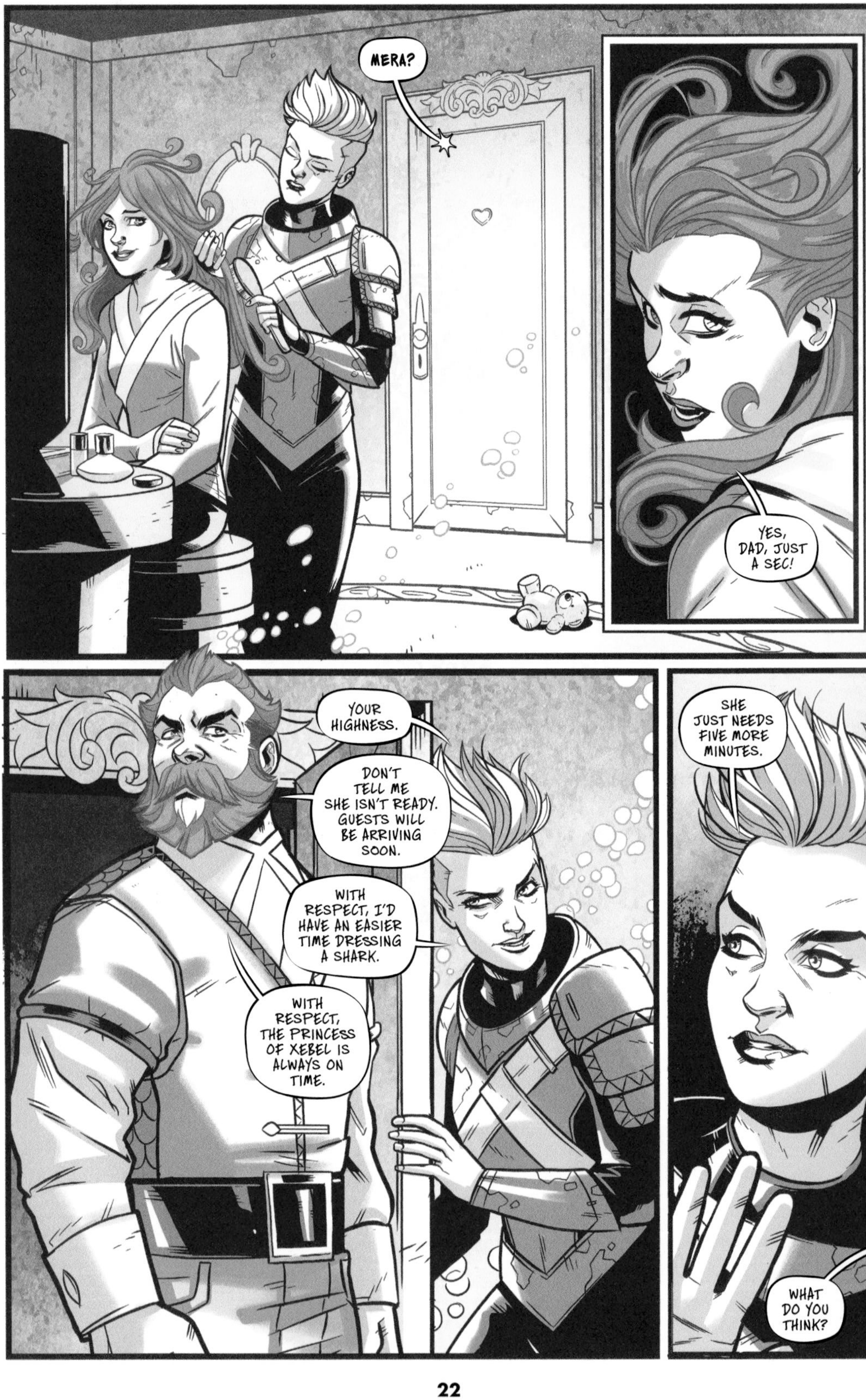
MERA?
YES, DAD, JUST A SEC!
YOUR HIGHNESS.
DON'T TELL ME SHE ISN'T READY. GUESTS WILL BE ARRIVING SOON.
WITH RESPECT, I'D HAVE AN EASIER TIME DRESSING A SHARK.
WITH RESPECT, THE PRINCESS OF XEBEL IS ALWAYS ON TIME.
SHE JUST NEEDS FIVE MORE MINUTES.
WHAT DO YOU THINK?

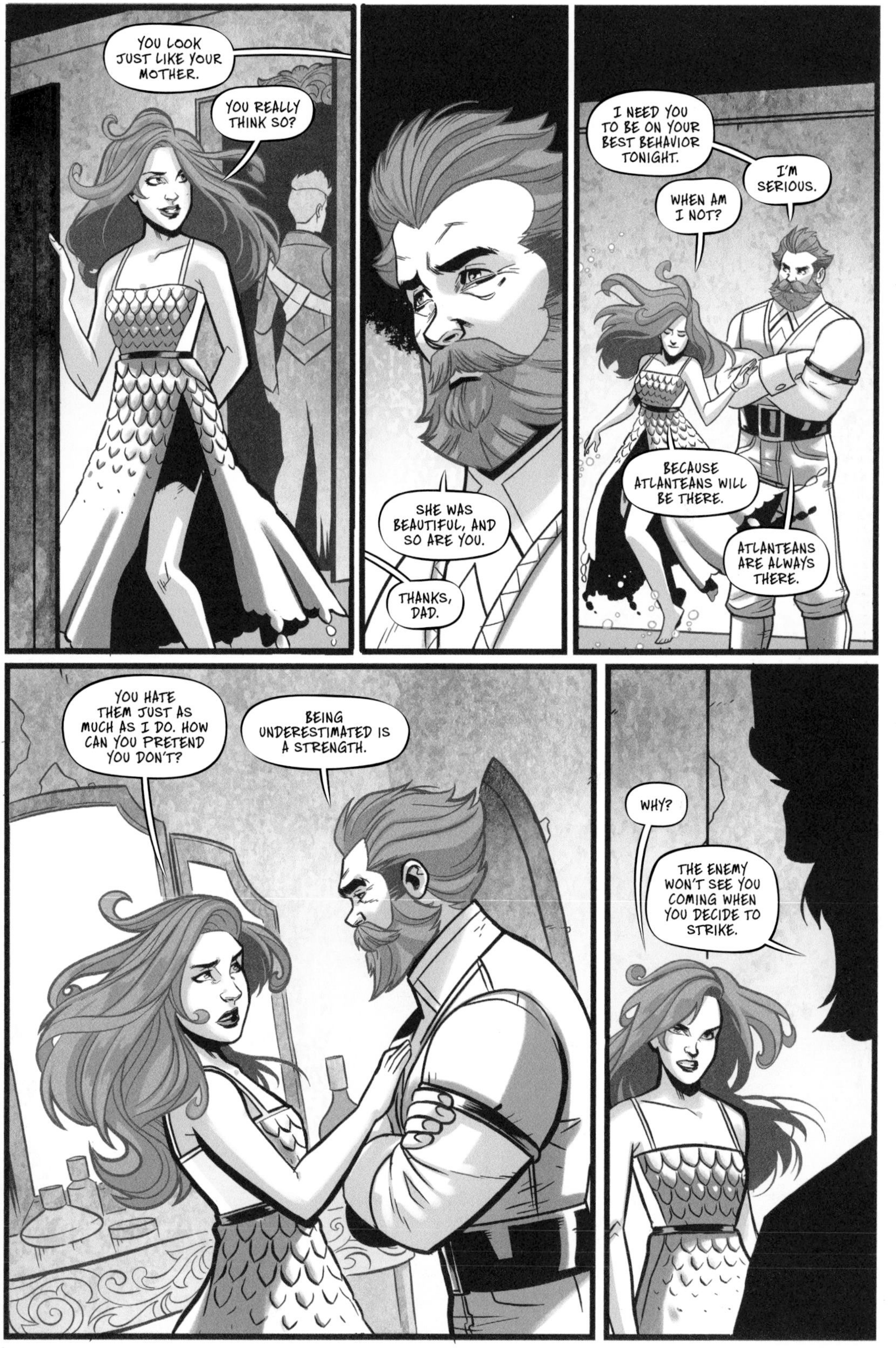
YOU LOOK JUST LIKE YOUR MOTHER.
YOU REALLY THINK SO?
SHE WAS BEAUTIFUL, AND SO ARE YOU.
THANKS, DAD.
I NEED YOU TO BE ON YOUR BEST BEHAVIOR TONIGHT.
I'M SERIOUS.
WHEN AM I NOT?
BECAUSE ATLANTEANS WILL BE THERE.
ATLANTEANS ARE ALWAYS THERE.
YOU HATE THEM JUST AS MUCH AS I DO. HOW CAN YOU PRETEND YOU DON'T?
BEING UNDERESTIMATED IS A STRENGTH.
WHY?
THE ENEMY WON'T SEE YOU COMING WHEN YOU DECIDE TO STRIKE.

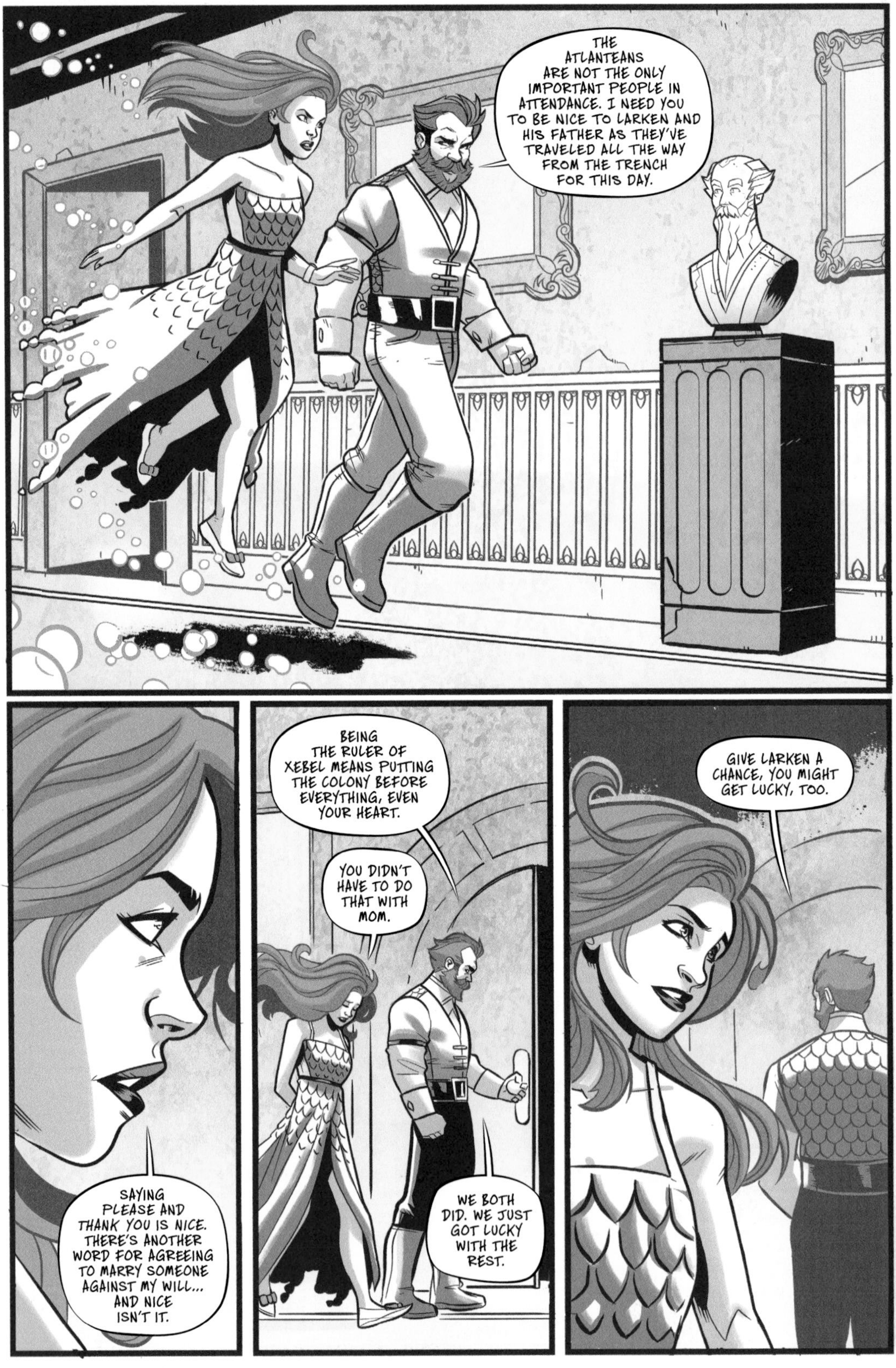
THE ATLANTEANS ARE NOT THE ONLY IMPORTANT PEOPLE IN ATTENDANCE. I NEED YOU TO BE NICE TO LARKEN AND HIS FATHER AS THEY'VE TRAVELED ALL THE WAY FROM THE TRENCH FOR THIS DAY.
SAYING PLEASE AND THANK YOU IS NICE. THERE'S ANOTHER WORD FOR AGREEING TO MARRY SOMEONE AGAINST MY WILL... AND NICE ISN'T IT.
BEING THE RULER OF XEBEL MEANS PUTTING THE COLONY BEFORE EVERYTHING, EVEN YOUR HEART.
YOU DIDN'T HAVE TO DO THAT WITH MOM.
WE BOTH DID. WE JUST GOT LUCKY WITH THE REST.
GIVE LARKEN A CHANCE, YOU MIGHT GET LUCKY, TOO.

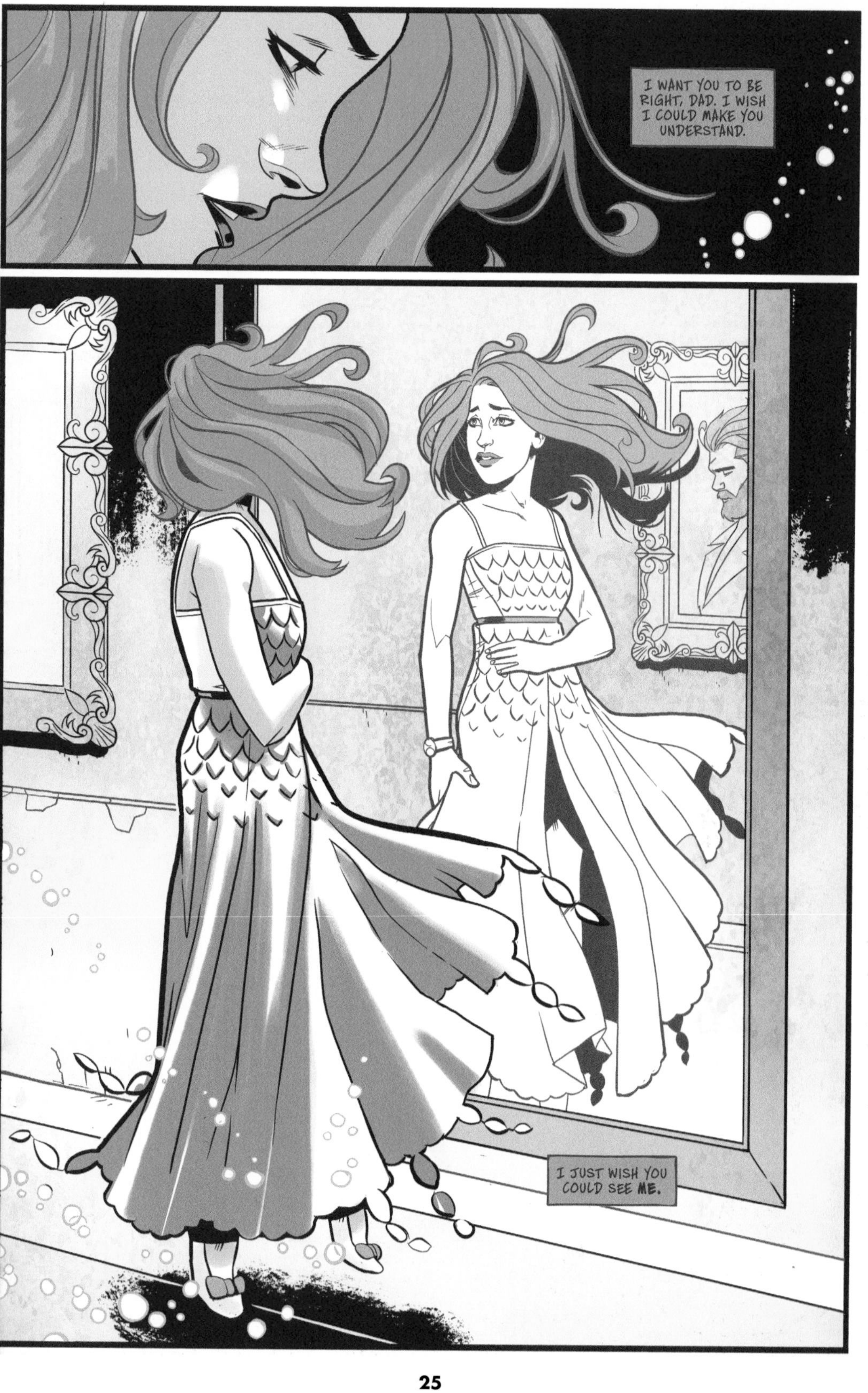
I WANT YOU TO BE RIGHT, DAD. I WISH I COULD MAKE YOU UNDERSTAND.
I JUST WISH YOU COULD SEE **ME.**

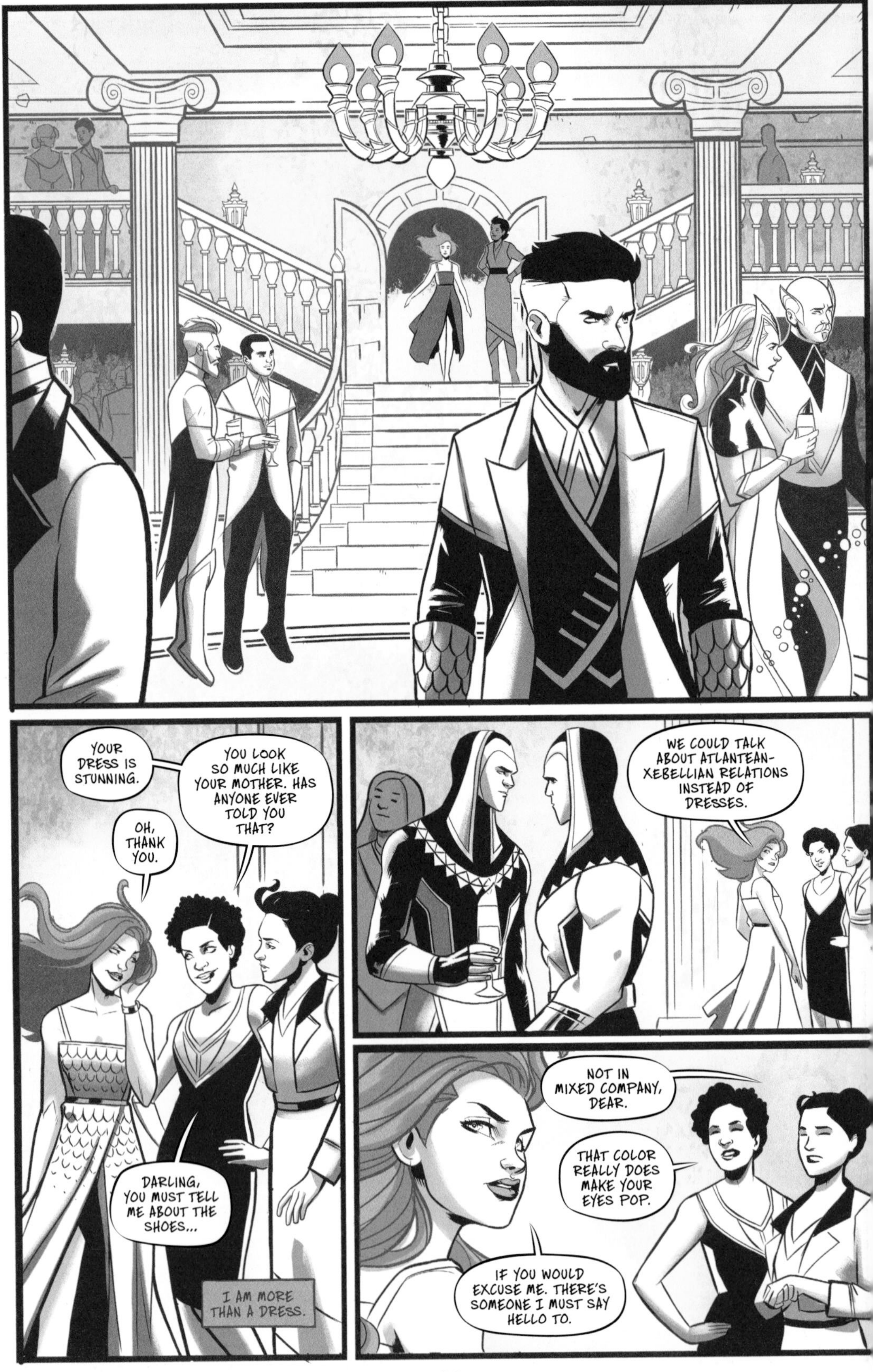
YOUR DRESS IS STUNNING.
YOU LOOK SO MUCH LIKE YOUR MOTHER. HAS ANYONE EVER TOLD YOU THAT?
OH, THANK YOU.
DARLING, YOU MUST TELL ME ABOUT THE SHOES...
I AM MORE THAN A DRESS.
WE COULD TALK ABOUT ATLANTEAN-XEBELLIAN RELATIONS INSTEAD OF DRESSES.
NOT IN MIXED COMPANY, DEAR.
THAT COLOR REALLY DOES MAKE YOUR EYES POP.
IF YOU WOULD EXCUSE ME. THERE'S SOMEONE I MUST SAY HELLO TO.

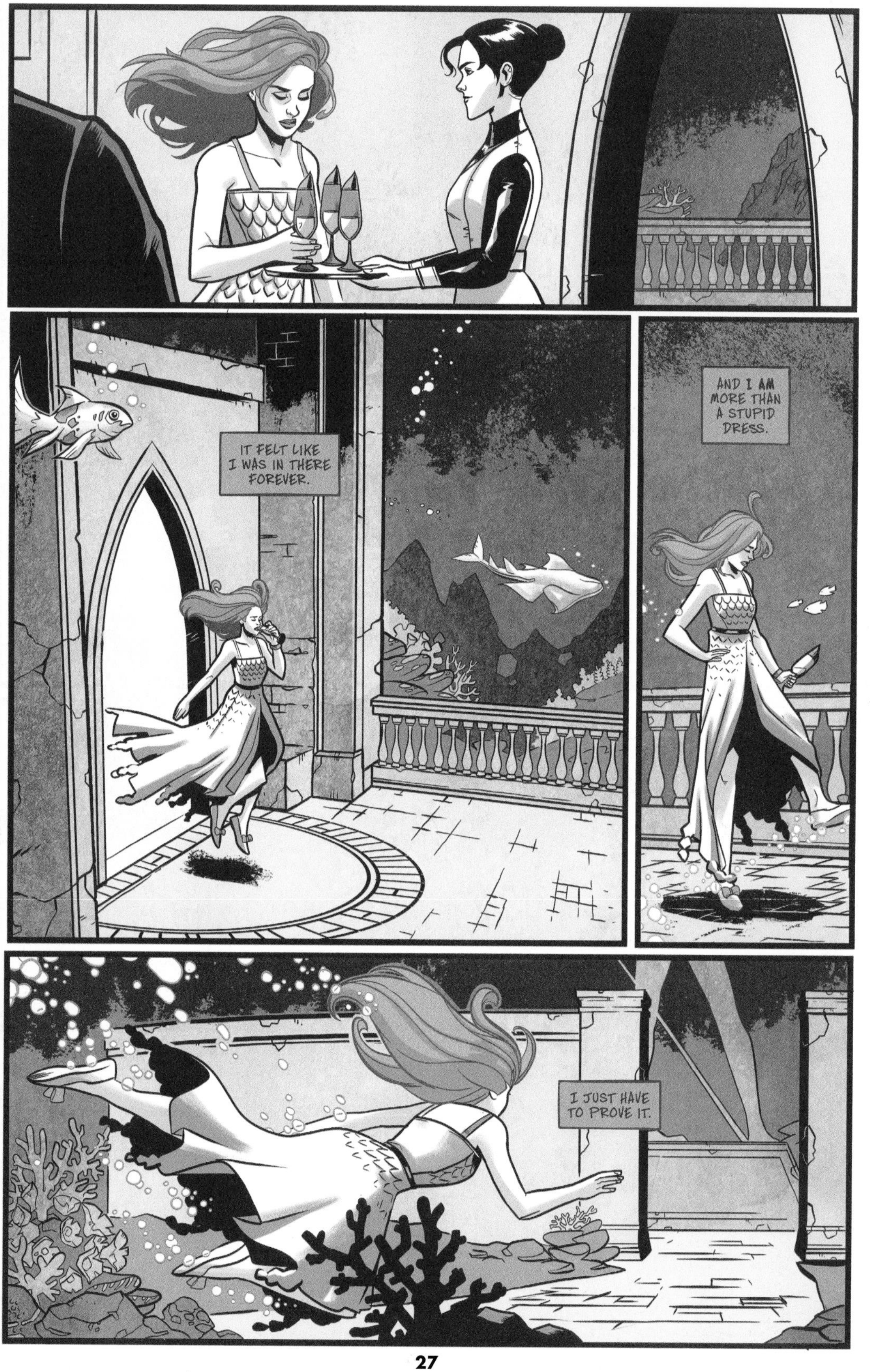
IT FELT LIKE I WAS IN THERE FOREVER.
AND I AM MORE THAN A STUPID DRESS.
I JUST HAVE TO PROVE IT.

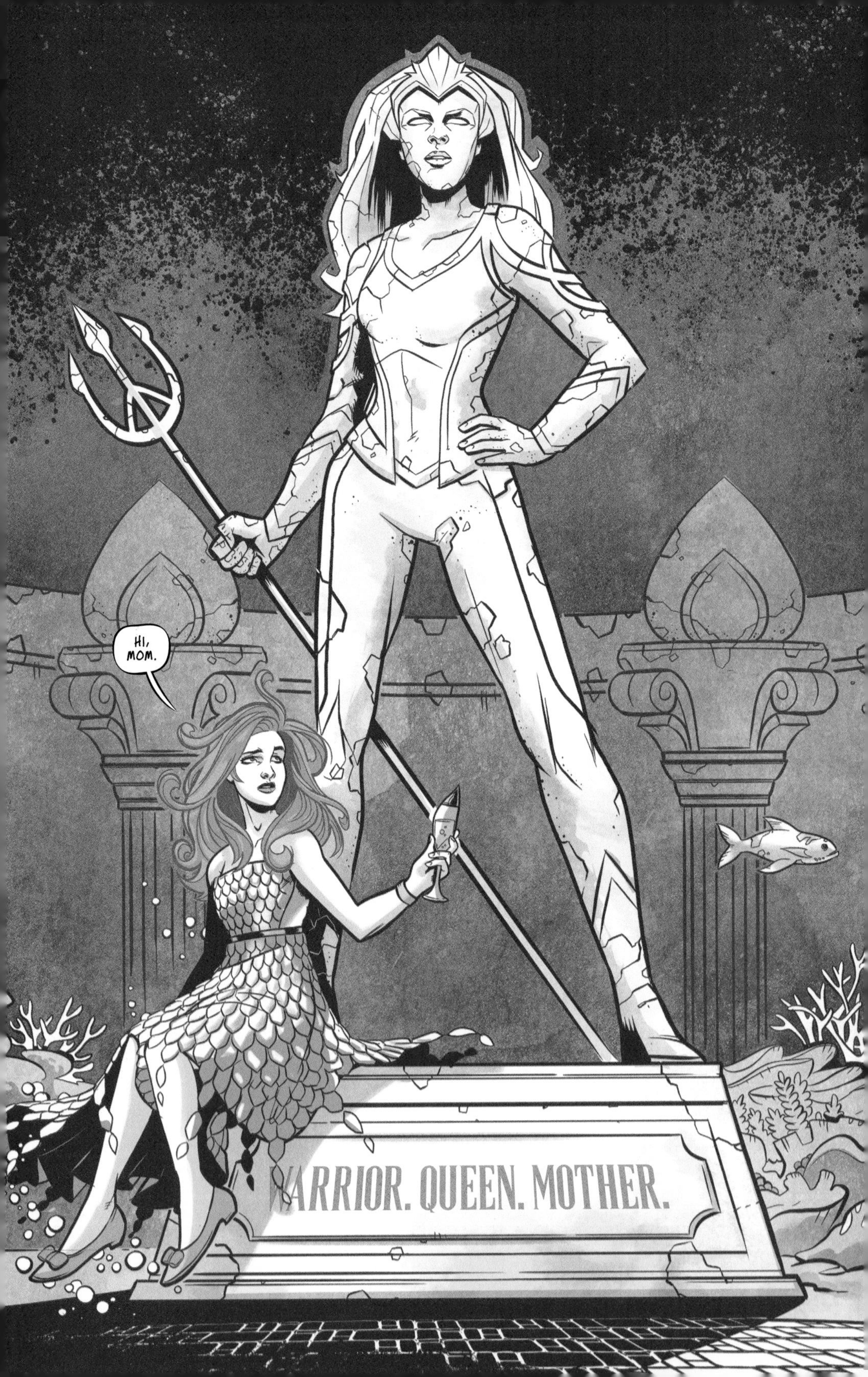
HI, MOM.
WARRIOR. QUEEN. MOTHER.

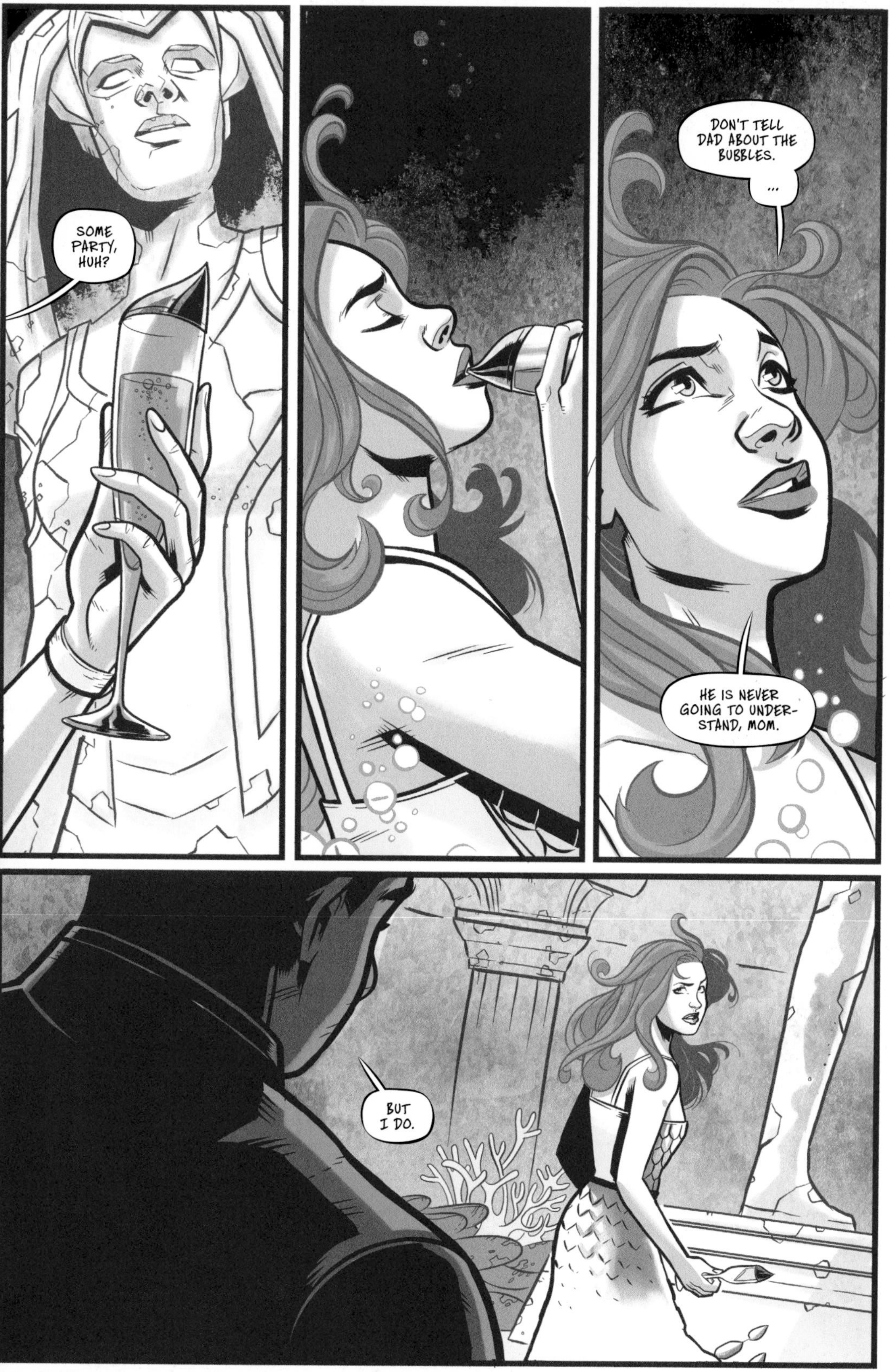
SOME PARTY, HUH?
DON'T TELL DAD ABOUT THE BUBBLES.
...
HE IS NEVER GOING TO UNDER-STAND, MOM.
BUT I DO.

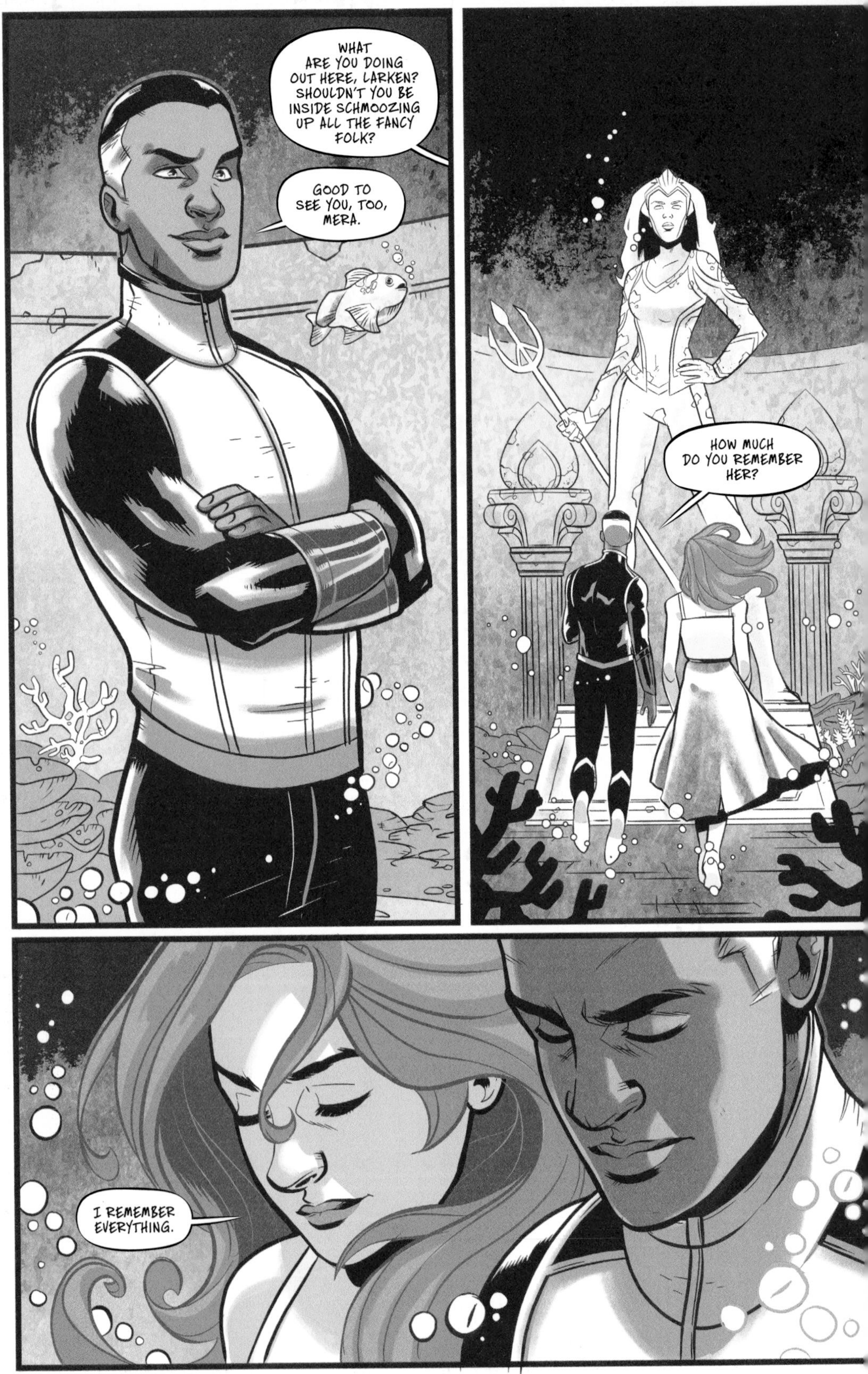
WHAT ARE YOU DOING OUT HERE, LARKEN? SHOULDN'T YOU BE INSIDE SCHMOOZING UP ALL THE FANCY FOLK?
GOOD TO SEE YOU, TOO, MERA.
HOW MUCH DO YOU REMEMBER HER?
I REMEMBER EVERYTHING.

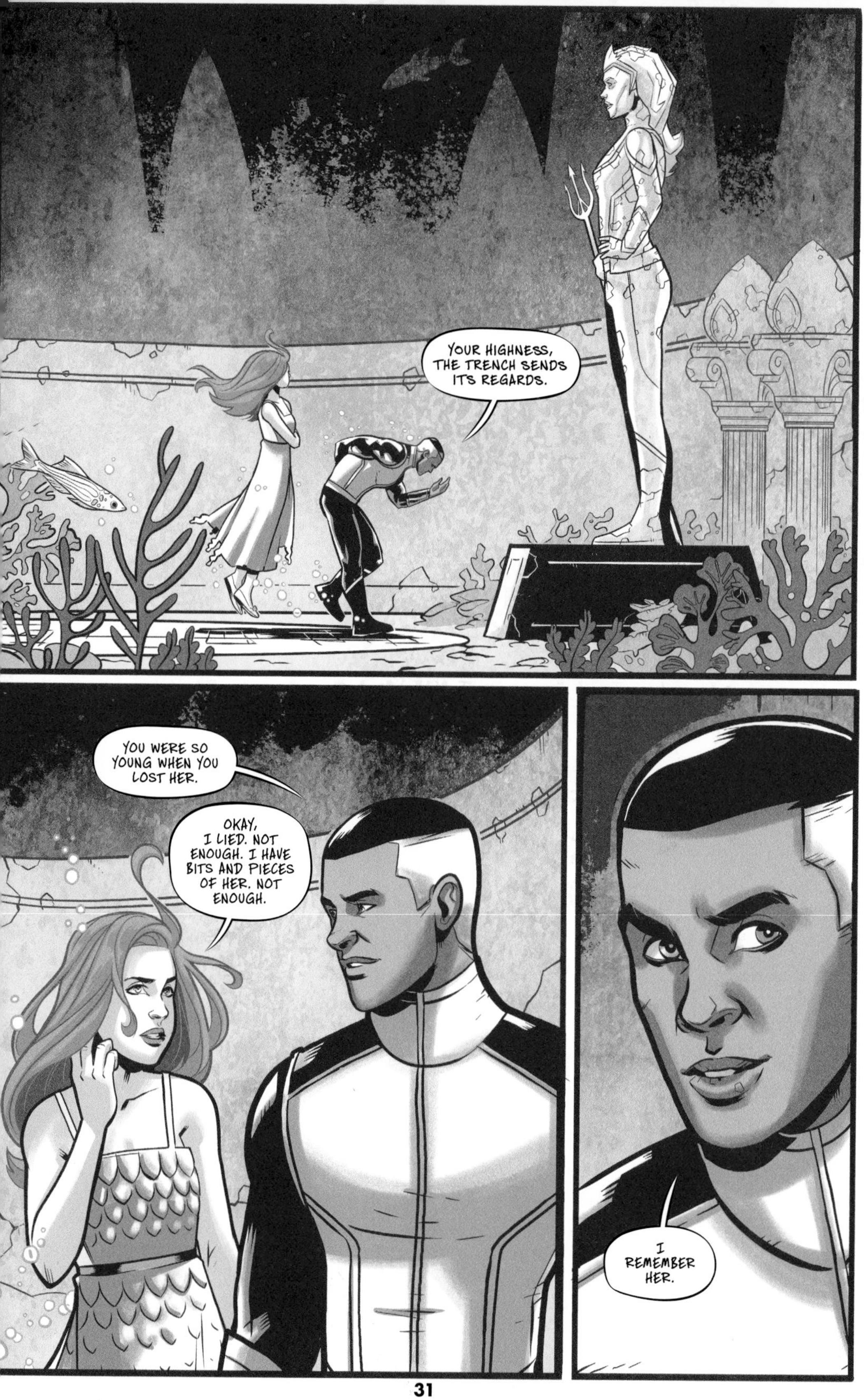
YOUR HIGHNESS, THE TRENCH SENDS ITS REGARDS.
YOU WERE SO YOUNG WHEN YOU LOST HER.
OKAY, I LIED. NOT ENOUGH. I HAVE BITS AND PIECES OF HER. NOT ENOUGH.
I REMEMBER HER.

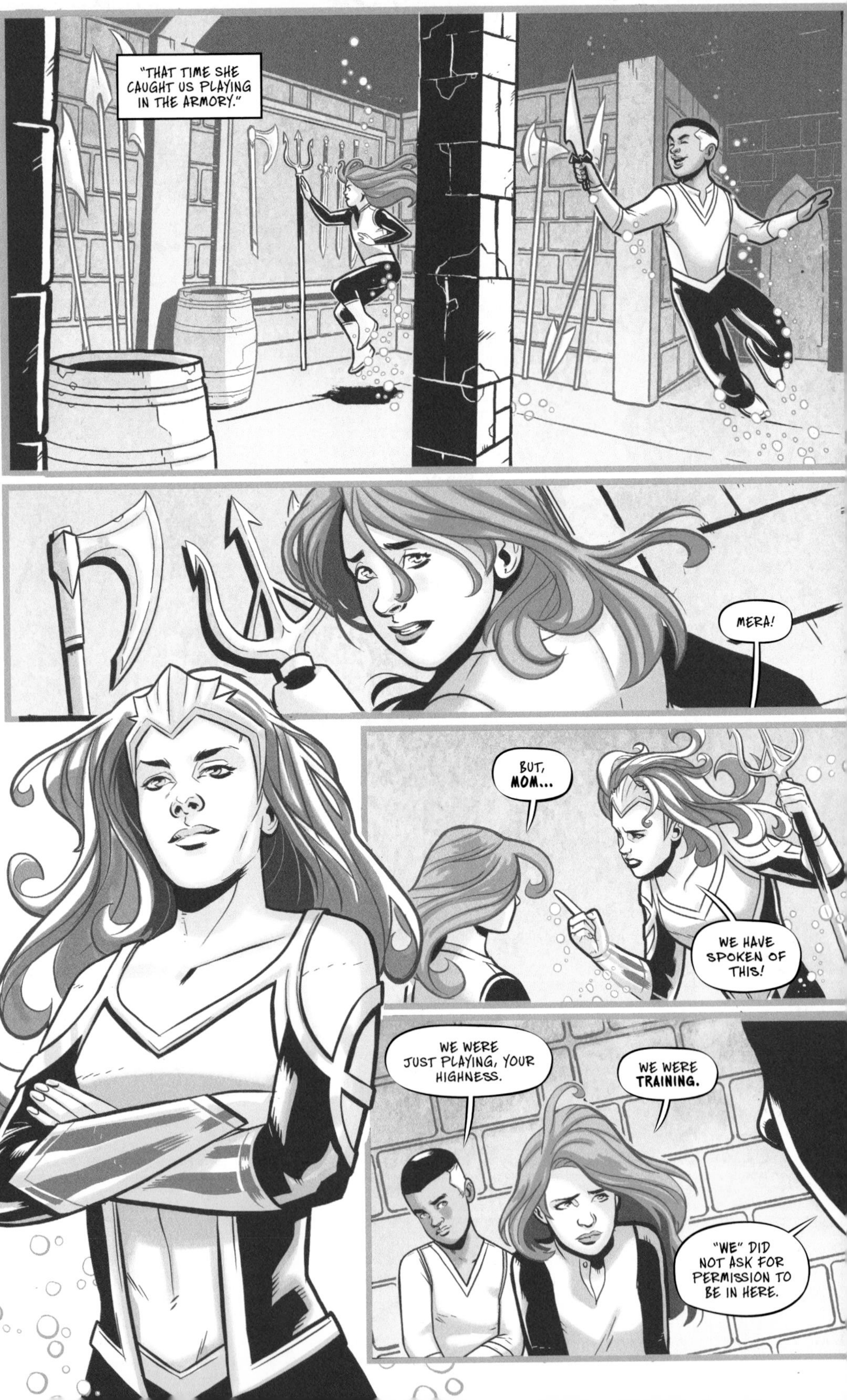
"THAT TIME SHE CAUGHT US PLAYING IN THE ARMORY."
MERA!
BUT, MOM...
WE HAVE SPOKEN OF THIS!
WE WERE JUST PLAYING, YOUR HIGHNESS.
WE WERE TRAINING.
"WE" DID NOT ASK FOR PERMISSION TO BE IN HERE.

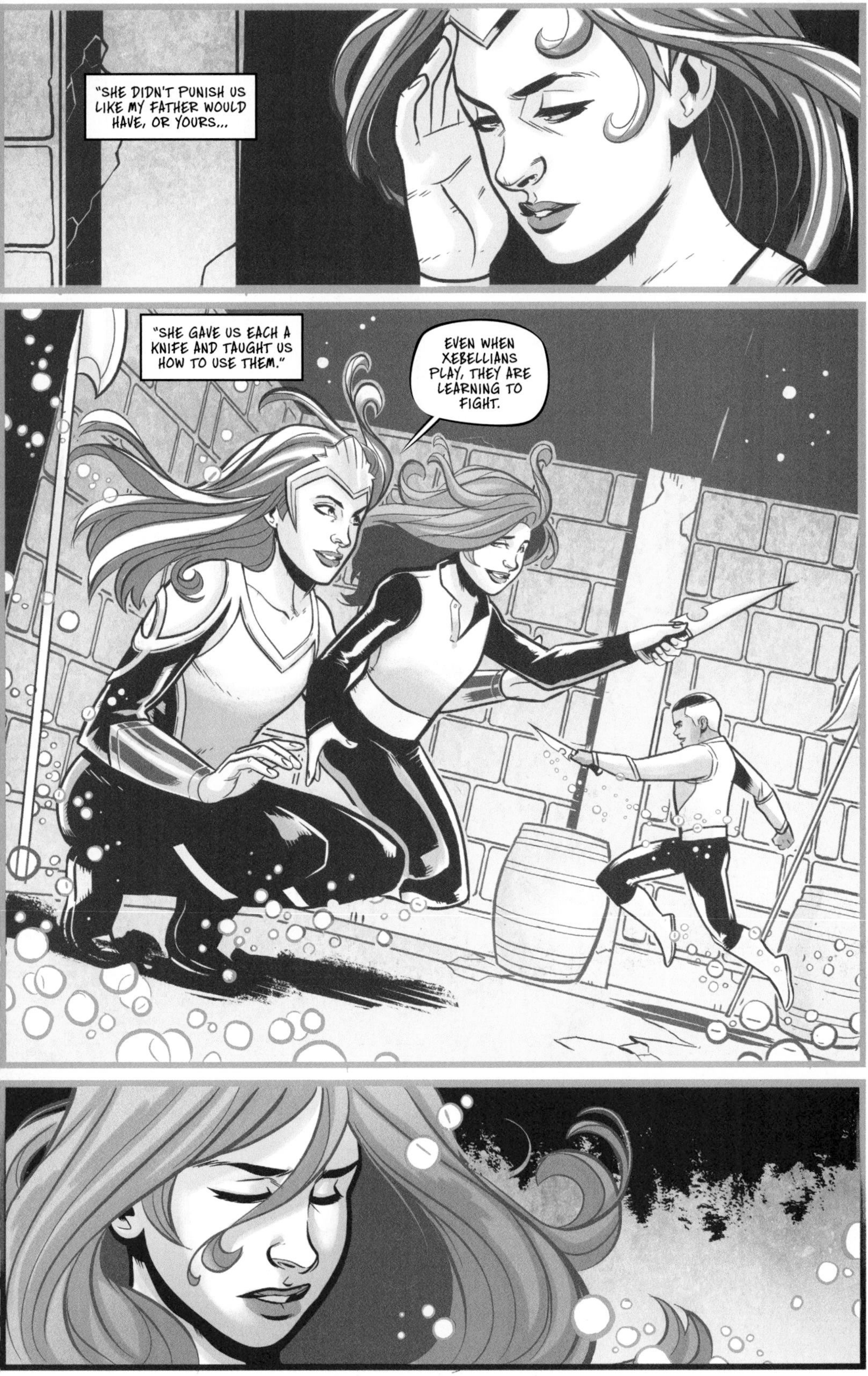
"SHE DIDN'T PUNISH US LIKE MY FATHER WOULD HAVE, OR YOURS...
"SHE GAVE US EACH A KNIFE AND TAUGHT US HOW TO USE THEM."
EVEN WHEN XEBELLIANS PLAY, THEY ARE LEARNING TO FIGHT.

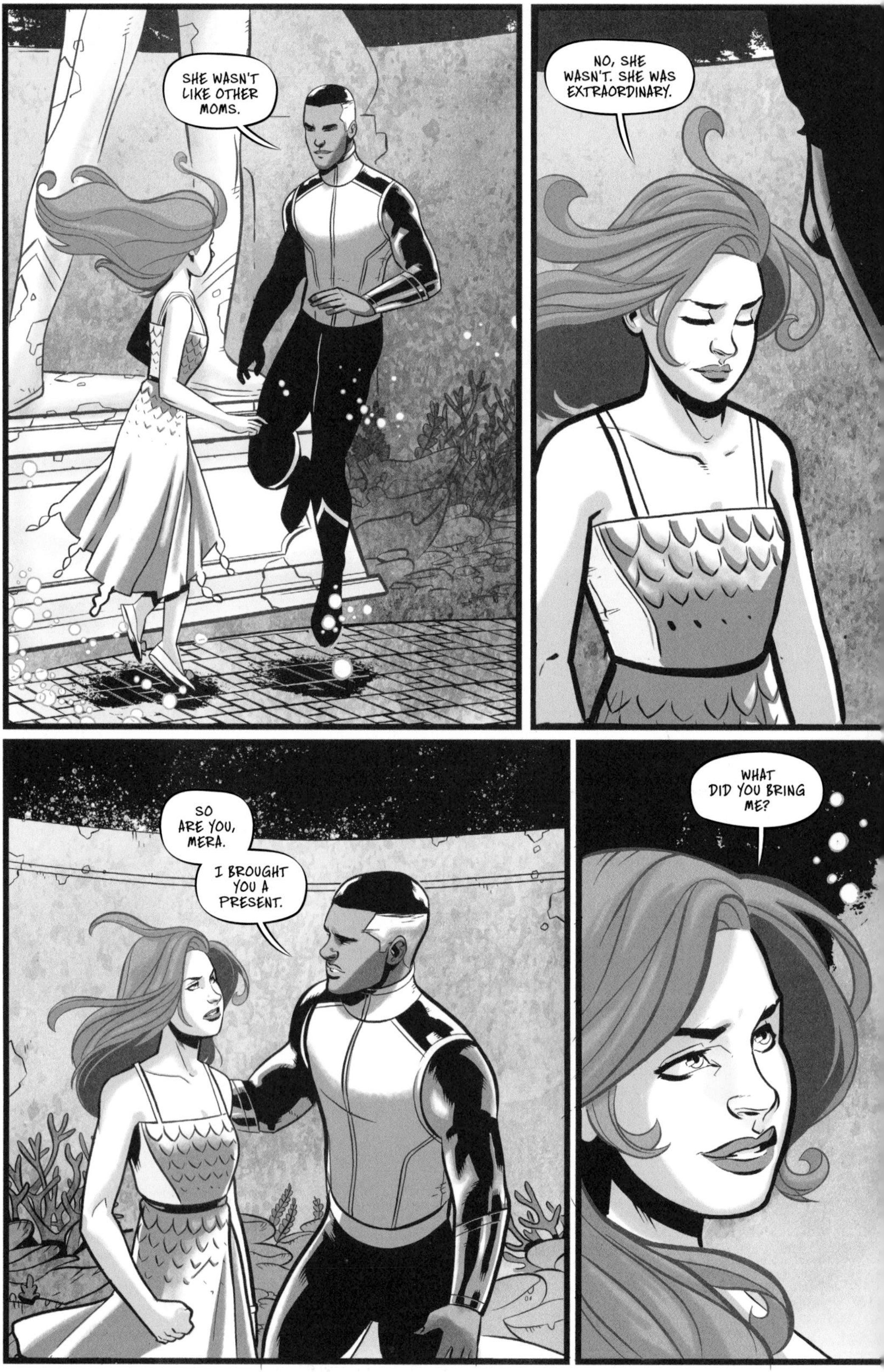
SHE WASN'T LIKE OTHER MOMS.
NO, SHE WASN'T. SHE WAS EXTRAORDINARY.
SO ARE YOU, MERA.
I BROUGHT YOU A PRESENT.
WHAT DID YOU BRING ME?

THAT'S NOT HOW A PRESENT WORKS.

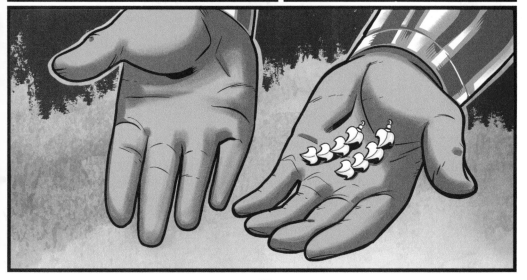

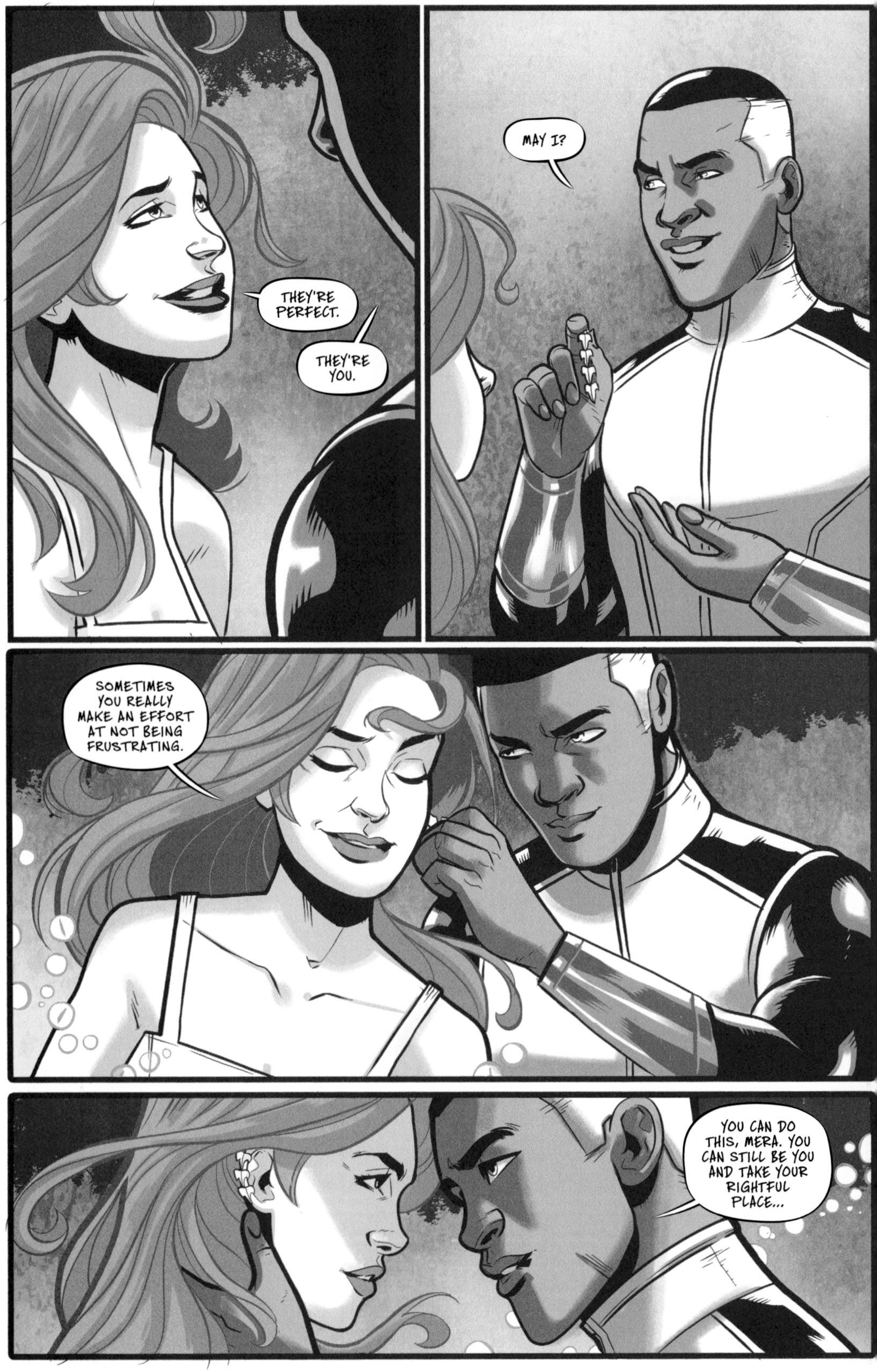
THEY'RE PERFECT.
THEY'RE YOU.
MAY I?
SOMETIMES YOU REALLY MAKE AN EFFORT AT NOT BEING FRUSTRATING.
YOU CAN DO THIS, MERA. YOU CAN STILL BE YOU AND TAKE YOUR RIGHTFUL PLACE...

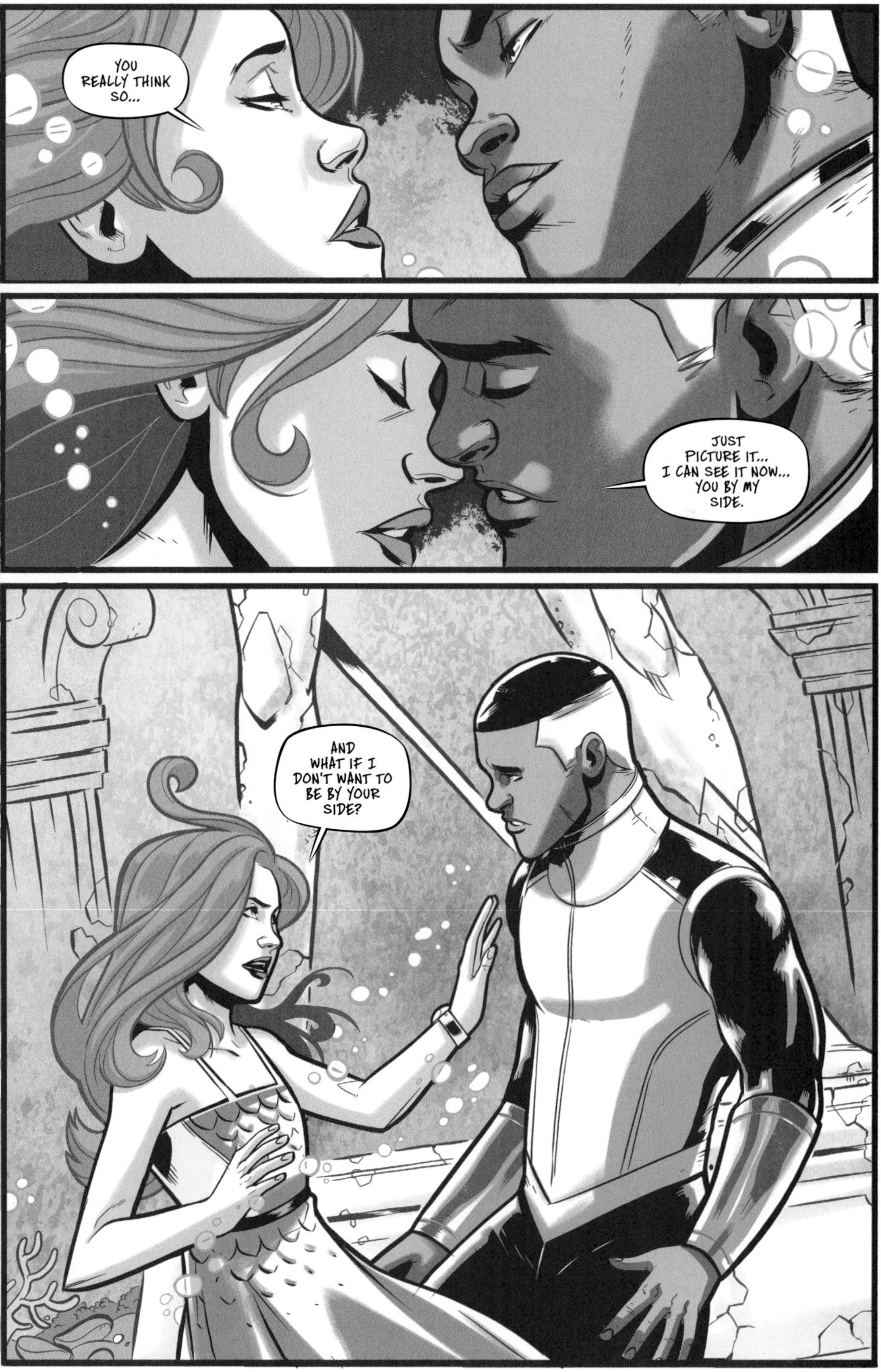
YOU REALLY THINK SO...
JUST PICTURE IT... I CAN SEE IT NOW... YOU BY MY SIDE.
AND WHAT IF I DON'T WANT TO BE BY YOUR SIDE?

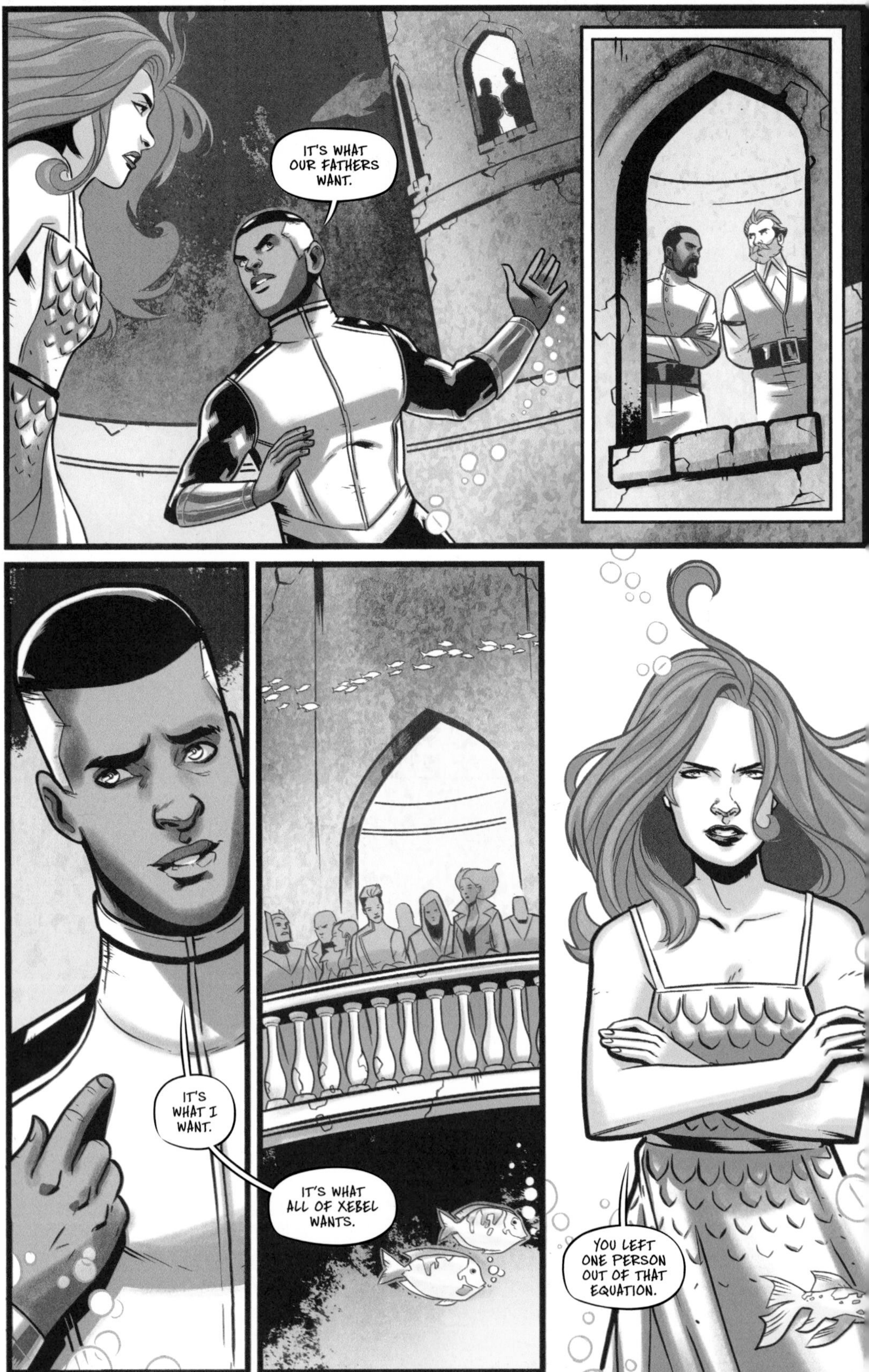
IT'S WHAT OUR FATHERS WANT.
IT'S WHAT I WANT.
IT'S WHAT ALL OF XEBEL WANTS.
YOU LEFT ONE PERSON OUT OF THAT EQUATION.

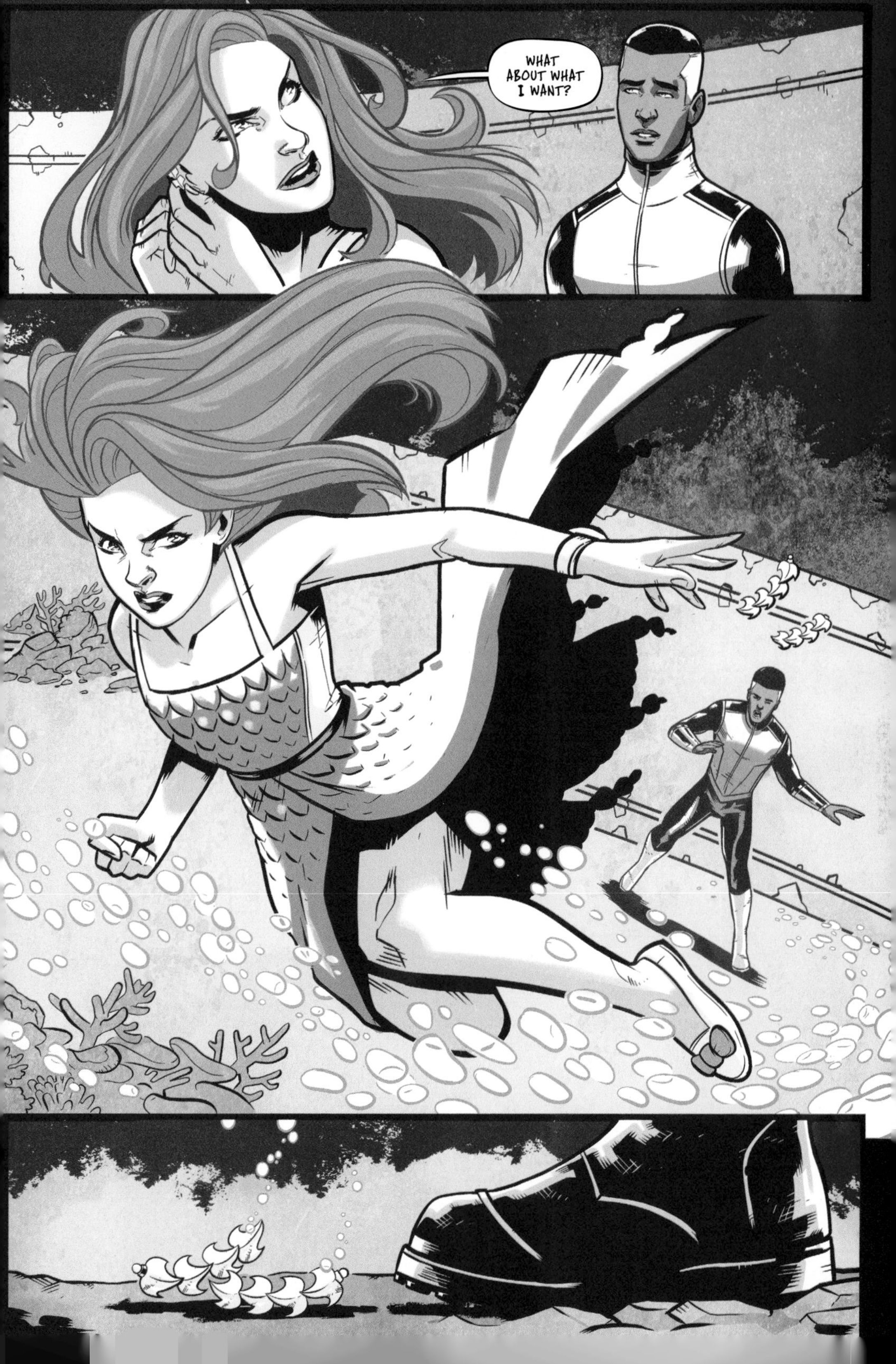
WHAT ABOUT WHAT I WANT?

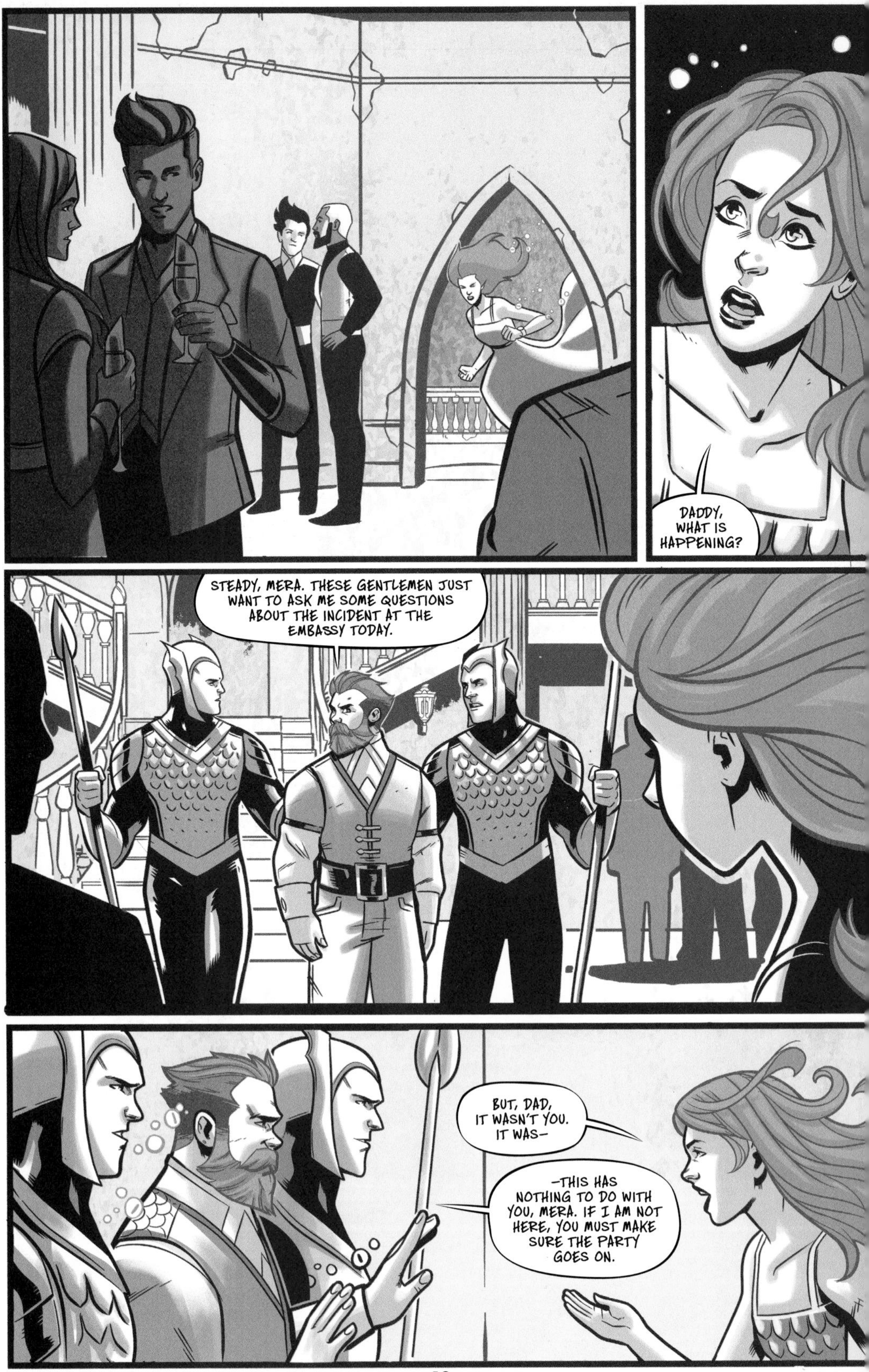
DADDY, WHAT IS HAPPENING?
STEADY, MERA. THESE GENTLEMEN JUST WANT TO ASK ME SOME QUESTIONS ABOUT THE INCIDENT AT THE EMBASSY TODAY.
BUT, DAD, IT WASN'T YOU. IT WAS—
—THIS HAS NOTHING TO DO WITH YOU, MERA. IF I AM NOT HERE, YOU MUST MAKE SURE THE PARTY GOES ON.

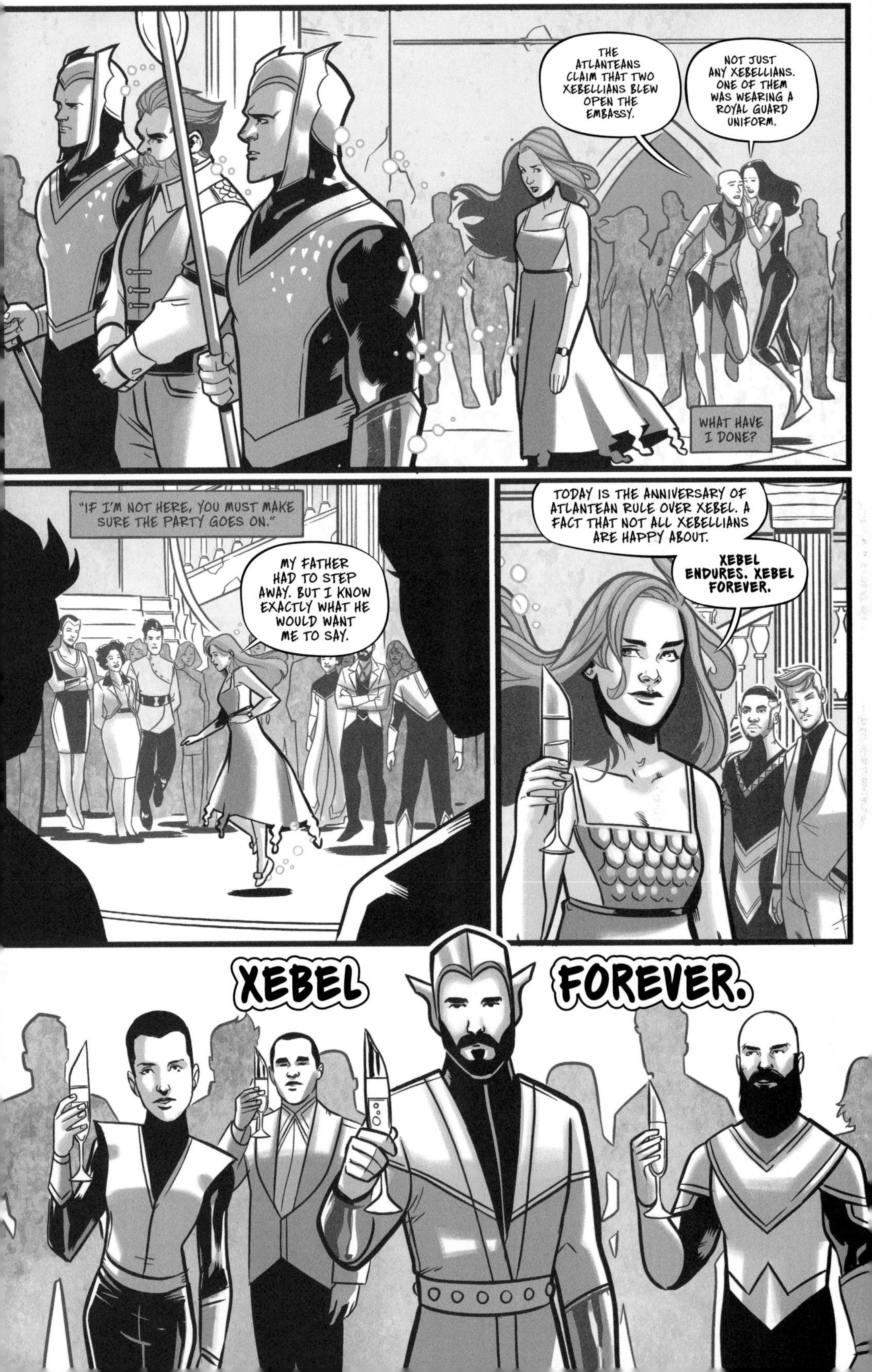
THE ATLANTEANS CLAIM THAT TWO XEBELLIANS BLEW OPEN THE EMBASSY.
NOT JUST ANY XEBELLIANS. ONE OF THEM WAS WEARING A ROYAL GUARD UNIFORM.
WHAT HAVE I DONE?
"IF I'M NOT HERE, YOU MUST MAKE SURE THE PARTY GOES ON."
MY FATHER HAD TO STEP AWAY. BUT I KNOW EXACTLY WHAT HE WOULD WANT ME TO SAY.
TODAY IS THE ANNIVERSARY OF ATLANTEAN RULE OVER XEBEL. A FACT THAT NOT ALL XEBELLIANS ARE HAPPY ABOUT.
XEBEL ENDURES. XEBEL FOREVER.
XEBEL FOREVER.

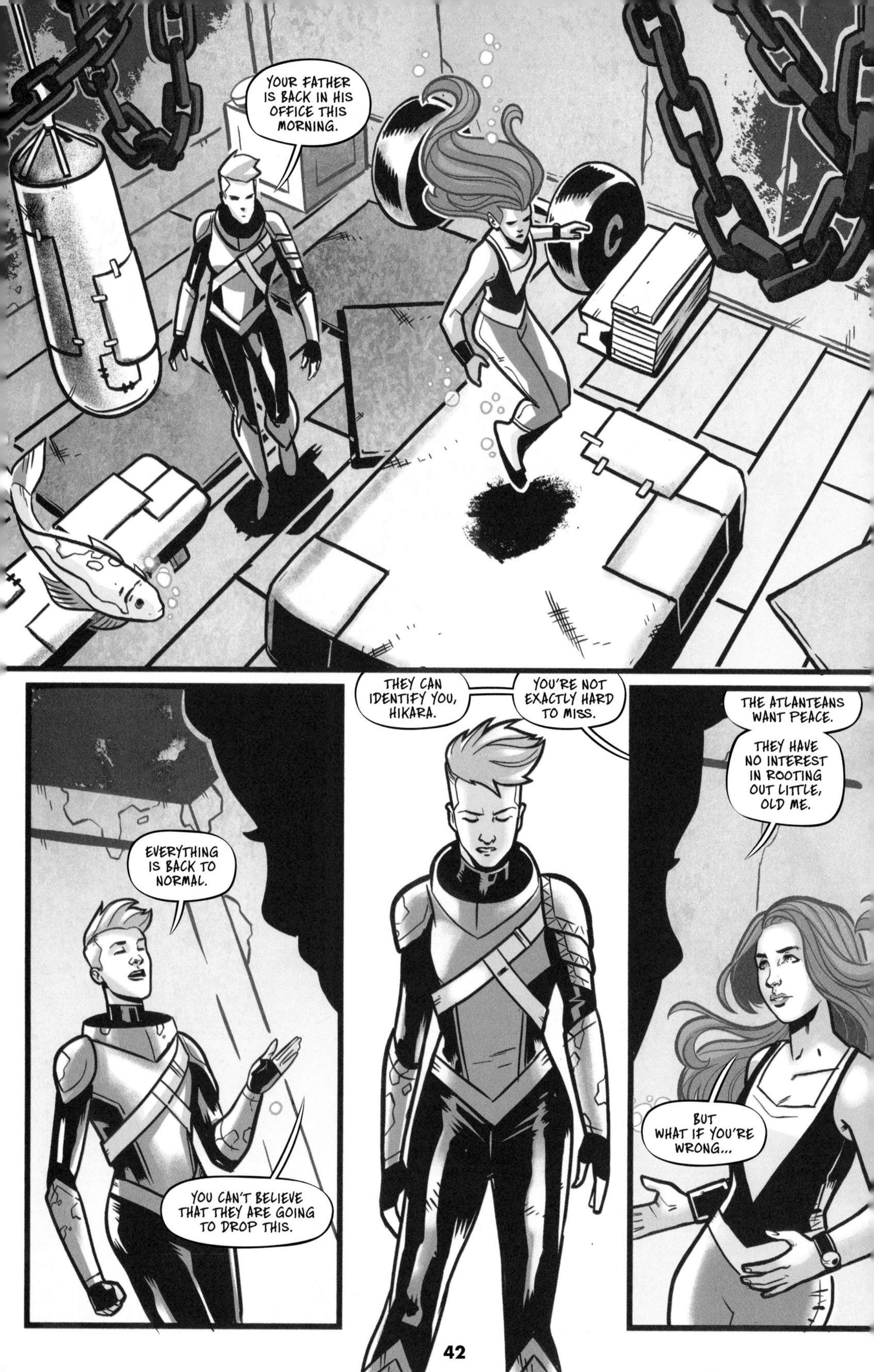
YOUR FATHER IS BACK IN HIS OFFICE THIS MORNING.
EVERYTHING IS BACK TO NORMAL.
YOU CAN'T BELIEVE THAT THEY ARE GOING TO DROP THIS.
THEY CAN IDENTIFY YOU, HIKARA.
YOU'RE NOT EXACTLY HARD TO MISS.
THE ATLANTEANS WANT PEACE.
THEY HAVE NO INTEREST IN ROOTING OUT LITTLE, OLD ME.
BUT WHAT IF YOU'RE WRONG...

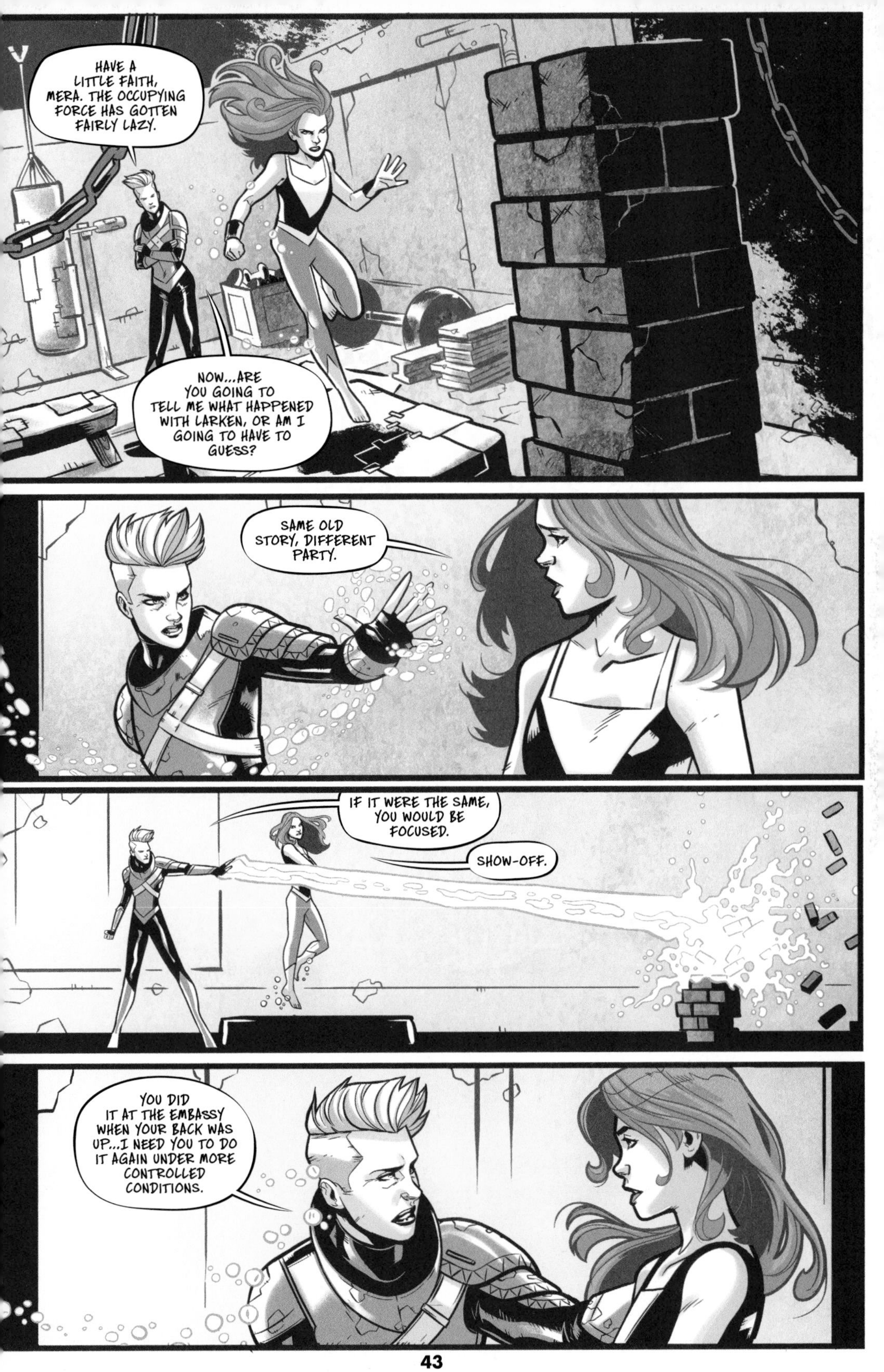
HAVE A LITTLE FAITH, MERA. THE OCCUPYING FORCE HAS GOTTEN FAIRLY LAZY.
NOW...ARE YOU GOING TO TELL ME WHAT HAPPENED WITH LARKEN, OR AM I GOING TO HAVE TO GUESS?
SAME OLD STORY, DIFFERENT PARTY.
IF IT WERE THE SAME, YOU WOULD BE FOCUSED.
SHOW-OFF.
YOU DID IT AT THE EMBASSY WHEN YOUR BACK WAS UP...I NEED YOU TO DO IT AGAIN UNDER MORE CONTROLLED CONDITIONS.

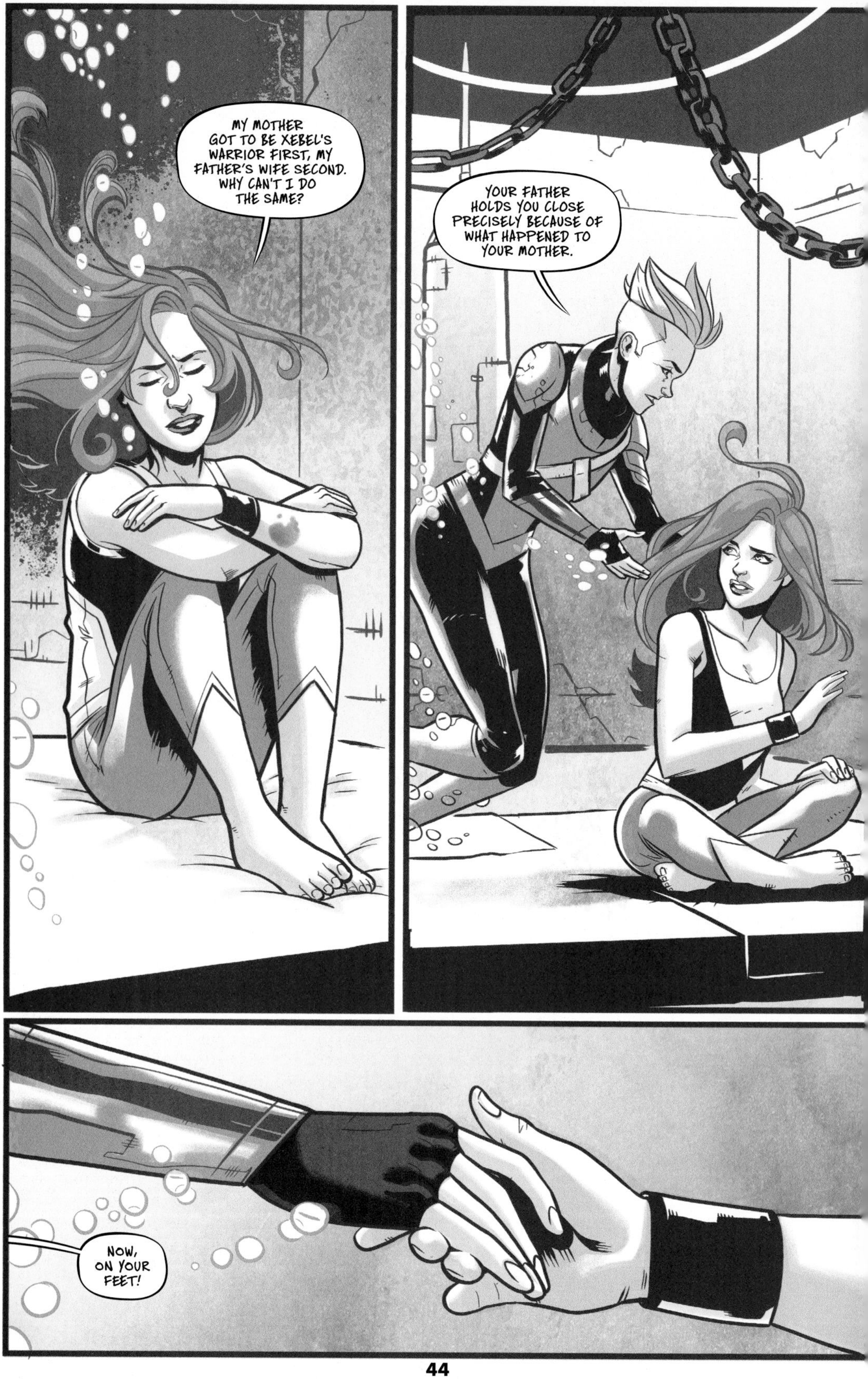
MY MOTHER GOT TO BE XEBEL'S WARRIOR FIRST, MY FATHER'S WIFE SECOND. WHY CAN'T I DO THE SAME?
YOUR FATHER HOLDS YOU CLOSE PRECISELY BECAUSE OF WHAT HAPPENED TO YOUR MOTHER.
NOW, ON YOUR FEET!

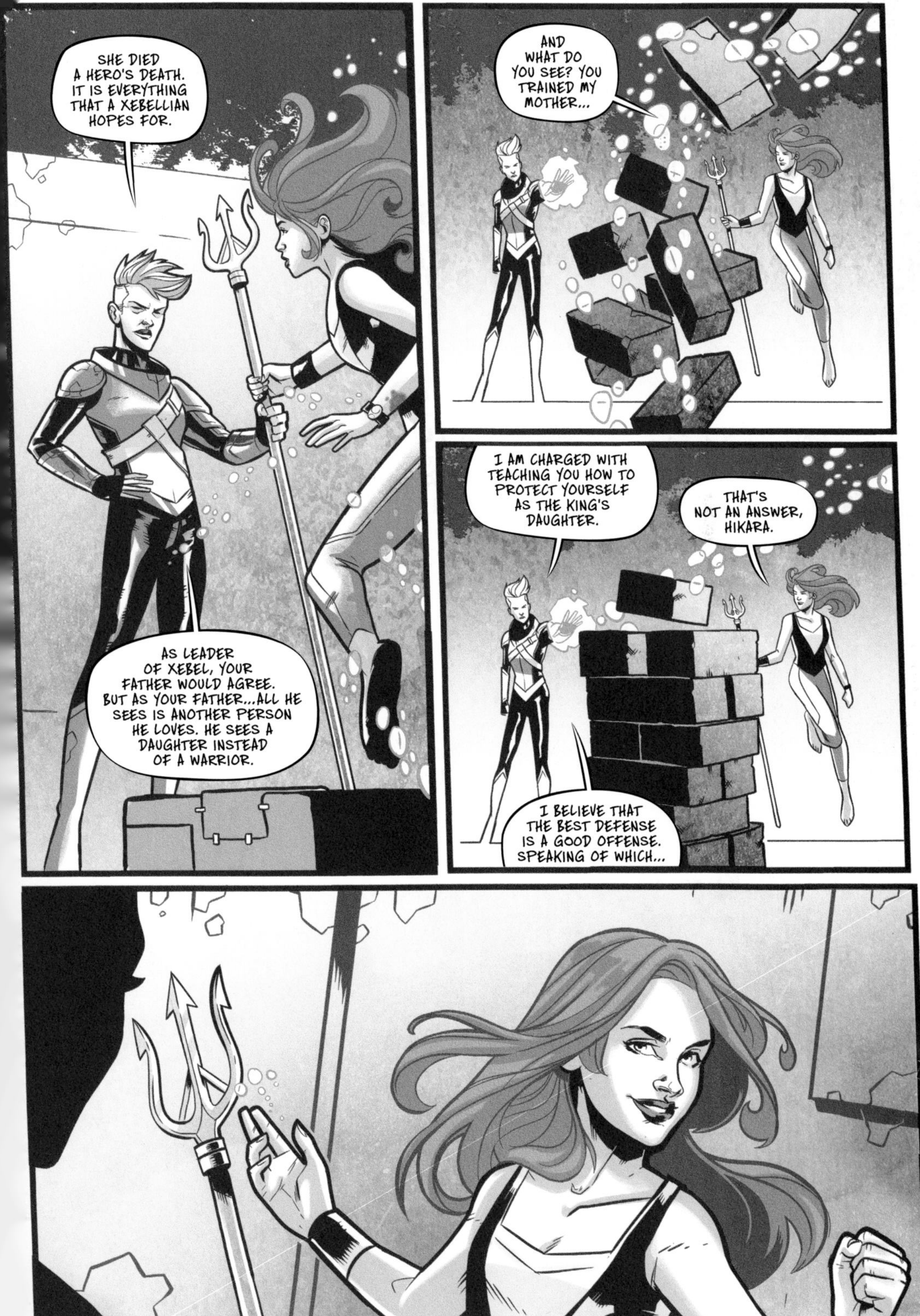

SHE DIED A HERO'S DEATH. IT IS EVERYTHING THAT A XEBELLIAN HOPES FOR.
AS LEADER OF XEBEL, YOUR FATHER WOULD AGREE. BUT AS YOUR FATHER...ALL HE SEES IS ANOTHER PERSON HE LOVES. HE SEES A DAUGHTER INSTEAD OF A WARRIOR.
AND WHAT DO YOU SEE? YOU TRAINED MY MOTHER...
I AM CHARGED WITH TEACHING YOU HOW TO PROTECT YOURSELF AS THE KING'S DAUGHTER.
THAT'S NOT AN ANSWER, HIKARA.
I BELIEVE THAT THE BEST DEFENSE IS A GOOD OFFENSE. SPEAKING OF WHICH...

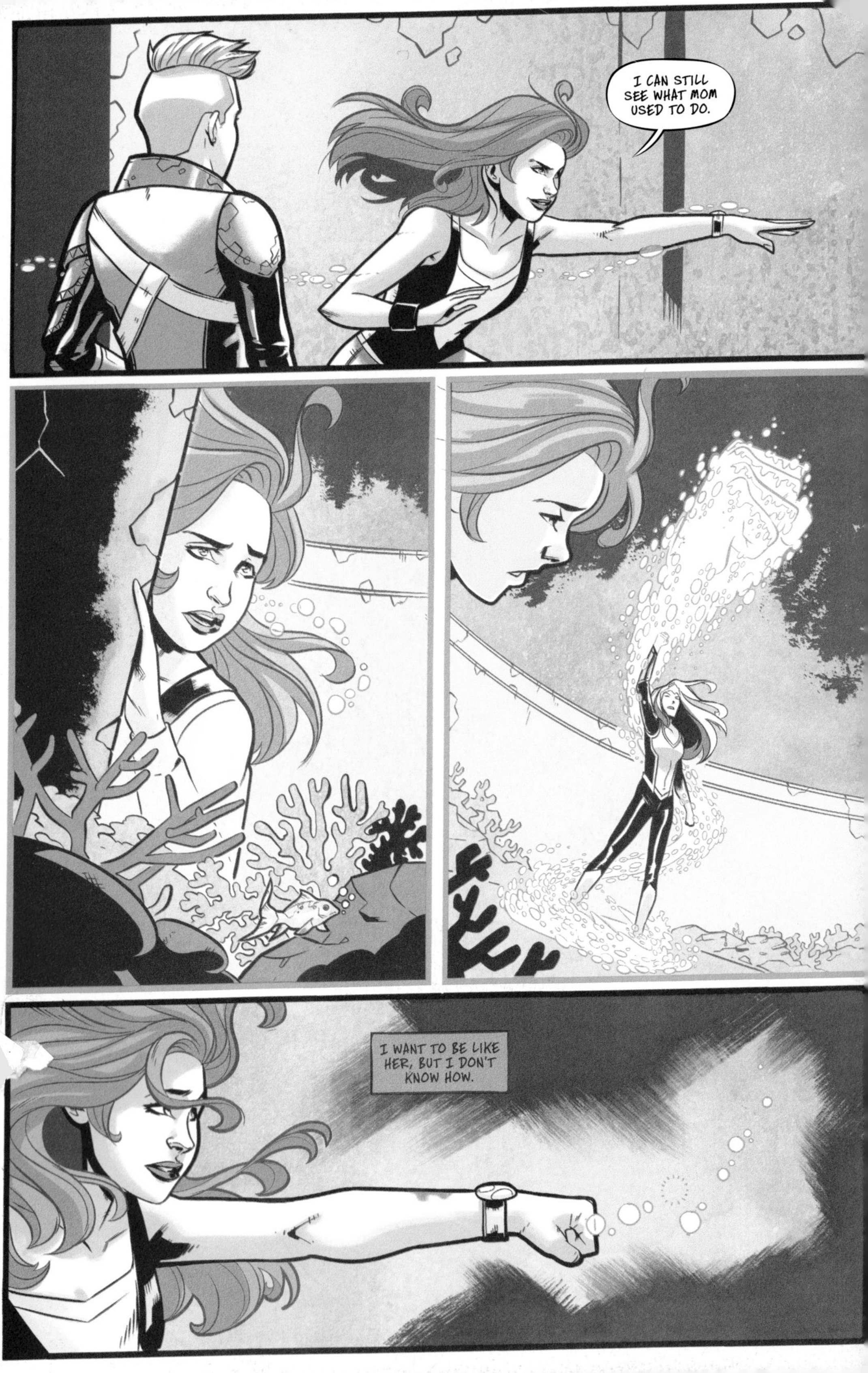
I CAN STILL SEE WHAT MOM USED TO DO.
I WANT TO BE LIKE HER, BUT I DON'T KNOW HOW.

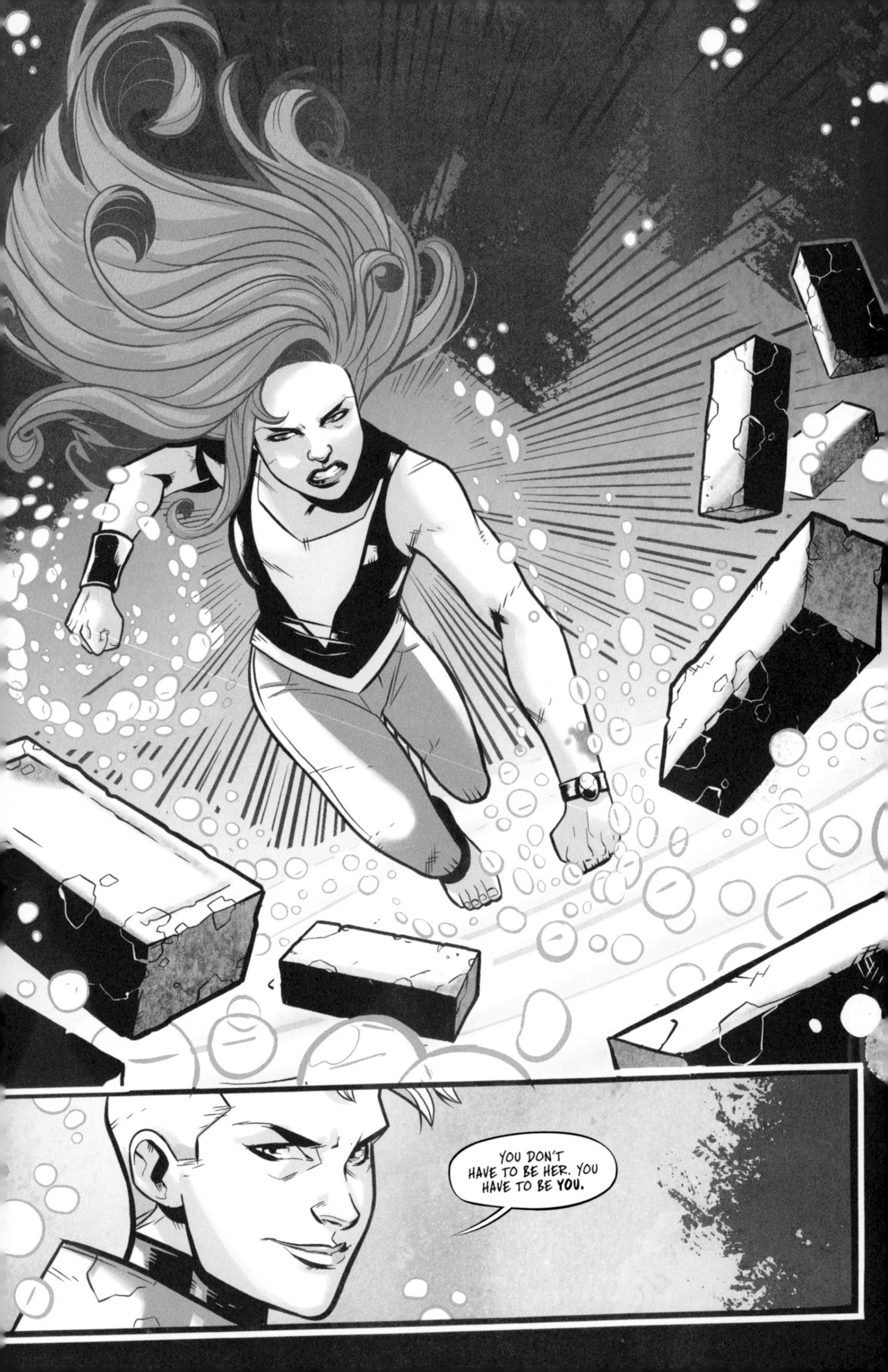
YOU DON'T HAVE TO BE HER. YOU HAVE TO BE **YOU.**

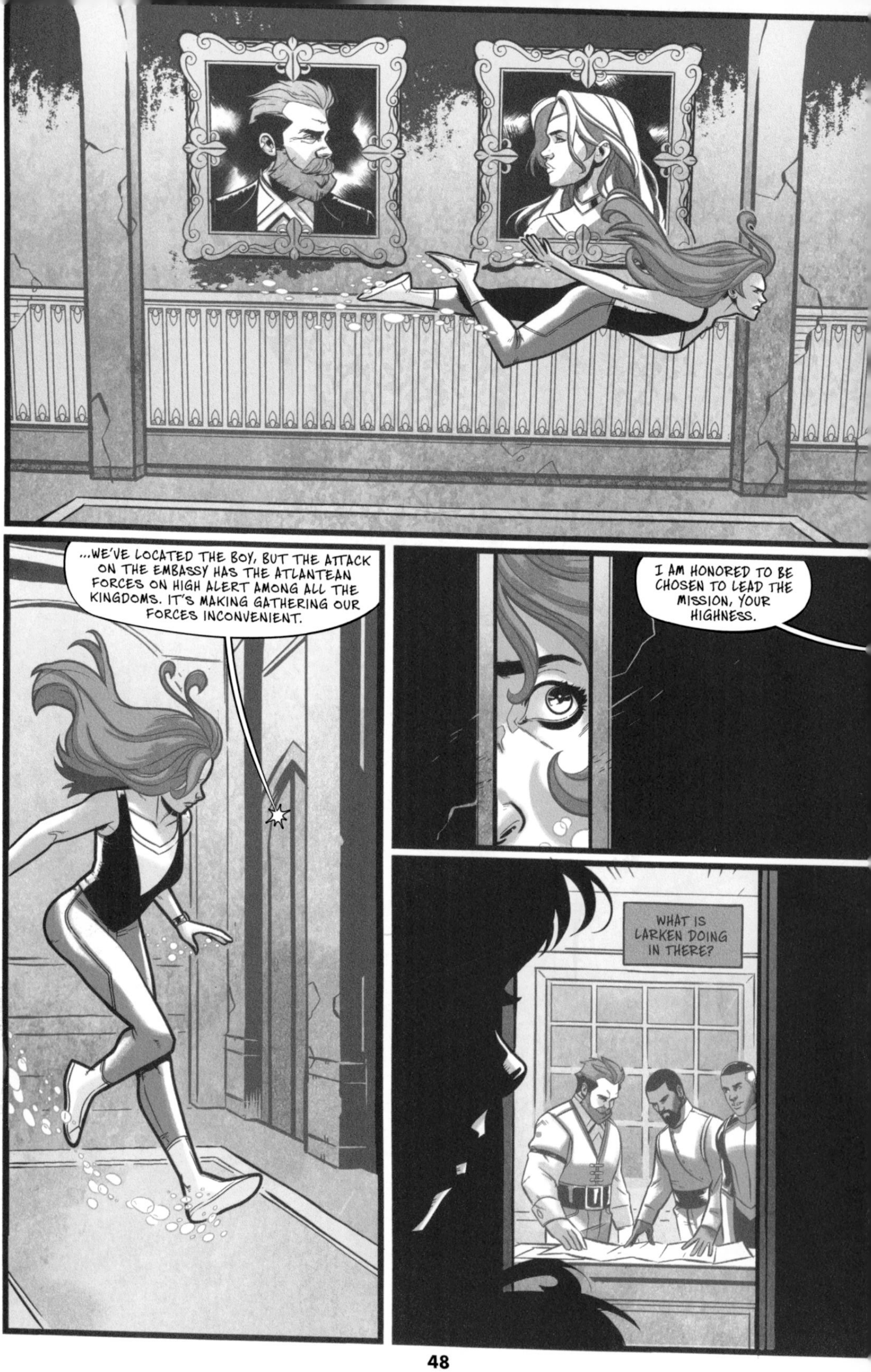
...WE'VE LOCATED THE BOY, BUT THE ATTACK ON THE EMBASSY HAS THE ATLANTEAN FORCES ON HIGH ALERT AMONG ALL THE KINGDOMS. IT'S MAKING GATHERING OUR FORCES INCONVENIENT.
I AM HONORED TO BE CHOSEN TO LEAD THE MISSION, YOUR HIGHNESS.
WHAT IS LARKEN DOING IN THERE?

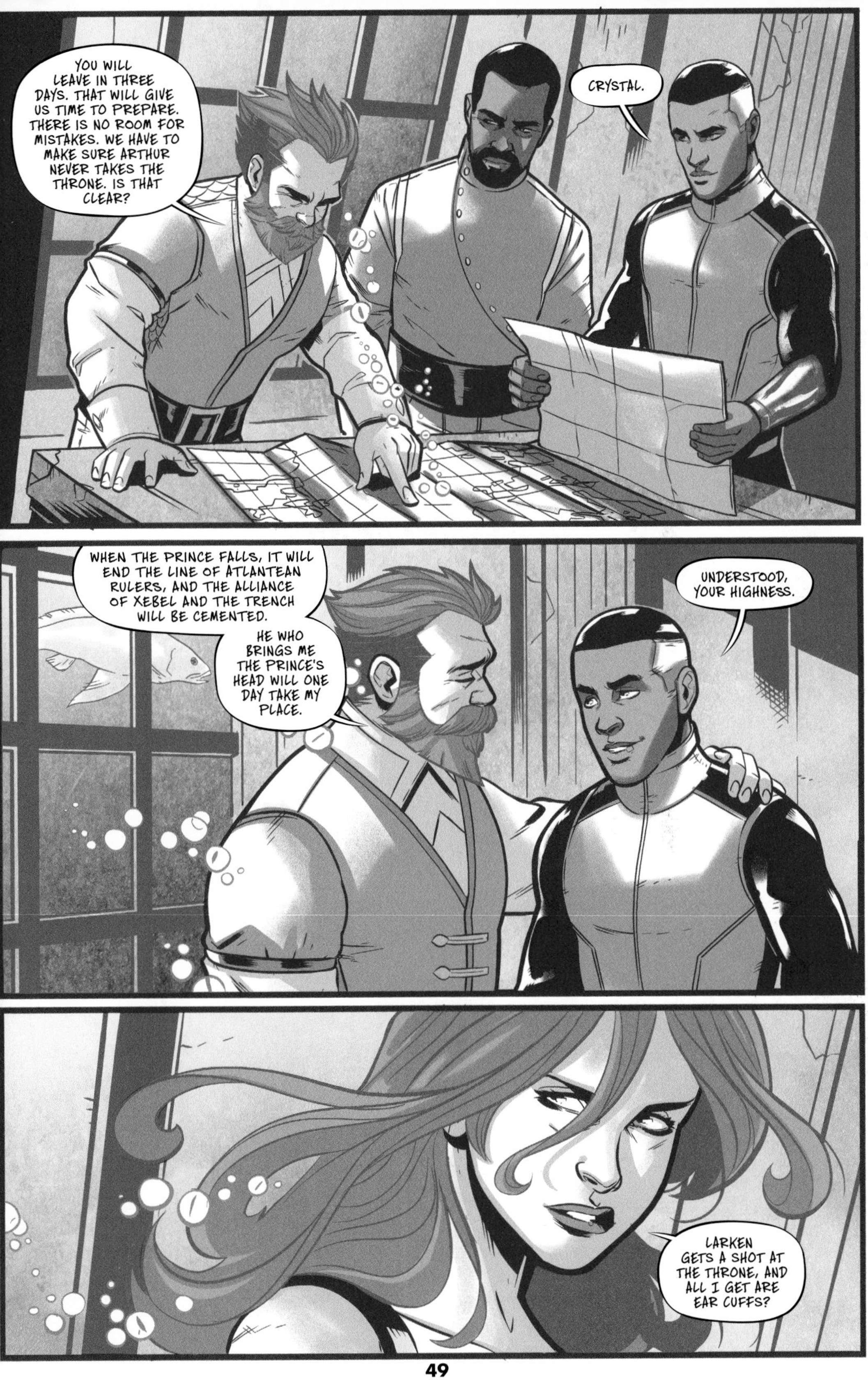
YOU WILL LEAVE IN THREE DAYS. THAT WILL GIVE US TIME TO PREPARE. THERE IS NO ROOM FOR MISTAKES. WE HAVE TO MAKE SURE ARTHUR NEVER TAKES THE THRONE. IS THAT CLEAR?
CRYSTAL.
WHEN THE PRINCE FALLS, IT WILL END THE LINE OF ATLANTEAN RULERS, AND THE ALLIANCE OF XEBEL AND THE TRENCH WILL BE CEMENTED.
HE WHO BRINGS ME THE PRINCE'S HEAD WILL ONE DAY TAKE MY PLACE.
UNDERSTOOD, YOUR HIGHNESS.
LARKEN GETS A SHOT AT THE THRONE, AND ALL I GET ARE EAR CUFFS?

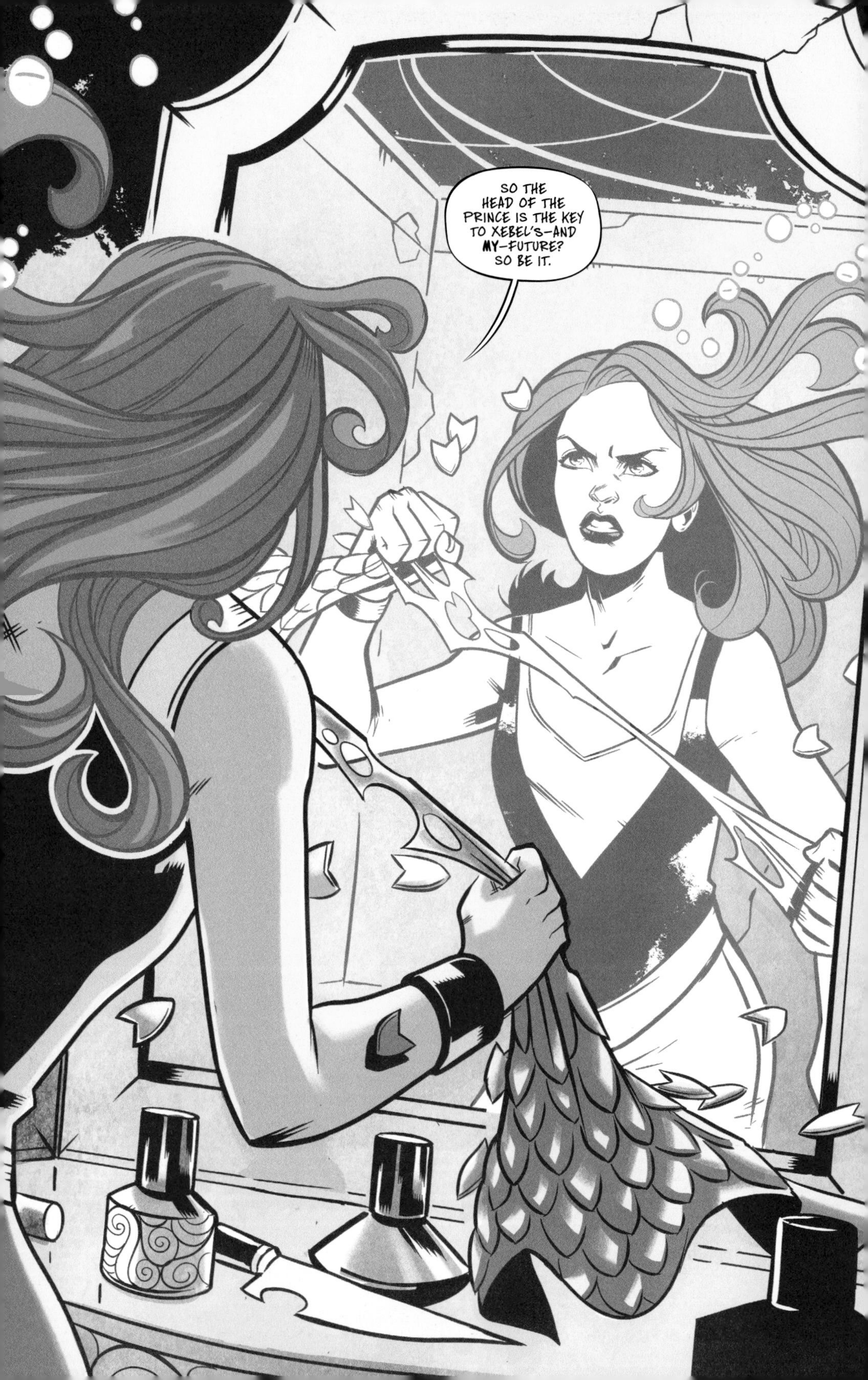
SO THE HEAD OF THE PRINCE IS THE KEY TO XEBEL'S—AND MY—FUTURE? SO BE IT.

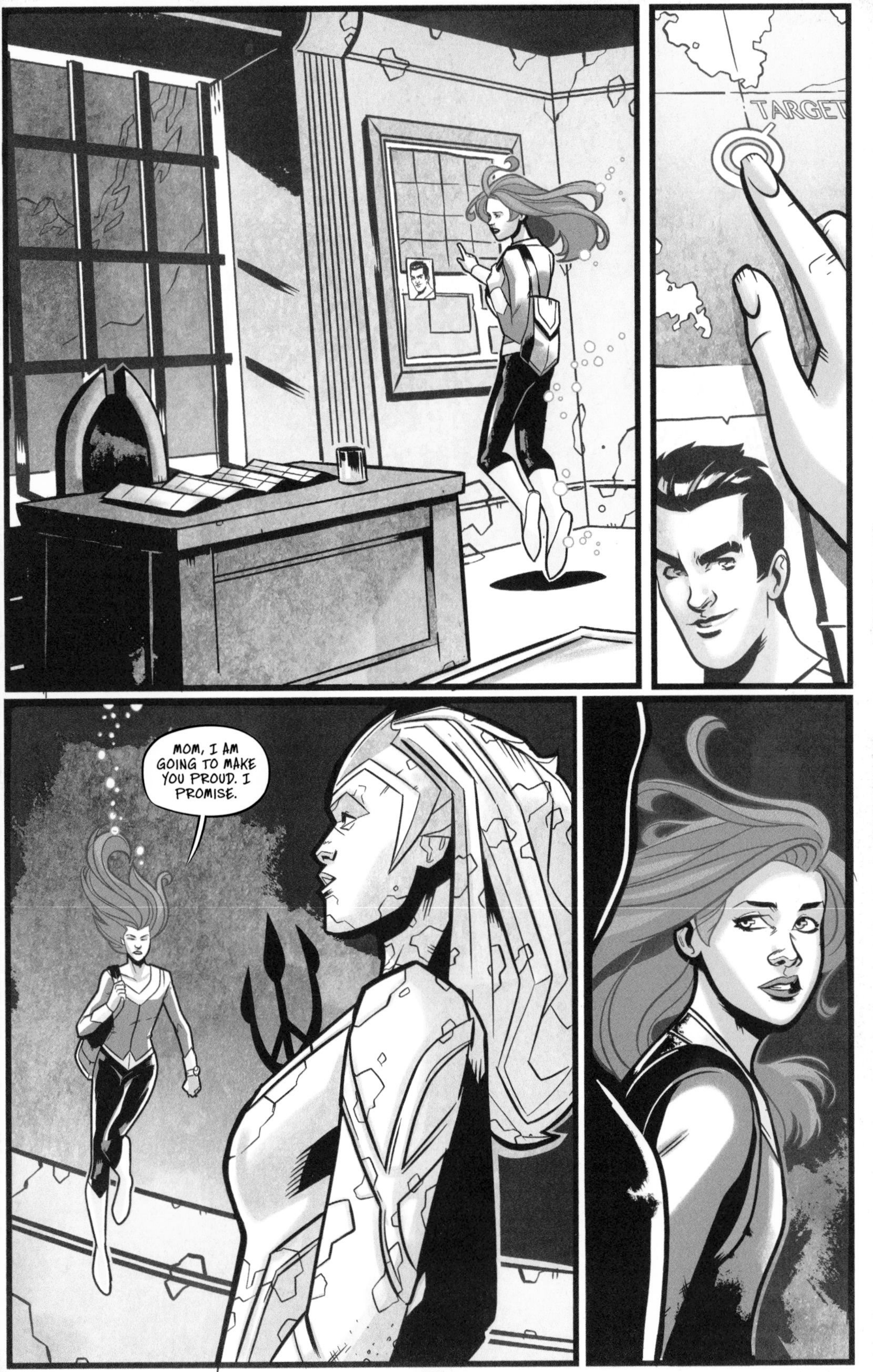
MOM, I AM GOING TO MAKE YOU PROUD. I PROMISE.

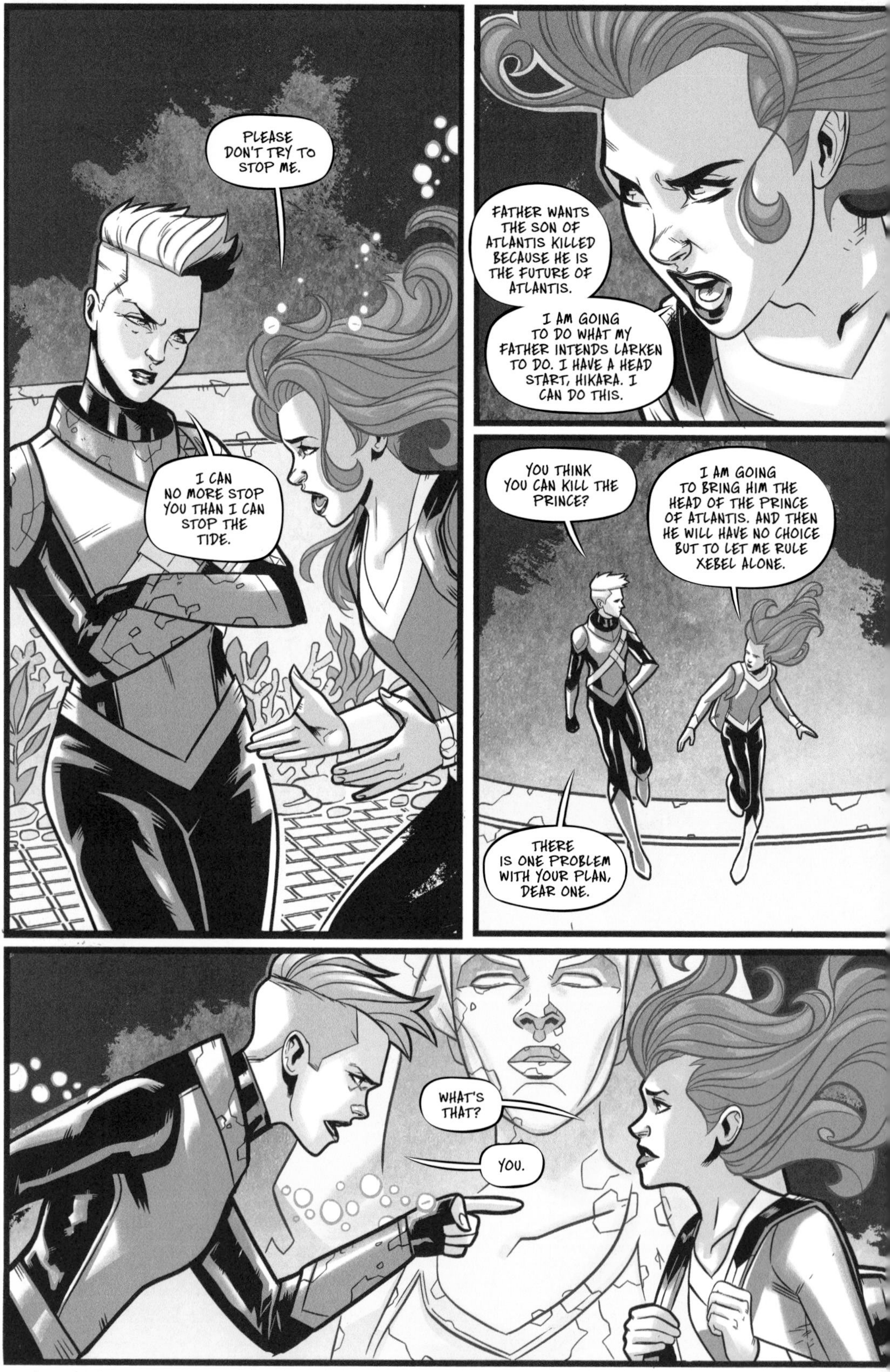
PLEASE DON'T TRY TO STOP ME.
I CAN NO MORE STOP YOU THAN I CAN STOP THE TIDE.
FATHER WANTS THE SON OF ATLANTIS KILLED BECAUSE HE IS THE FUTURE OF ATLANTIS.
I AM GOING TO DO WHAT MY FATHER INTENDS LARKEN TO DO. I HAVE A HEAD START, HIKARA. I CAN DO THIS.
YOU THINK YOU CAN KILL THE PRINCE?
I AM GOING TO BRING HIM THE HEAD OF THE PRINCE OF ATLANTIS. AND THEN HE WILL HAVE NO CHOICE BUT TO LET ME RULE XEBEL ALONE.
THERE IS ONE PROBLEM WITH YOUR PLAN, DEAR ONE.
WHAT'S THAT?
YOU.

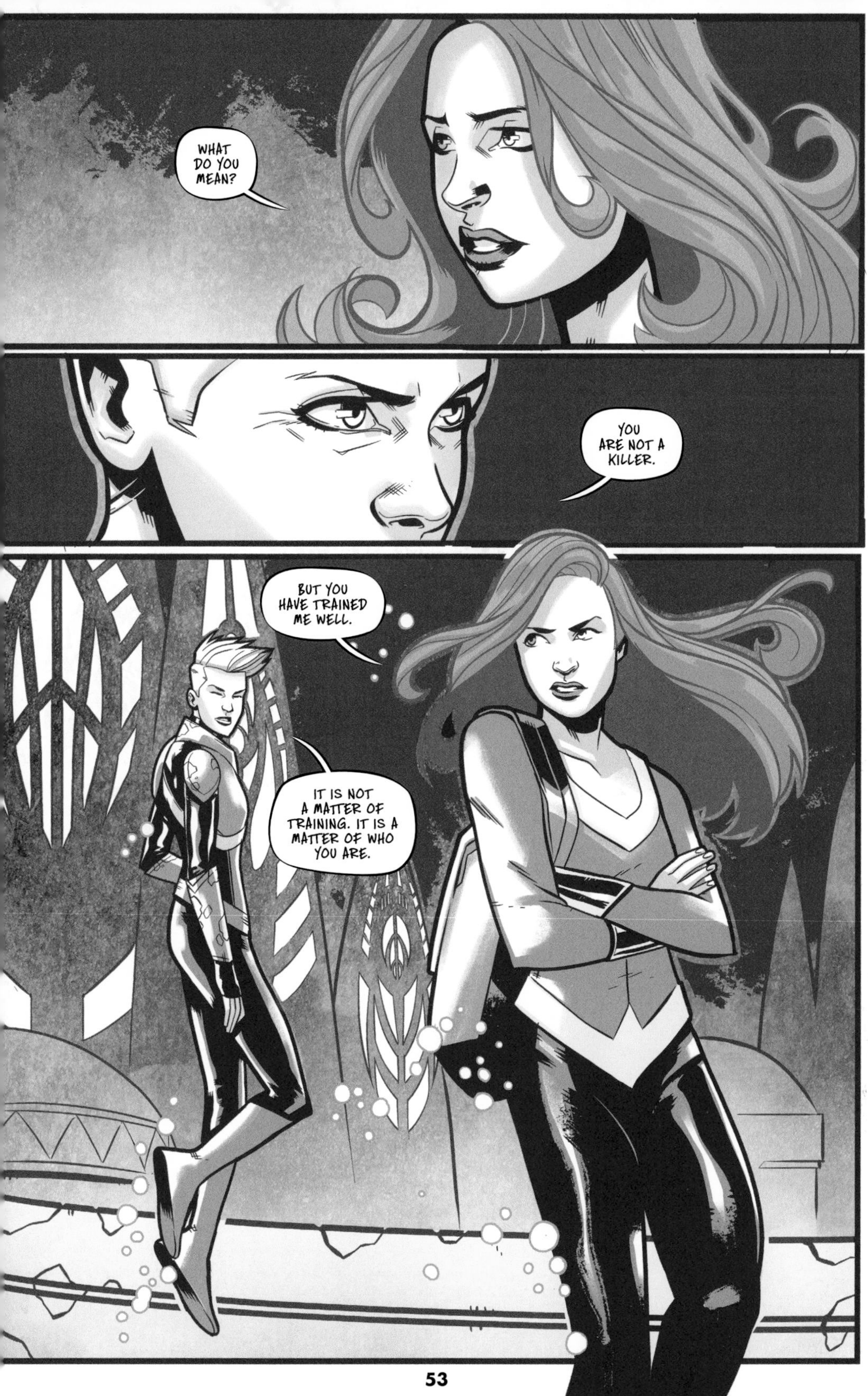
WHAT DO YOU MEAN?
YOU ARE NOT A KILLER.
BUT YOU HAVE TRAINED ME WELL.
IT IS NOT A MATTER OF TRAINING. IT IS A MATTER OF WHO YOU ARE.

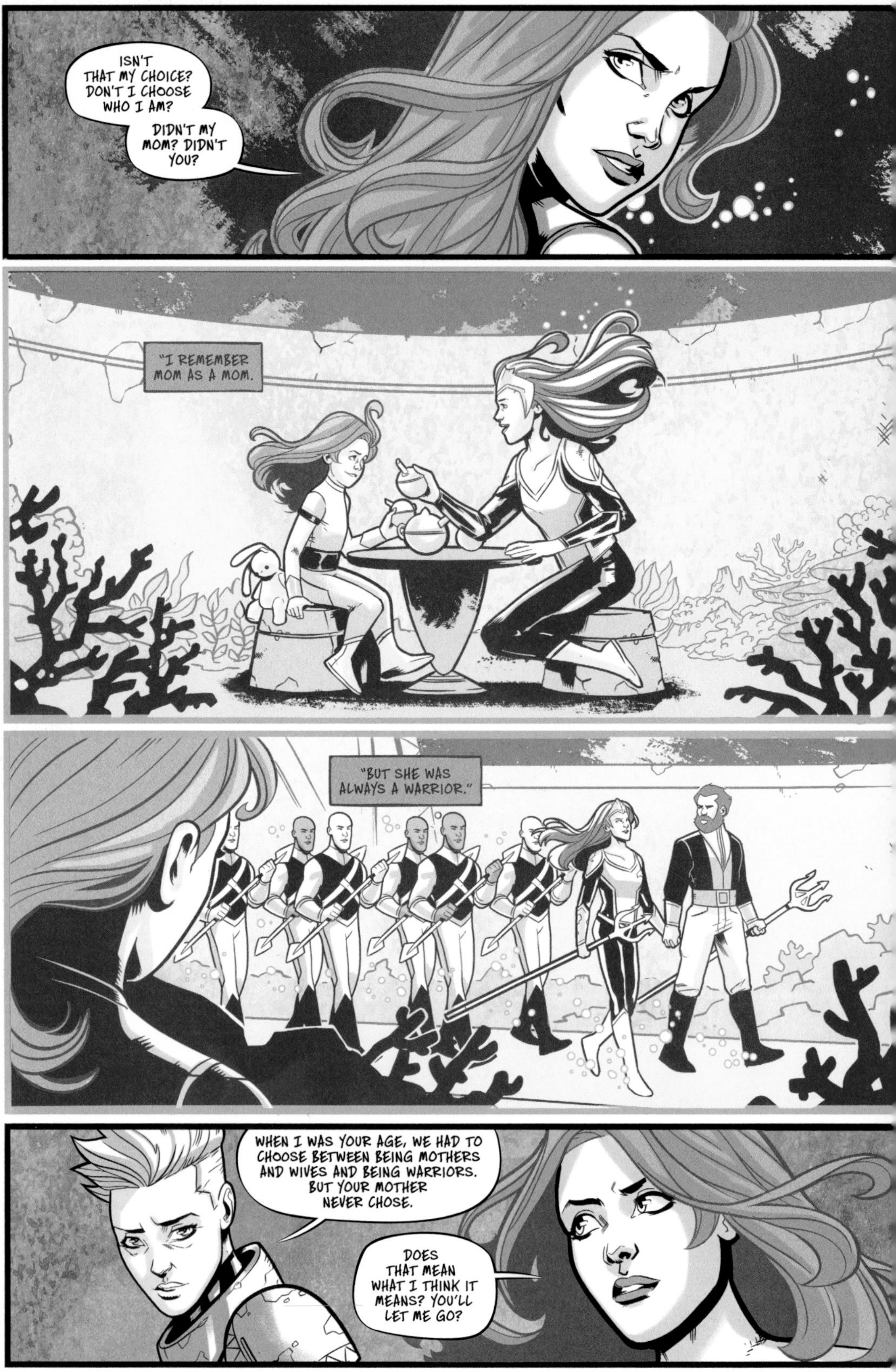
ISN'T THAT MY CHOICE? DON'T I CHOOSE WHO I AM?
DIDN'T MY MOM? DIDN'T YOU?
"I REMEMBER MOM AS A MOM.
"BUT SHE WAS ALWAYS A WARRIOR."
WHEN I WAS YOUR AGE, WE HAD TO CHOOSE BETWEEN BEING MOTHERS AND WIVES AND BEING WARRIORS. BUT YOUR MOTHER NEVER CHOSE.
DOES THAT MEAN WHAT I THINK IT MEANS? YOU'LL LET ME GO?

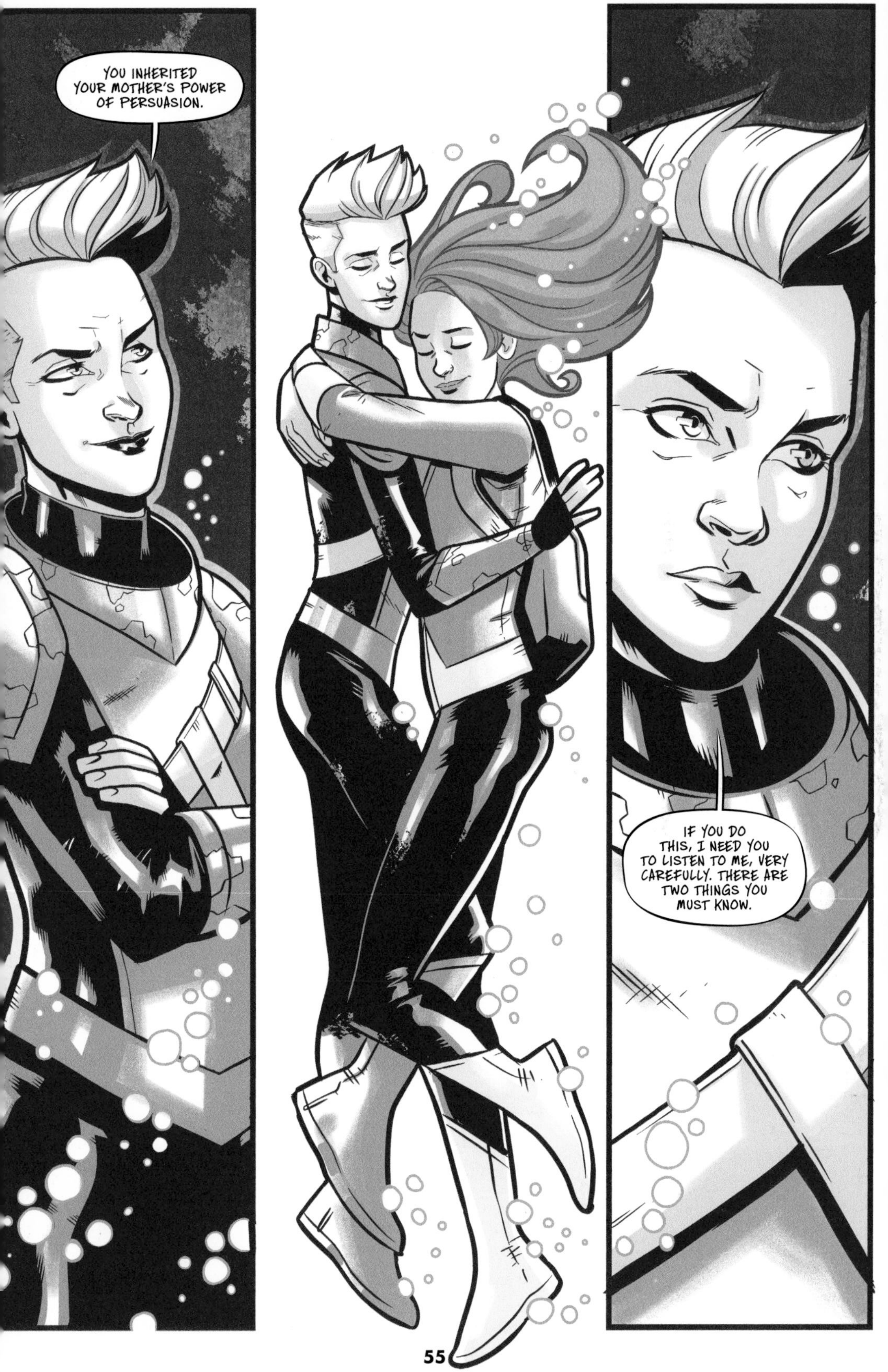
YOU INHERITED YOUR MOTHER'S POWER OF PERSUASION.
IF YOU DO THIS, I NEED YOU TO LISTEN TO ME, VERY CAREFULLY. THERE ARE TWO THINGS YOU MUST KNOW.

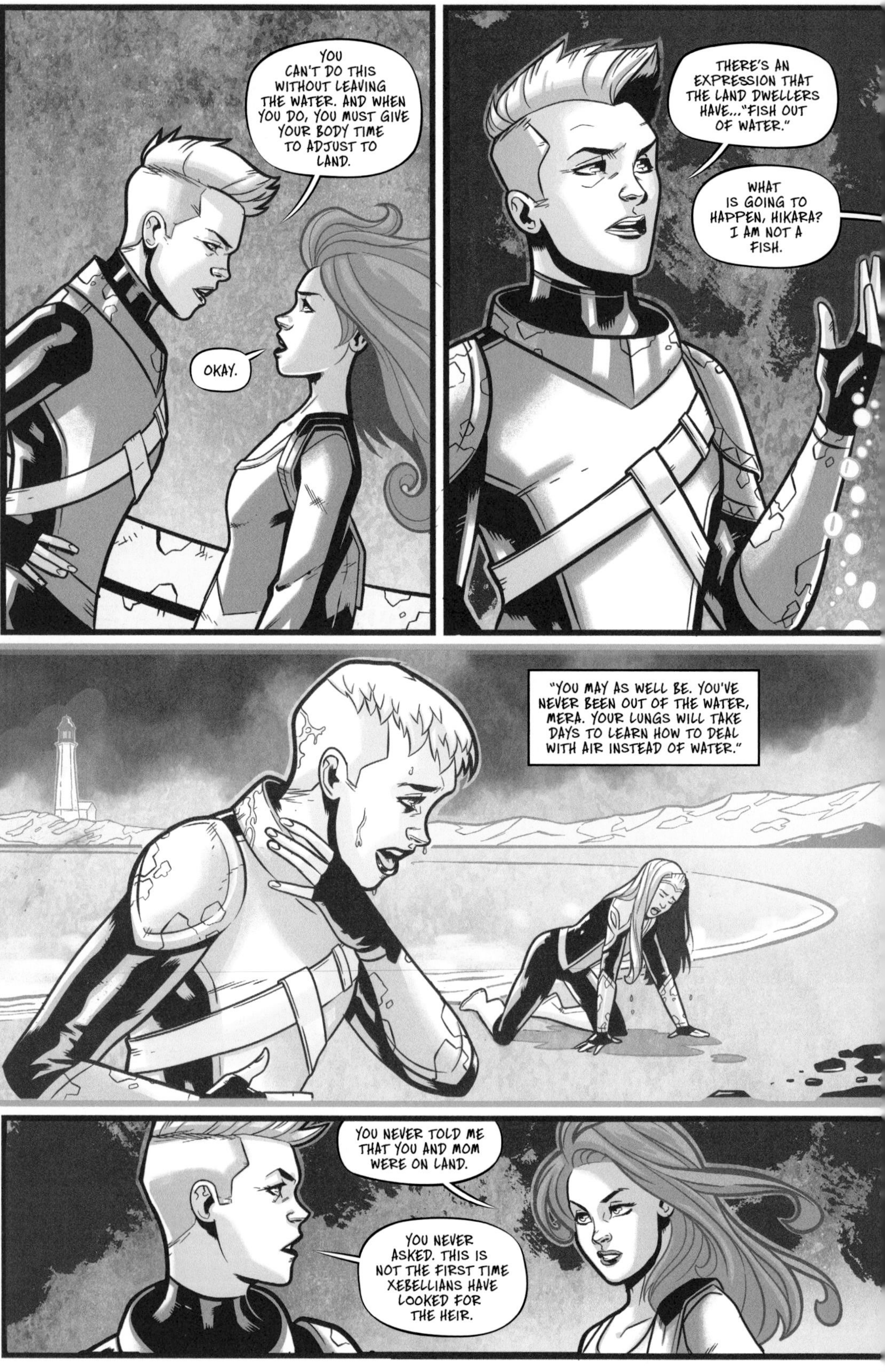
YOU CAN'T DO THIS WITHOUT LEAVING THE WATER. AND WHEN YOU DO, YOU MUST GIVE YOUR BODY TIME TO ADJUST TO LAND.
OKAY.
THERE'S AN EXPRESSION THAT THE LAND DWELLERS HAVE..."FISH OUT OF WATER."
WHAT IS GOING TO HAPPEN, HIKARA? I AM NOT A FISH.
"YOU MAY AS WELL BE. YOU'VE NEVER BEEN OUT OF THE WATER, MERA. YOUR LUNGS WILL TAKE DAYS TO LEARN HOW TO DEAL WITH AIR INSTEAD OF WATER."
YOU NEVER TOLD ME THAT YOU AND MOM WERE ON LAND.
YOU NEVER ASKED. THIS IS NOT THE FIRST TIME XEBELLIANS HAVE LOOKED FOR THE HEIR.

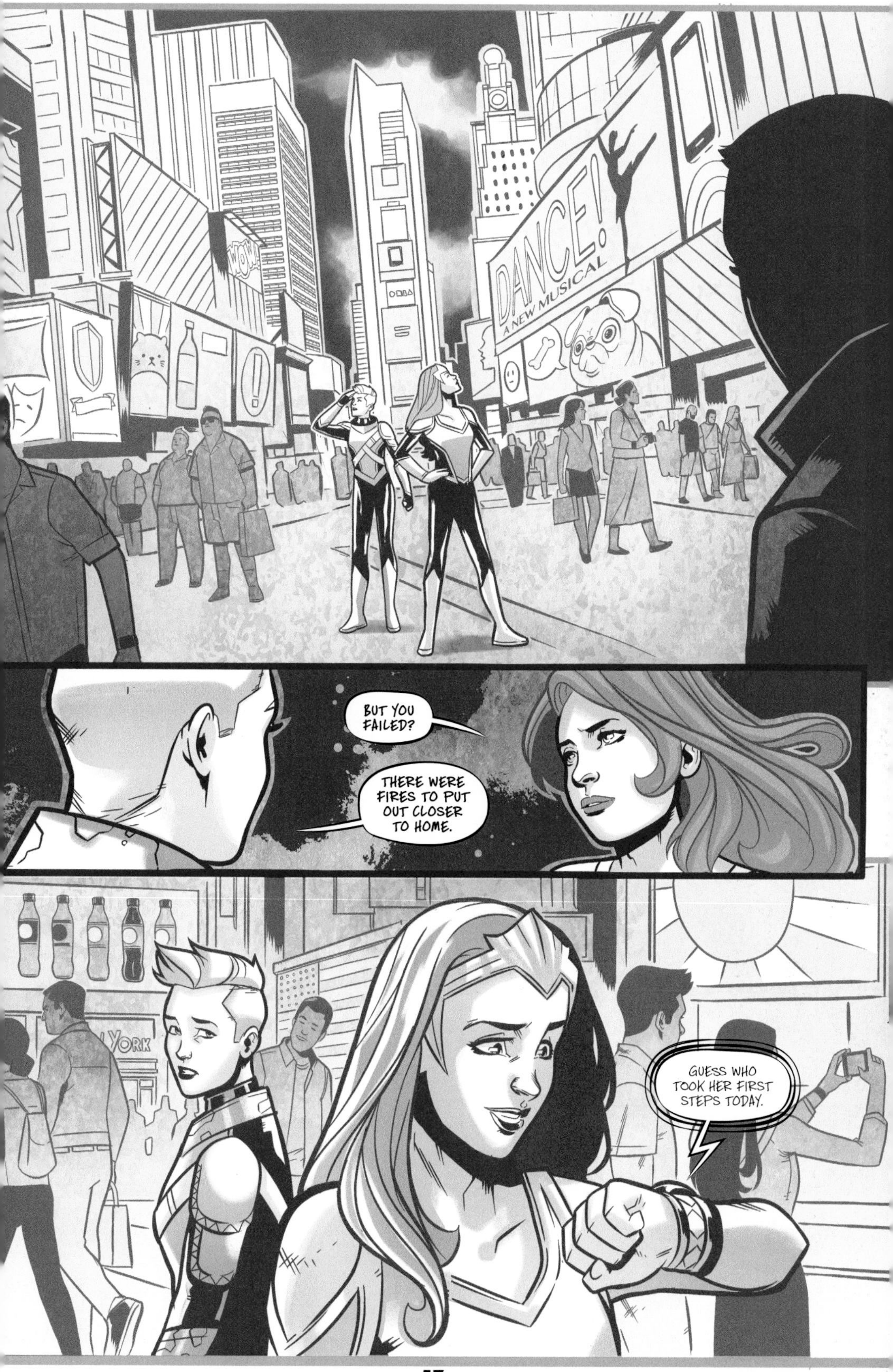
WOW!
DANCE!
A NEW MUSICAL
BUT YOU FAILED?
THERE WERE FIRES TO PUT OUT CLOSER TO HOME.
YORK
GUESS WHO TOOK HER FIRST STEPS TODAY.

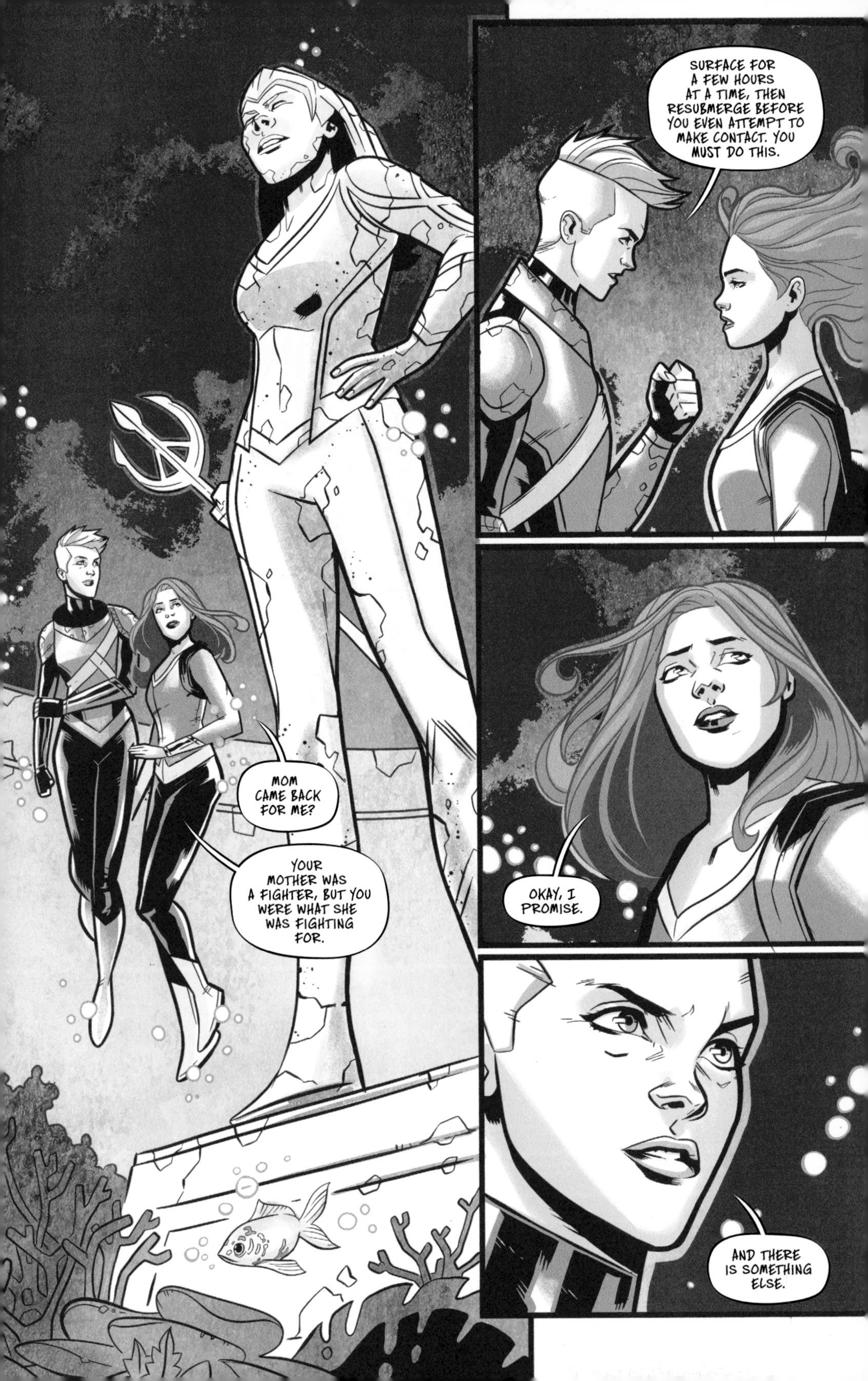
MOM CAME BACK FOR ME?
YOUR MOTHER WAS A FIGHTER, BUT YOU WERE WHAT SHE WAS FIGHTING FOR.
SURFACE FOR A FEW HOURS AT A TIME, THEN RESUBMERGE BEFORE YOU EVEN ATTEMPT TO MAKE CONTACT. YOU MUST DO THIS.
OKAY, I PROMISE.
AND THERE IS SOMETHING ELSE.

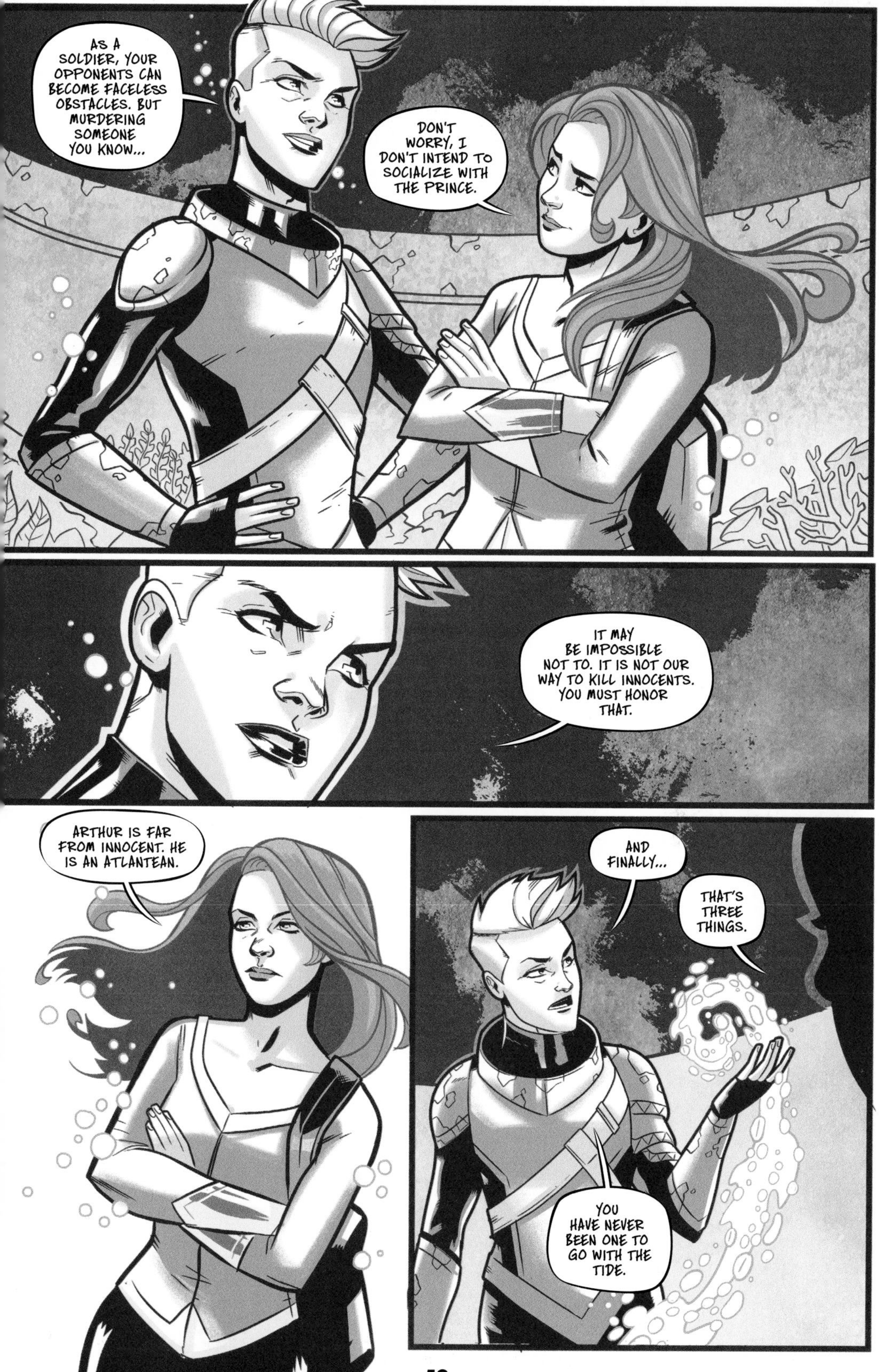
AS A SOLDIER, YOUR OPPONENTS CAN BECOME FACELESS OBSTACLES. BUT MURDERING SOMEONE YOU KNOW...
DON'T WORRY, I DON'T INTEND TO SOCIALIZE WITH THE PRINCE.
IT MAY BE IMPOSSIBLE NOT TO. IT IS NOT OUR WAY TO KILL INNOCENTS. YOU MUST HONOR THAT.
ARTHUR IS FAR FROM INNOCENT. HE IS AN ATLANTEAN.
AND FINALLY...
THAT'S THREE THINGS.
YOU HAVE NEVER BEEN ONE TO GO WITH THE TIDE.

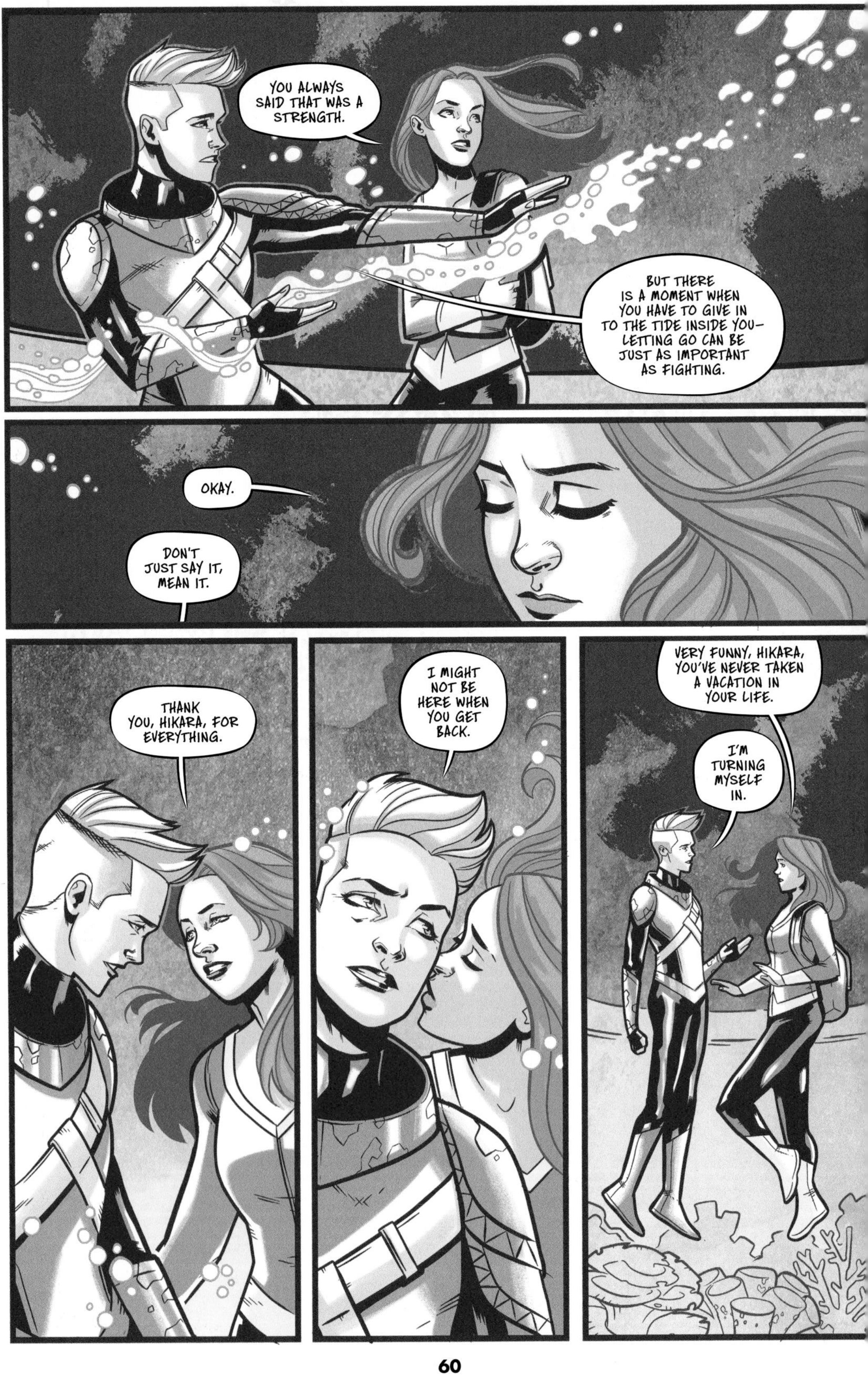
YOU ALWAYS SAID THAT WAS A STRENGTH.
BUT THERE IS A MOMENT WHEN YOU HAVE TO GIVE IN TO THE TIDE INSIDE YOU-LETTING GO CAN BE JUST AS IMPORTANT AS FIGHTING.
OKAY.
DON'T JUST SAY IT, MEAN IT.
THANK YOU, HIKARA, FOR EVERYTHING.
I MIGHT NOT BE HERE WHEN YOU GET BACK.
VERY FUNNY, HIKARA, YOU'VE NEVER TAKEN A VACATION IN YOUR LIFE.
I'M TURNING MYSELF IN.

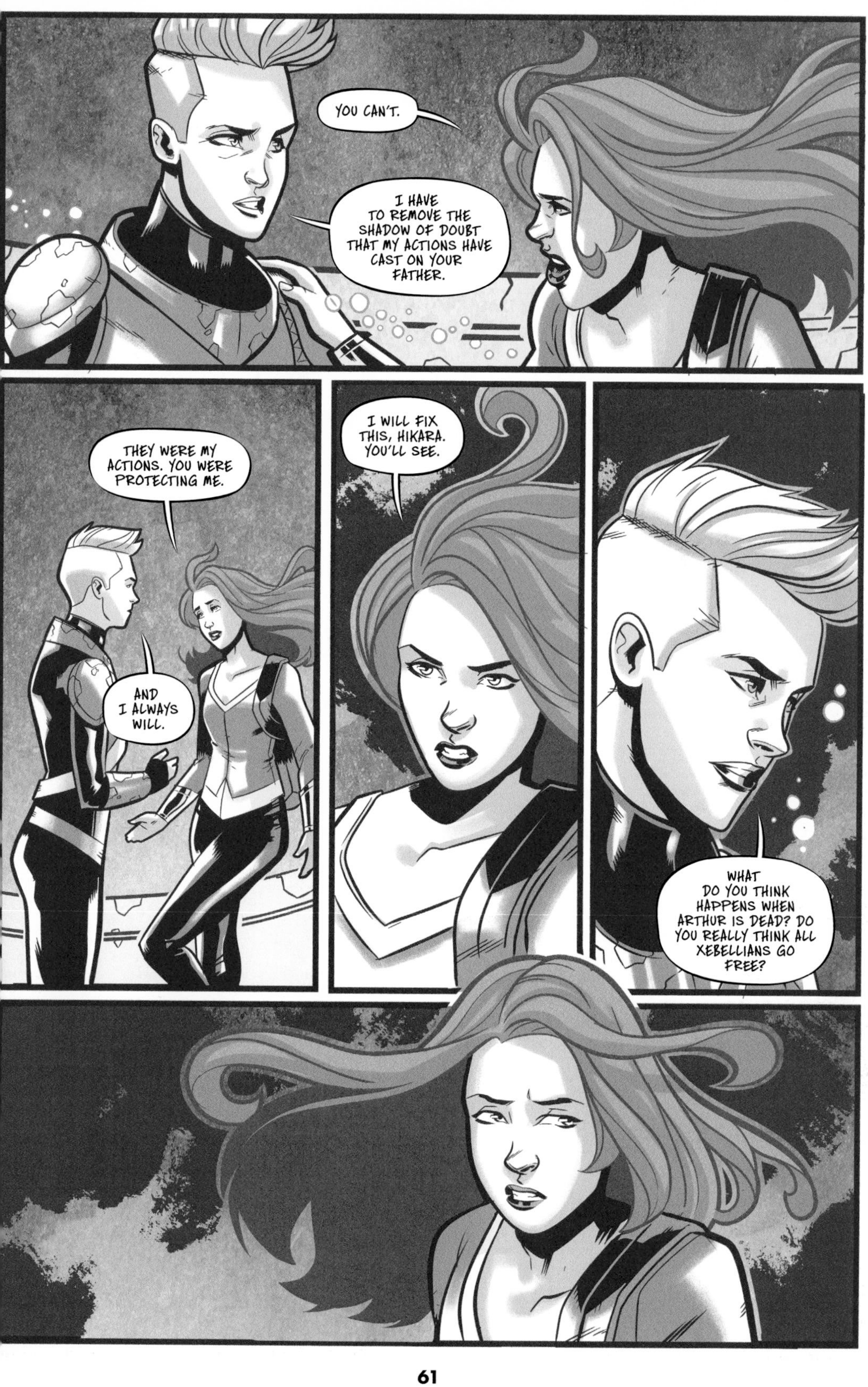
YOU CAN'T.
I HAVE TO REMOVE THE SHADOW OF DOUBT THAT MY ACTIONS HAVE CAST ON YOUR FATHER.
THEY WERE MY ACTIONS. YOU WERE PROTECTING ME.
AND I ALWAYS WILL.
I WILL FIX THIS, HIKARA. YOU'LL SEE.
WHAT DO YOU THINK HAPPENS WHEN ARTHUR IS DEAD? DO YOU REALLY THINK ALL XEBELLIANS GO FREE?

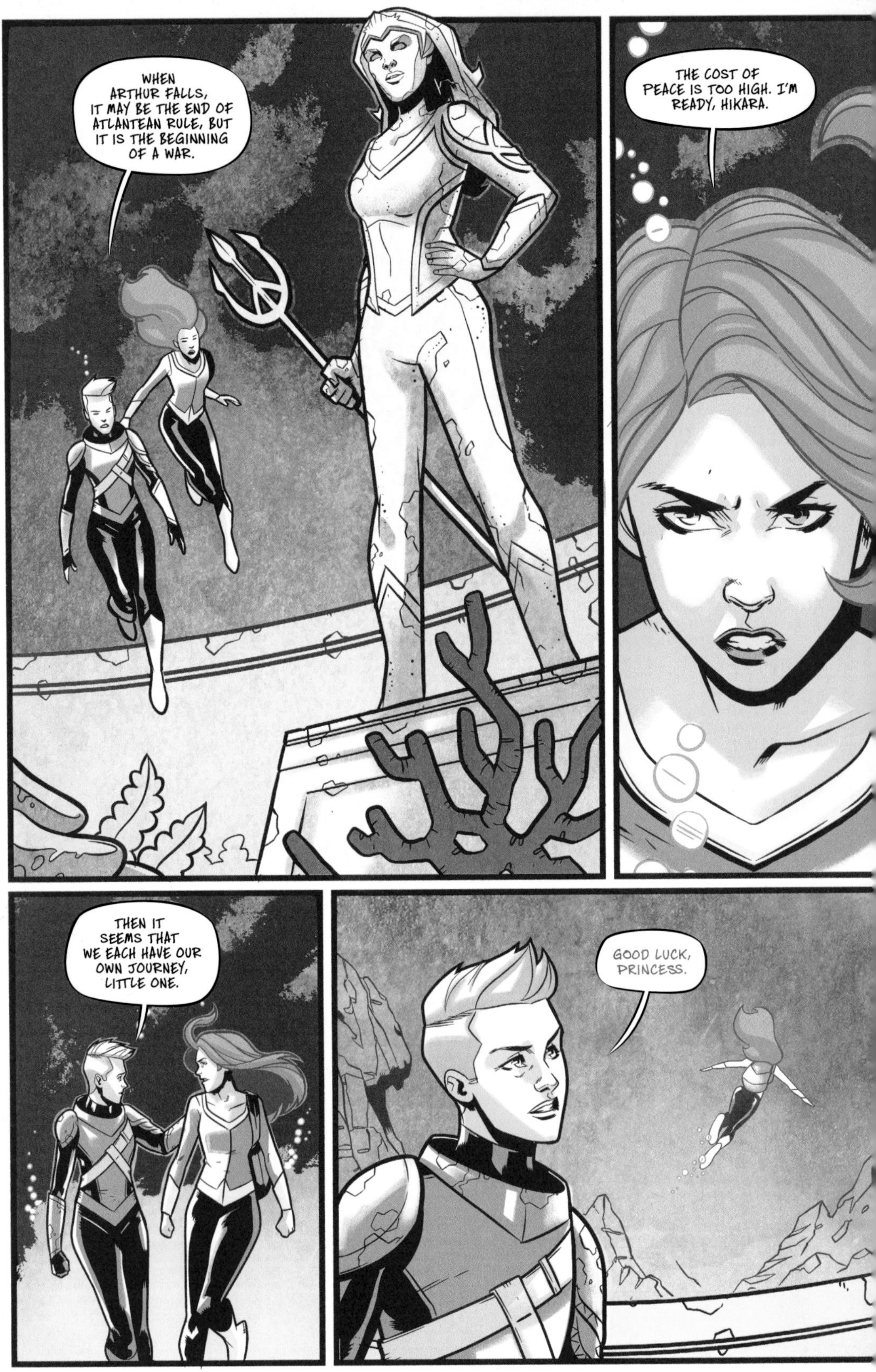
WHEN ARTHUR FALLS, IT MAY BE THE END OF ATLANTEAN RULE, BUT IT IS THE BEGINNING OF A WAR.
THE COST OF PEACE IS TOO HIGH. I'M READY, HIKARA.
THEN IT SEEMS THAT WE EACH HAVE OUR OWN JOURNEY, LITTLE ONE.
GOOD LUCK, PRINCESS.

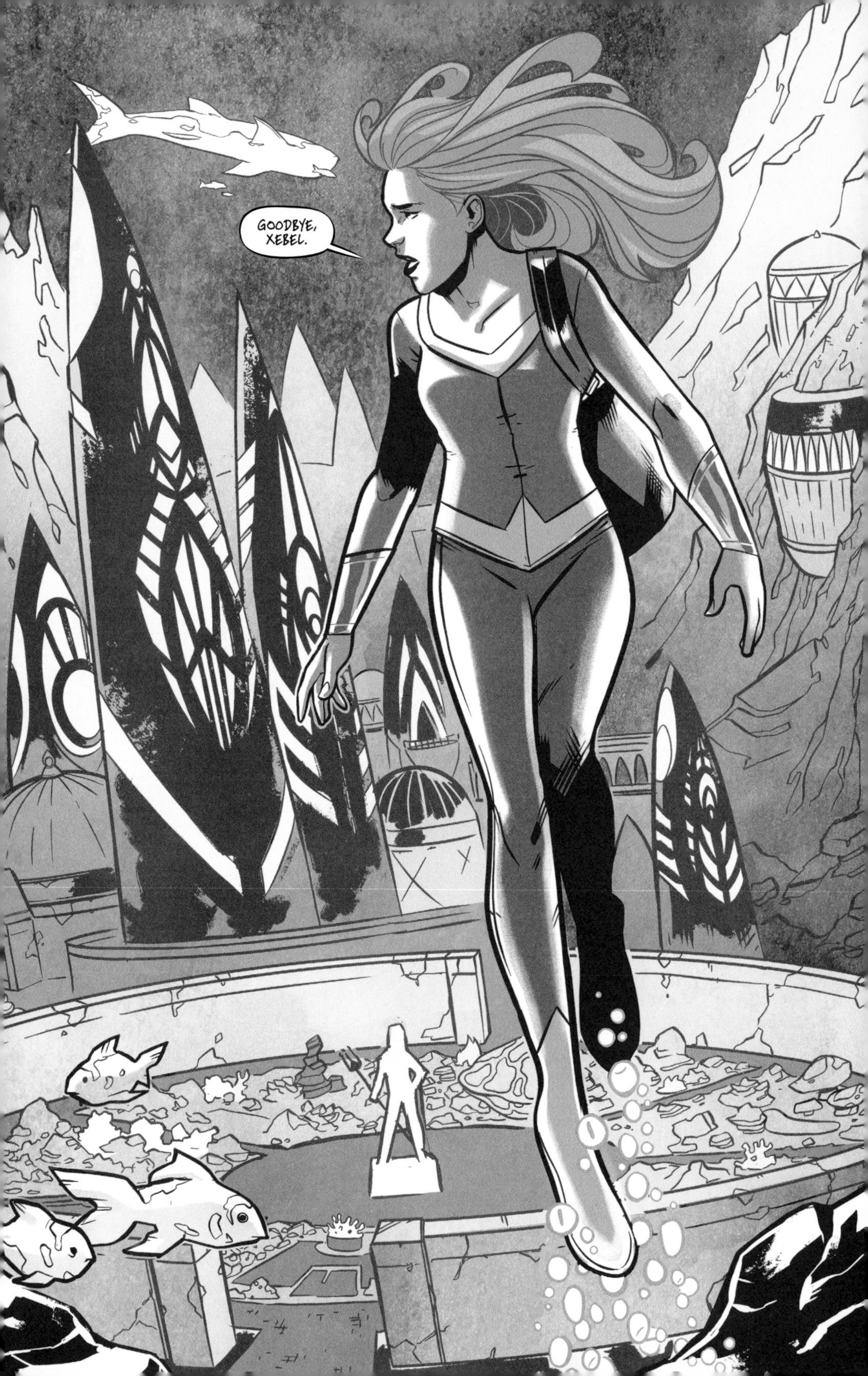
GOODBYE, XEBEL.

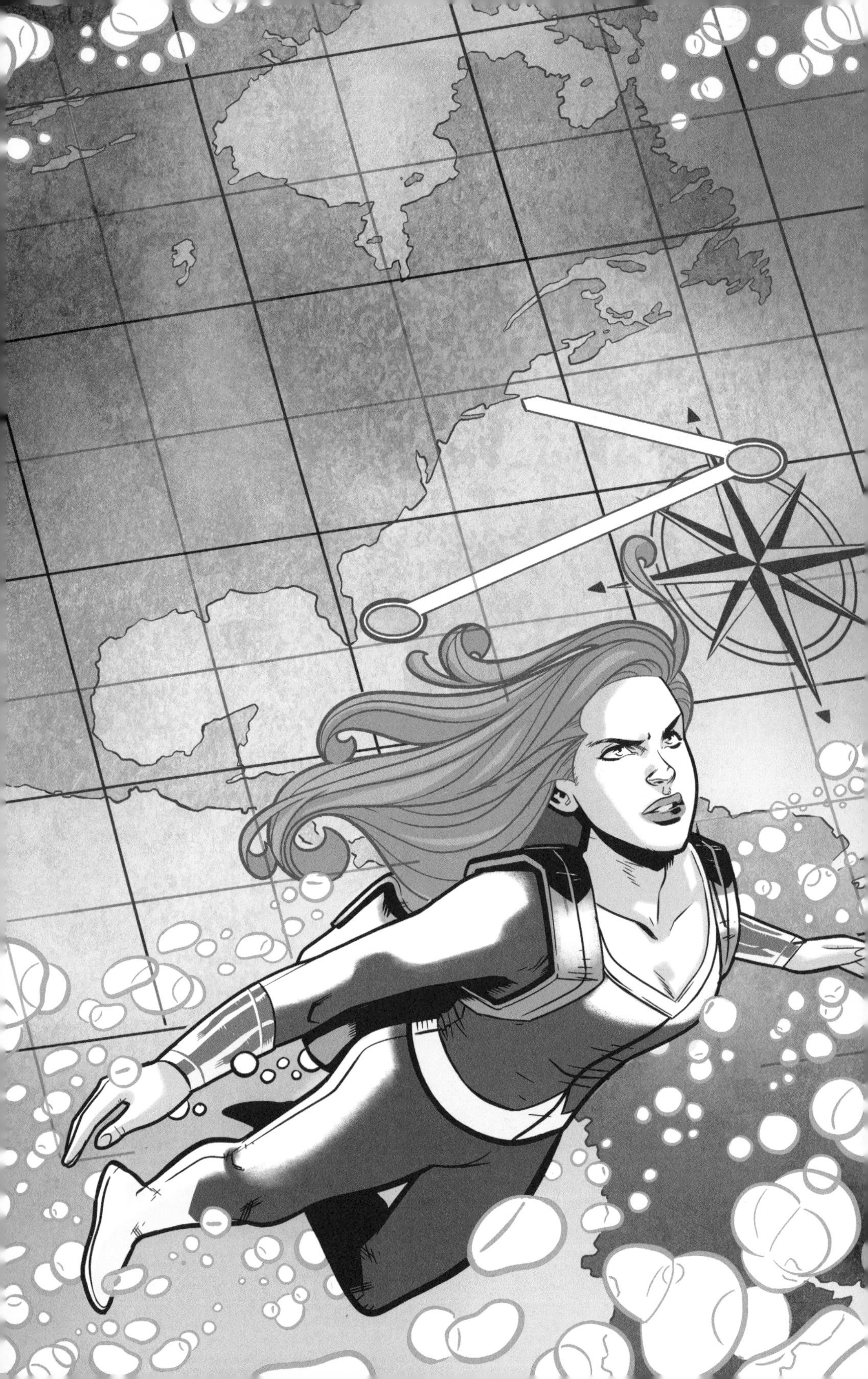

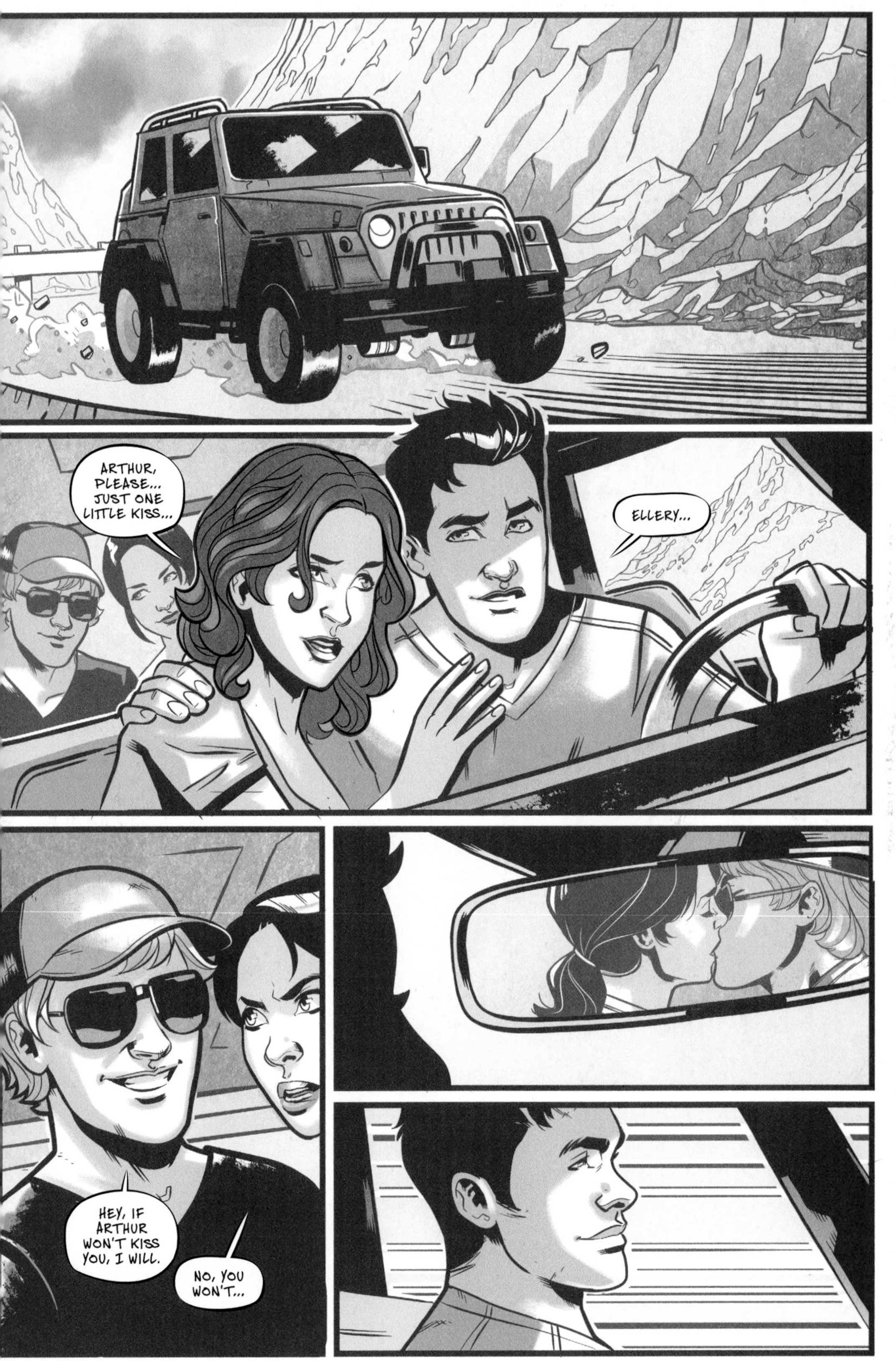
ARTHUR, PLEASE... JUST ONE LITTLE KISS...
ELLERY...
HEY, IF ARTHUR WON'T KISS YOU, I WILL.
NO, YOU WON'T...

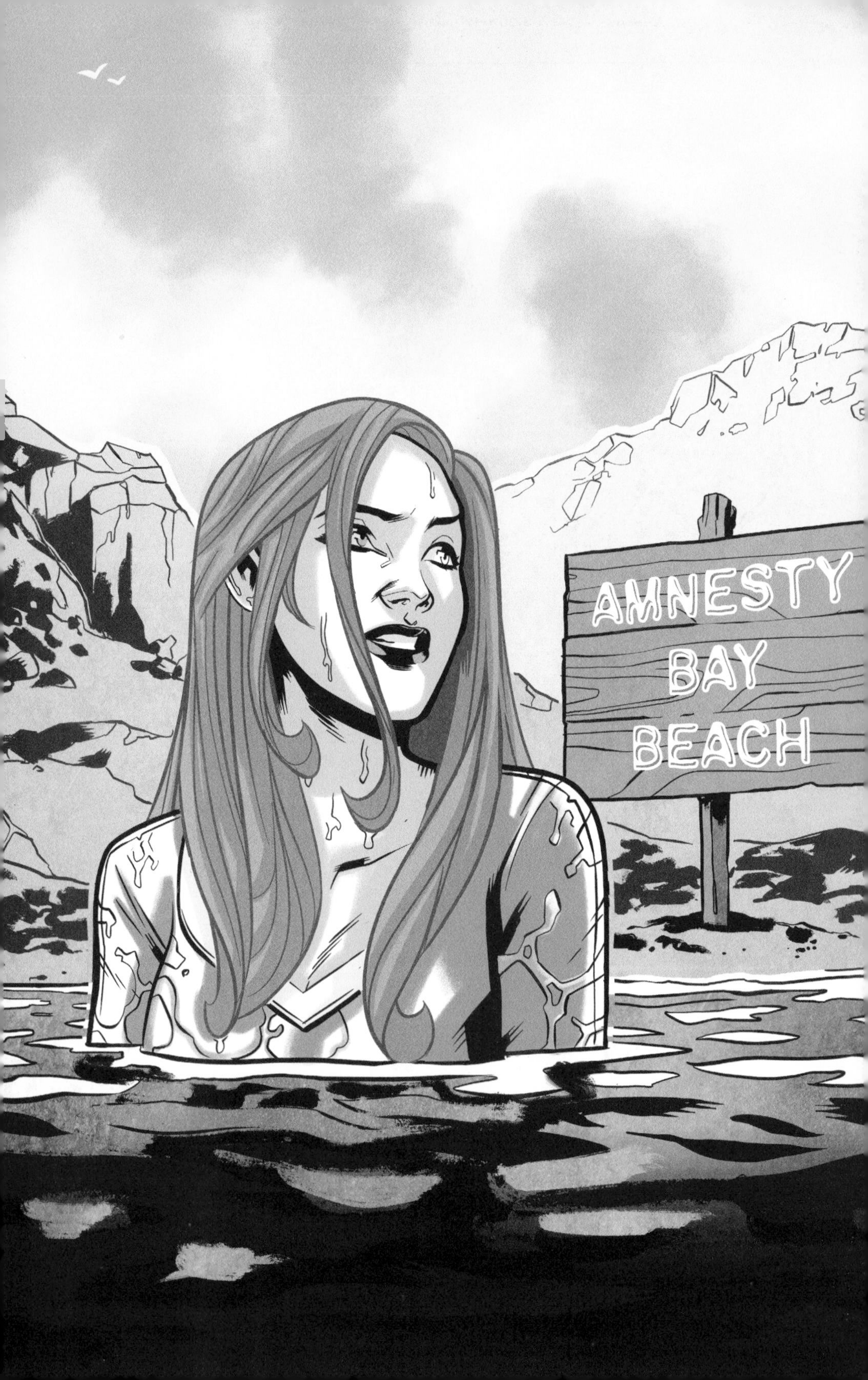
AMNESTY
BAY
BEACH

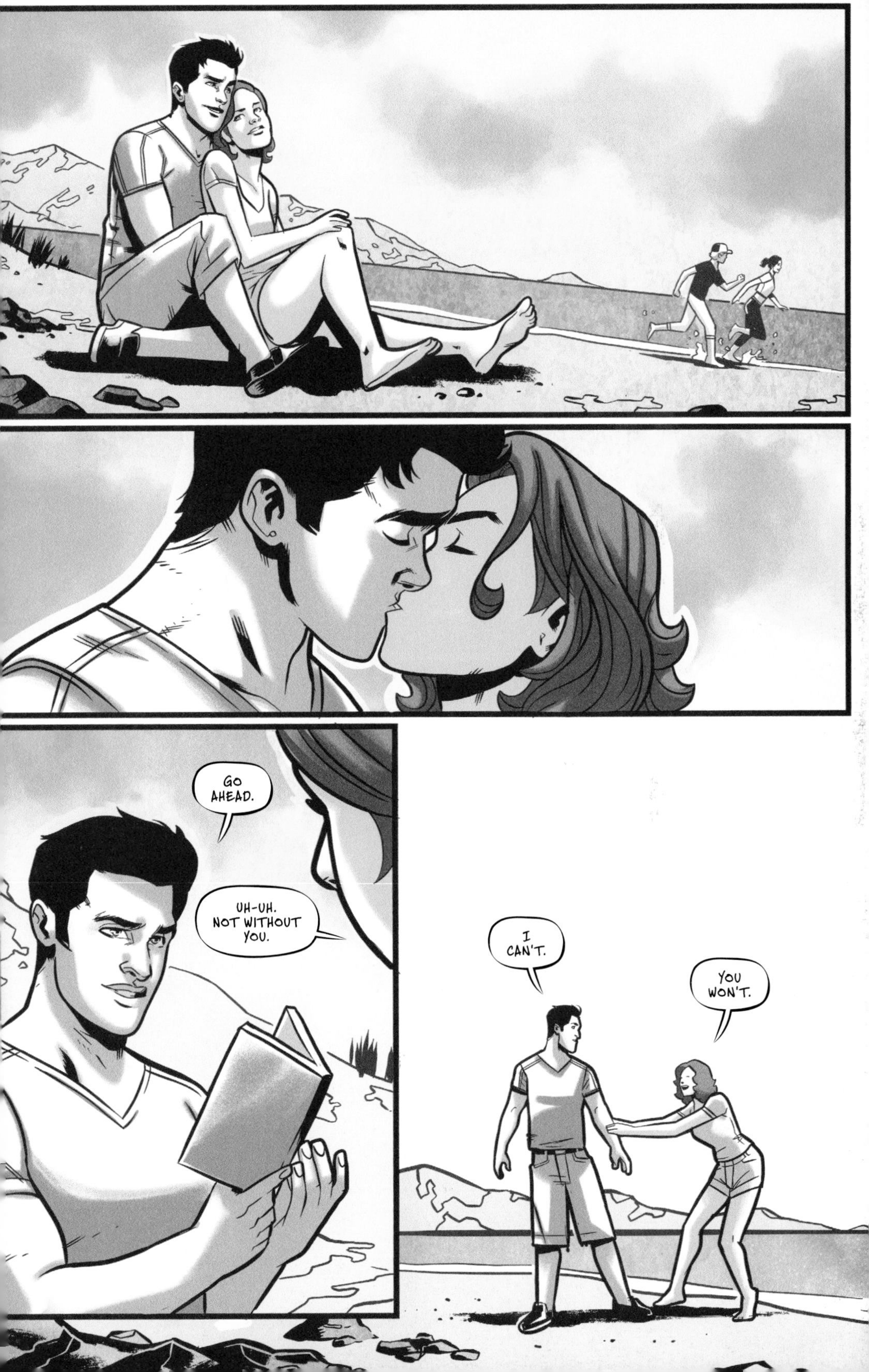
GO AHEAD.
UH-UH. NOT WITHOUT YOU.
I CAN'T.
YOU WON'T.

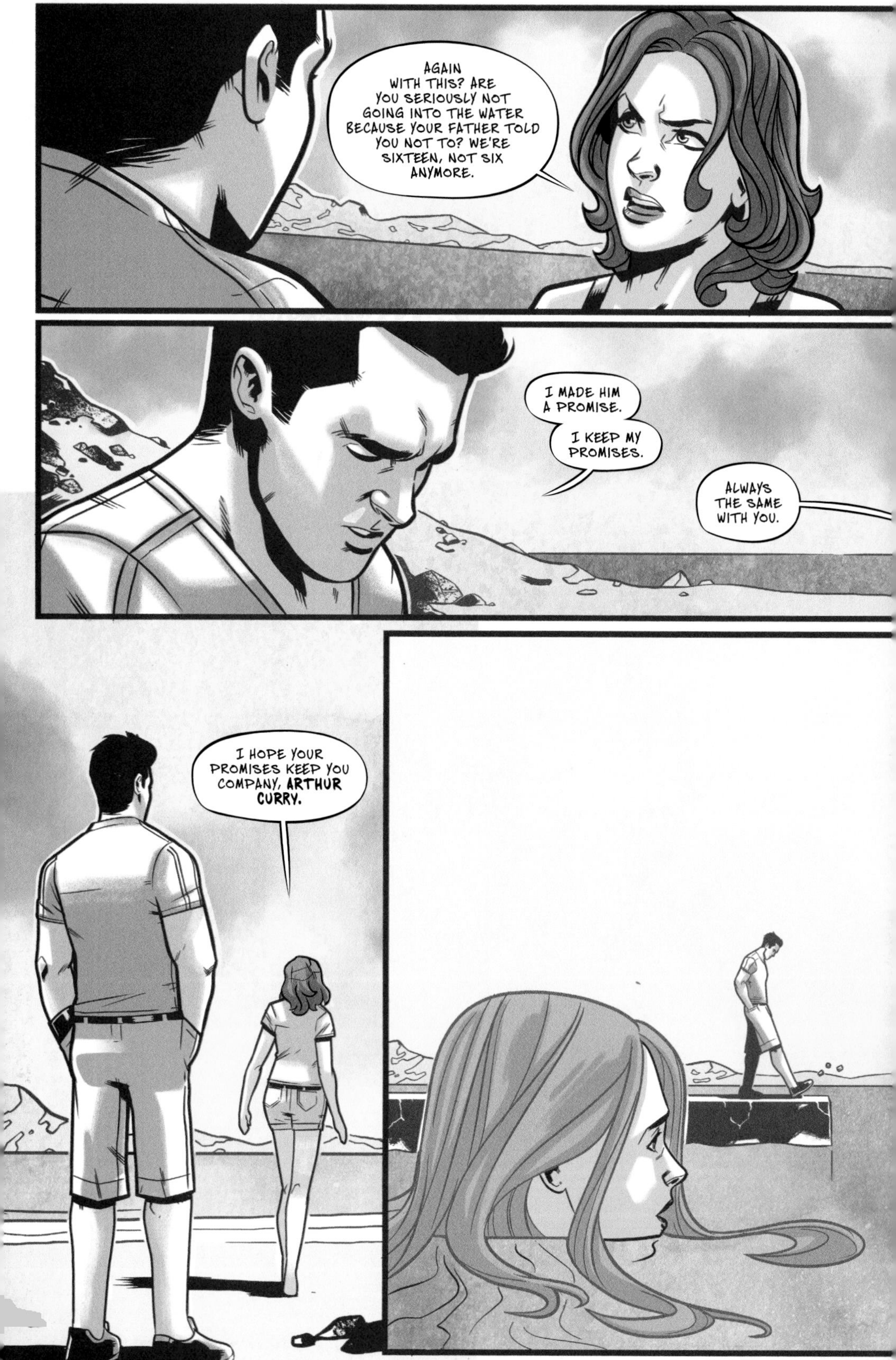
AGAIN WITH THIS? ARE YOU SERIOUSLY NOT GOING INTO THE WATER BECAUSE YOUR FATHER TOLD YOU NOT TO? WE'RE SIXTEEN, NOT SIX ANYMORE.
I MADE HIM A PROMISE.
I KEEP MY PROMISES.
ALWAYS THE SAME WITH YOU.
I HOPE YOUR PROMISES KEEP YOU COMPANY, **ARTHUR CURRY.**

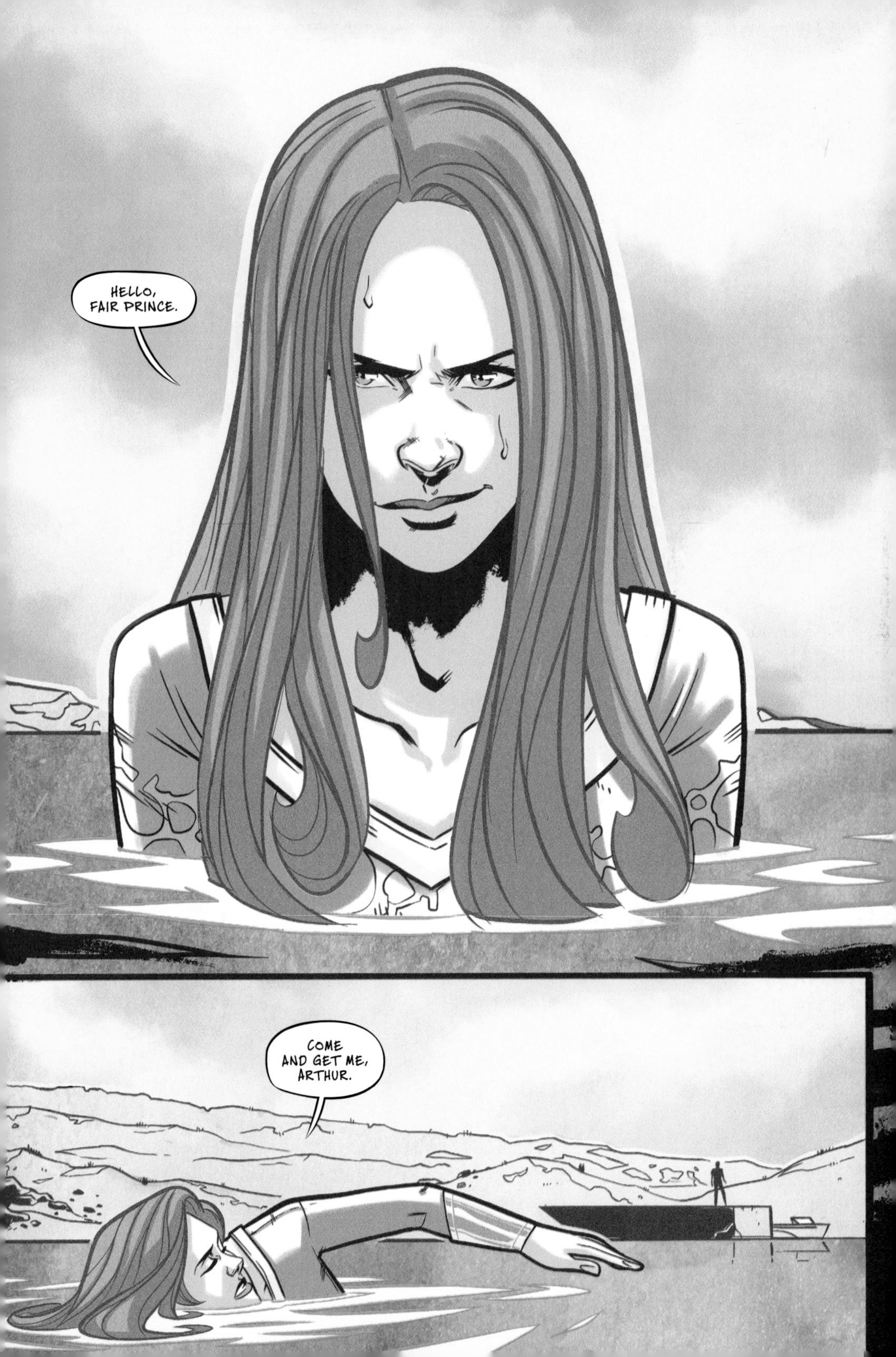
HELLO, FAIR PRINCE.
COME AND GET ME, ARTHUR.

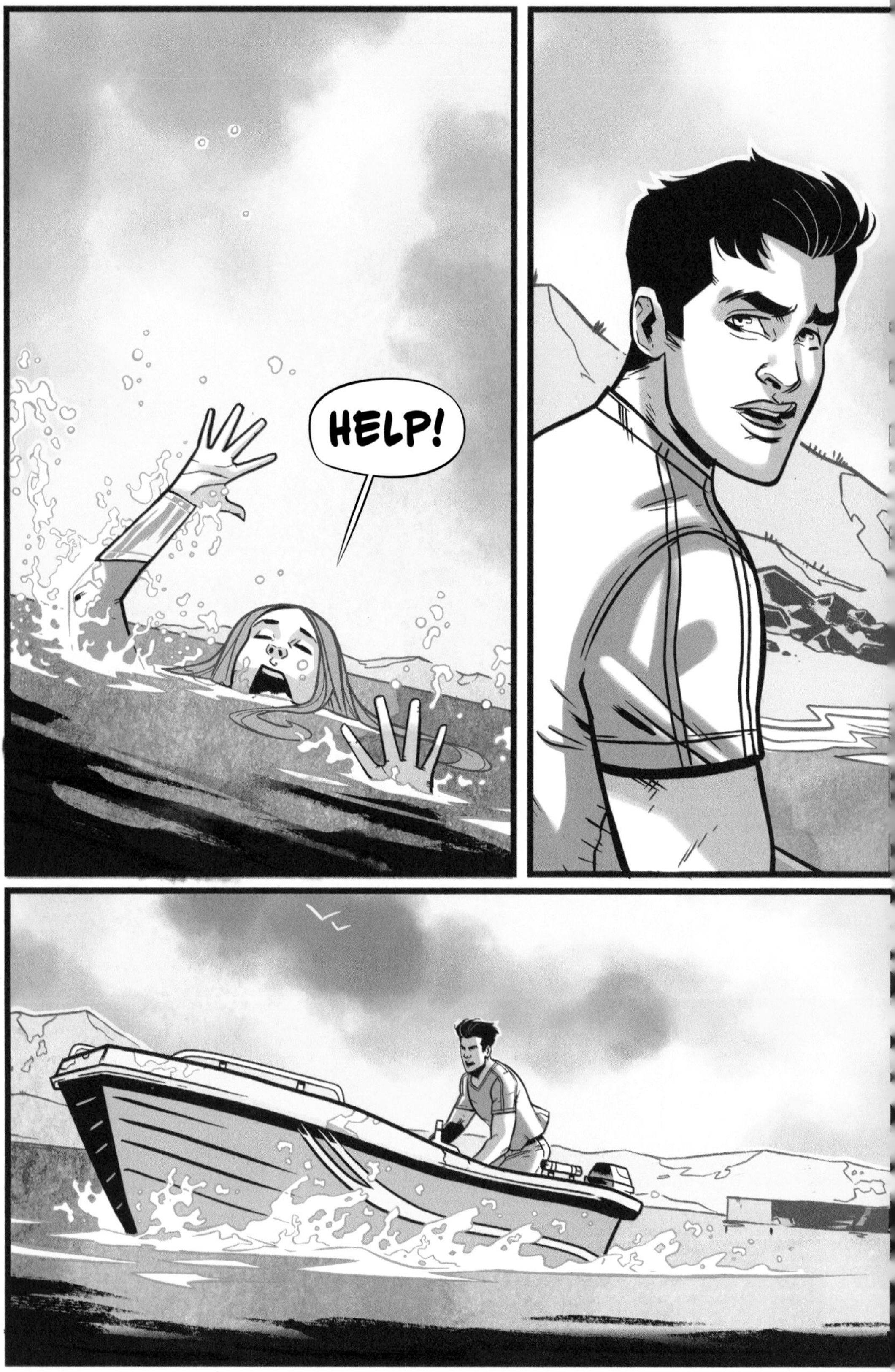
HELP!

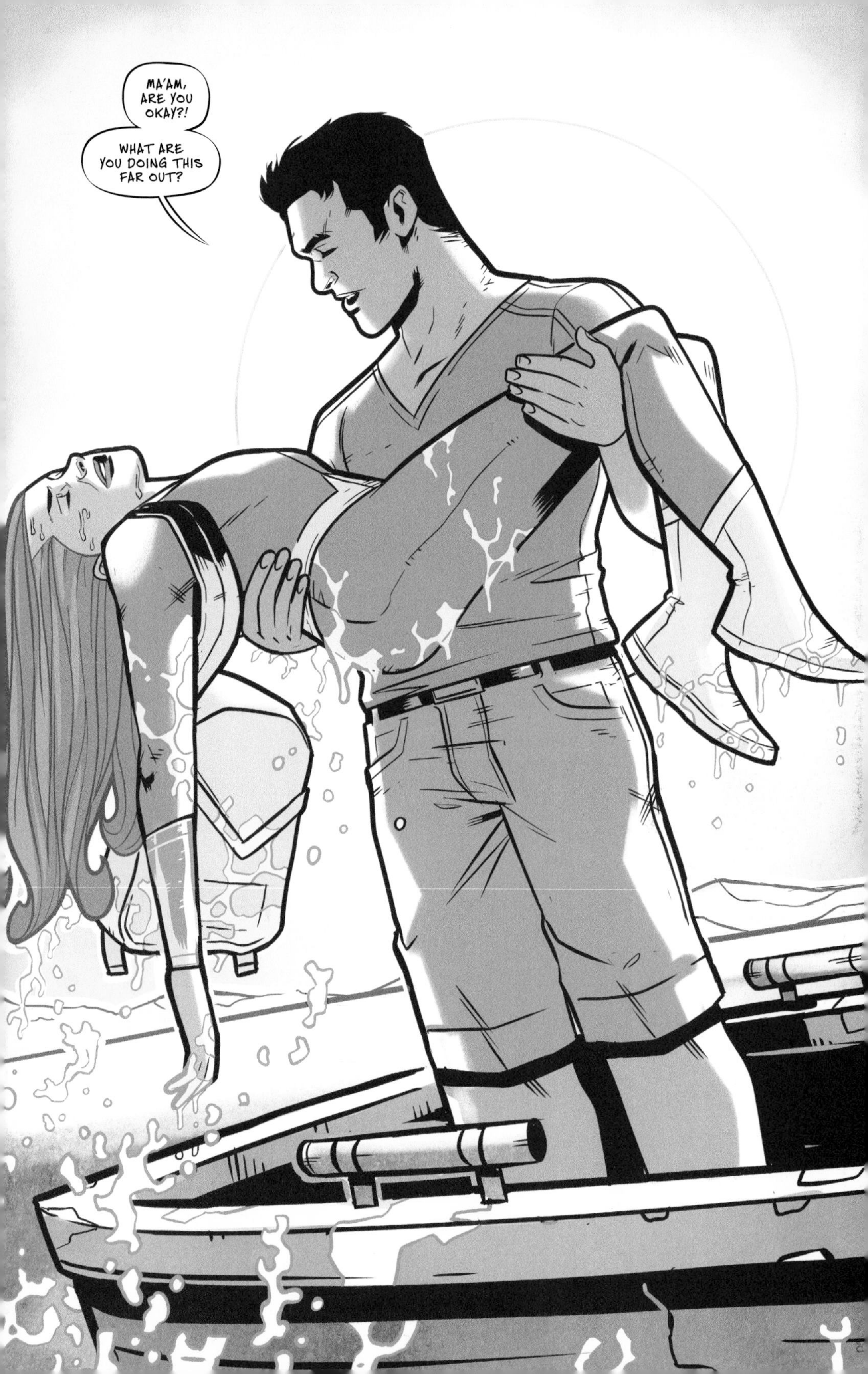
MA'AM, ARE YOU OKAY?!
WHAT ARE YOU DOING THIS FAR OUT?

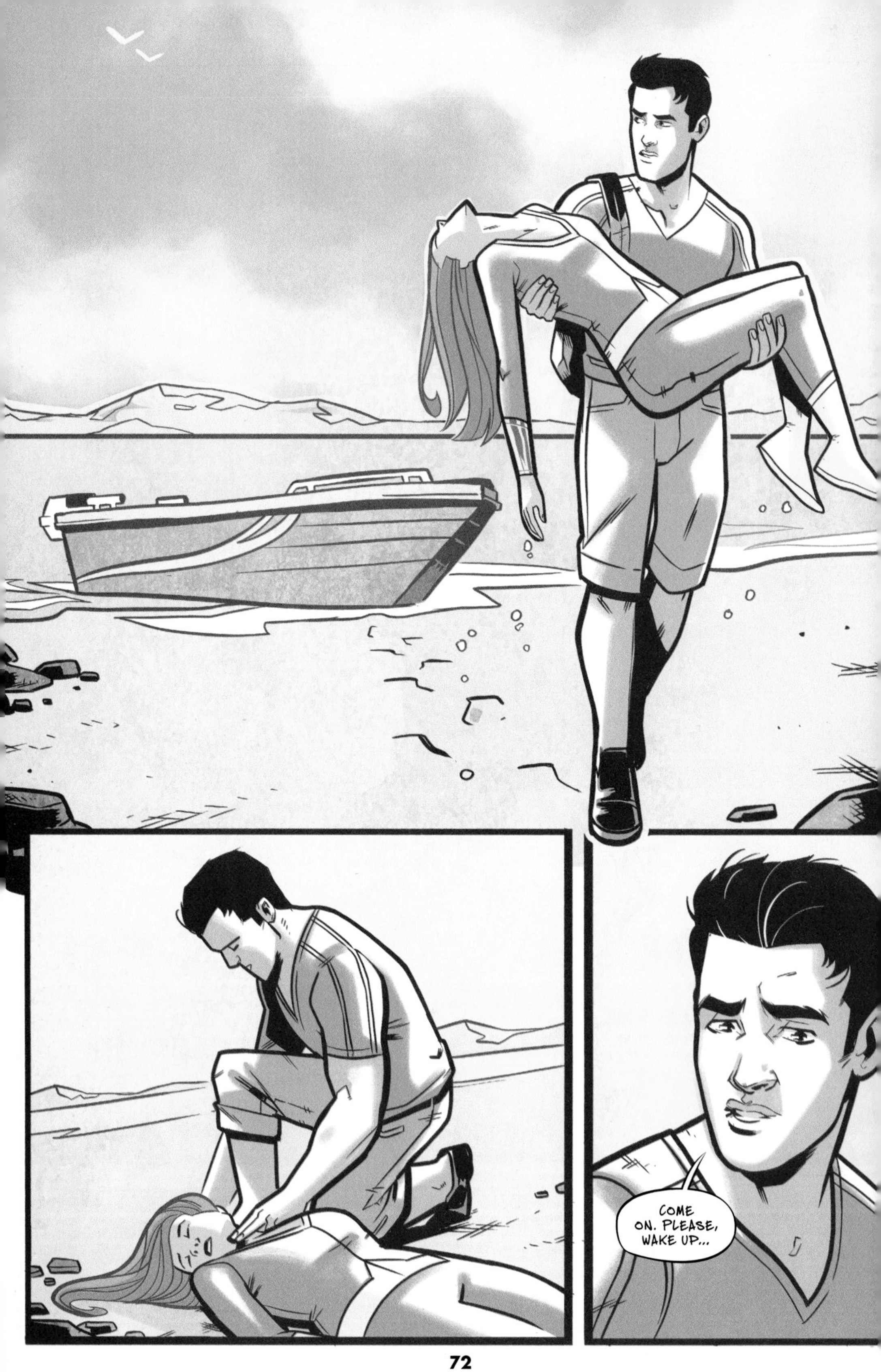
COME ON. PLEASE, WAKE UP...

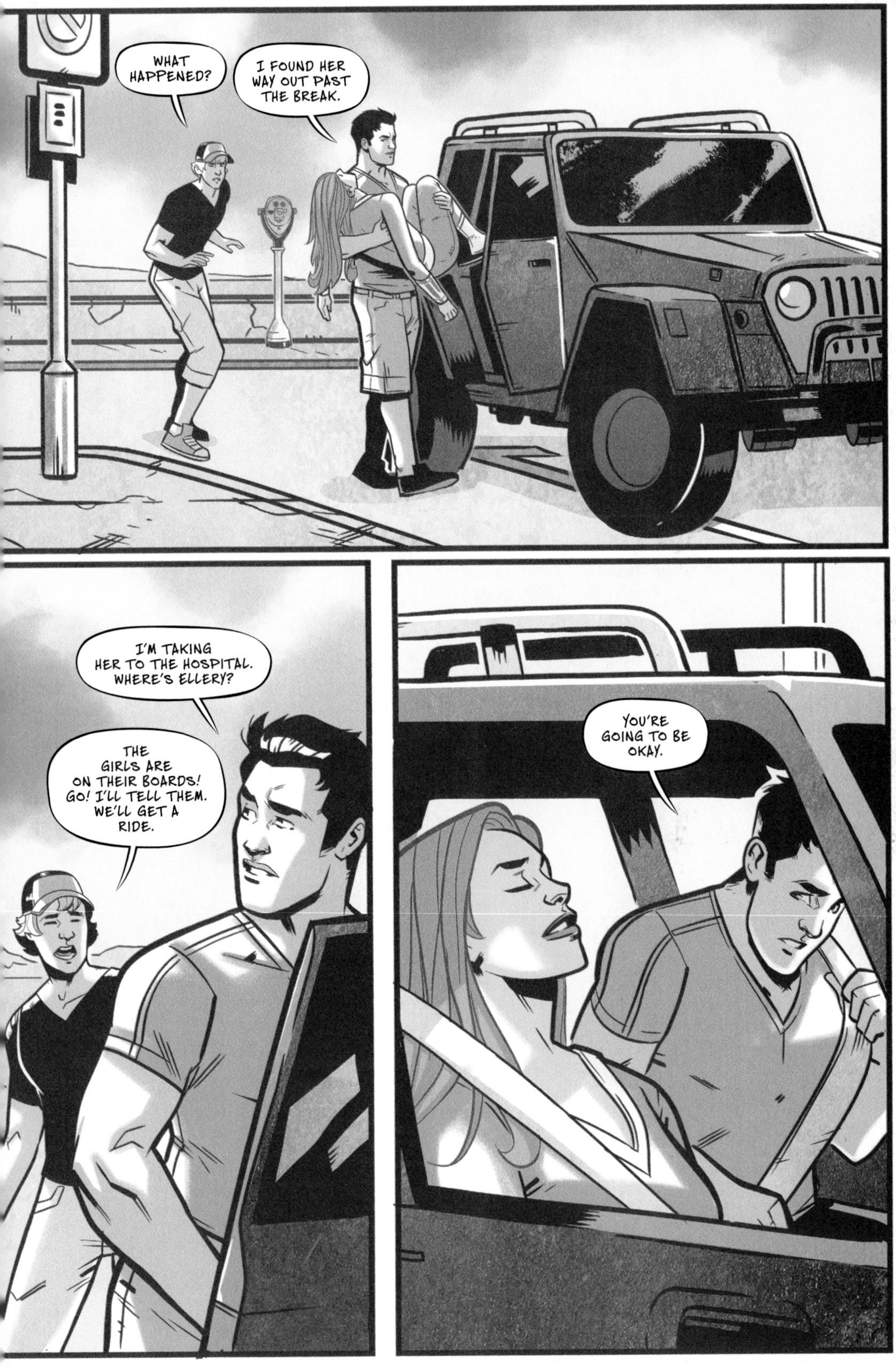
WHAT HAPPENED?
I FOUND HER WAY OUT PAST THE BREAK.
I'M TAKING HER TO THE HOSPITAL. WHERE'S ELLERY?
THE GIRLS ARE ON THEIR BOARDS! GO! I'LL TELL THEM. WE'LL GET A RIDE.
YOU'RE GOING TO BE OKAY.

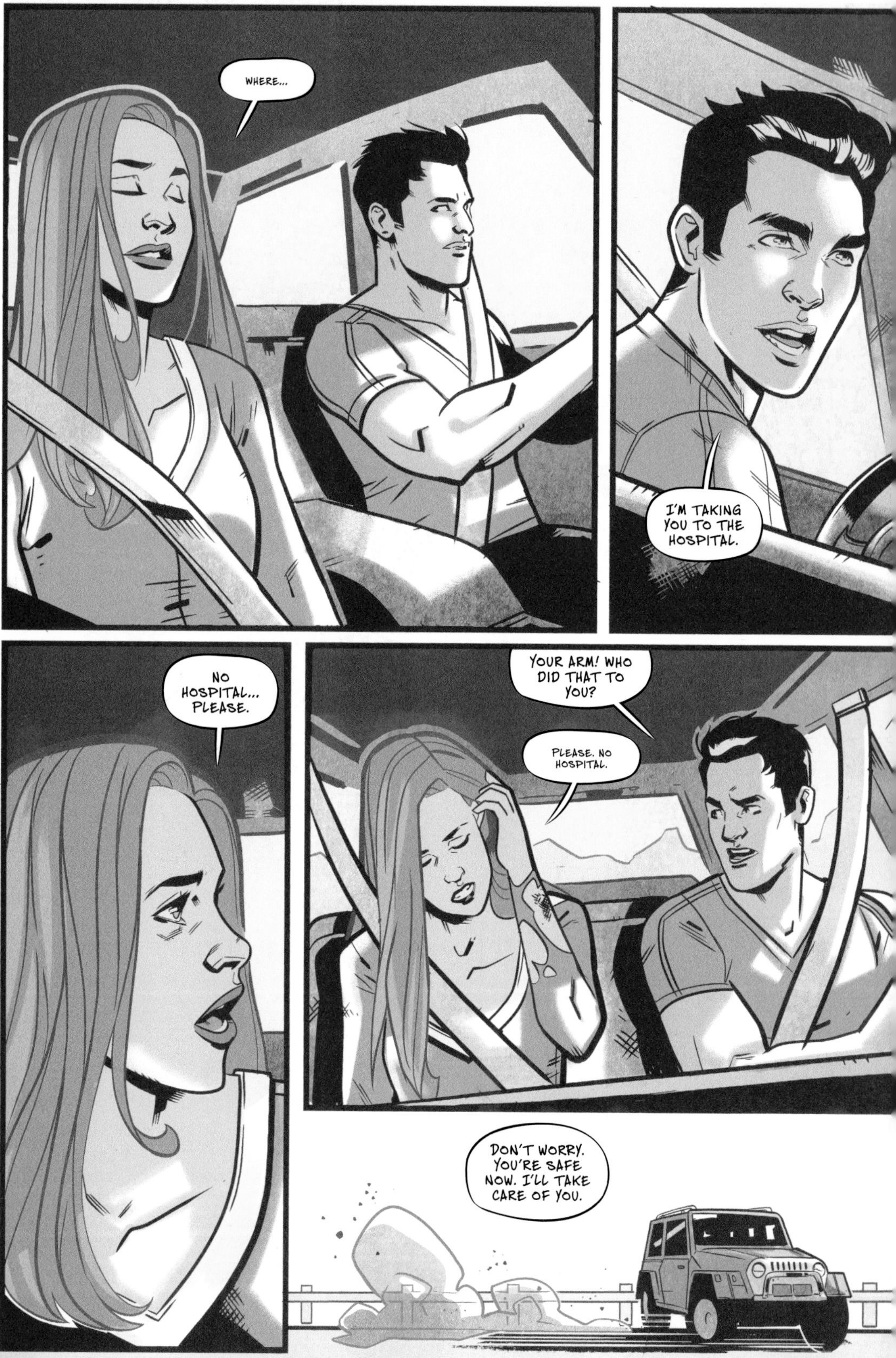

WHERE...
I'M TAKING YOU TO THE HOSPITAL.
NO HOSPITAL... PLEASE.
YOUR ARM! WHO DID THAT TO YOU?
PLEASE. NO HOSPITAL.
DON'T WORRY. YOU'RE SAFE NOW. I'LL TAKE CARE OF YOU.

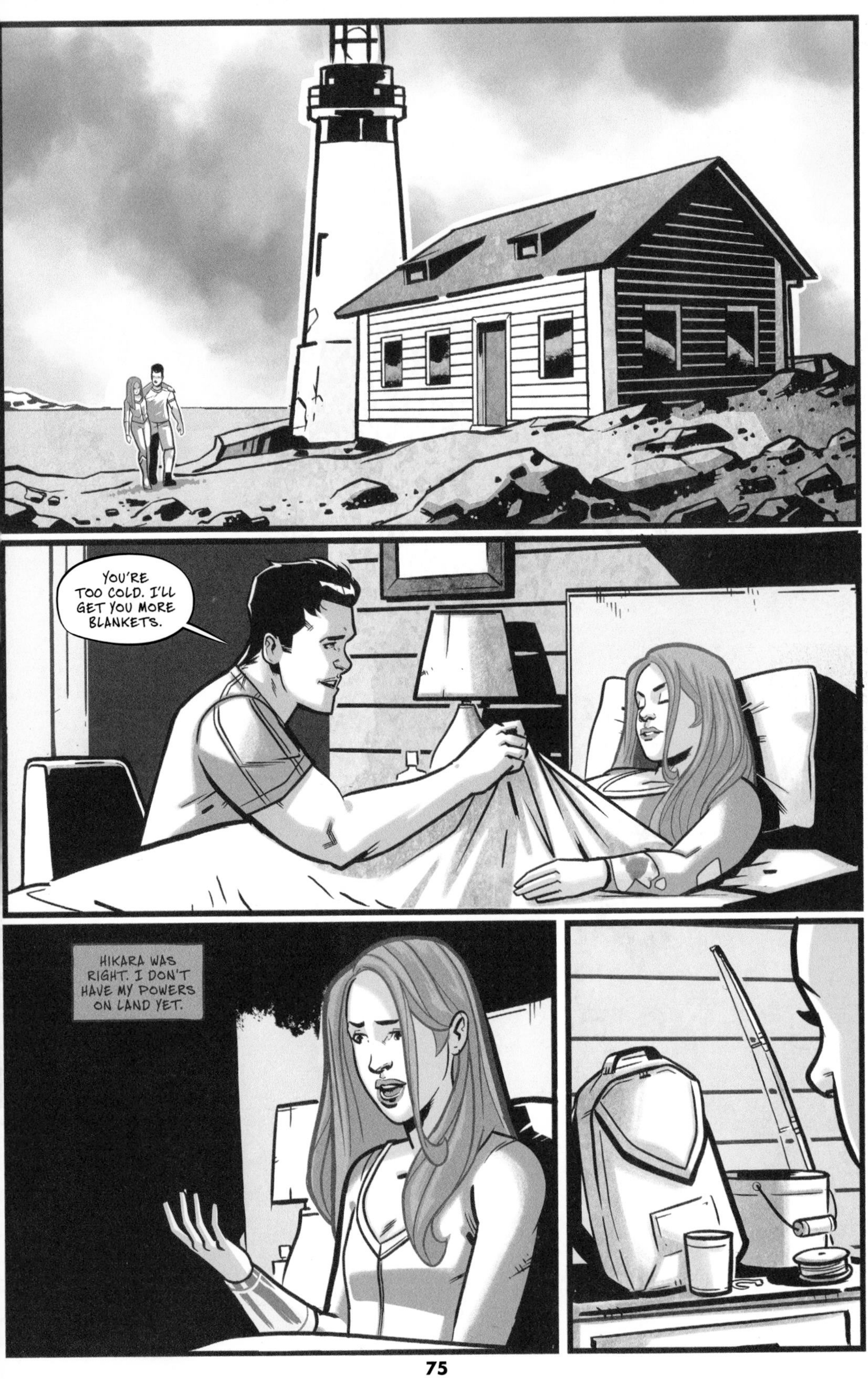
YOU'RE TOO COLD. I'LL GET YOU MORE BLANKETS.
HIKARA WAS RIGHT. I DON'T HAVE MY POWERS ON LAND YET.

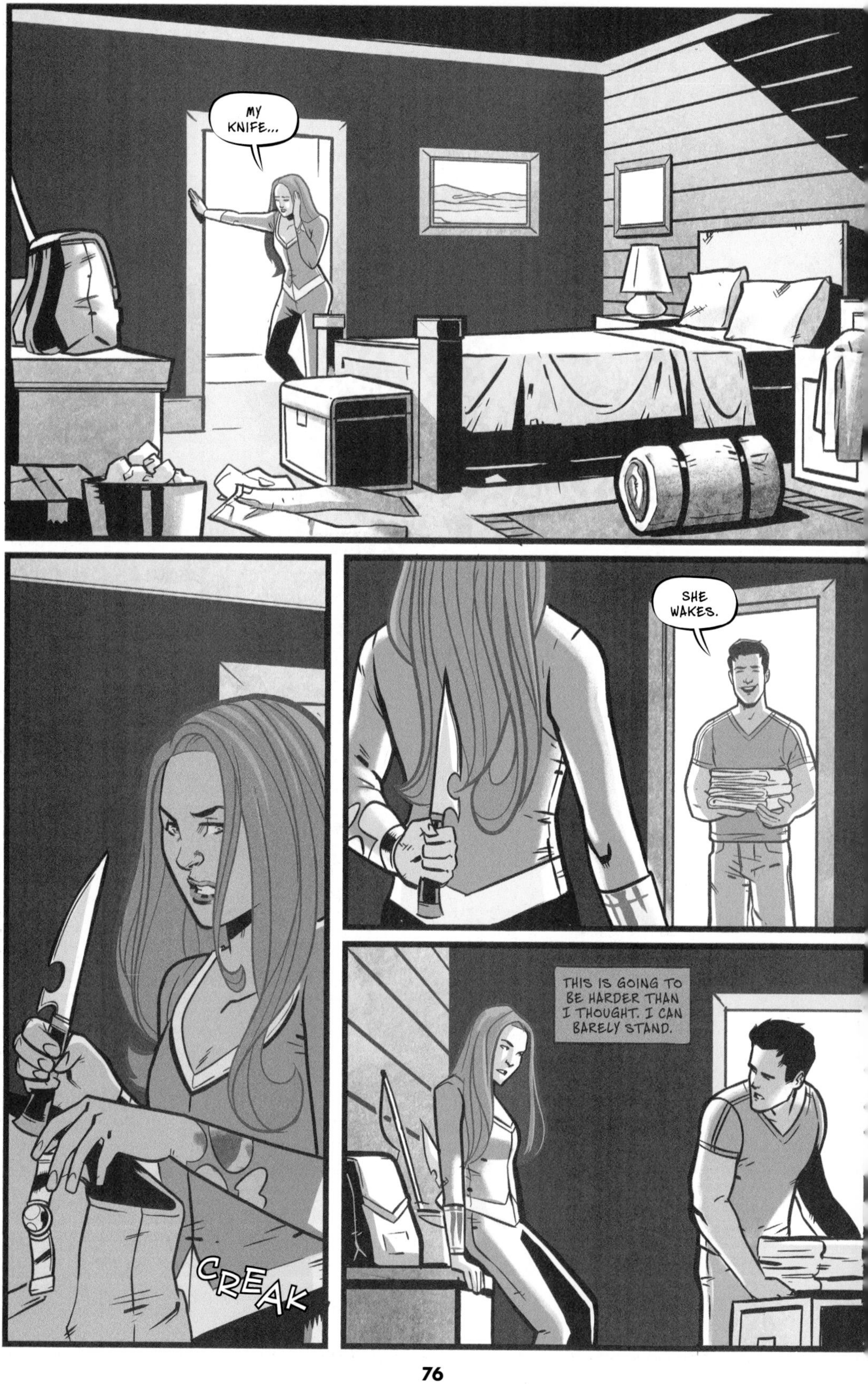
MY KNIFE...
CREAK
SHE WAKES.
THIS IS GOING TO BE HARDER THAN I THOUGHT. I CAN BARELY STAND.

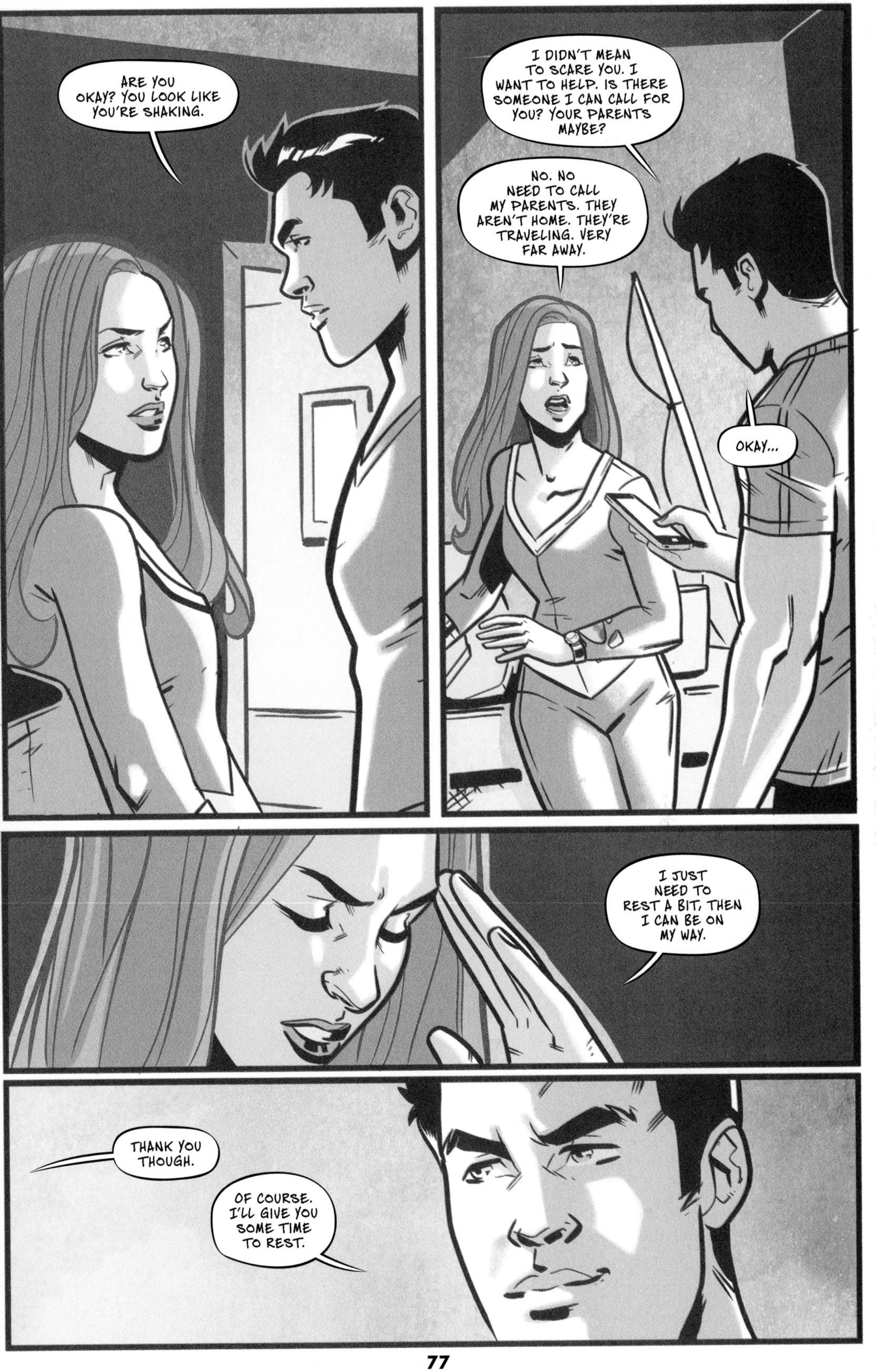
ARE YOU OKAY? YOU LOOK LIKE YOU'RE SHAKING.
I DIDN'T MEAN TO SCARE YOU. I WANT TO HELP. IS THERE SOMEONE I CAN CALL FOR YOU? YOUR PARENTS MAYBE?
NO. NO NEED TO CALL MY PARENTS. THEY AREN'T HOME. THEY'RE TRAVELING. VERY FAR AWAY.
OKAY...
I JUST NEED TO REST A BIT, THEN I CAN BE ON MY WAY.
THANK YOU THOUGH.
OF COURSE. I'LL GIVE YOU SOME TIME TO REST.

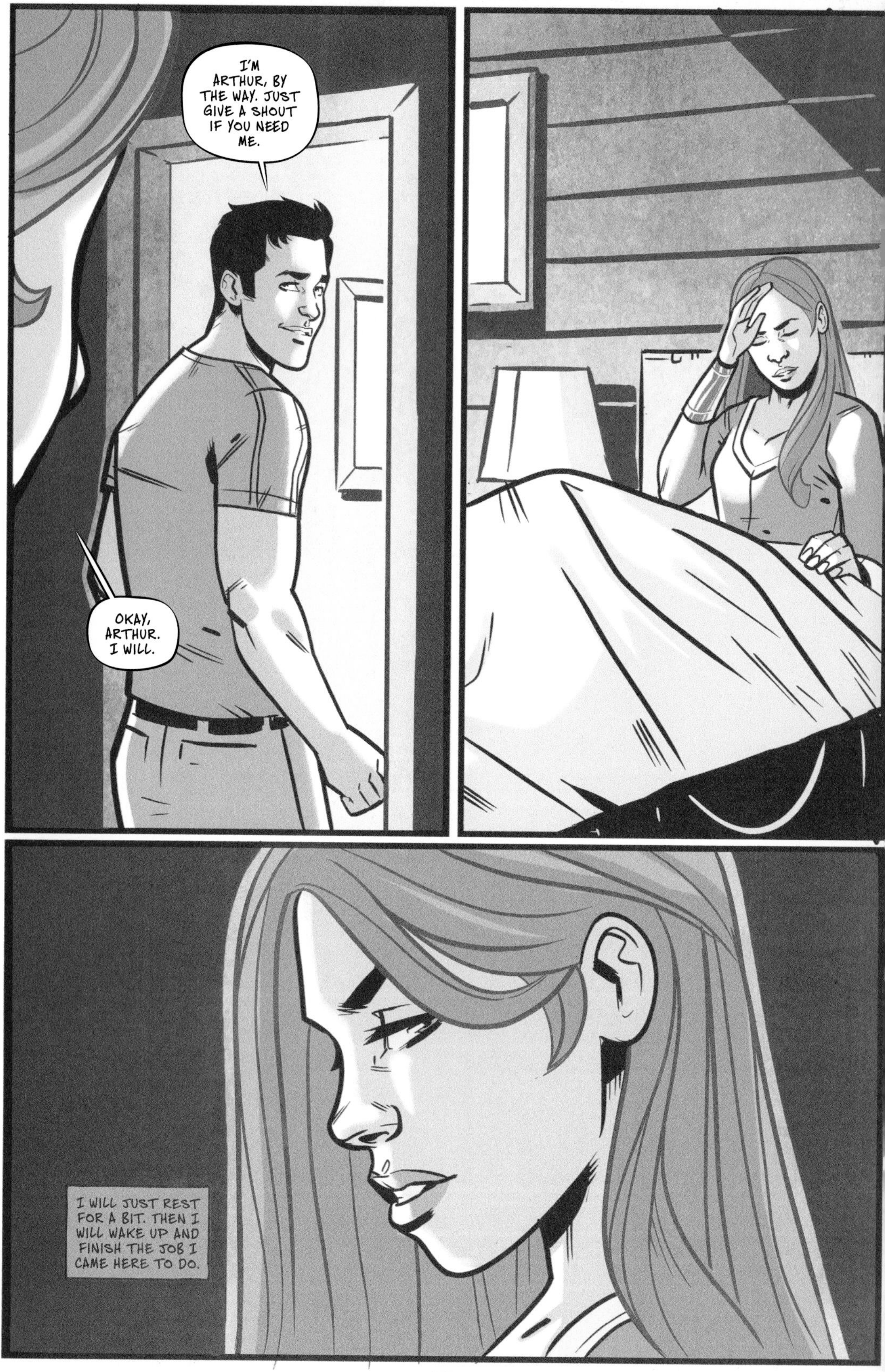
I'M ARTHUR, BY THE WAY. JUST GIVE A SHOUT IF YOU NEED ME.
OKAY, ARTHUR. I WILL.
I WILL JUST REST FOR A BIT. THEN I WILL WAKE UP AND FINISH THE JOB I CAME HERE TO DO.

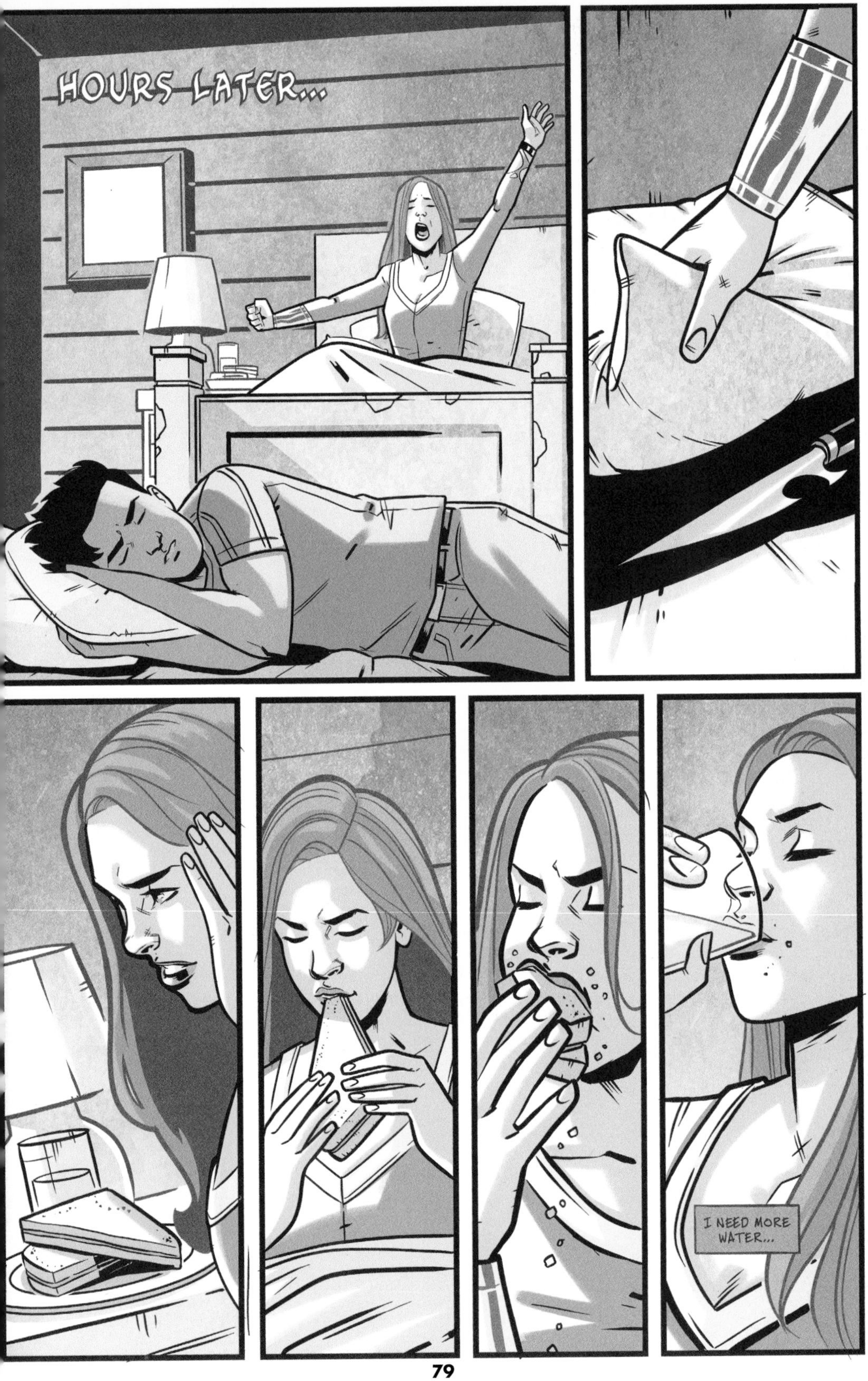
HOURS LATER...
I NEED MORE WATER...

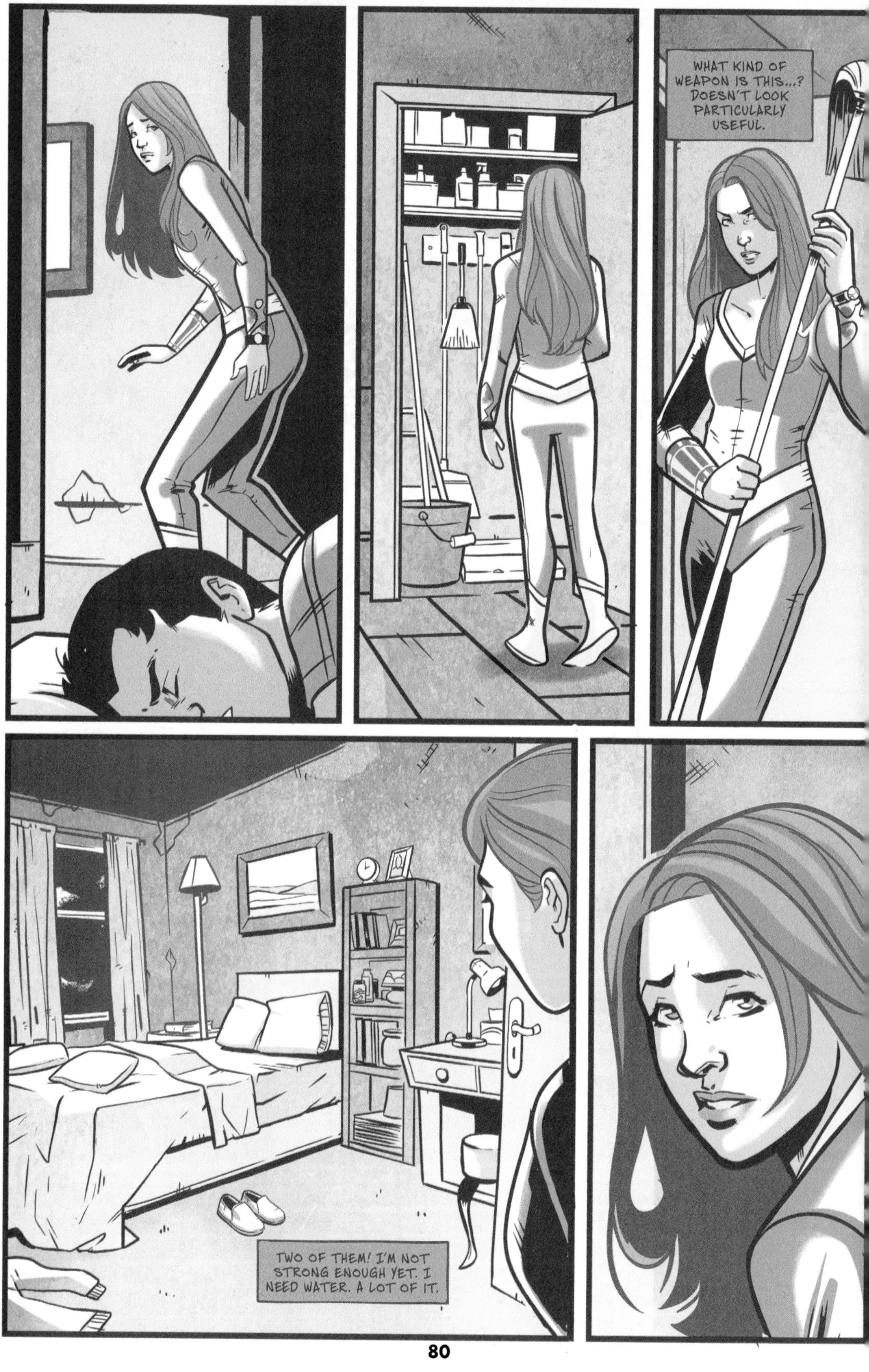
WHAT KIND OF WEAPON IS THIS...? DOESN'T LOOK PARTICULARLY USEFUL.
TWO OF THEM! I'M NOT STRONG ENOUGH YET. I NEED WATER. A LOT OF IT.

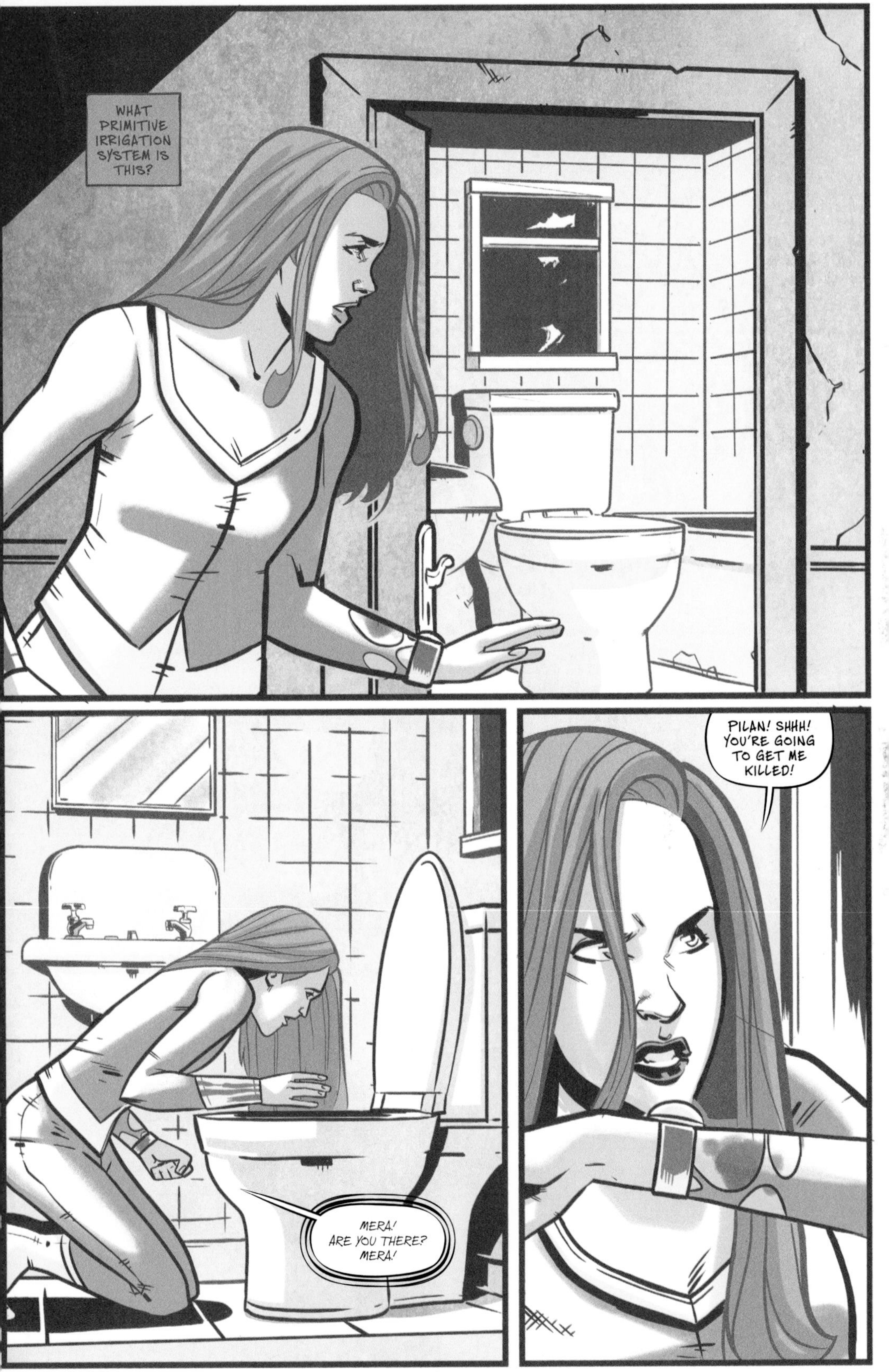
WHAT PRIMITIVE IRRIGATION SYSTEM IS THIS?
MERA! ARE YOU THERE? MERA!
PILAN! SHHH! YOU'RE GOING TO GET ME KILLED!

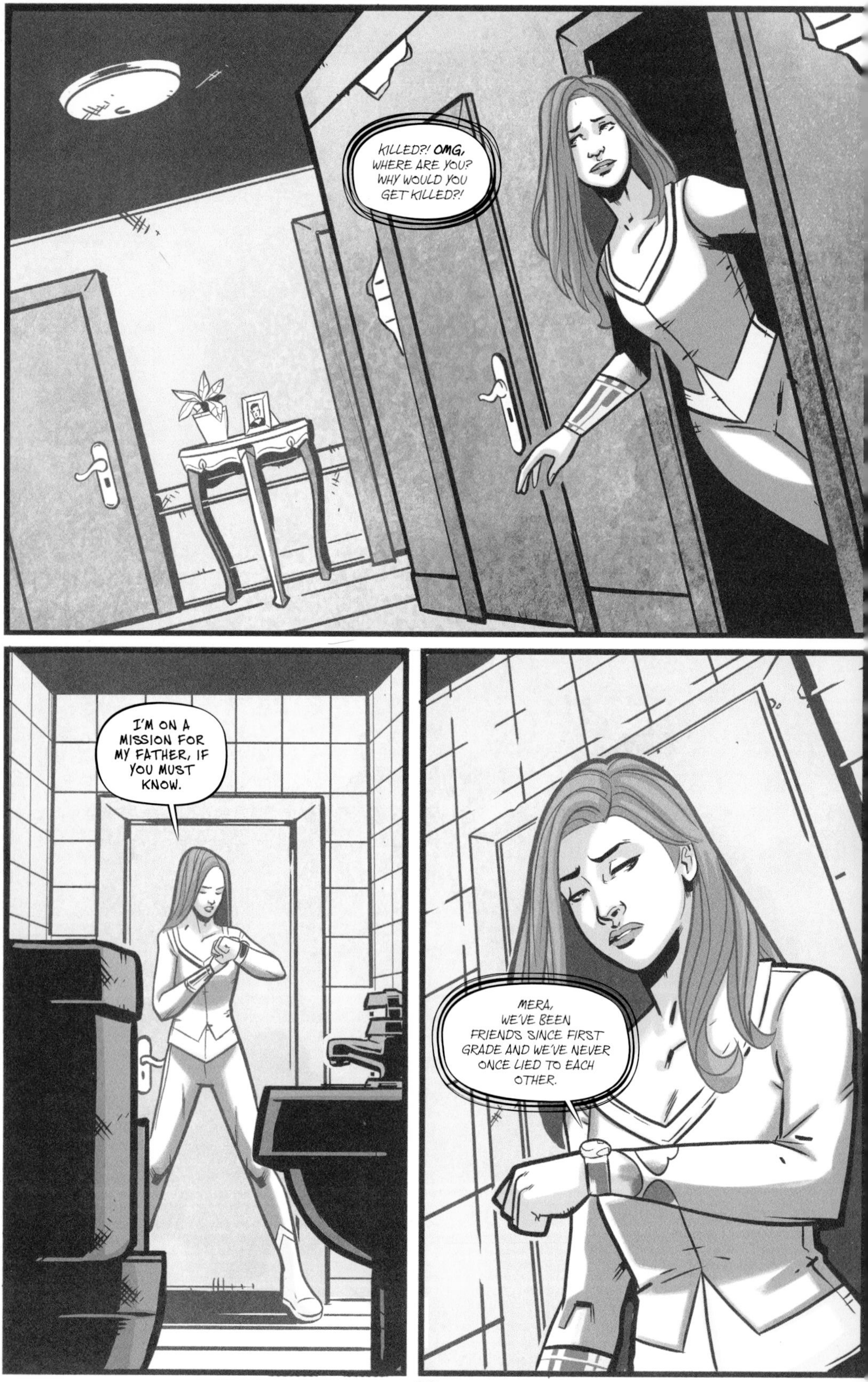
KILLED?! OMG, WHERE ARE YOU? WHY WOULD YOU GET KILLED?!
I'M ON A MISSION FOR MY FATHER, IF YOU MUST KNOW.
MERA, WE'VE BEEN FRIENDS SINCE FIRST GRADE AND WE'VE NEVER ONCE LIED TO EACH OTHER.

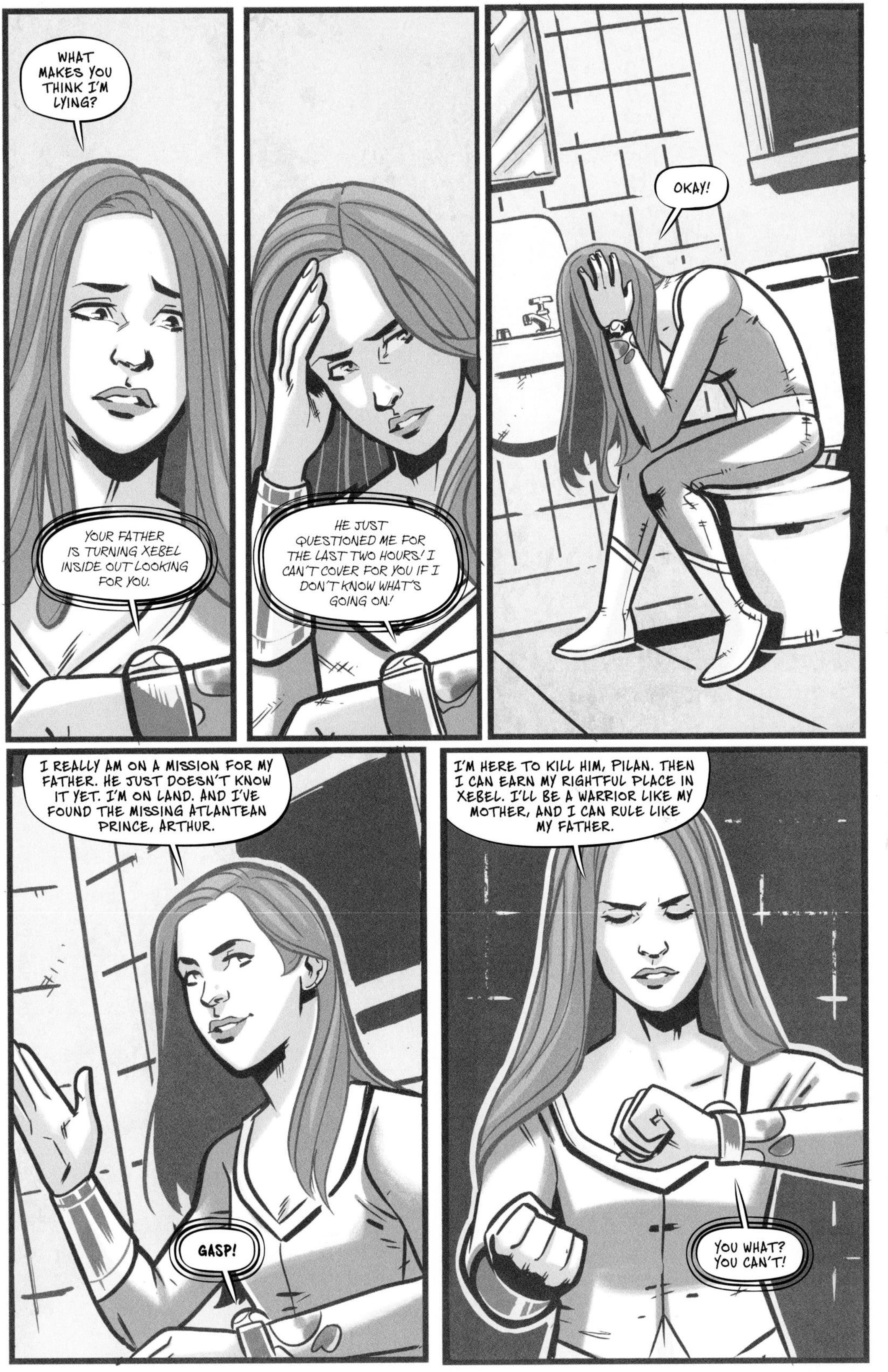
WHAT MAKES YOU THINK I'M LYING?
YOUR FATHER IS TURNING XEBEL INSIDE OUT LOOKING FOR YOU.
HE JUST QUESTIONED ME FOR THE LAST TWO HOURS! I CAN'T COVER FOR YOU IF I DON'T KNOW WHAT'S GOING ON!
OKAY!
I REALLY AM ON A MISSION FOR MY FATHER. HE JUST DOESN'T KNOW IT YET. I'M ON LAND. AND I'VE FOUND THE MISSING ATLANTEAN PRINCE, ARTHUR.
GASP!
I'M HERE TO KILL HIM, PILAN. THEN I CAN EARN MY RIGHTFUL PLACE IN XEBEL. I'LL BE A WARRIOR LIKE MY MOTHER, AND I CAN RULE LIKE MY FATHER.
YOU WHAT? YOU CAN'T!

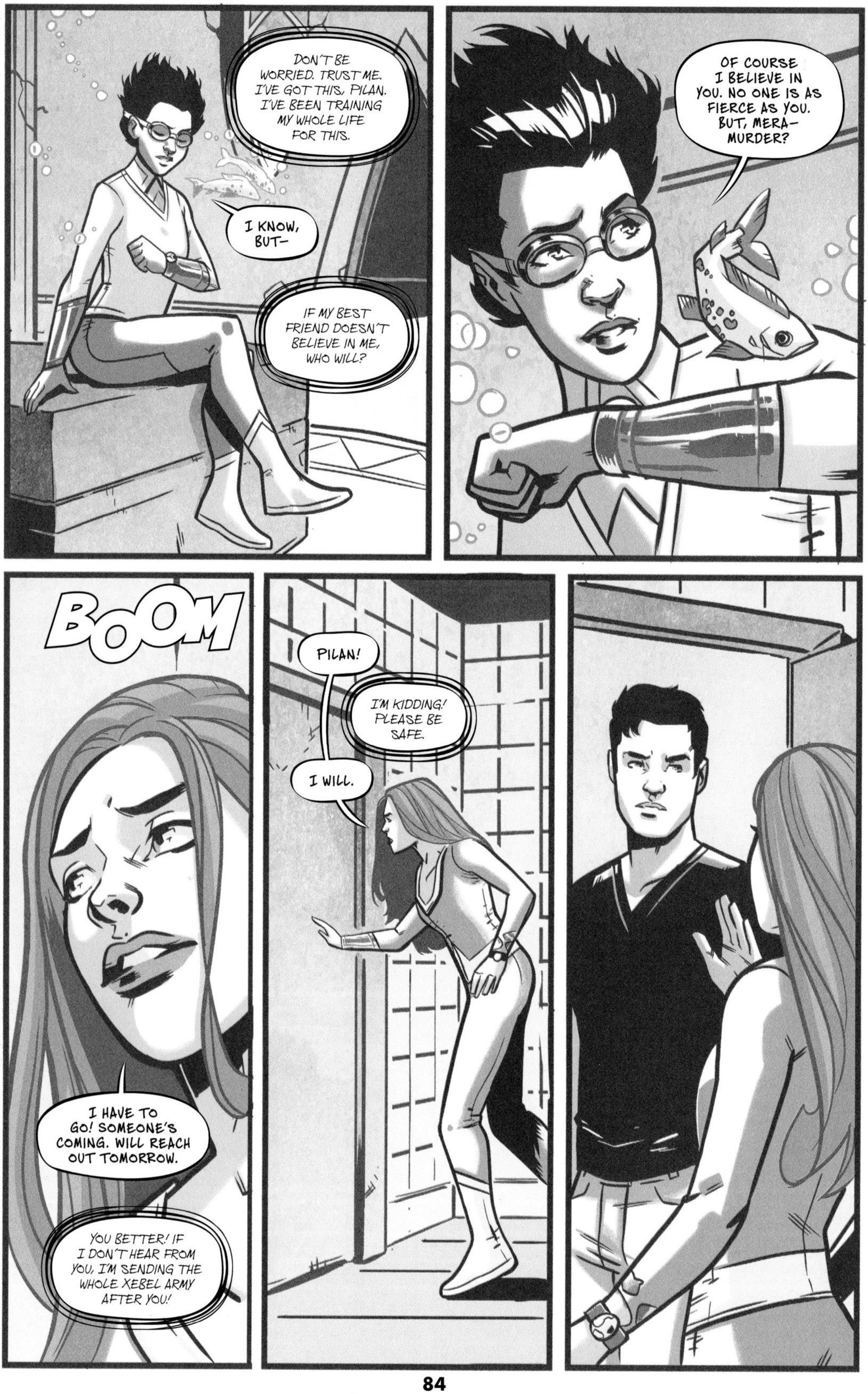
DON'T BE WORRIED. TRUST ME. I'VE GOT THIS, PILAN. I'VE BEEN TRAINING MY WHOLE LIFE FOR THIS.
I KNOW, BUT–
IF MY BEST FRIEND DOESN'T BELIEVE IN ME, WHO WILL?
OF COURSE I BELIEVE IN YOU. NO ONE IS AS FIERCE AS YOU. BUT, MERA–MURDER?
BOOM
I HAVE TO GO! SOMEONE'S COMING. WILL REACH OUT TOMORROW.
YOU BETTER! IF I DON'T HEAR FROM YOU, I'M SENDING THE WHOLE XEBEL ARMY AFTER YOU!
PILAN!
I'M KIDDING! PLEASE BE SAFE.
I WILL.

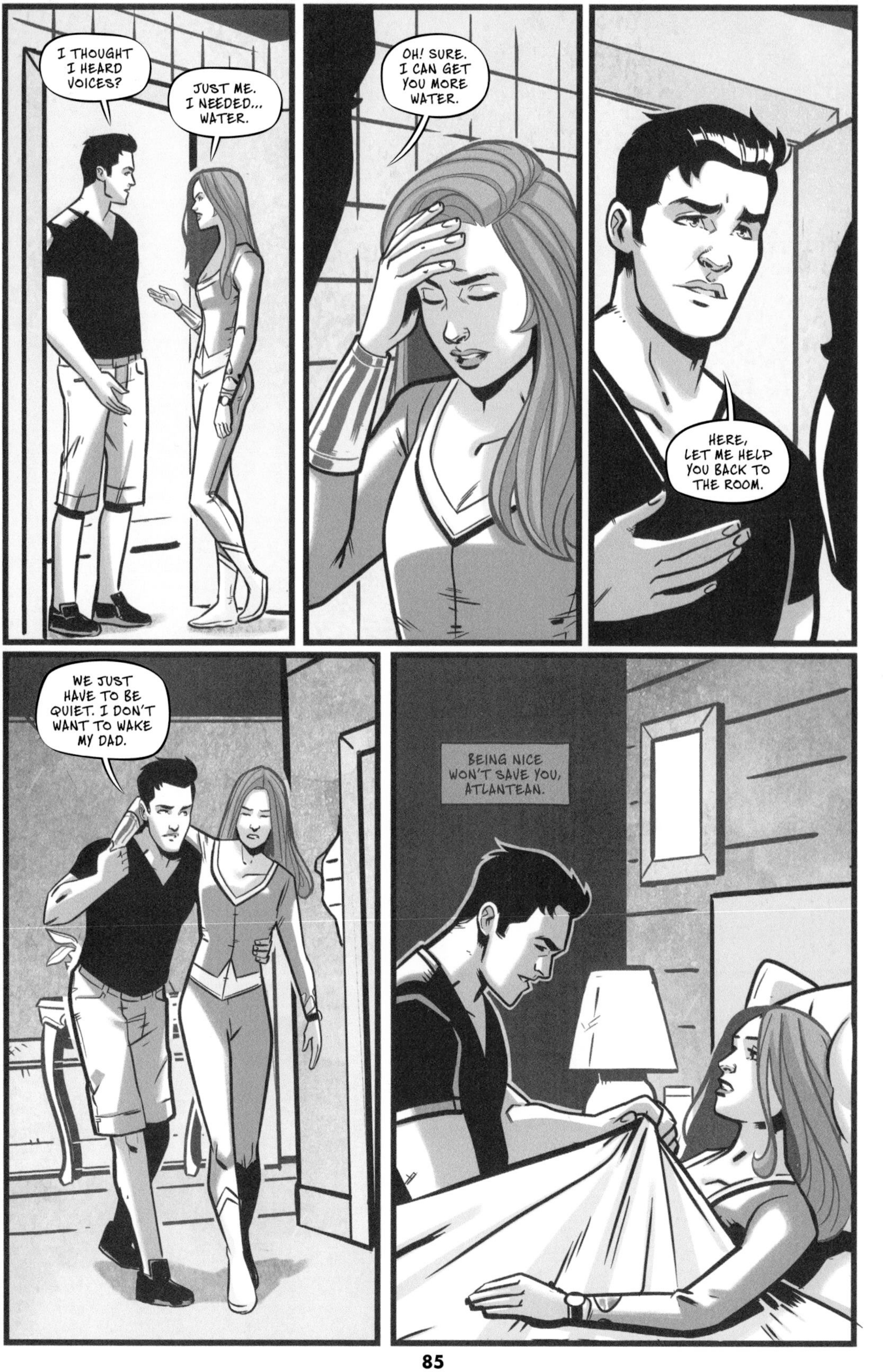
I THOUGHT I HEARD VOICES?
JUST ME. I NEEDED... WATER.
OH! SURE. I CAN GET YOU MORE WATER.
HERE, LET ME HELP YOU BACK TO THE ROOM.
WE JUST HAVE TO BE QUIET. I DON'T WANT TO WAKE MY DAD.
BEING NICE WON'T SAVE YOU, ATLANTEAN.

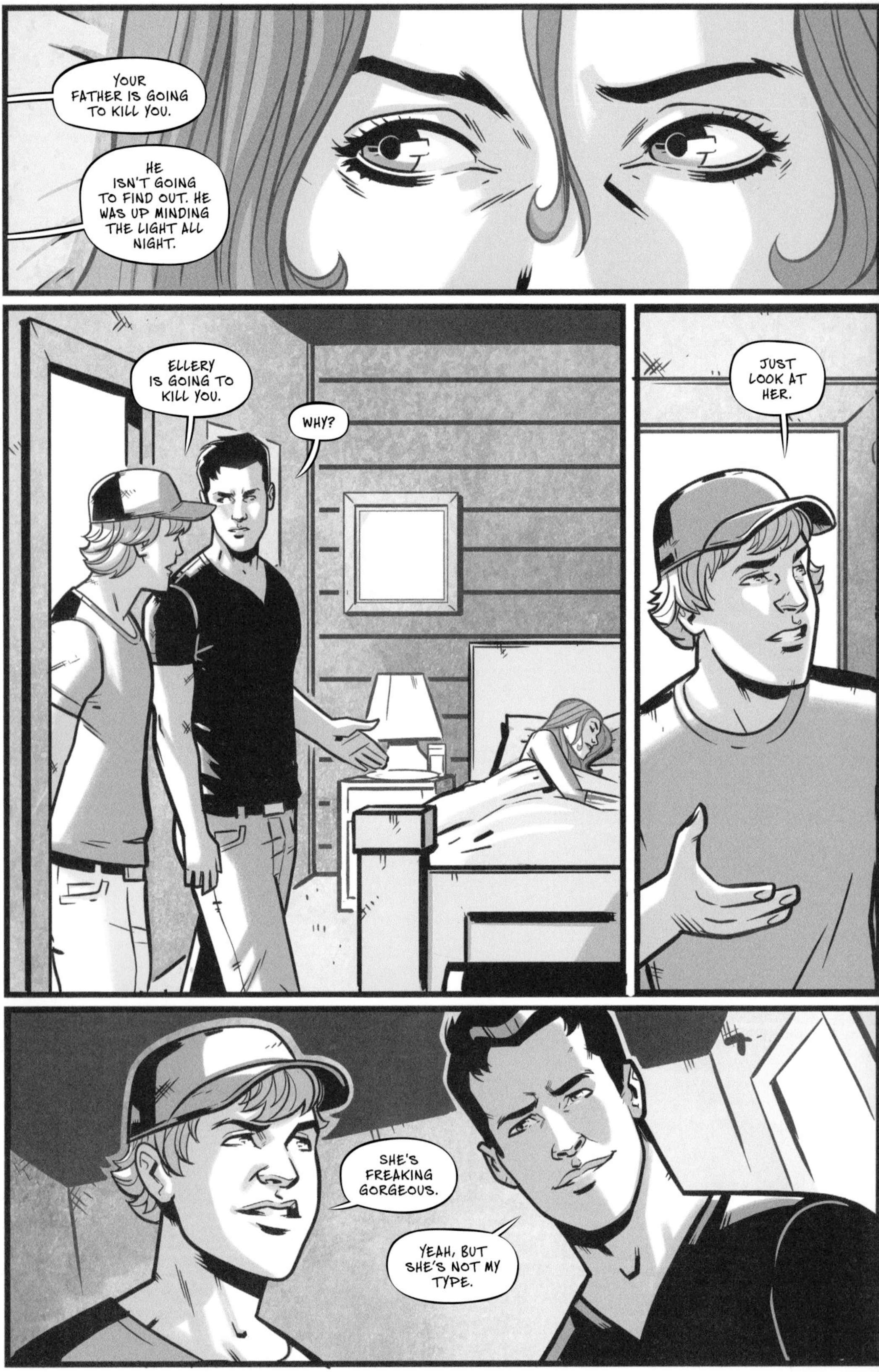
YOUR FATHER IS GOING TO KILL YOU.
HE ISN'T GOING TO FIND OUT. HE WAS UP MINDING THE LIGHT ALL NIGHT.
ELLERY IS GOING TO KILL YOU.
WHY?
JUST LOOK AT HER.
SHE'S FREAKING GORGEOUS.
YEAH, BUT SHE'S NOT MY TYPE.

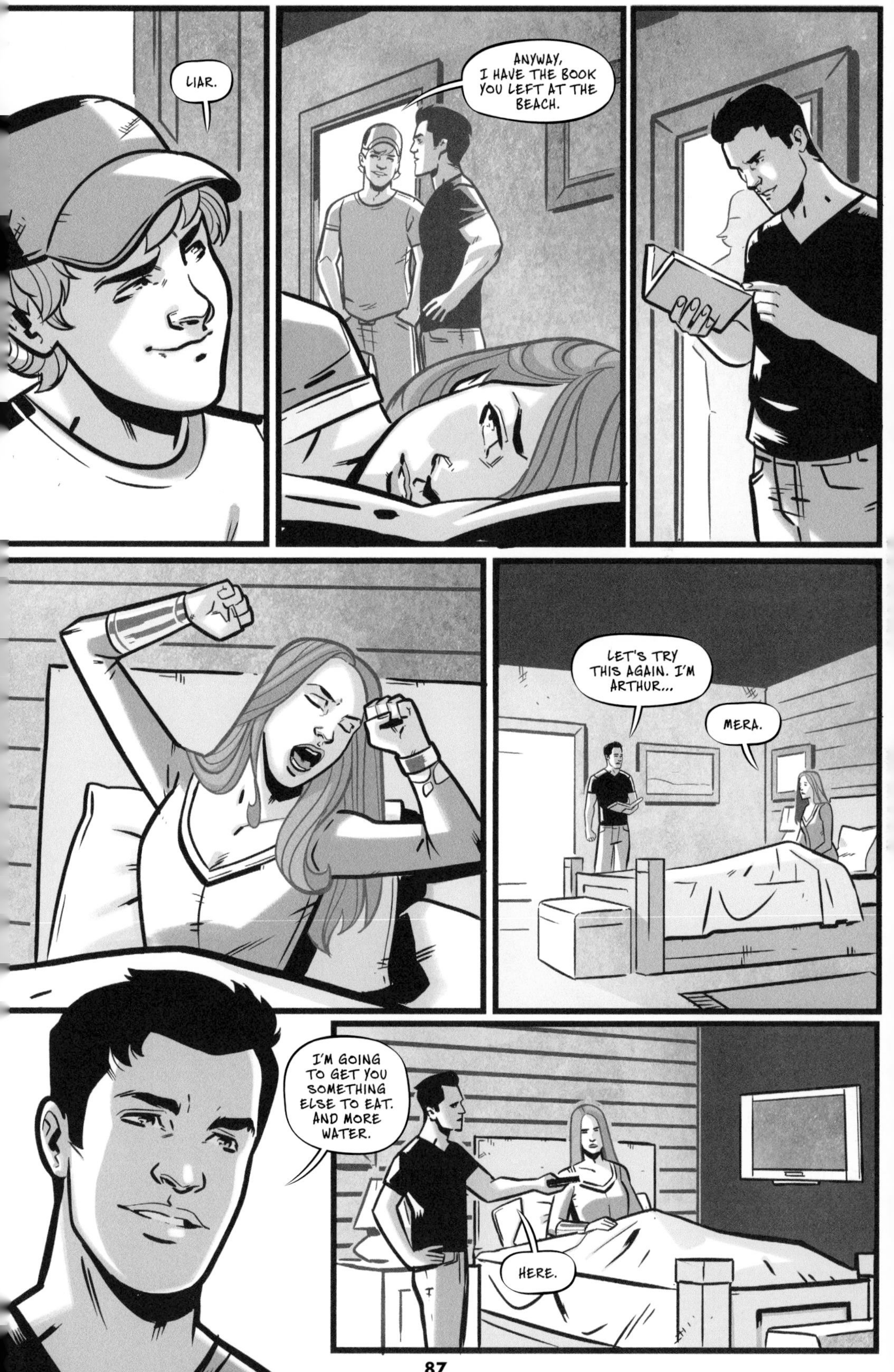
LIAR.
ANYWAY, I HAVE THE BOOK YOU LEFT AT THE BEACH.
LET'S TRY THIS AGAIN. I'M ARTHUR...
MERA.
I'M GOING TO GET YOU SOMETHING ELSE TO EAT. AND MORE WATER.
HERE.

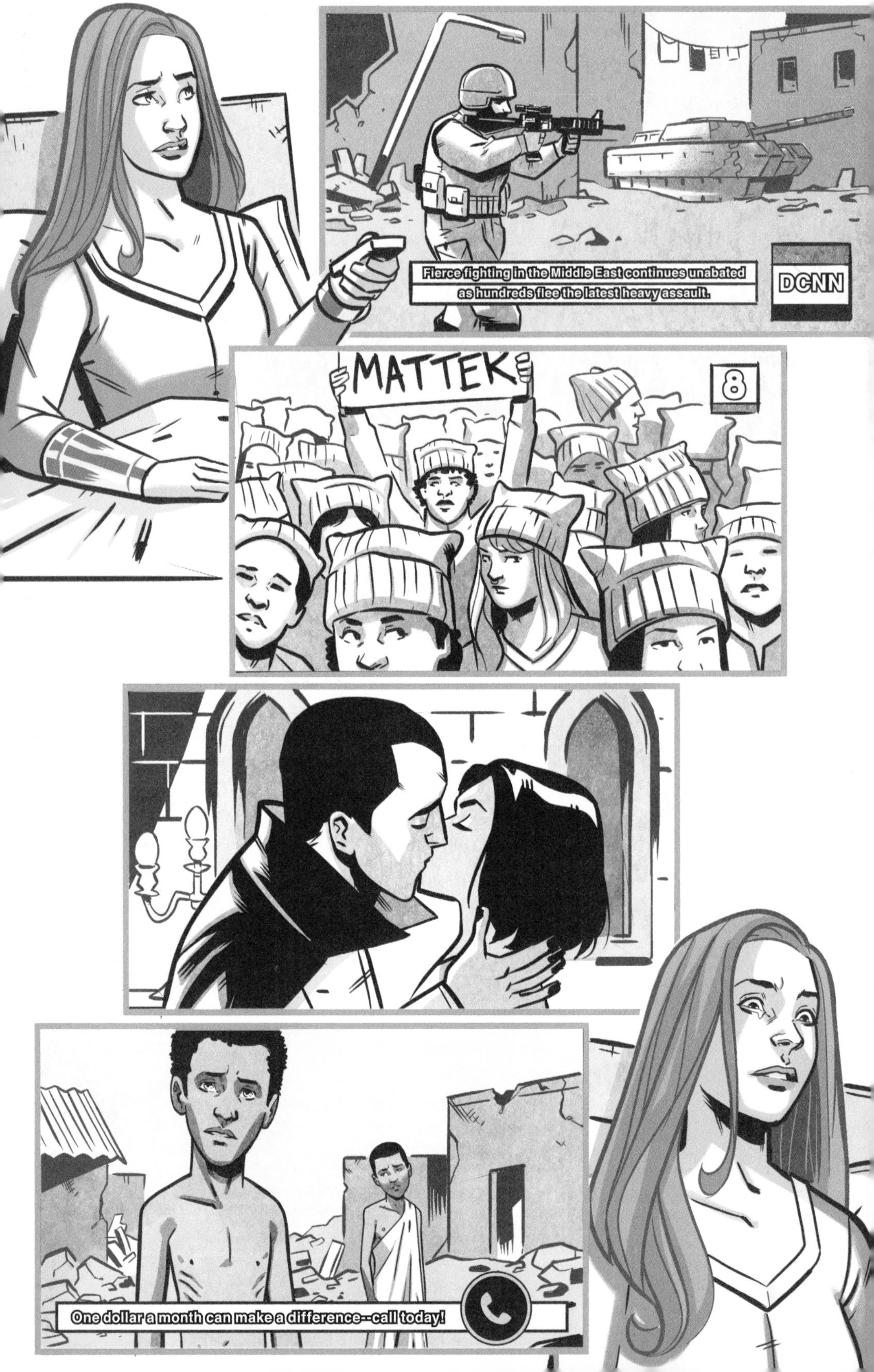

Fierce fighting in the Middle East continues unabated as hundreds flee the latest heavy assault.
DCNN
MATTEK
8
One dollar a month can make a difference--call today!

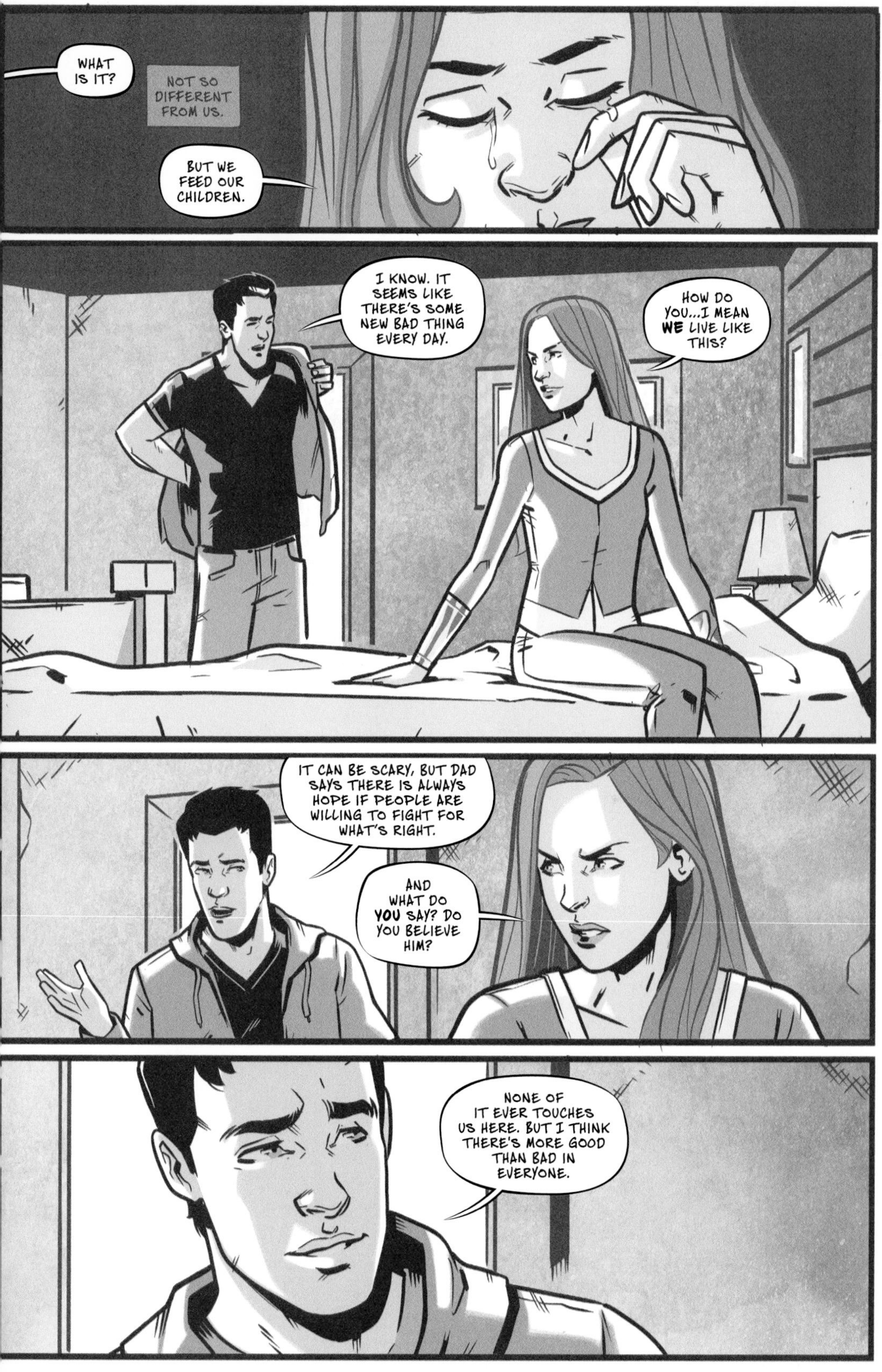
WHAT IS IT?
NOT SO DIFFERENT FROM US.
BUT WE FEED OUR CHILDREN.
I KNOW. IT SEEMS LIKE THERE'S SOME NEW BAD THING EVERY DAY.
HOW DO YOU...I MEAN WE LIVE LIKE THIS?
IT CAN BE SCARY, BUT DAD SAYS THERE IS ALWAYS HOPE IF PEOPLE ARE WILLING TO FIGHT FOR WHAT'S RIGHT.
AND WHAT DO YOU SAY? DO YOU BELIEVE HIM?
NONE OF IT EVER TOUCHES US HERE. BUT I THINK THERE'S MORE GOOD THAN BAD IN EVERYONE.

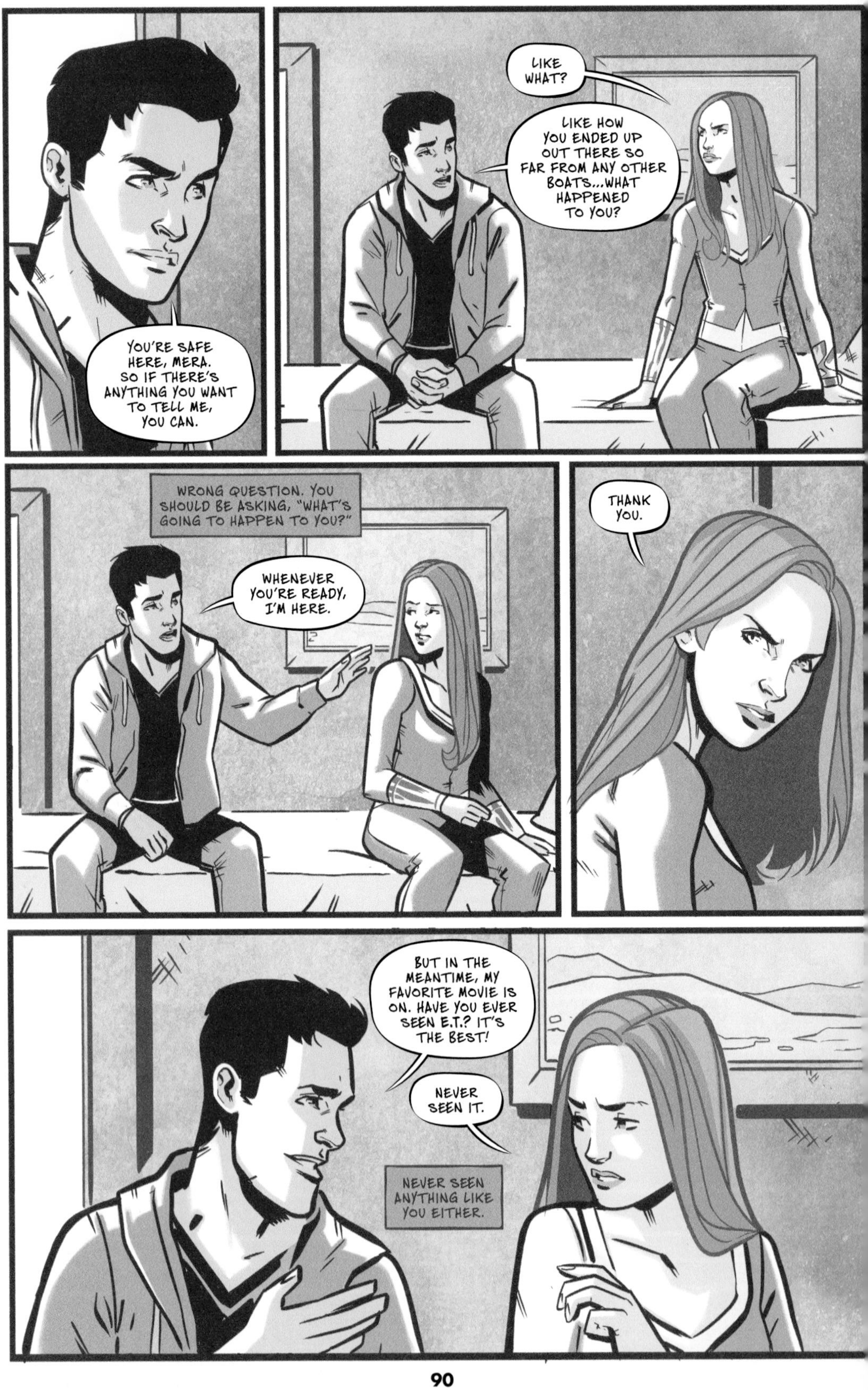
YOU'RE SAFE HERE, MERA. SO IF THERE'S ANYTHING YOU WANT TO TELL ME, YOU CAN.
LIKE WHAT?
LIKE HOW YOU ENDED UP OUT THERE SO FAR FROM ANY OTHER BOATS...WHAT HAPPENED TO YOU?
WRONG QUESTION. YOU SHOULD BE ASKING, "WHAT'S GOING TO HAPPEN TO YOU?"
WHENEVER YOU'RE READY, I'M HERE.
THANK YOU.
BUT IN THE MEANTIME, MY FAVORITE MOVIE IS ON. HAVE YOU EVER SEEN E.T.? IT'S THE BEST!
NEVER SEEN IT.
NEVER SEEN ANYTHING LIKE YOU EITHER.

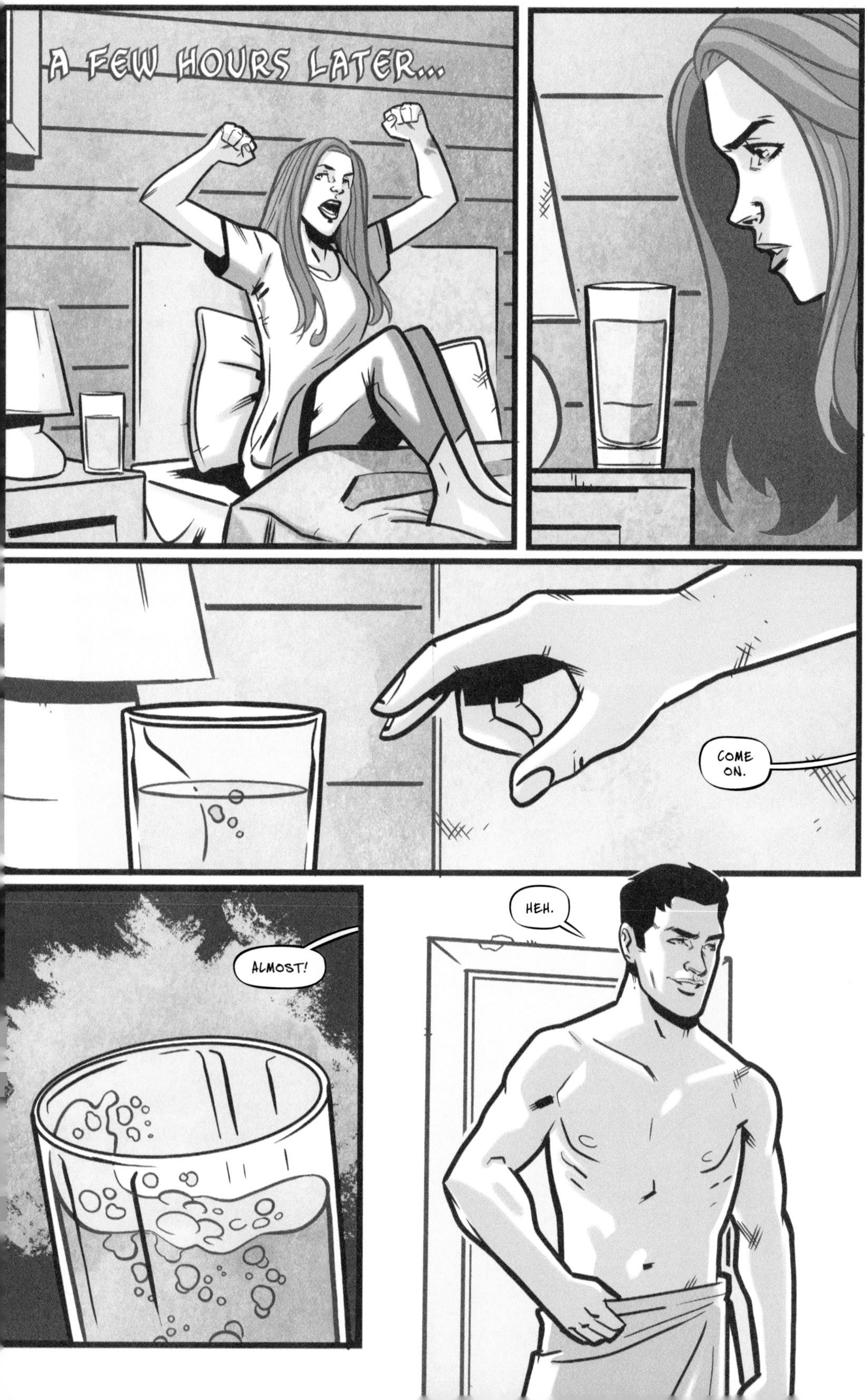
A FEW HOURS LATER...
COME ON.
ALMOST!
HEH.

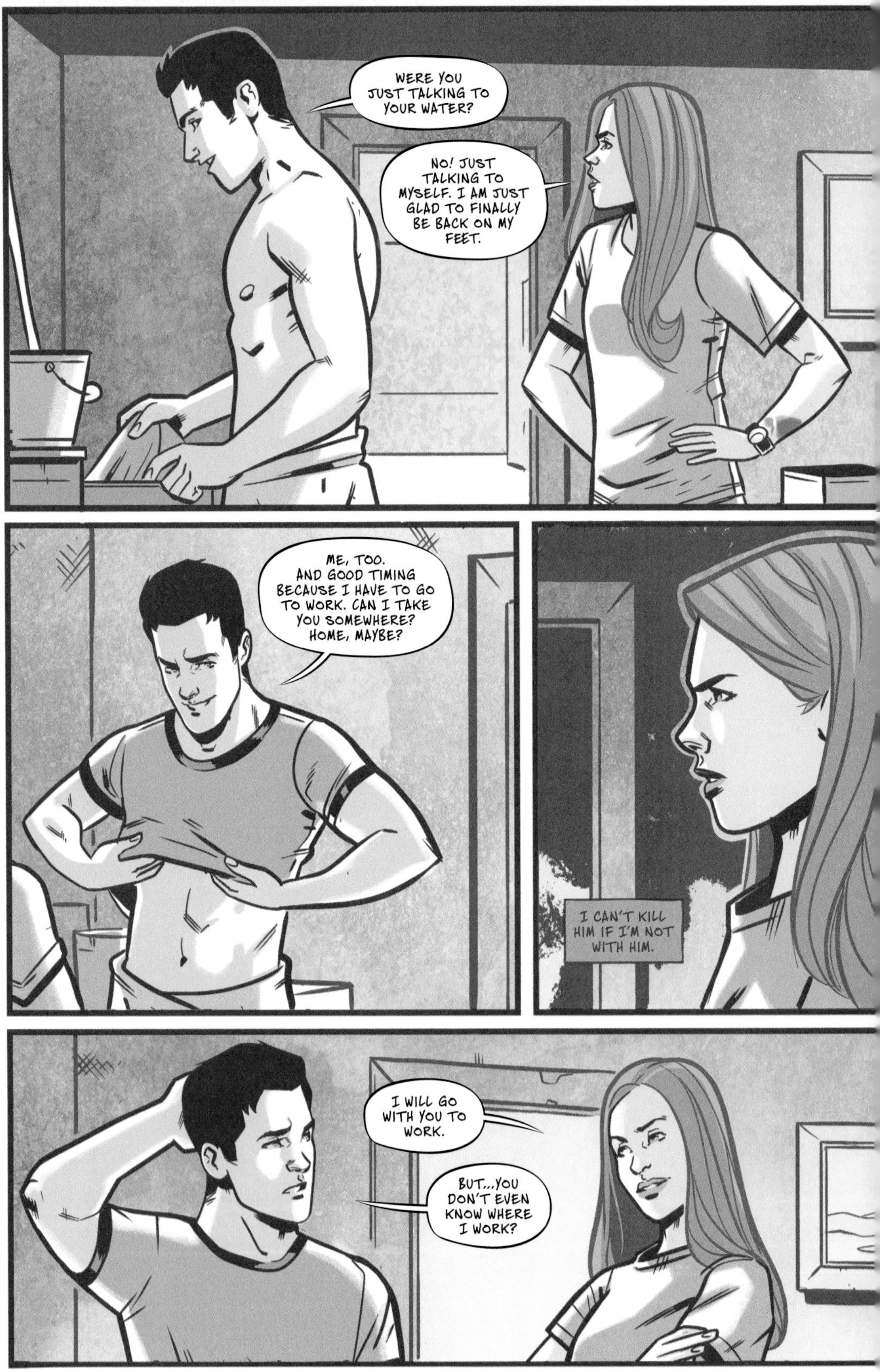
WERE YOU JUST TALKING TO YOUR WATER?
NO! JUST TALKING TO MYSELF. I AM JUST GLAD TO FINALLY BE BACK ON MY FEET.
ME, TOO. AND GOOD TIMING BECAUSE I HAVE TO GO TO WORK. CAN I TAKE YOU SOMEWHERE? HOME, MAYBE?
I CAN'T KILL HIM IF I'M NOT WITH HIM.
I WILL GO WITH YOU TO WORK.
BUT...YOU DON'T EVEN KNOW WHERE I WORK?

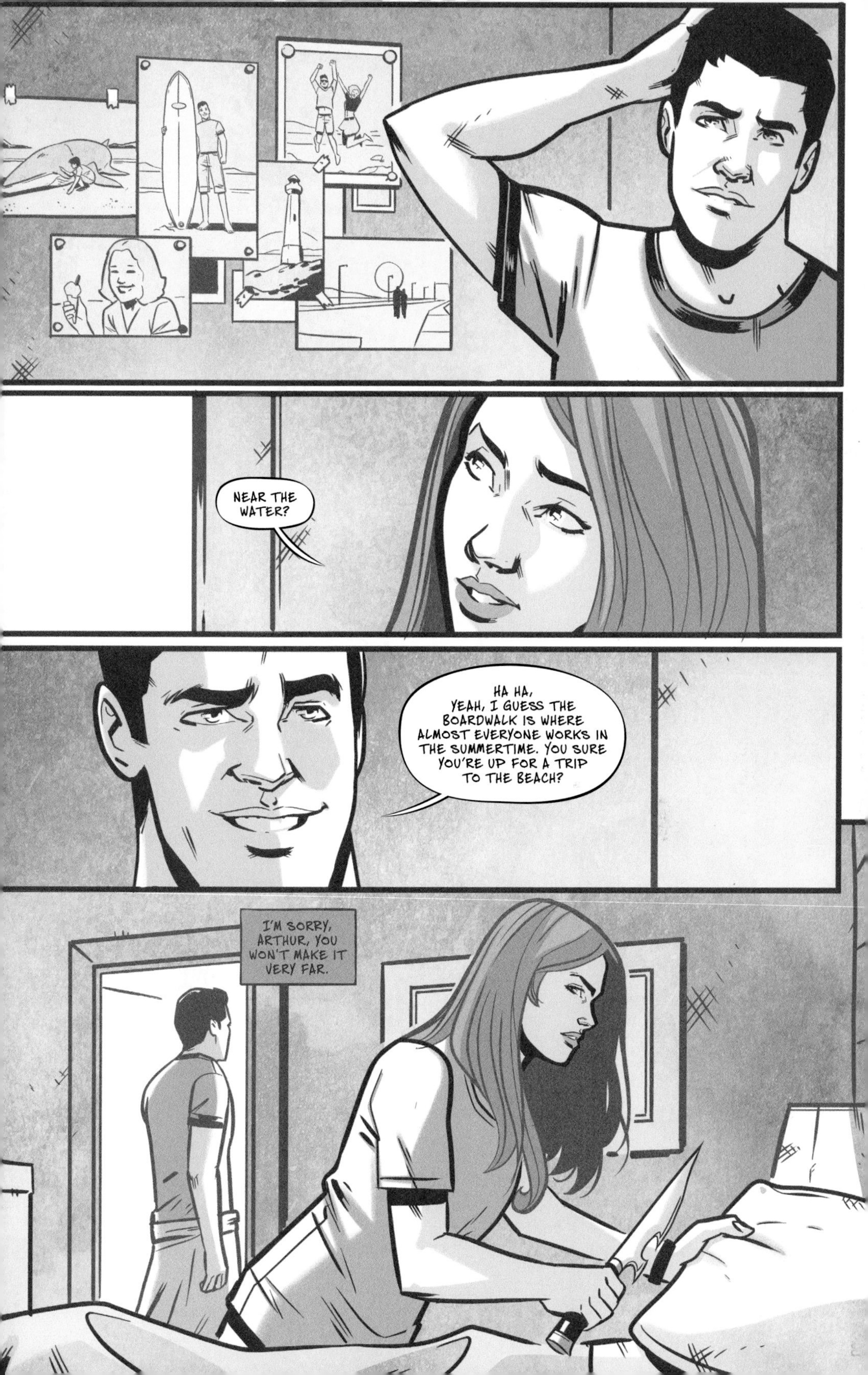
NEAR THE WATER?
HA HA, YEAH, I GUESS THE BOARDWALK IS WHERE ALMOST EVERYONE WORKS IN THE SUMMERTIME. YOU SURE YOU'RE UP FOR A TRIP TO THE BEACH?
I'M SORRY, ARTHUR, YOU WON'T MAKE IT VERY FAR.

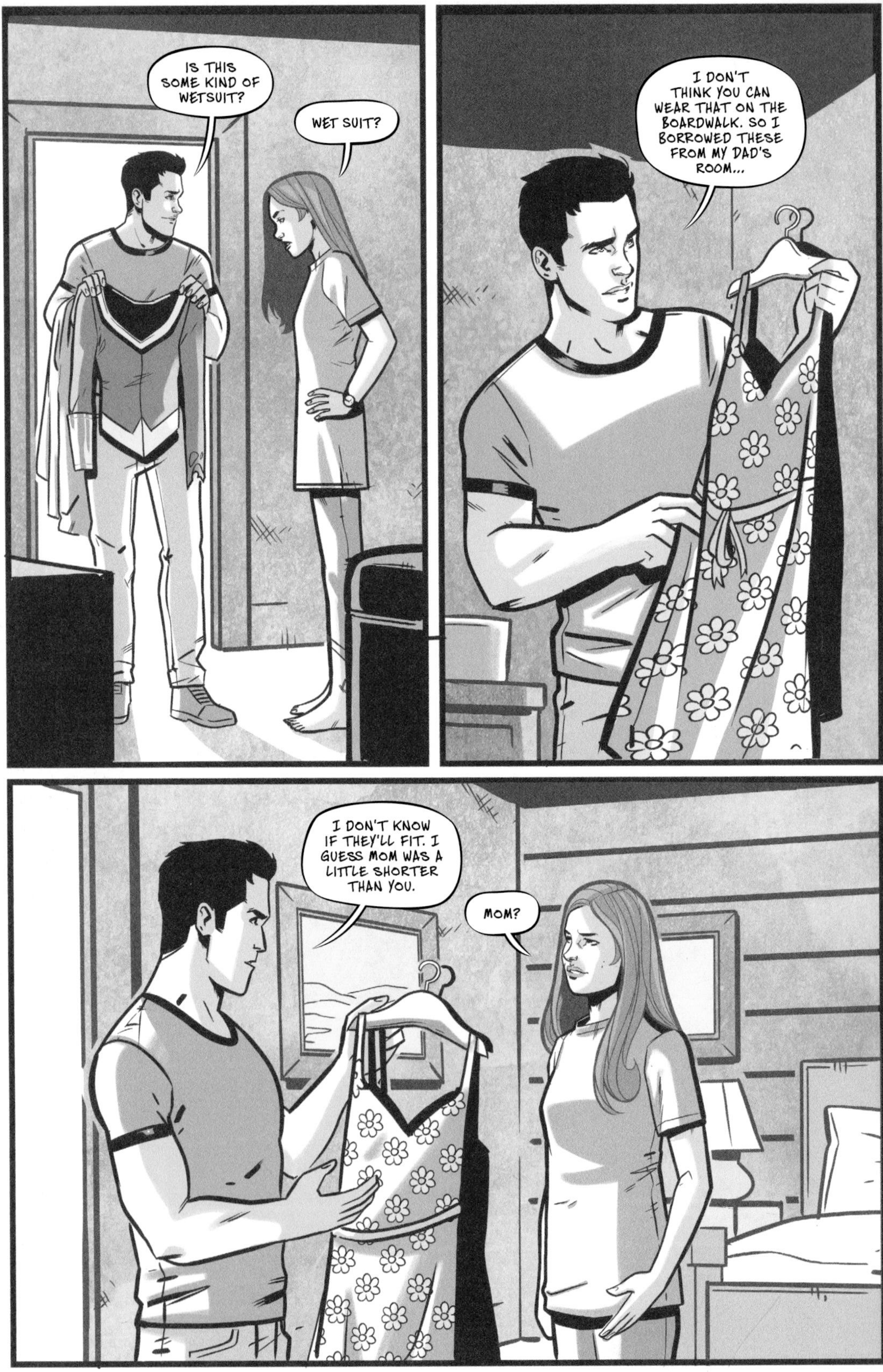
IS THIS SOME KIND OF WETSUIT?
WET SUIT?
I DON'T THINK YOU CAN WEAR THAT ON THE BOARDWALK. SO I BORROWED THESE FROM MY DAD'S ROOM...
I DON'T KNOW IF THEY'LL FIT. I GUESS MOM WAS A LITTLE SHORTER THAN YOU.
MOM?

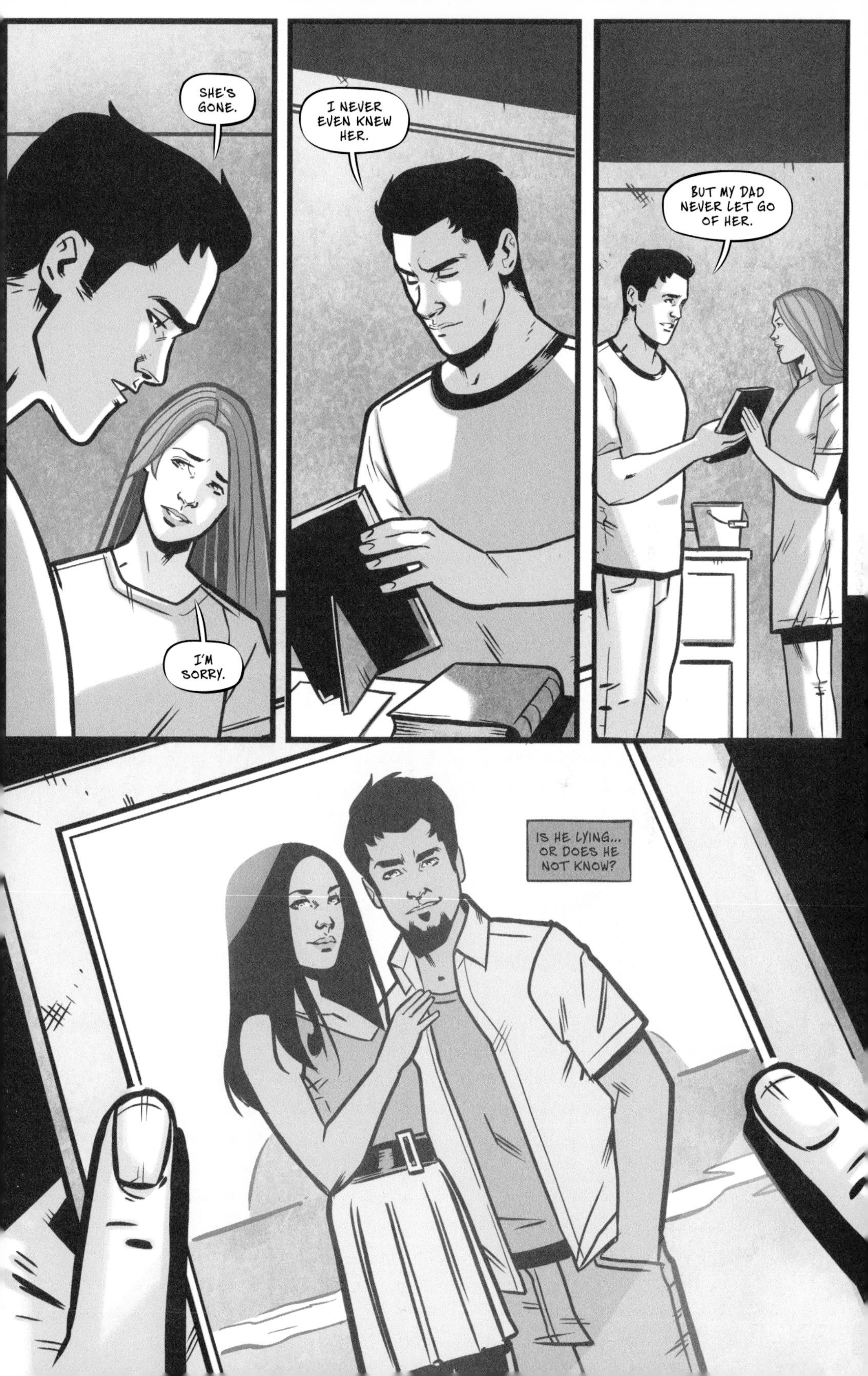
SHE'S GONE.
I'M SORRY.
I NEVER EVEN KNEW HER.
BUT MY DAD NEVER LET GO OF HER.
IS HE LYING... OR DOES HE NOT KNOW?

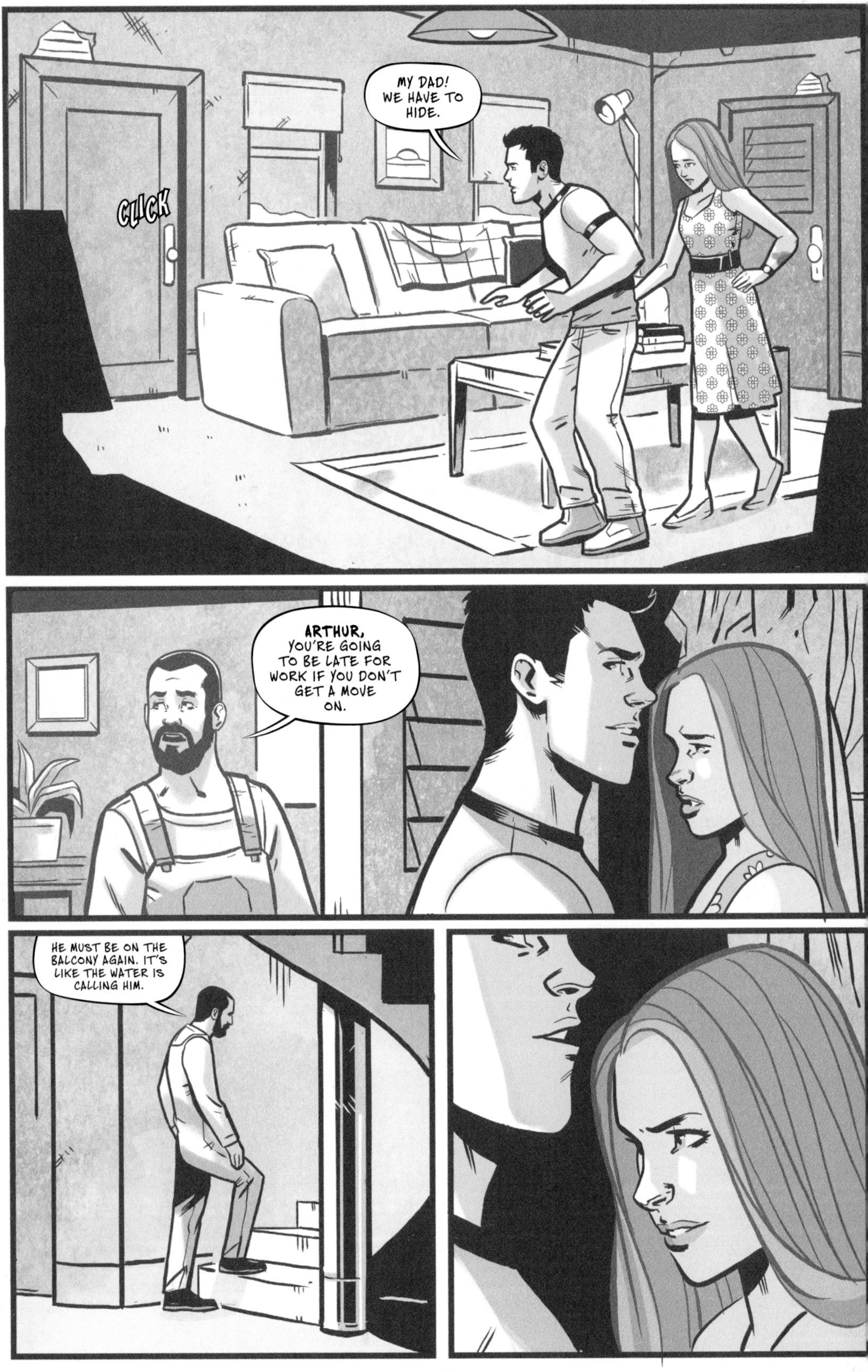
MY DAD! WE HAVE TO HIDE.
CLICK
ARTHUR, YOU'RE GOING TO BE LATE FOR WORK IF YOU DON'T GET A MOVE ON.
HE MUST BE ON THE BALCONY AGAIN. IT'S LIKE THE WATER IS CALLING HIM.

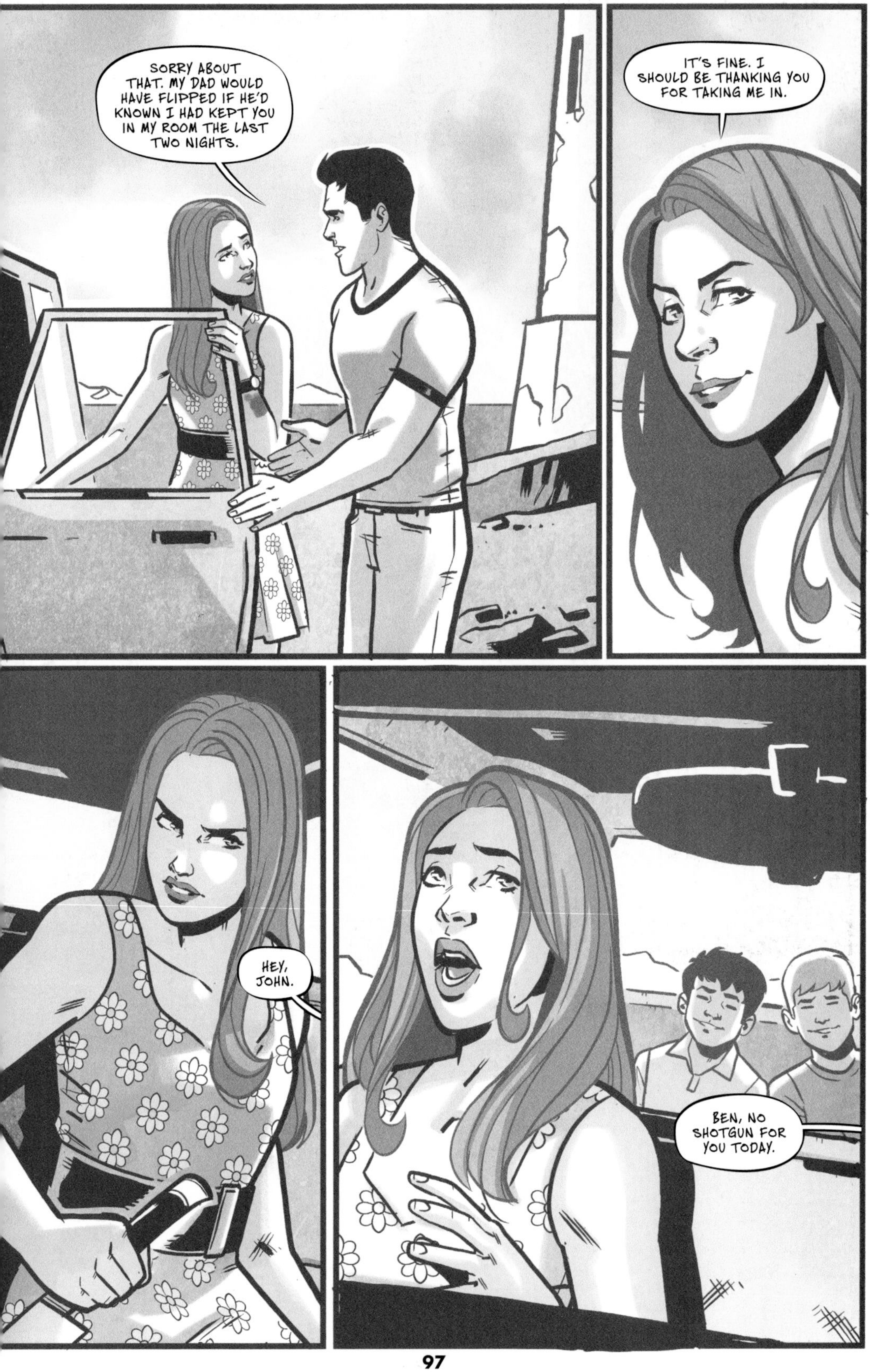
SORRY ABOUT THAT. MY DAD WOULD HAVE FLIPPED IF HE'D KNOWN I HAD KEPT YOU IN MY ROOM THE LAST TWO NIGHTS.
IT'S FINE. I SHOULD BE THANKING YOU FOR TAKING ME IN.
HEY, JOHN.
BEN, NO SHOTGUN FOR YOU TODAY.

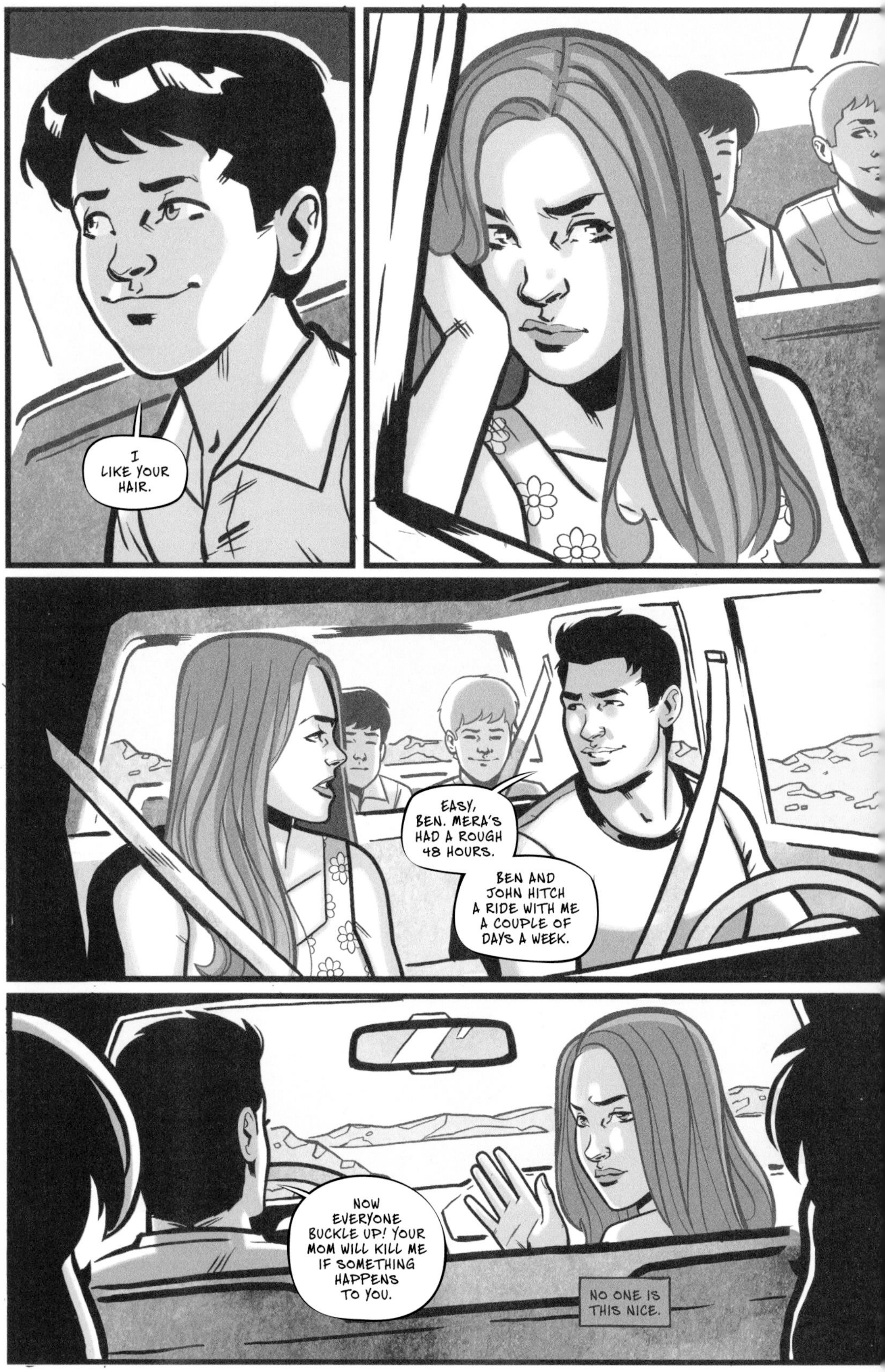
I LIKE YOUR HAIR.
EASY, BEN. MERA'S HAD A ROUGH 48 HOURS.
BEN AND JOHN HITCH A RIDE WITH ME A COUPLE OF DAYS A WEEK.
NOW EVERYONE BUCKLE UP! YOUR MOM WILL KILL ME IF SOMETHING HAPPENS TO YOU.
NO ONE IS THIS NICE.

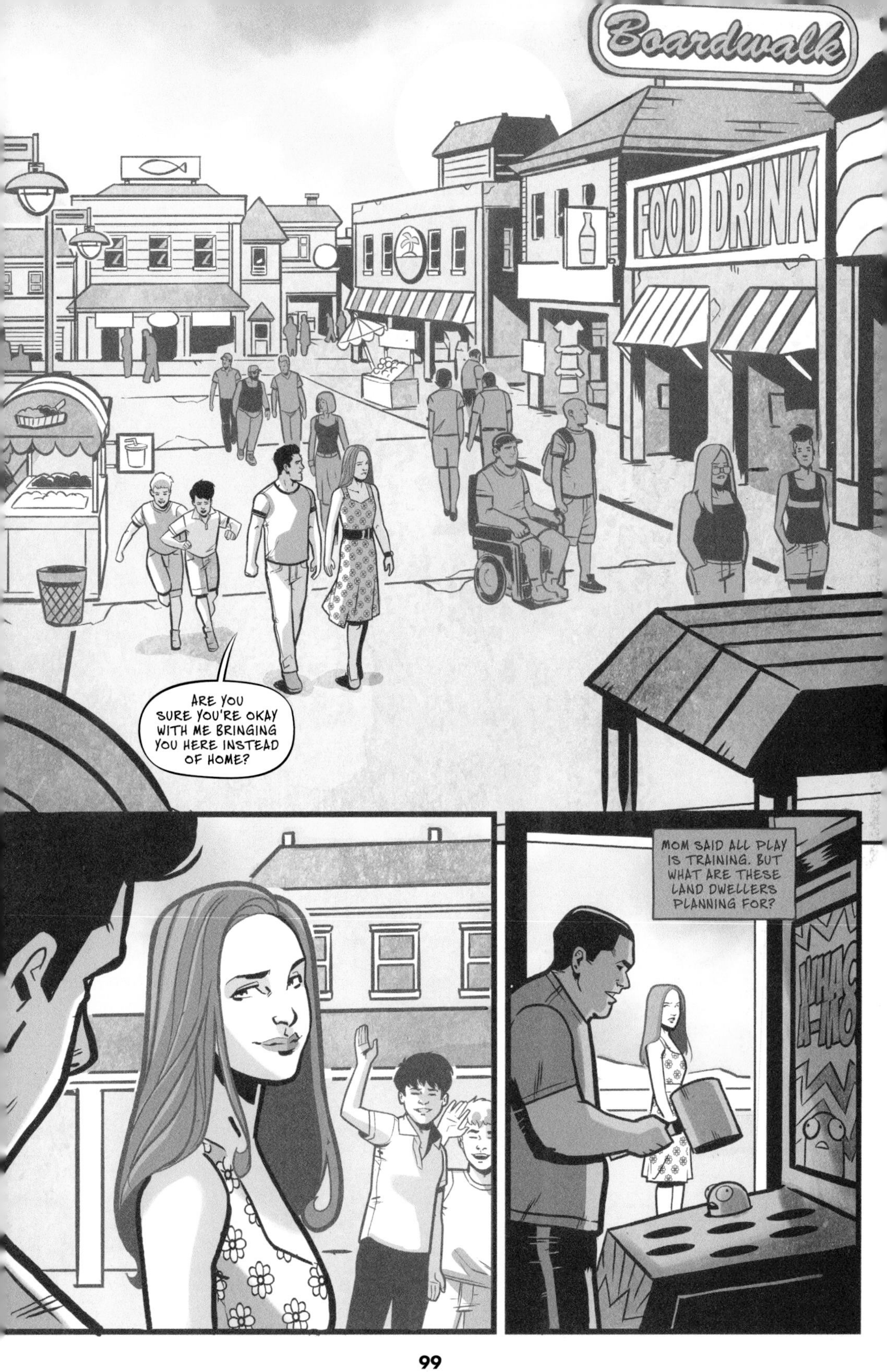
Boardwalk
FOOD DRINK
ARE YOU SURE YOU'RE OKAY WITH ME BRINGING YOU HERE INSTEAD OF HOME?
MOM SAID ALL PLAY IS TRAINING. BUT WHAT ARE THESE LAND DWELLERS PLANNING FOR?

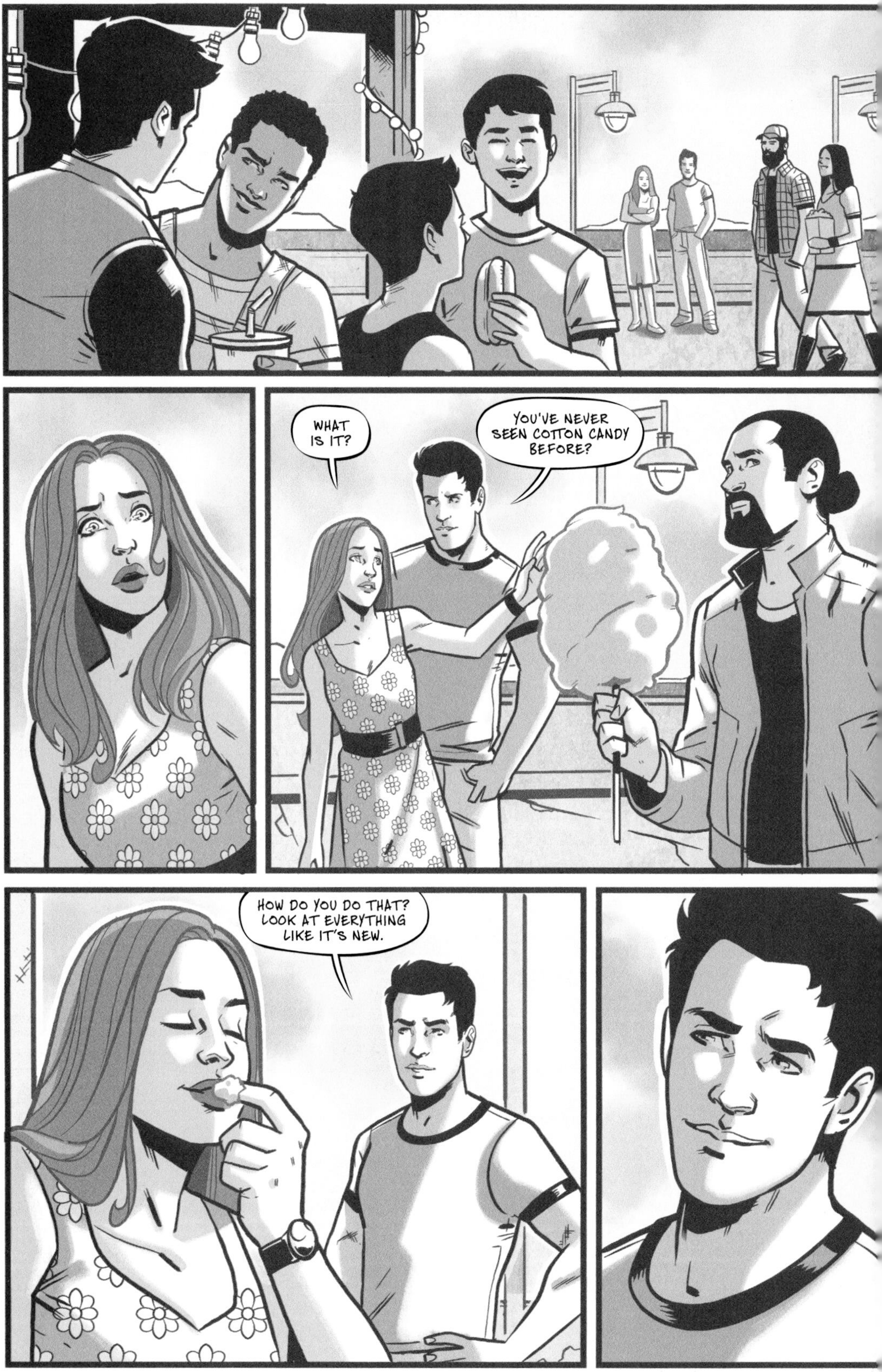
WHAT IS IT?
YOU'VE NEVER SEEN COTTON CANDY BEFORE?
HOW DO YOU DO THAT? LOOK AT EVERYTHING LIKE IT'S NEW.

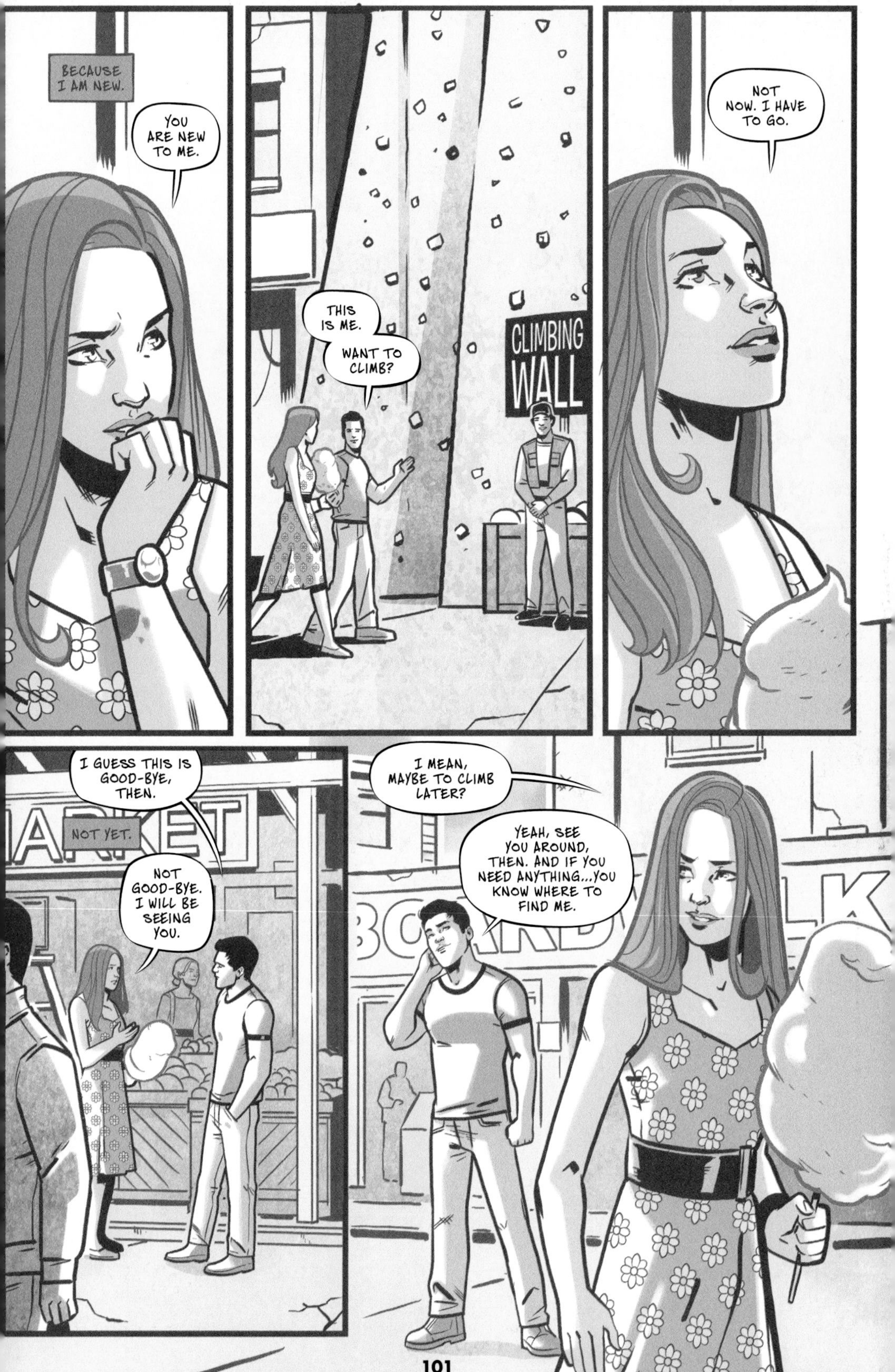
BECAUSE I AM NEW.
YOU ARE NEW TO ME.
THIS IS ME.
WANT TO CLIMB?
CLIMBING WALL
NOT NOW. I HAVE TO GO.
I GUESS THIS IS GOOD-BYE, THEN.
NOT YET.
NOT GOOD-BYE. I WILL BE SEEING YOU.
I MEAN, MAYBE TO CLIMB LATER?
YEAH, SEE YOU AROUND, THEN. AND IF YOU NEED ANYTHING...YOU KNOW WHERE TO FIND ME.

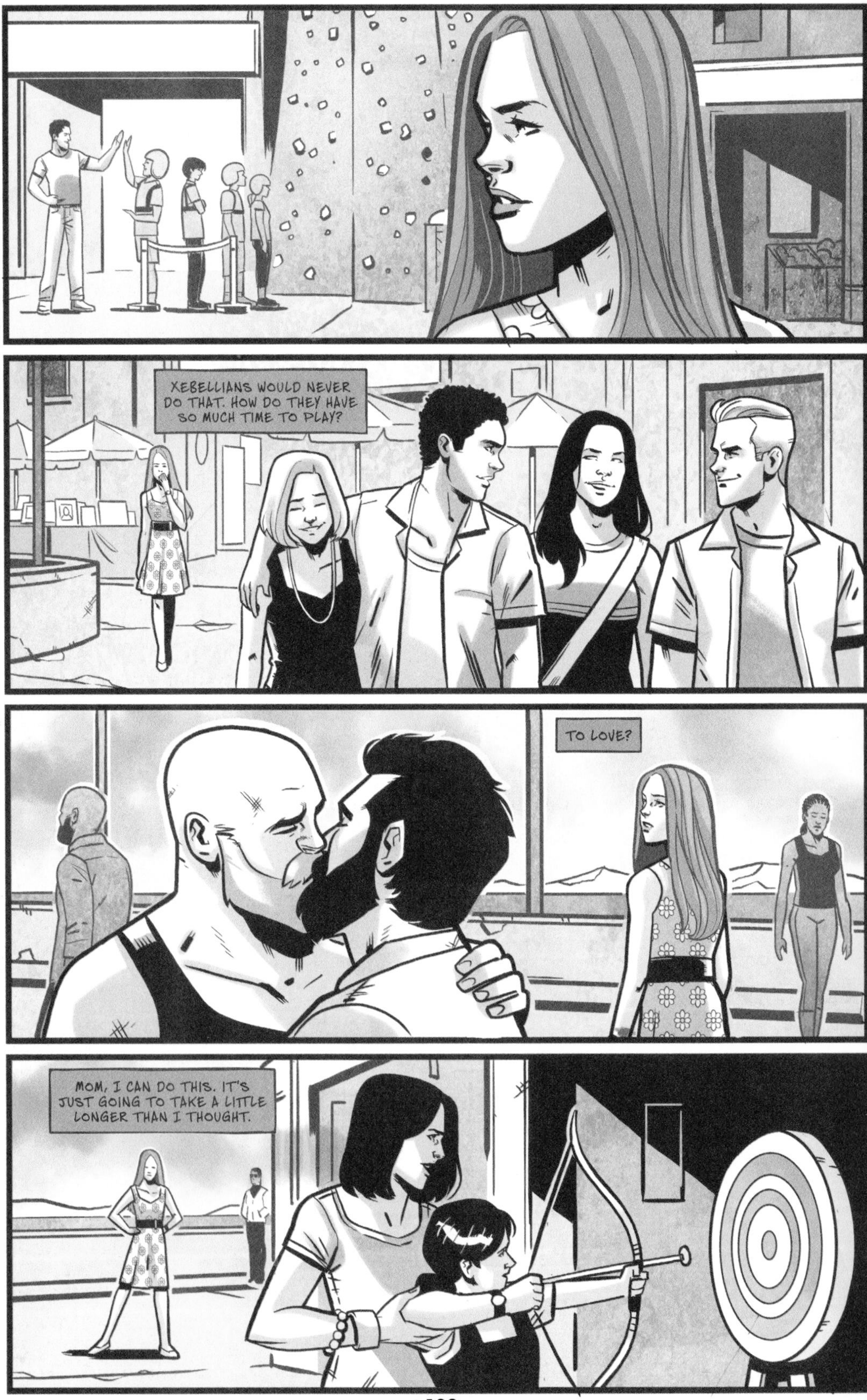
XEBELLIANS WOULD NEVER DO THAT. HOW DO THEY HAVE SO MUCH TIME TO PLAY?
TO LOVE?
MOM, I CAN DO THIS. IT'S JUST GOING TO TAKE A LITTLE LONGER THAN I THOUGHT.

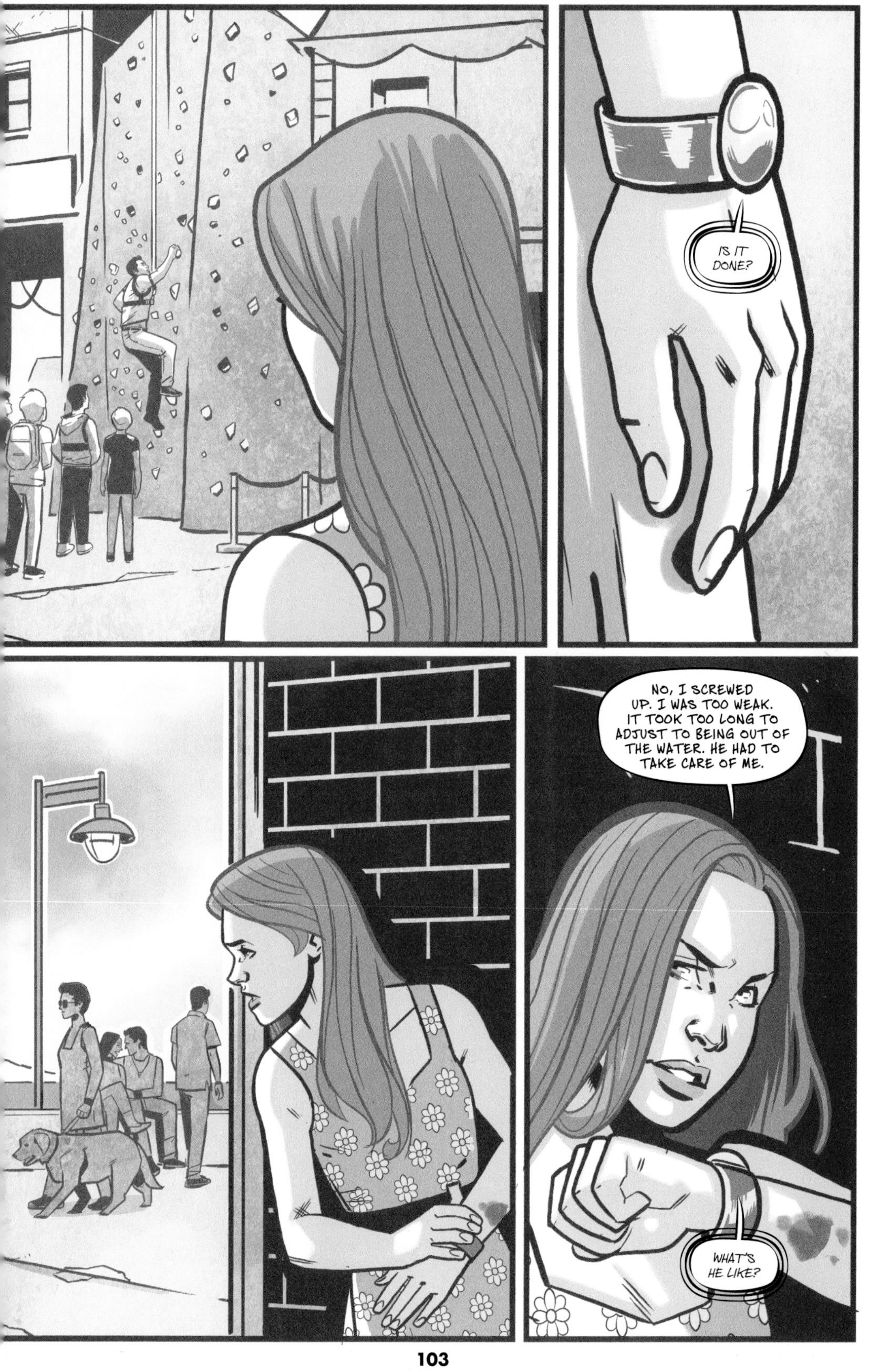
IS IT DONE?
NO, I SCREWED UP. I WAS TOO WEAK. IT TOOK TOO LONG TO ADJUST TO BEING OUT OF THE WATER. HE HAD TO TAKE CARE OF ME.
WHAT'S HE LIKE?

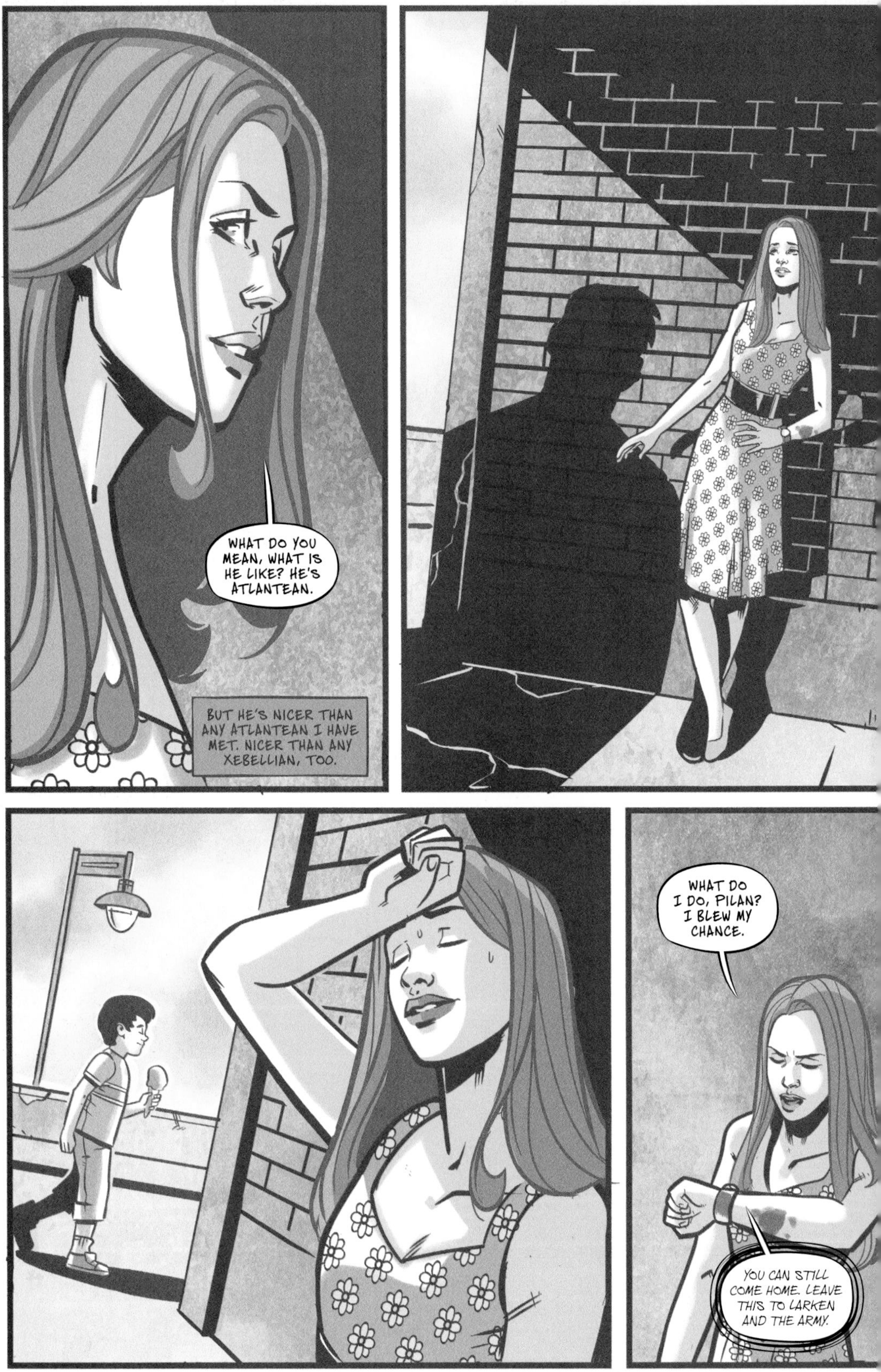
WHAT DO YOU MEAN, WHAT IS HE LIKE? HE'S ATLANTEAN.
BUT HE'S NICER THAN ANY ATLANTEAN I HAVE MET. NICER THAN ANY XEBELLIAN, TOO.
WHAT DO I DO, PILAN? I BLEW MY CHANCE.
YOU CAN STILL COME HOME. LEAVE THIS TO LARKEN AND THE ARMY.

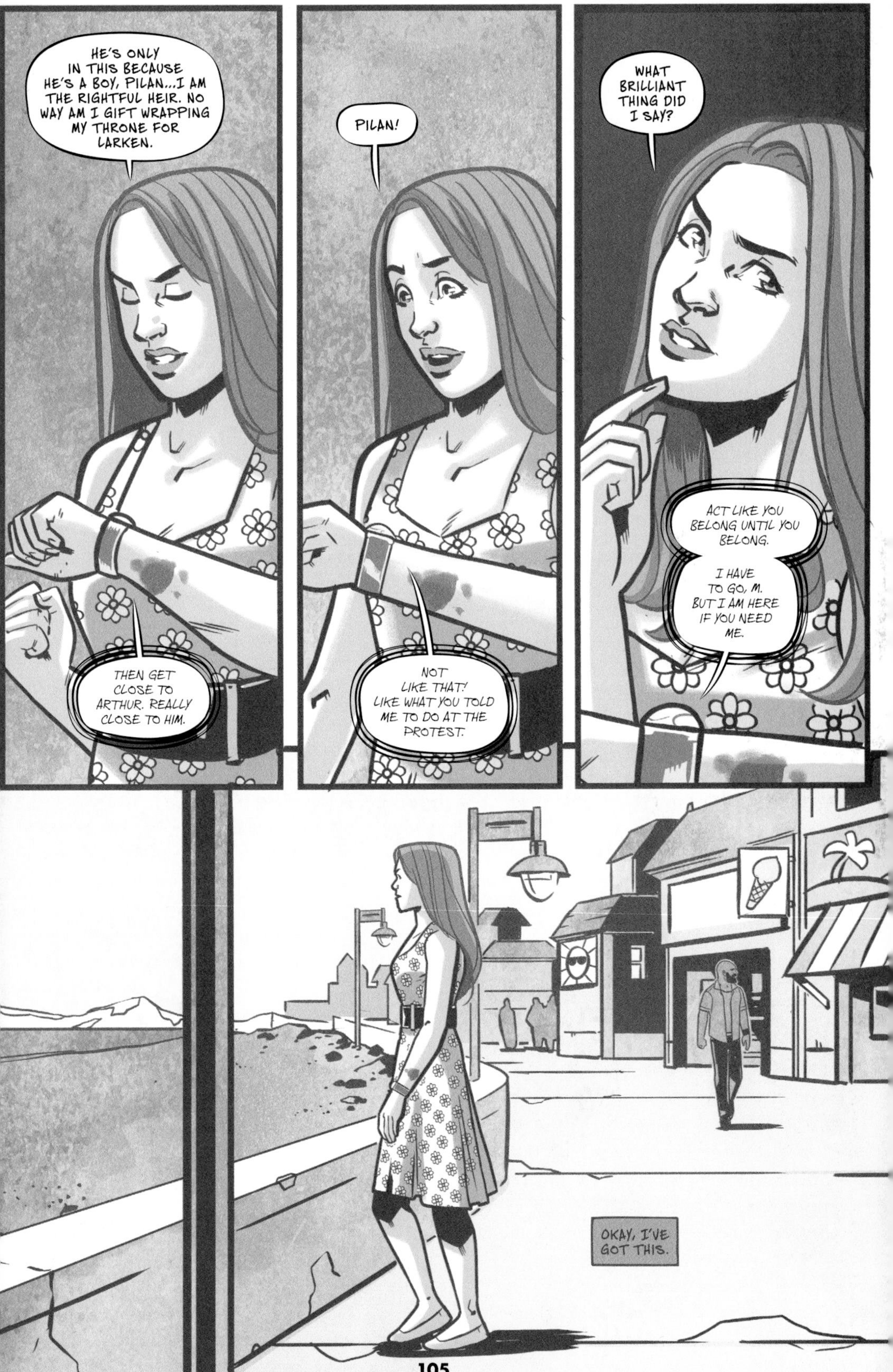
HE'S ONLY IN THIS BECAUSE HE'S A BOY, PILAN...I AM THE RIGHTFUL HEIR. NO WAY AM I GIFT WRAPPING MY THRONE FOR LARKEN.
THEN GET CLOSE TO ARTHUR. REALLY CLOSE TO HIM.
PILAN!
NOT LIKE THAT! LIKE WHAT YOU TOLD ME TO DO AT THE PROTEST.
WHAT BRILLIANT THING DID I SAY?
ACT LIKE YOU BELONG UNTIL YOU BELONG.
I HAVE TO GO, M. BUT I AM HERE IF YOU NEED ME.
OKAY, I'VE GOT THIS.

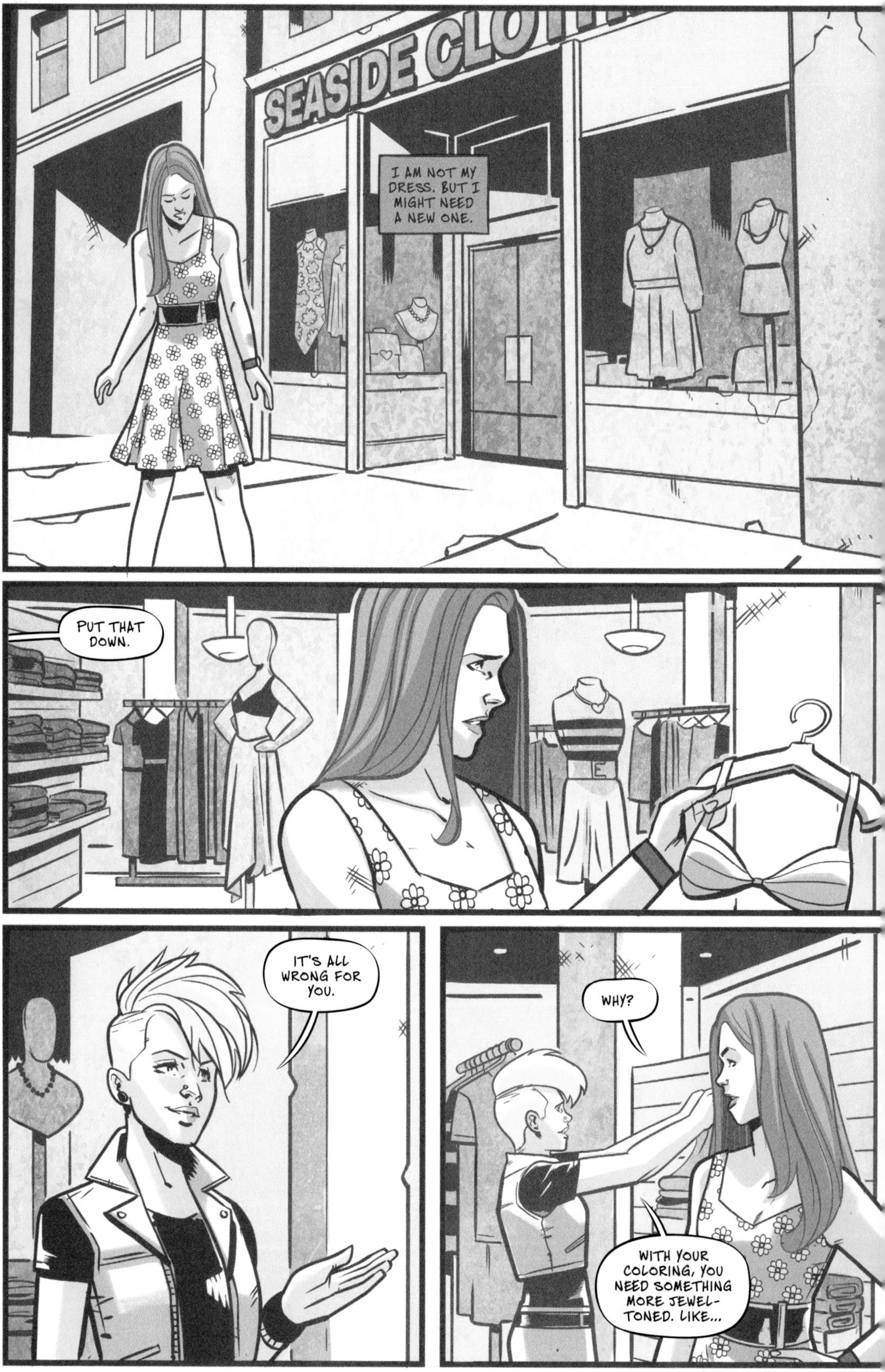
SEASIDE CLO
I AM NOT MY DRESS. BUT I MIGHT NEED A NEW ONE.
PUT THAT DOWN.
IT'S ALL WRONG FOR YOU.
WHY?
WITH YOUR COLORING, YOU NEED SOMETHING MORE JEWEL-TONED. LIKE...

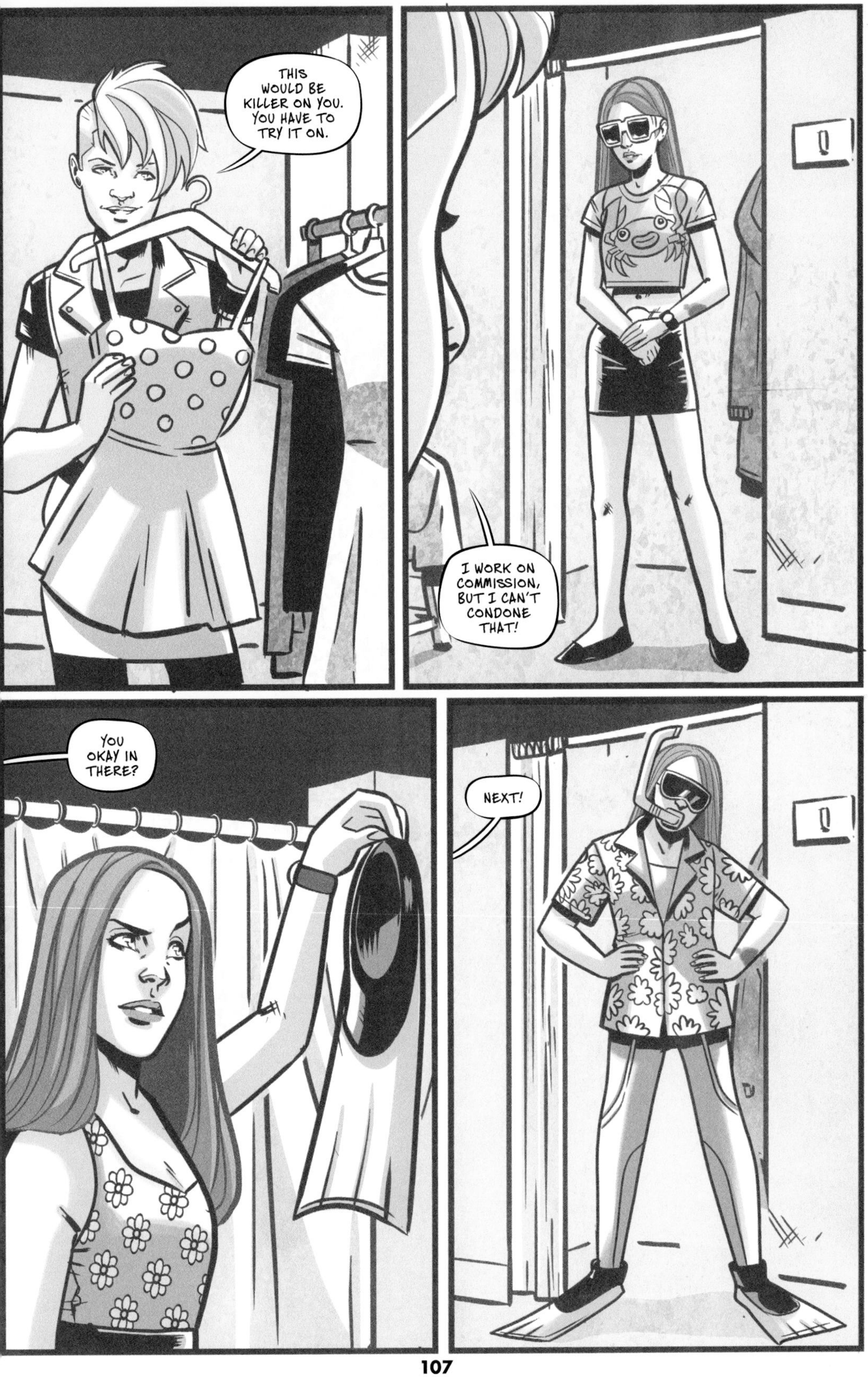
THIS WOULD BE KILLER ON YOU. YOU HAVE TO TRY IT ON.
I WORK ON COMMISSION, BUT I CAN'T CONDONE THAT!
YOU OKAY IN THERE?
NEXT!

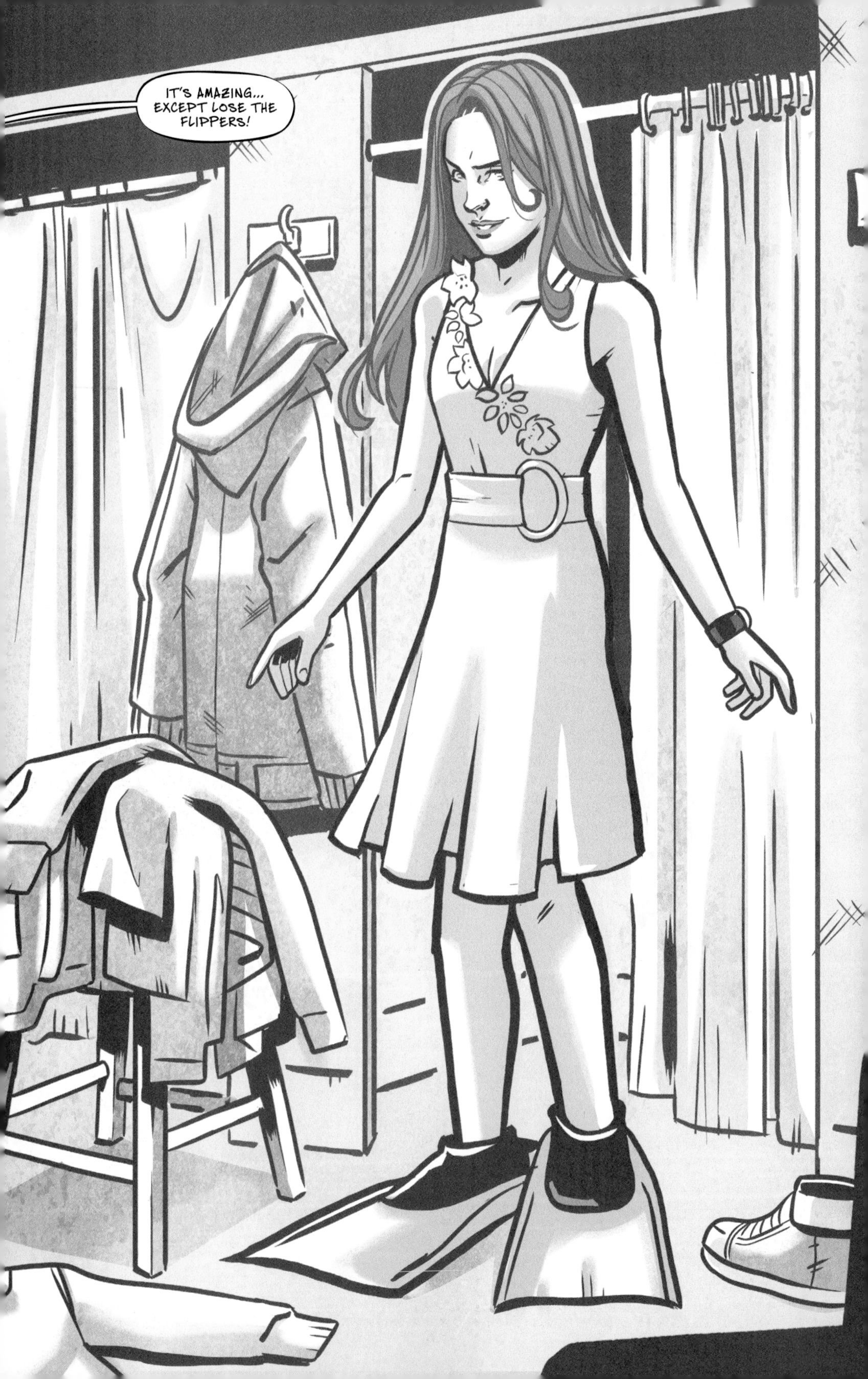
IT'S AMAZING... EXCEPT LOSE THE FLIPPERS!

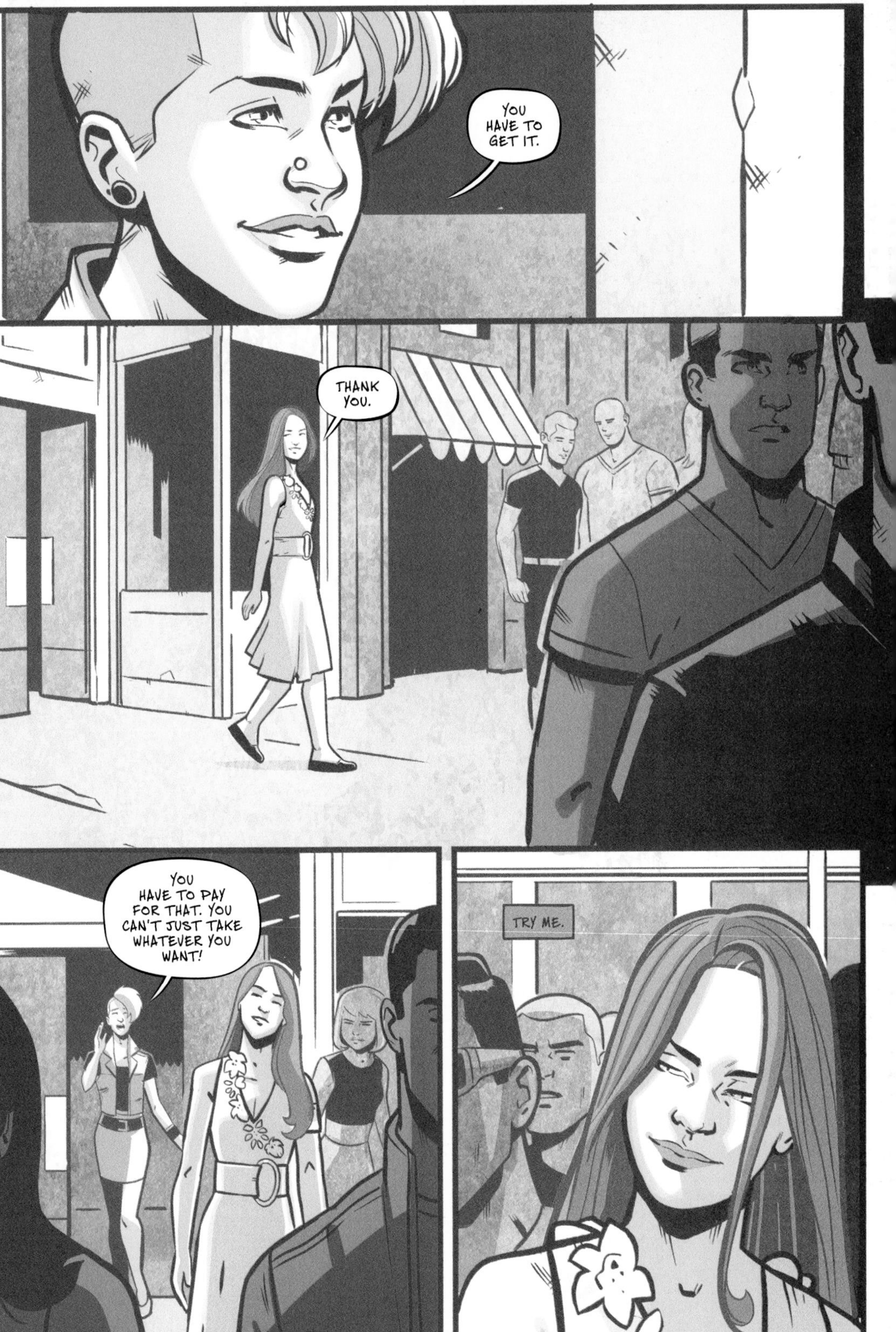
YOU HAVE TO GET IT.
THANK YOU.
YOU HAVE TO PAY FOR THAT. YOU CAN'T JUST TAKE WHATEVER YOU WANT!
TRY ME.

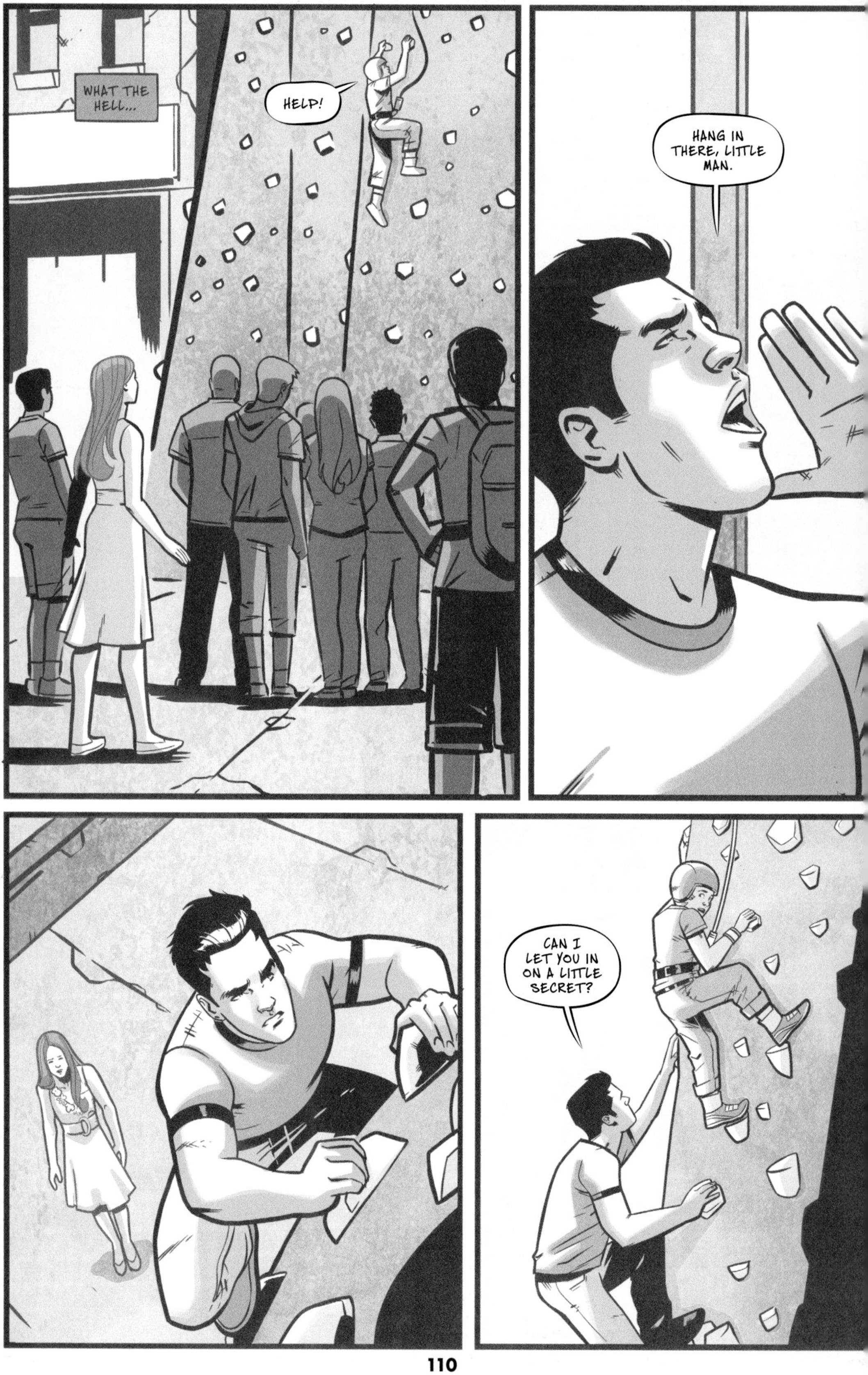
WHAT THE HELL...
HELP!
HANG IN THERE, LITTLE MAN.
CAN I LET YOU IN ON A LITTLE SECRET?

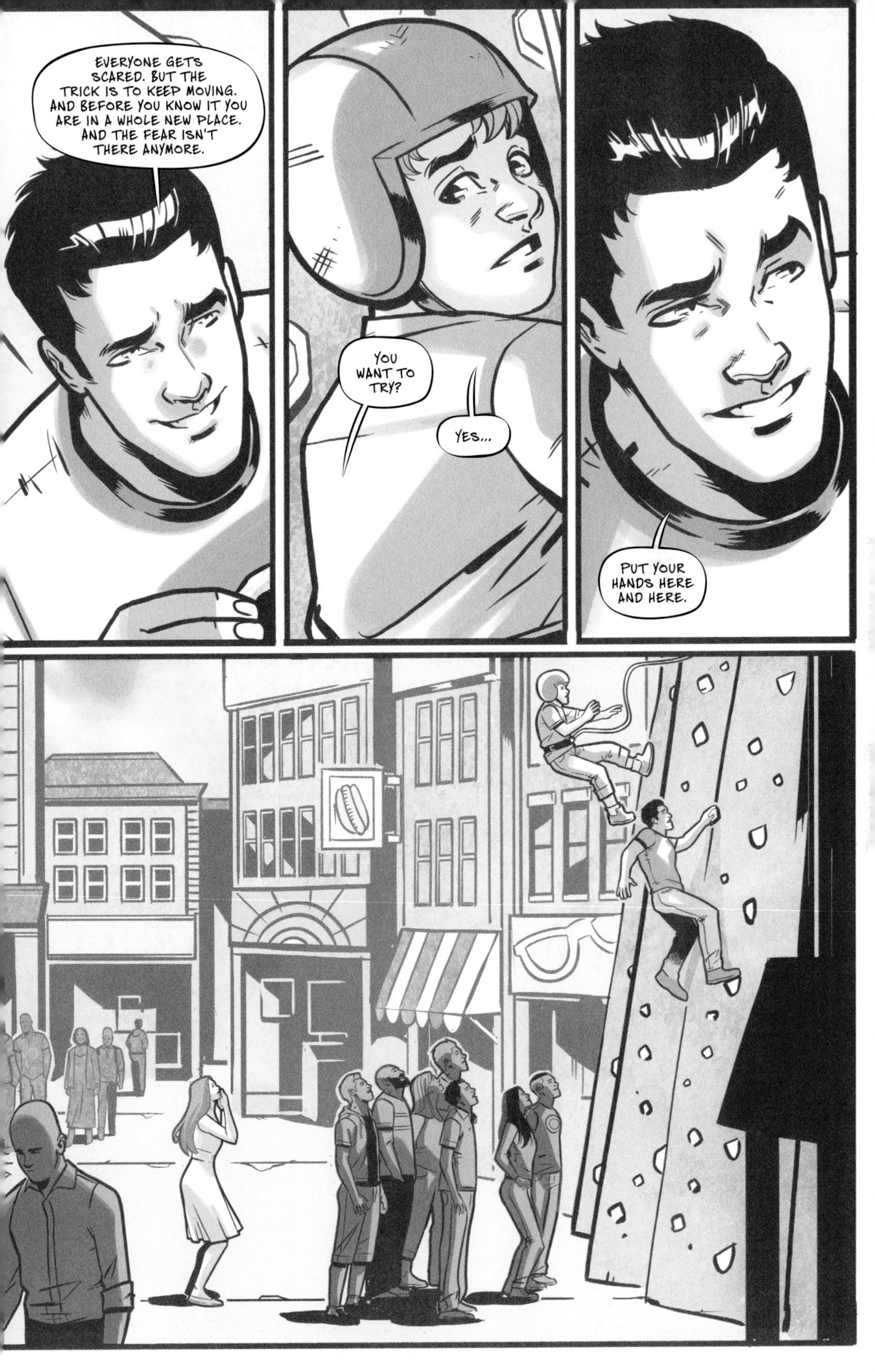
EVERYONE GETS SCARED. BUT THE TRICK IS TO KEEP MOVING. AND BEFORE YOU KNOW IT YOU ARE IN A WHOLE NEW PLACE. AND THE FEAR ISN'T THERE ANYMORE.
YOU WANT TO TRY?
YES...
PUT YOUR HANDS HERE AND HERE.

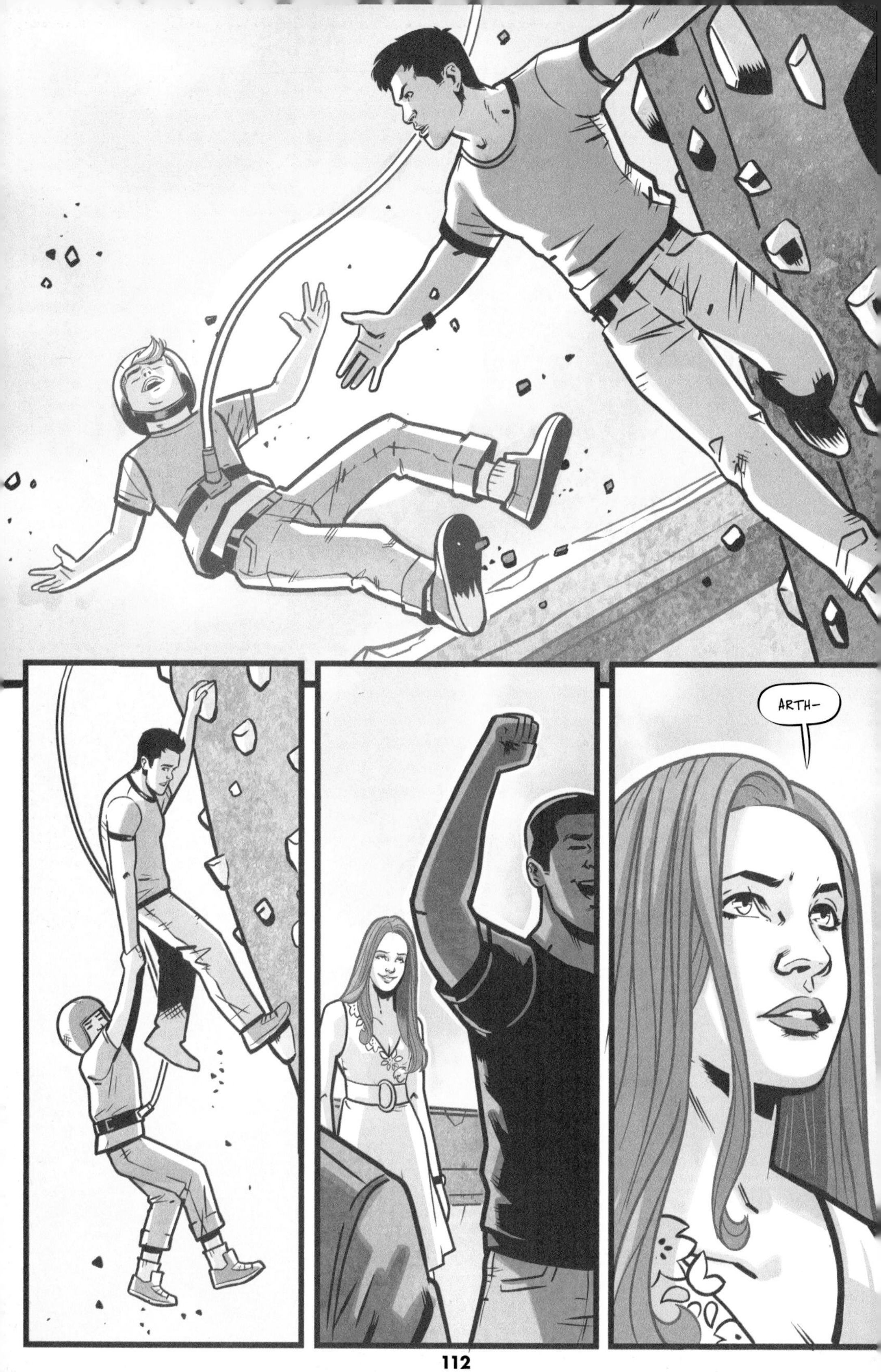
ARTH-

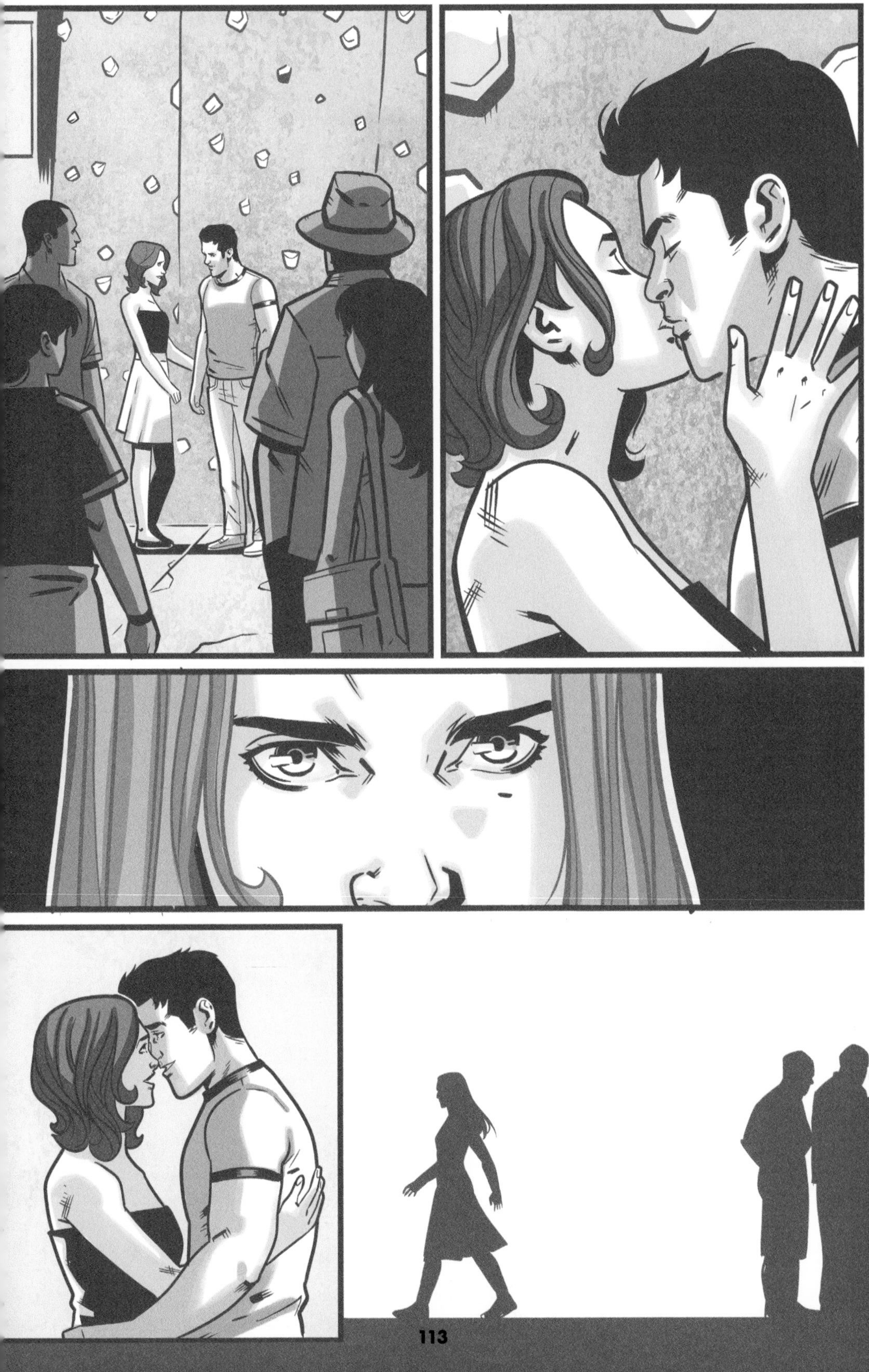

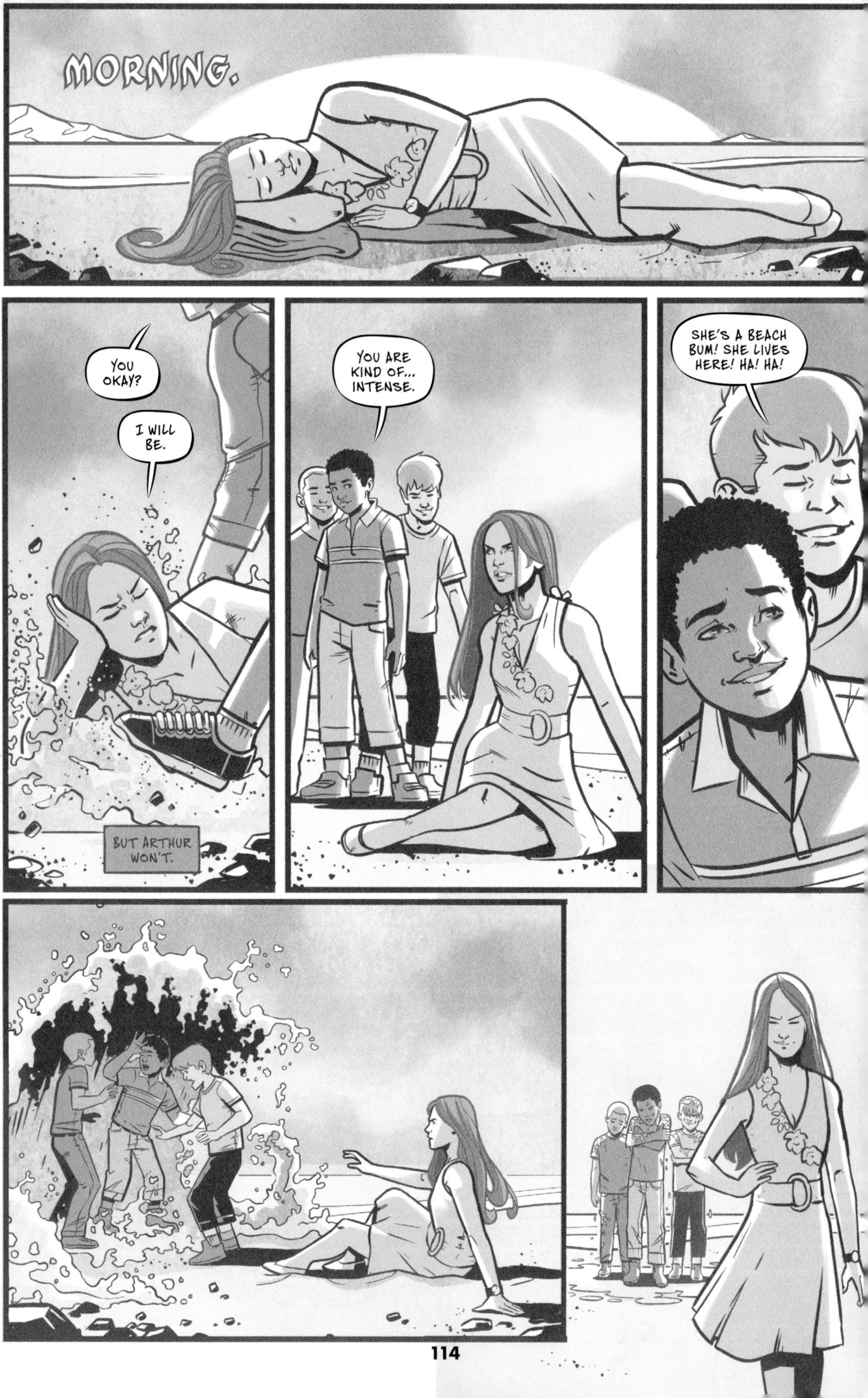
MORNING.
YOU OKAY?
I WILL BE.
BUT ARTHUR WON'T.
YOU ARE KIND OF... INTENSE.
SHE'S A BEACH BUM! SHE LIVES HERE! HA! HA!

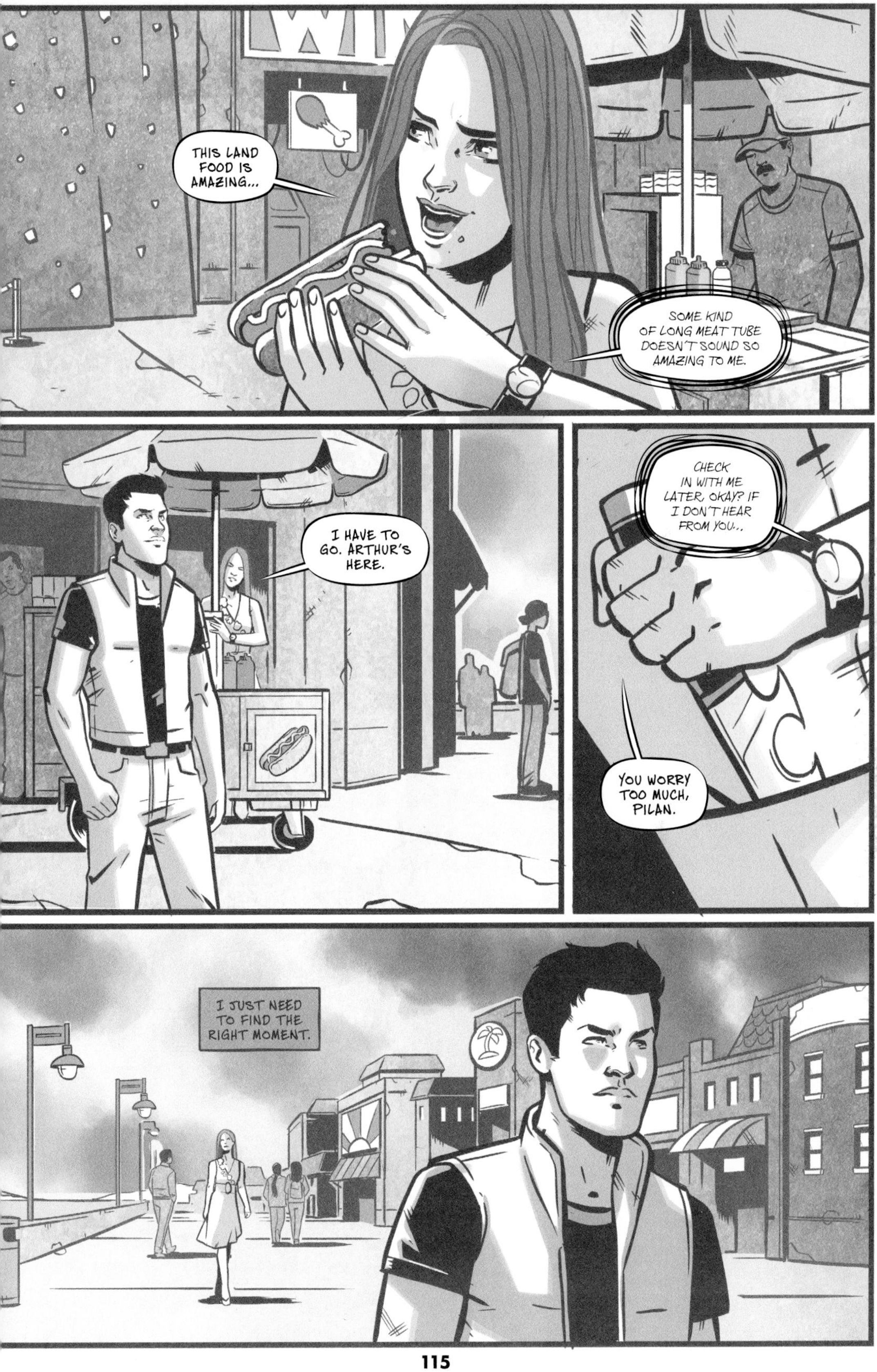
THIS LAND FOOD IS AMAZING...
SOME KIND OF LONG MEAT TUBE DOESN'T SOUND SO AMAZING TO ME.
I HAVE TO GO. ARTHUR'S HERE.
CHECK IN WITH ME LATER, OKAY? IF I DON'T HEAR FROM YOU...
YOU WORRY TOO MUCH, PILAN.
I JUST NEED TO FIND THE RIGHT MOMENT.

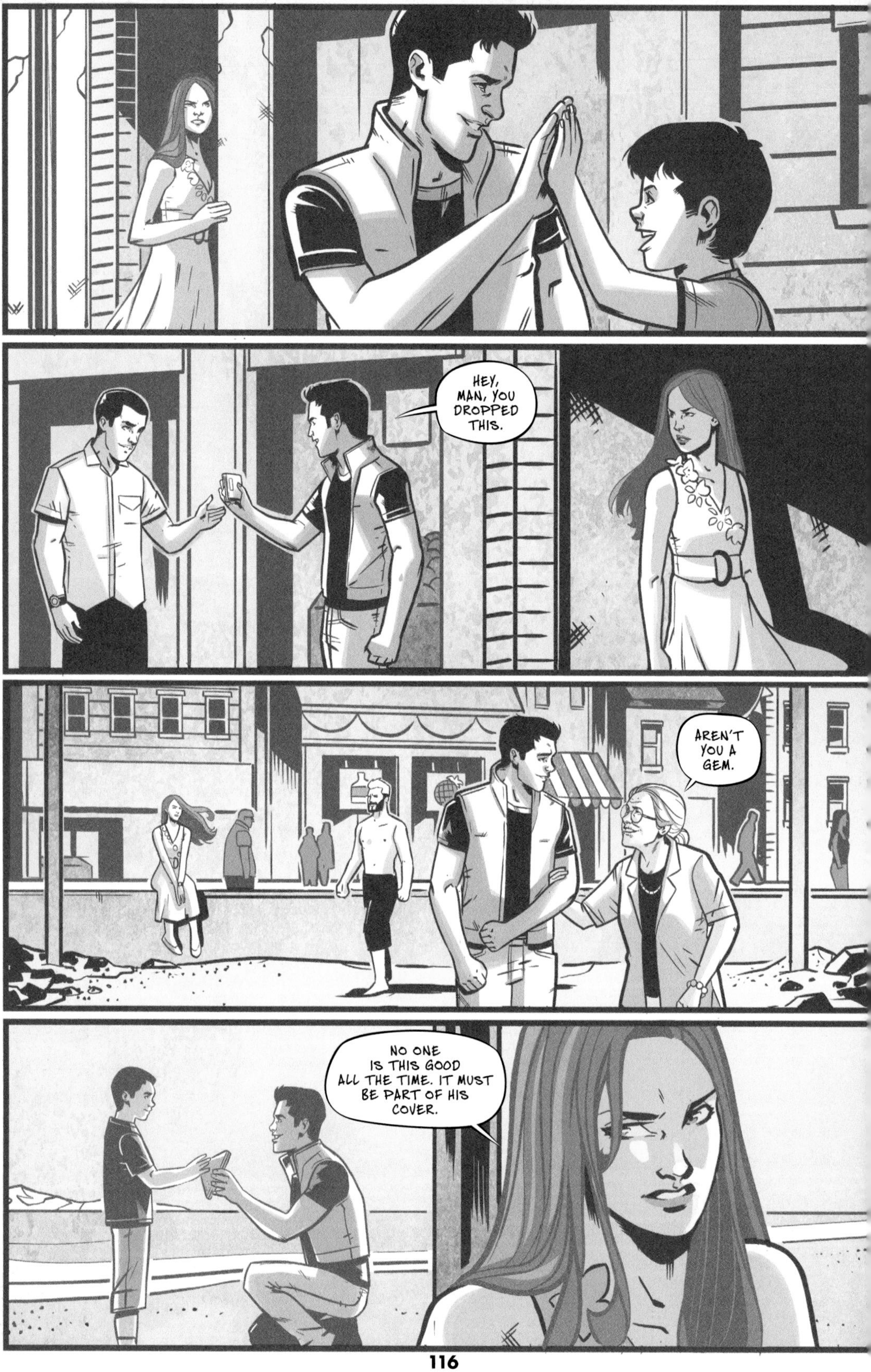
HEY, MAN, YOU DROPPED THIS.
AREN'T YOU A GEM.
NO ONE IS THIS GOOD ALL THE TIME. IT MUST BE PART OF HIS COVER.

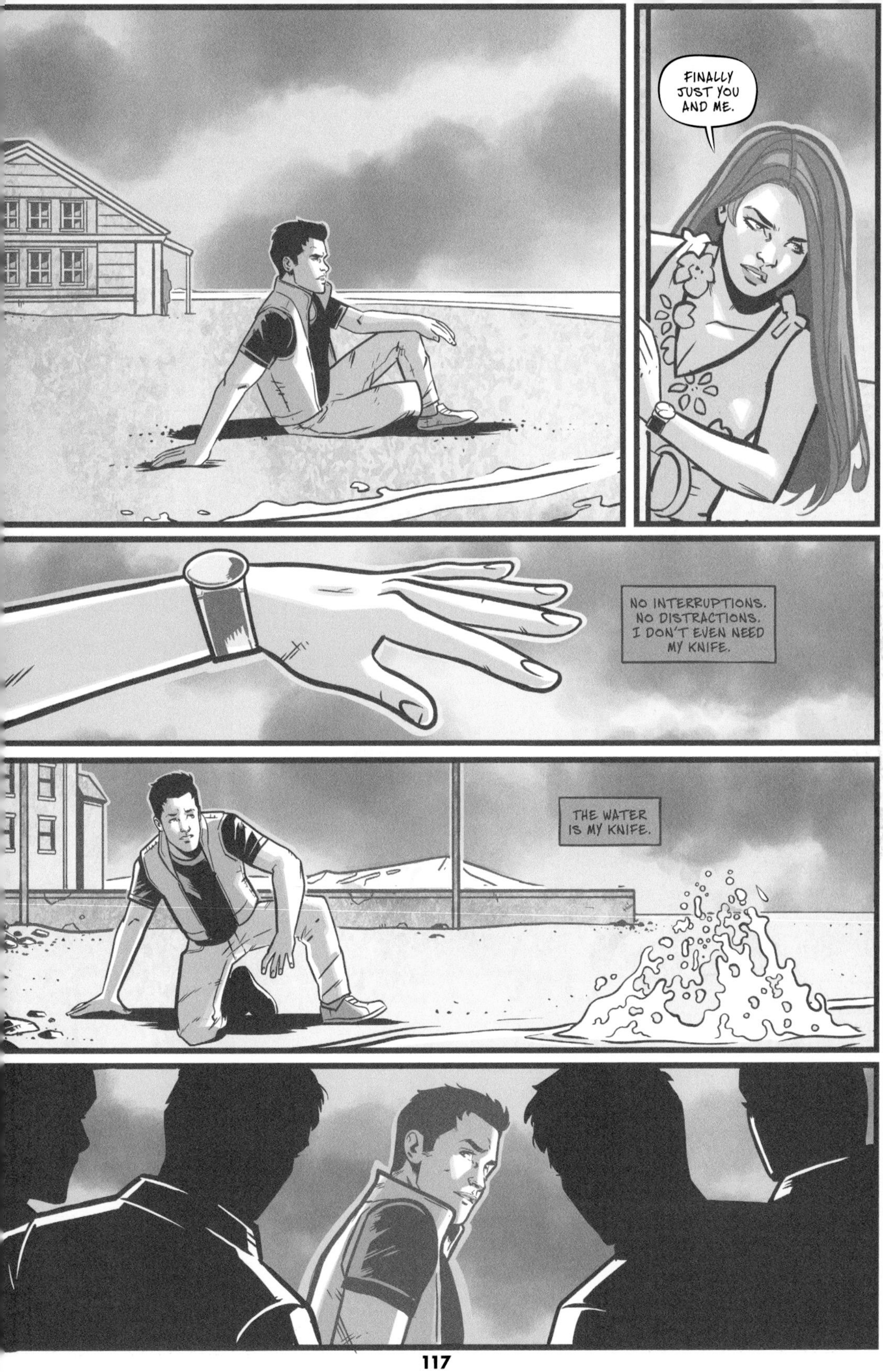
FINALLY JUST YOU AND ME.
NO INTERRUPTIONS. NO DISTRACTIONS. I DON'T EVEN NEED MY KNIFE.
THE WATER IS MY KNIFE.

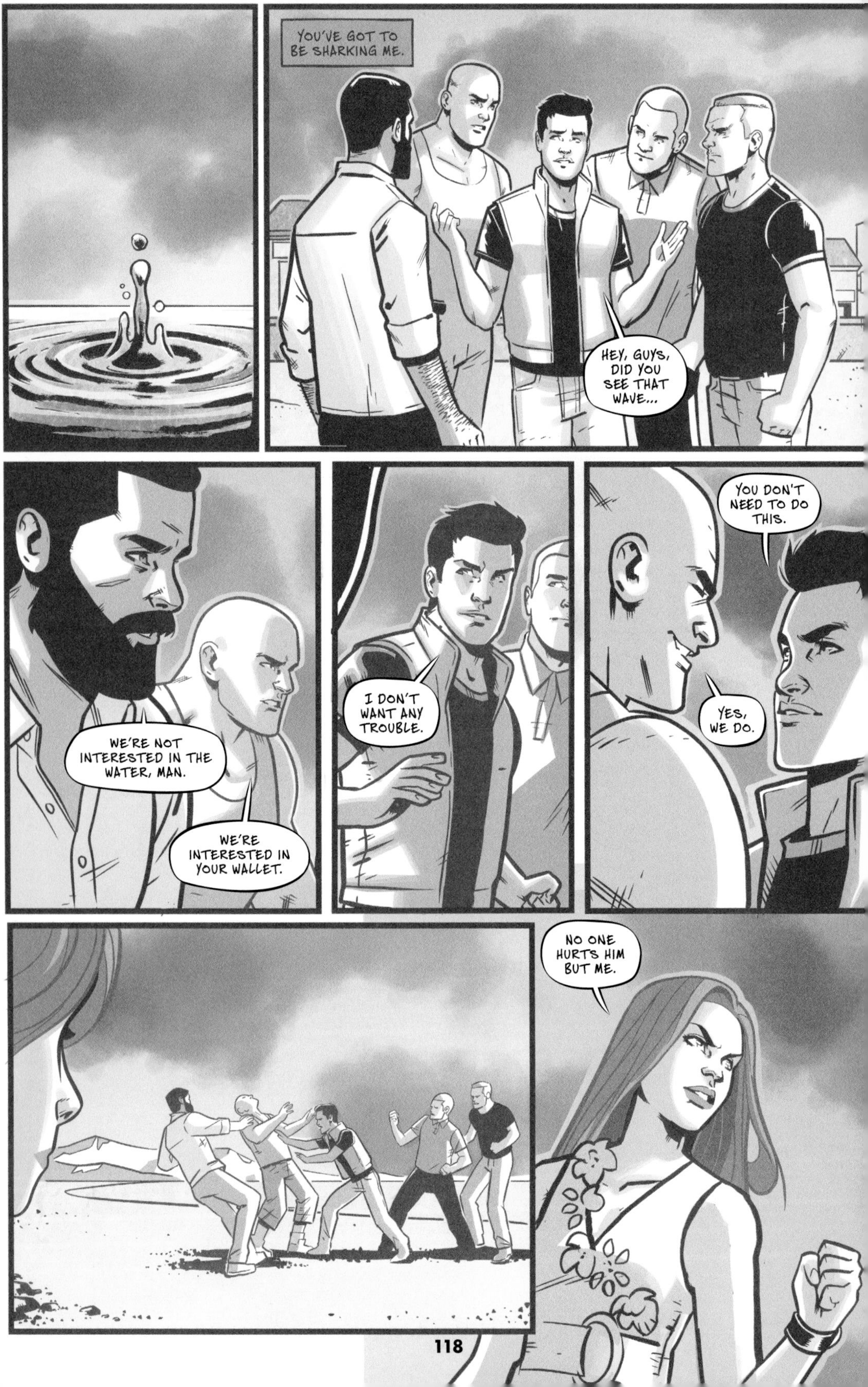
YOU'VE GOT TO BE SHARKING ME.
HEY, GUYS, DID YOU SEE THAT WAVE...
WE'RE NOT INTERESTED IN THE WATER, MAN.
WE'RE INTERESTED IN YOUR WALLET.
I DON'T WANT ANY TROUBLE.
YOU DON'T NEED TO DO THIS.
YES, WE DO.
NO ONE HURTS HIM BUT ME.

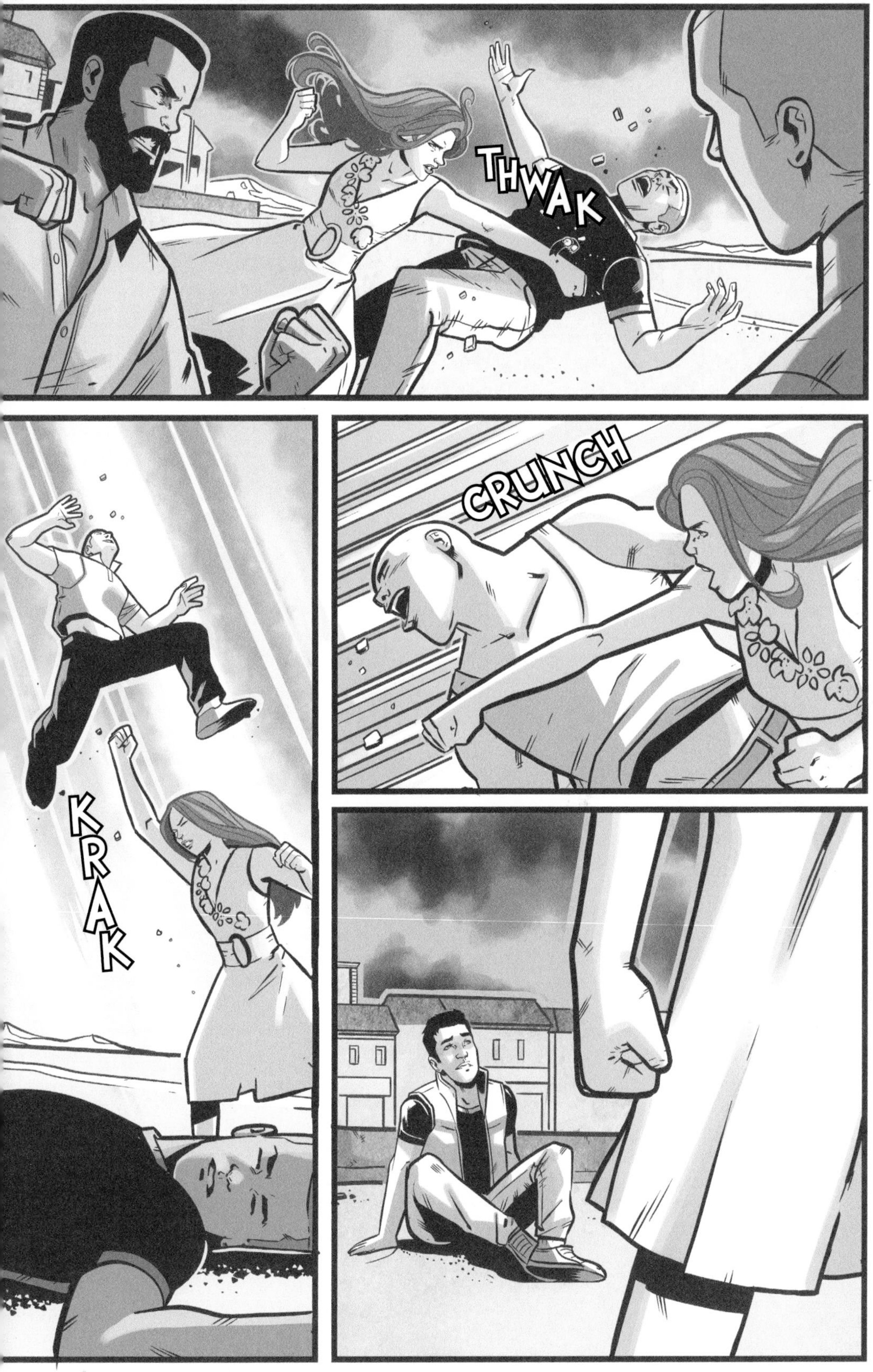
THWAK
CRUNCH
KRAK

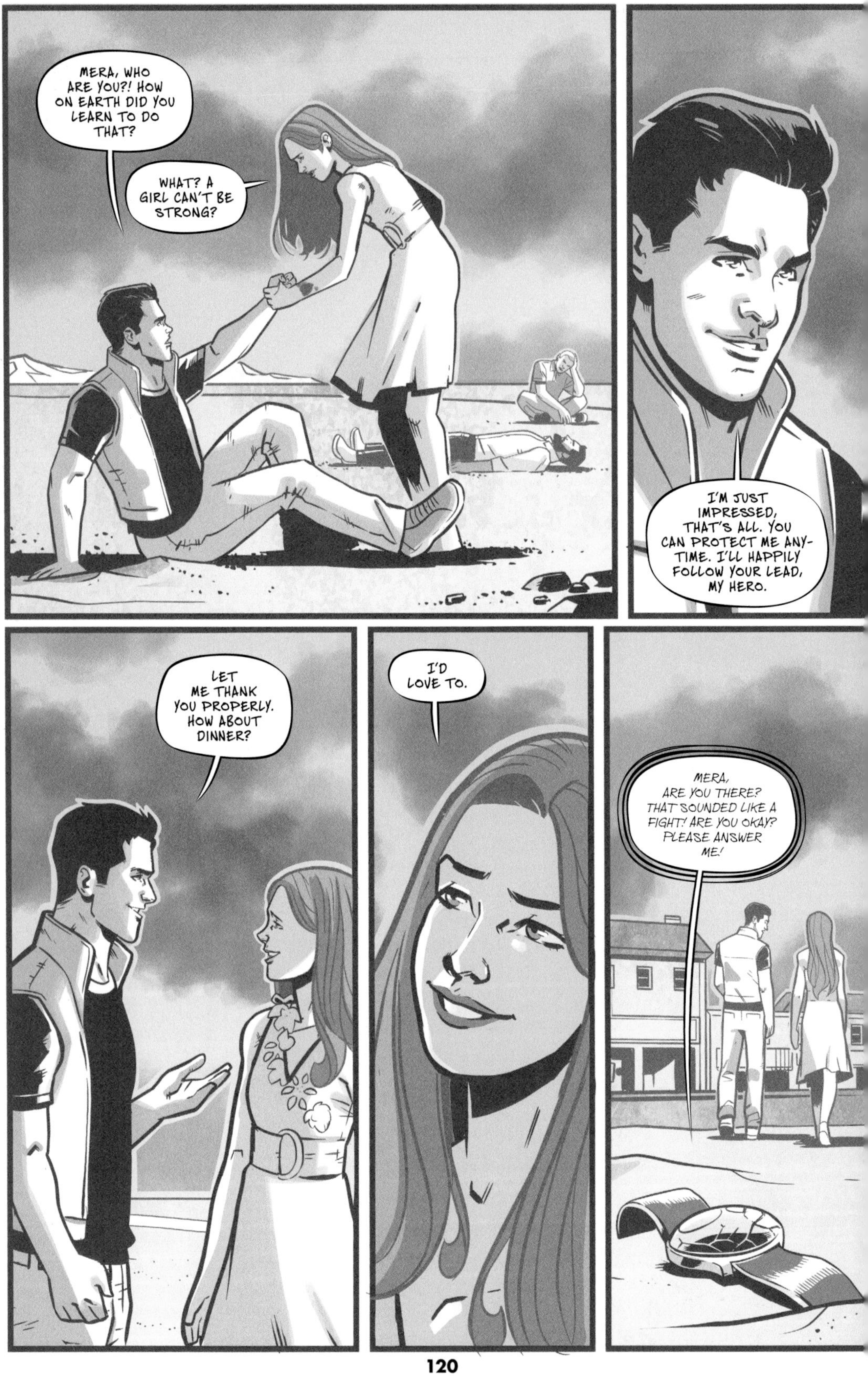
MERA, WHO ARE YOU?! HOW ON EARTH DID YOU LEARN TO DO THAT?
WHAT? A GIRL CAN'T BE STRONG?
I'M JUST IMPRESSED, THAT'S ALL. YOU CAN PROTECT ME ANY-TIME. I'LL HAPPILY FOLLOW YOUR LEAD, MY HERO.
LET ME THANK YOU PROPERLY. HOW ABOUT DINNER?
I'D LOVE TO.
MERA, ARE YOU THERE? THAT SOUNDED LIKE A FIGHT! ARE YOU OKAY? PLEASE ANSWER ME!

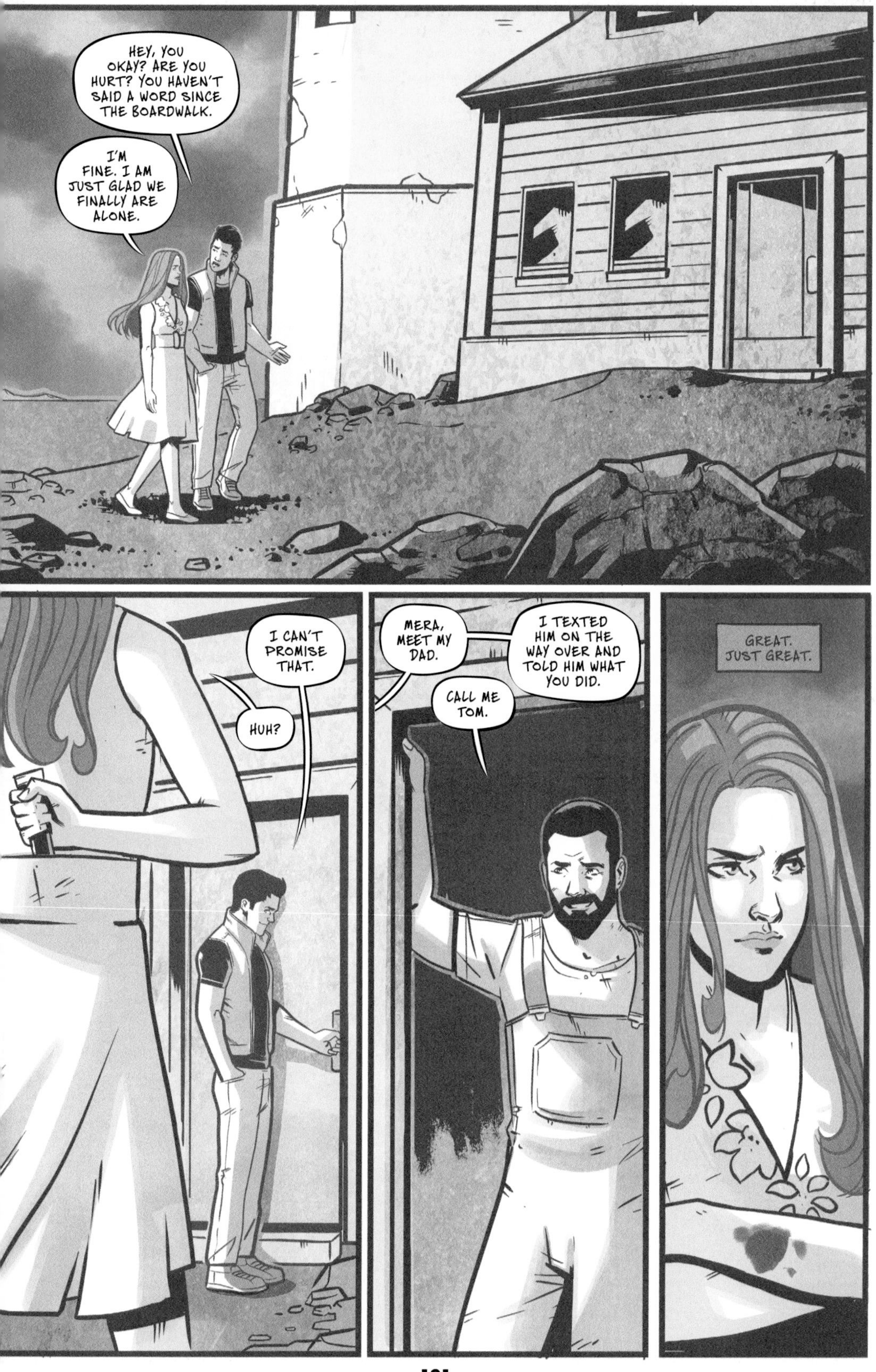
HEY, YOU OKAY? ARE YOU HURT? YOU HAVEN'T SAID A WORD SINCE THE BOARDWALK.
I'M FINE. I AM JUST GLAD WE FINALLY ARE ALONE.
I CAN'T PROMISE THAT.
HUH?
MERA, MEET MY DAD.
I TEXTED HIM ON THE WAY OVER AND TOLD HIM WHAT YOU DID.
CALL ME TOM.
GREAT. JUST GREAT.

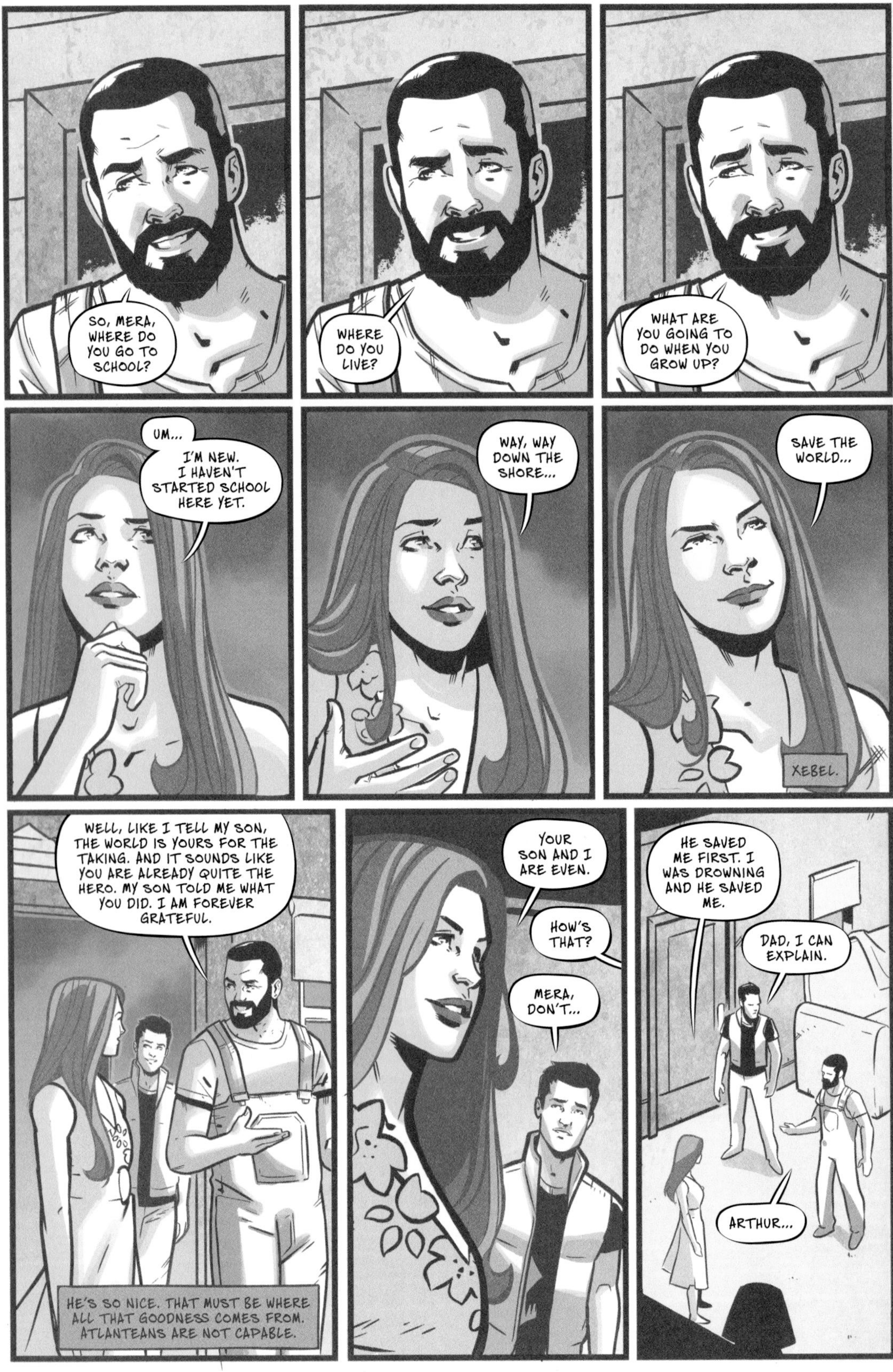
SO, MERA, WHERE DO YOU GO TO SCHOOL?
WHERE DO YOU LIVE?
WHAT ARE YOU GOING TO DO WHEN YOU GROW UP?
UM...
I'M NEW. I HAVEN'T STARTED SCHOOL HERE YET.
WAY, WAY DOWN THE SHORE...
SAVE THE WORLD...
XEBEL.
WELL, LIKE I TELL MY SON, THE WORLD IS YOURS FOR THE TAKING. AND IT SOUNDS LIKE YOU ARE ALREADY QUITE THE HERO. MY SON TOLD ME WHAT YOU DID. I AM FOREVER GRATEFUL.
HE'S SO NICE. THAT MUST BE WHERE ALL THAT GOODNESS COMES FROM. ATLANTEANS ARE NOT CAPABLE.
YOUR SON AND I ARE EVEN.
HOW'S THAT?
MERA, DON'T...
HE SAVED ME FIRST. I WAS DROWNING AND HE SAVED ME.
DAD, I CAN EXPLAIN.
ARTHUR...

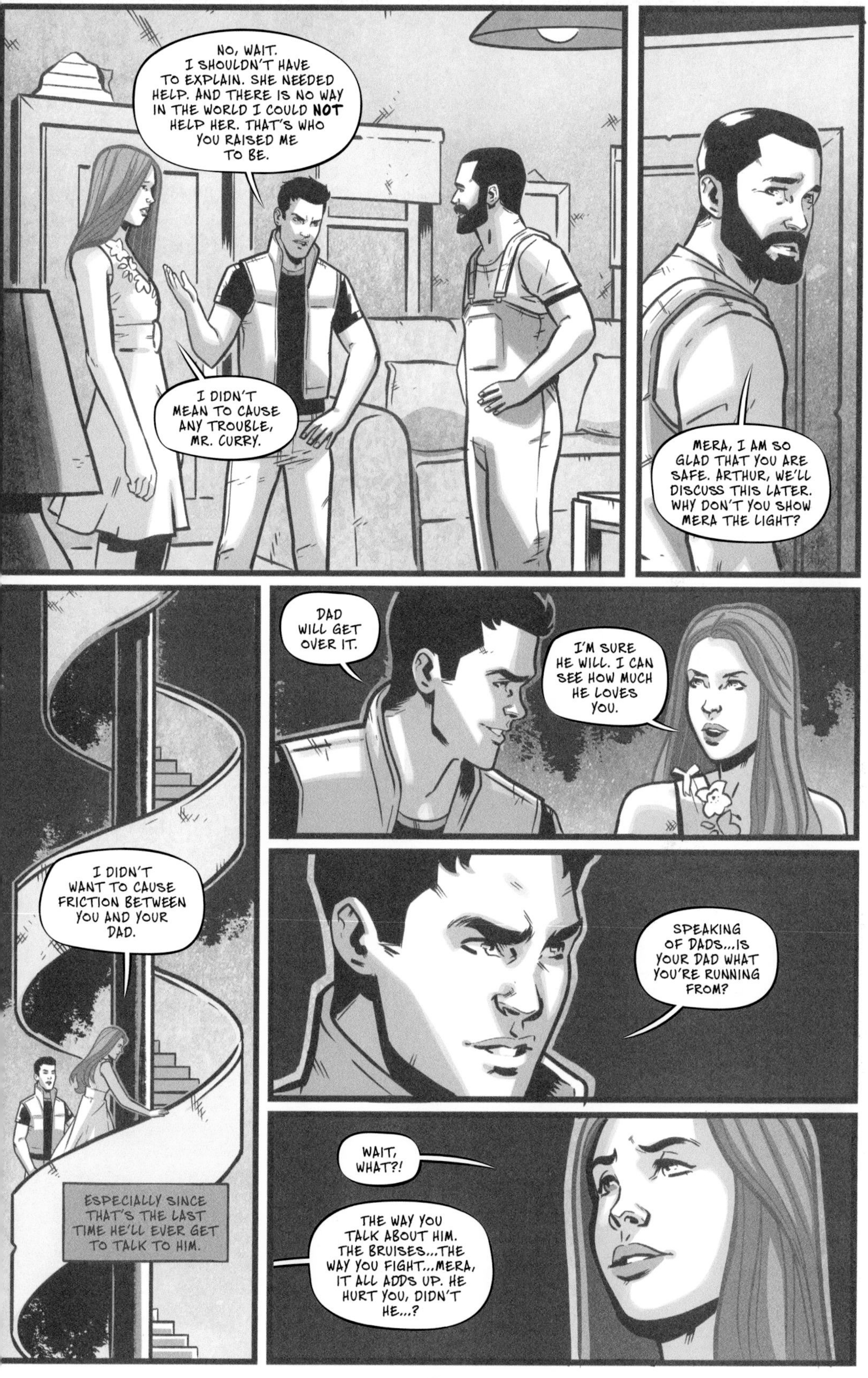
NO, WAIT. I SHOULDN'T HAVE TO EXPLAIN. SHE NEEDED HELP. AND THERE IS NO WAY IN THE WORLD I COULD **NOT** HELP HER. THAT'S WHO YOU RAISED ME TO BE.
I DIDN'T MEAN TO CAUSE ANY TROUBLE, MR. CURRY.
MERA, I AM SO GLAD THAT YOU ARE SAFE. ARTHUR, WE'LL DISCUSS THIS LATER. WHY DON'T YOU SHOW MERA THE LIGHT?
I DIDN'T WANT TO CAUSE FRICTION BETWEEN YOU AND YOUR DAD.
ESPECIALLY SINCE THAT'S THE LAST TIME HE'LL EVER GET TO TALK TO HIM.
DAD WILL GET OVER IT.
I'M SURE HE WILL. I CAN SEE HOW MUCH HE LOVES YOU.
SPEAKING OF DADS...IS YOUR DAD WHAT YOU'RE RUNNING FROM?
WAIT, WHAT?!
THE WAY YOU TALK ABOUT HIM. THE BRUISES...THE WAY YOU FIGHT...MERA, IT ALL ADDS UP. HE HURT YOU, DIDN'T HE...?

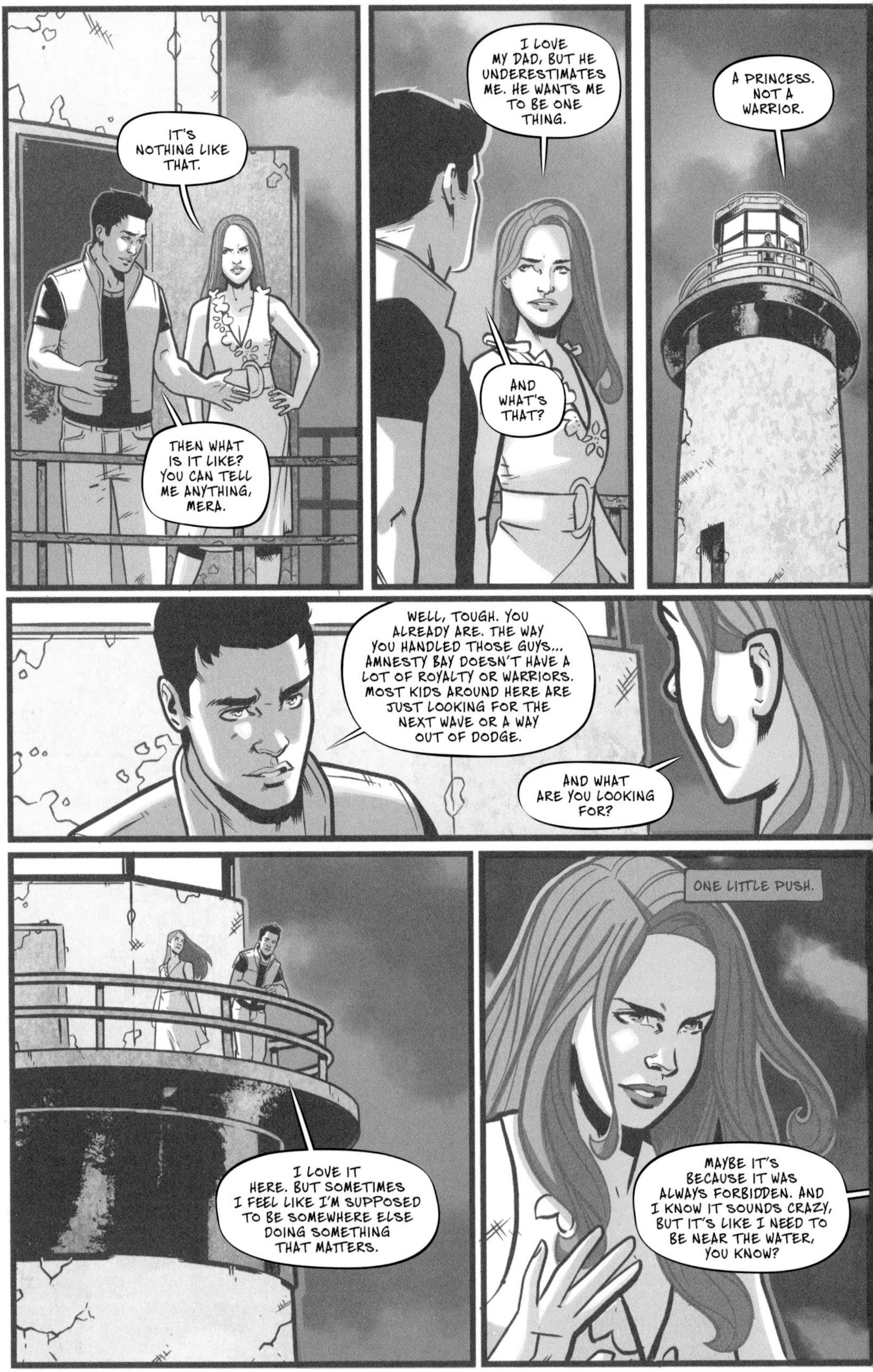
IT'S NOTHING LIKE THAT.
THEN WHAT IS IT LIKE? YOU CAN TELL ME ANYTHING, MERA.
I LOVE MY DAD, BUT HE UNDERESTIMATES ME. HE WANTS ME TO BE ONE THING.
AND WHAT'S THAT?
A PRINCESS. NOT A WARRIOR.
WELL, TOUGH. YOU ALREADY ARE. THE WAY YOU HANDLED THOSE GUYS... AMNESTY BAY DOESN'T HAVE A LOT OF ROYALTY OR WARRIORS. MOST KIDS AROUND HERE ARE JUST LOOKING FOR THE NEXT WAVE OR A WAY OUT OF DODGE.
AND WHAT ARE YOU LOOKING FOR?
I LOVE IT HERE. BUT SOMETIMES I FEEL LIKE I'M SUPPOSED TO BE SOMEWHERE ELSE DOING SOMETHING THAT MATTERS.
ONE LITTLE PUSH.
MAYBE IT'S BECAUSE IT WAS ALWAYS FORBIDDEN. AND I KNOW IT SOUNDS CRAZY, BUT IT'S LIKE I NEED TO BE NEAR THE WATER, YOU KNOW?

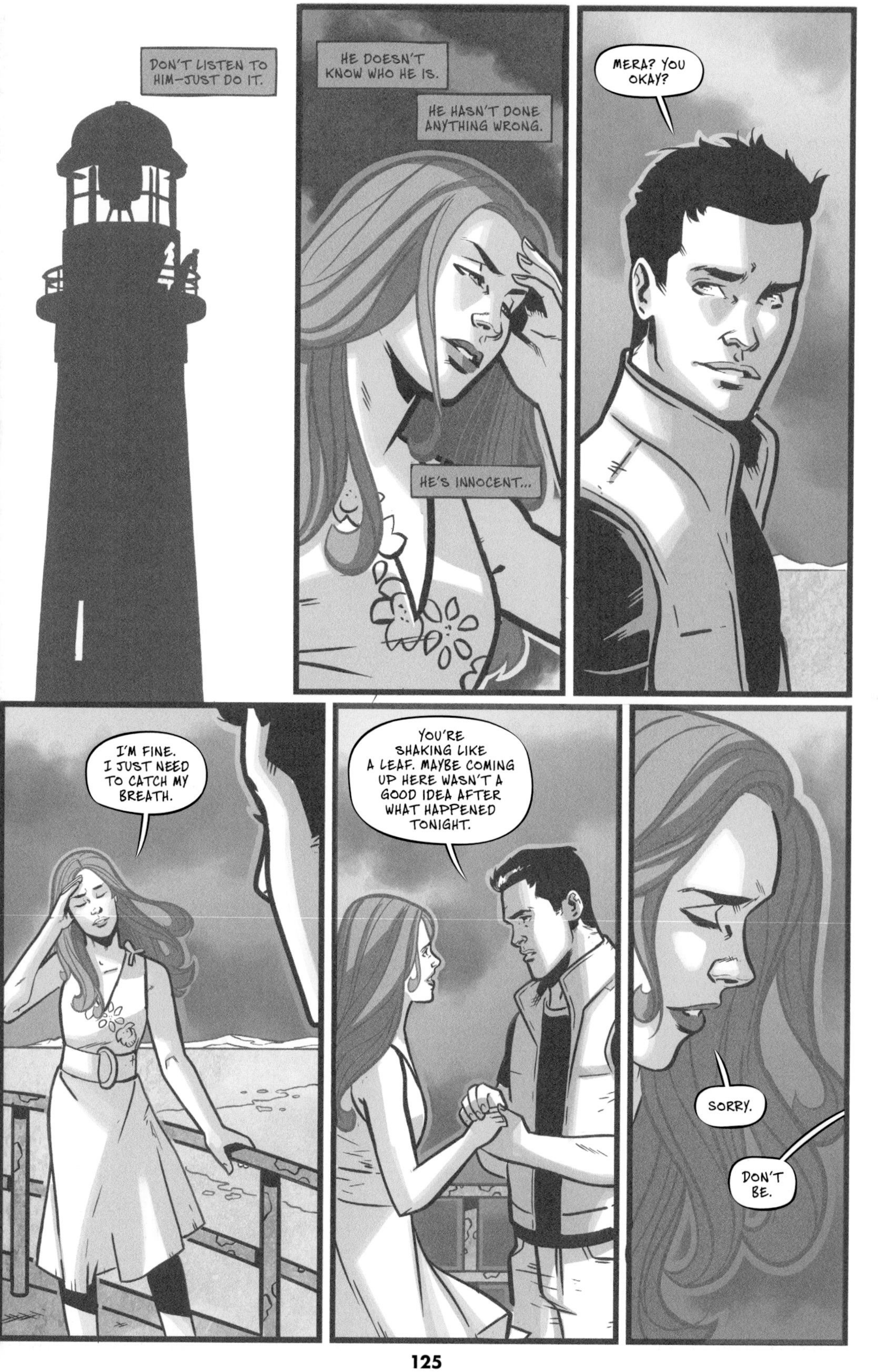
DON'T LISTEN TO HIM—JUST DO IT.
HE DOESN'T KNOW WHO HE IS.
HE HASN'T DONE ANYTHING WRONG.
HE'S INNOCENT...
MERA? YOU OKAY?
I'M FINE. I JUST NEED TO CATCH MY BREATH.
YOU'RE SHAKING LIKE A LEAF. MAYBE COMING UP HERE WASN'T A GOOD IDEA AFTER WHAT HAPPENED TONIGHT.
SORRY.
DON'T BE.

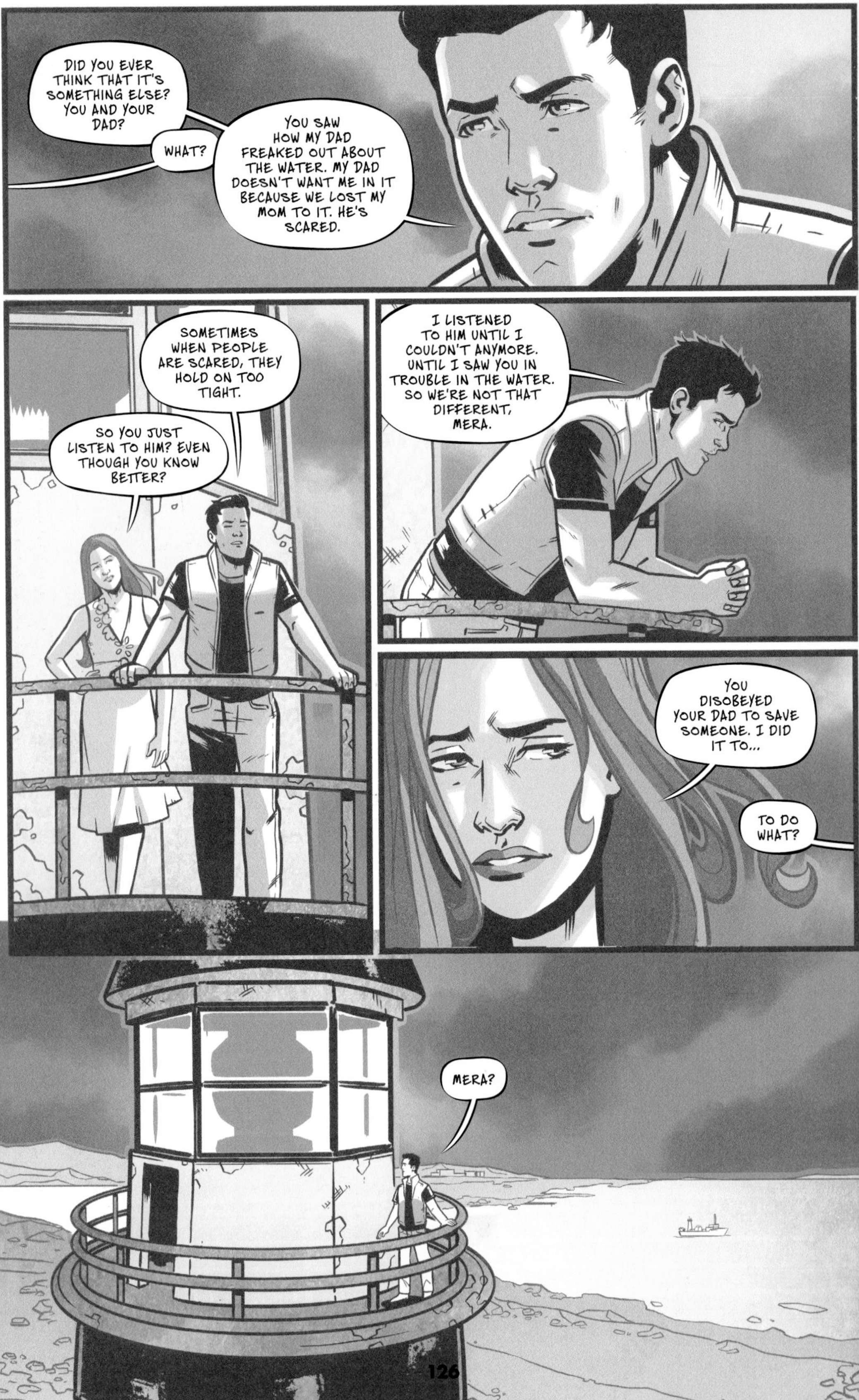
DID YOU EVER THINK THAT IT'S SOMETHING ELSE? YOU AND YOUR DAD?
WHAT?
YOU SAW HOW MY DAD FREAKED OUT ABOUT THE WATER. MY DAD DOESN'T WANT ME IN IT BECAUSE WE LOST MY MOM TO IT. HE'S SCARED.
SOMETIMES WHEN PEOPLE ARE SCARED, THEY HOLD ON TOO TIGHT.
SO YOU JUST LISTEN TO HIM? EVEN THOUGH YOU KNOW BETTER?
I LISTENED TO HIM UNTIL I COULDN'T ANYMORE. UNTIL I SAW YOU IN TROUBLE IN THE WATER. SO WE'RE NOT THAT DIFFERENT, MERA.
YOU DISOBEYED YOUR DAD TO SAVE SOMEONE. I DID IT TO...
TO DO WHAT?
MERA?

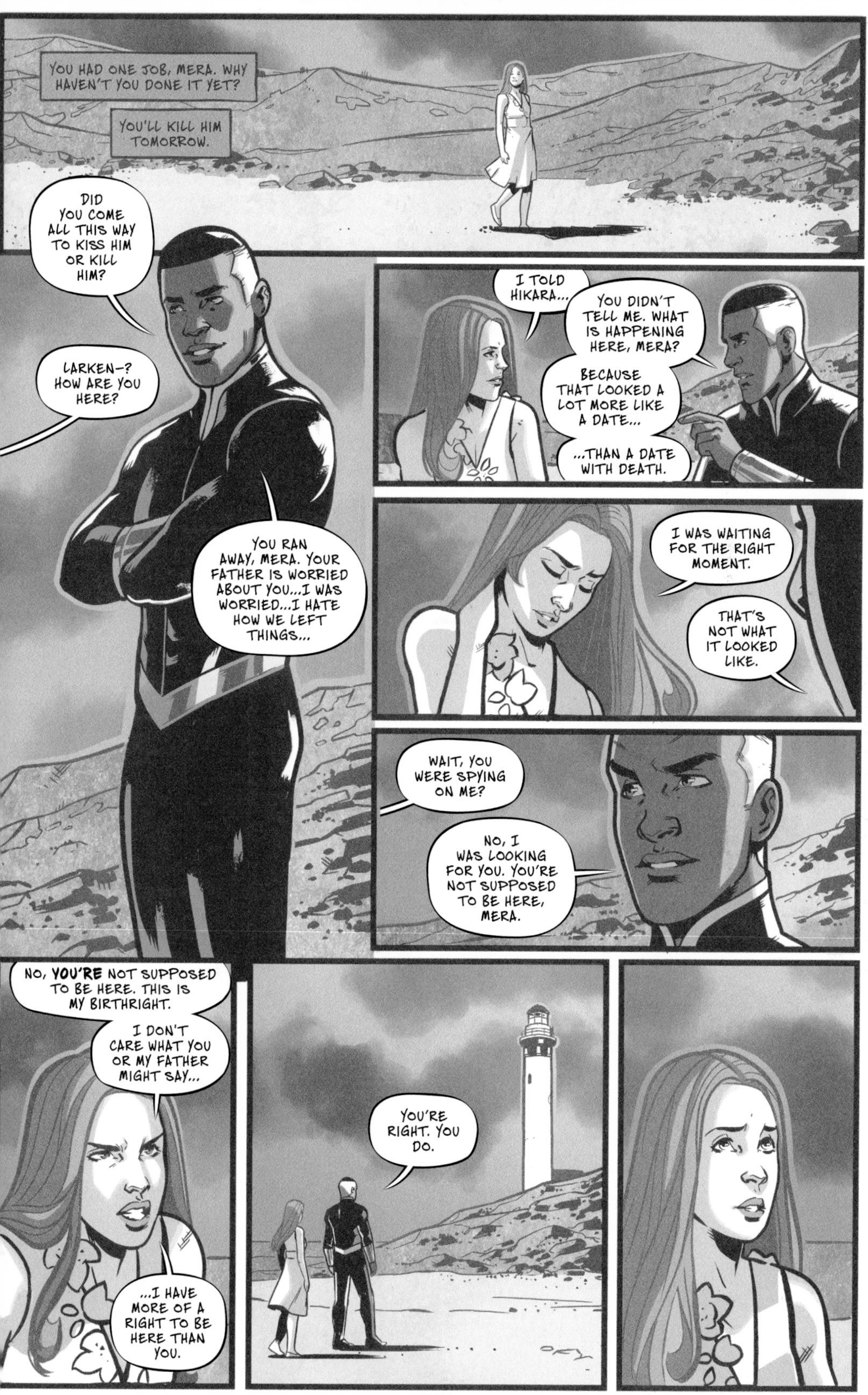
YOU HAD ONE JOB, MERA. WHY HAVEN'T YOU DONE IT YET?
YOU'LL KILL HIM TOMORROW.
DID YOU COME ALL THIS WAY TO KISS HIM OR KILL HIM?
LARKEN-? HOW ARE YOU HERE?
YOU RAN AWAY, MERA. YOUR FATHER IS WORRIED ABOUT YOU...I WAS WORRIED...I HATE HOW WE LEFT THINGS...
I TOLD HIKARA...
YOU DIDN'T TELL ME. WHAT IS HAPPENING HERE, MERA?
BECAUSE THAT LOOKED A LOT MORE LIKE A DATE...
...THAN A DATE WITH DEATH.
I WAS WAITING FOR THE RIGHT MOMENT.
THAT'S NOT WHAT IT LOOKED LIKE.
WAIT, YOU WERE SPYING ON ME?
NO, I WAS LOOKING FOR YOU. YOU'RE NOT SUPPOSED TO BE HERE, MERA.
NO, **YOU'RE** NOT SUPPOSED TO BE HERE. THIS IS MY BIRTHRIGHT.
I DON'T CARE WHAT YOU OR MY FATHER MIGHT SAY...
...I HAVE MORE OF A RIGHT TO BE HERE THAN YOU.
YOU'RE RIGHT. YOU DO.

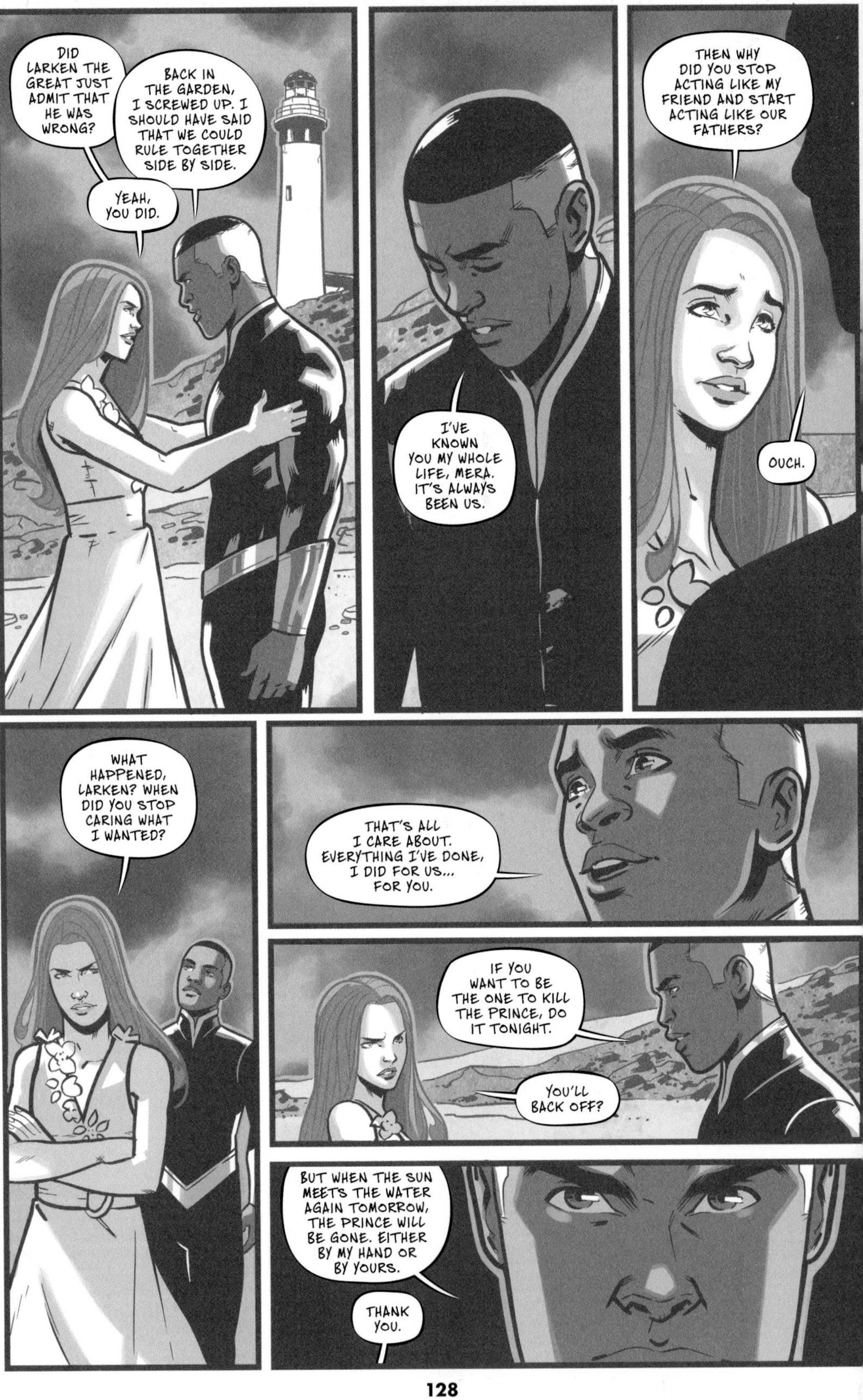

DID LARKEN THE GREAT JUST ADMIT THAT HE WAS WRONG?
BACK IN THE GARDEN, I SCREWED UP. I SHOULD HAVE SAID THAT WE COULD RULE TOGETHER SIDE BY SIDE.
YEAH, YOU DID.
I'VE KNOWN YOU MY WHOLE LIFE, MERA. IT'S ALWAYS BEEN US.
THEN WHY DID YOU STOP ACTING LIKE MY FRIEND AND START ACTING LIKE OUR FATHERS?
OUCH.
WHAT HAPPENED, LARKEN? WHEN DID YOU STOP CARING WHAT I WANTED?
THAT'S ALL I CARE ABOUT. EVERYTHING I'VE DONE, I DID FOR US... FOR YOU.
IF YOU WANT TO BE THE ONE TO KILL THE PRINCE, DO IT TONIGHT.
YOU'LL BACK OFF?
BUT WHEN THE SUN MEETS THE WATER AGAIN TOMORROW, THE PRINCE WILL BE GONE. EITHER BY MY HAND OR BY YOURS.
THANK YOU.

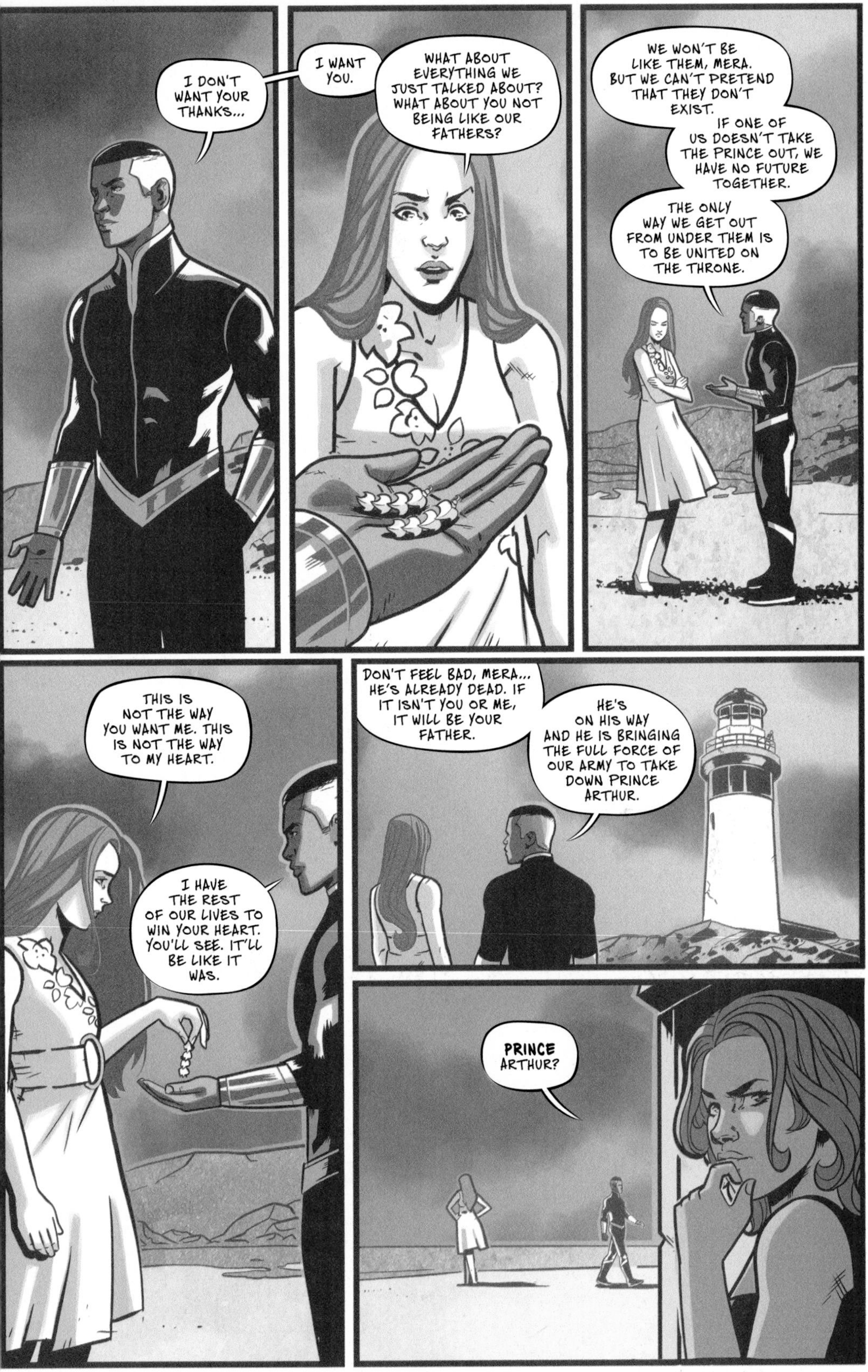
I DON'T WANT YOUR THANKS...
I WANT YOU.
WHAT ABOUT EVERYTHING WE JUST TALKED ABOUT? WHAT ABOUT YOU NOT BEING LIKE OUR FATHERS?
WE WON'T BE LIKE THEM, MERA. BUT WE CAN'T PRETEND THAT THEY DON'T EXIST.
IF ONE OF US DOESN'T TAKE THE PRINCE OUT, WE HAVE NO FUTURE TOGETHER.
THE ONLY WAY WE GET OUT FROM UNDER THEM IS TO BE UNITED ON THE THRONE.
THIS IS NOT THE WAY YOU WANT ME. THIS IS NOT THE WAY TO MY HEART.
I HAVE THE REST OF OUR LIVES TO WIN YOUR HEART. YOU'LL SEE. IT'LL BE LIKE IT WAS.
DON'T FEEL BAD, MERA... HE'S ALREADY DEAD. IF IT ISN'T YOU OR ME, IT WILL BE YOUR FATHER.
HE'S ON HIS WAY AND HE IS BRINGING THE FULL FORCE OF OUR ARMY TO TAKE DOWN PRINCE ARTHUR.
PRINCE ARTHUR?

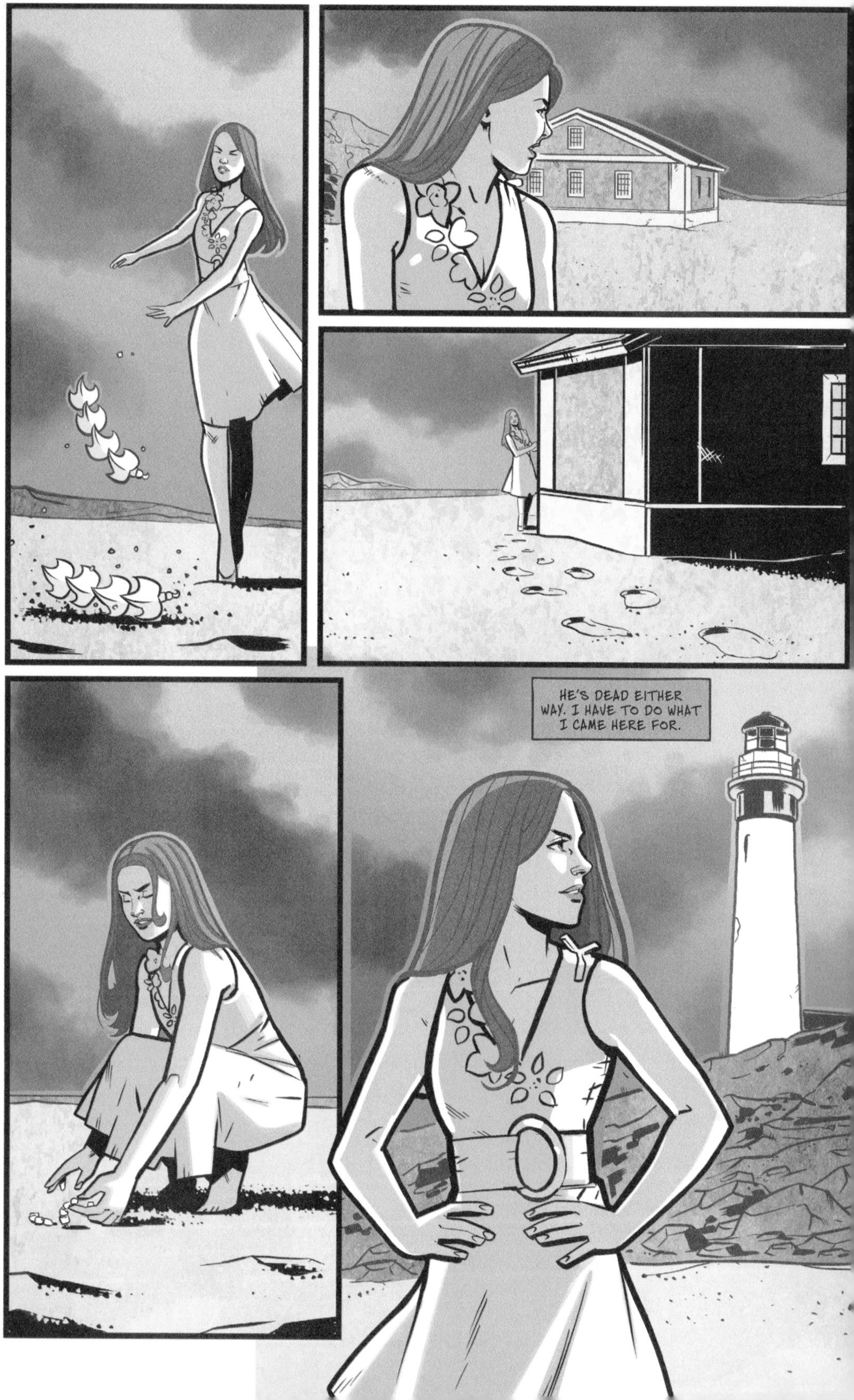
HE'S DEAD EITHER WAY. I HAVE TO DO WHAT I CAME HERE FOR.

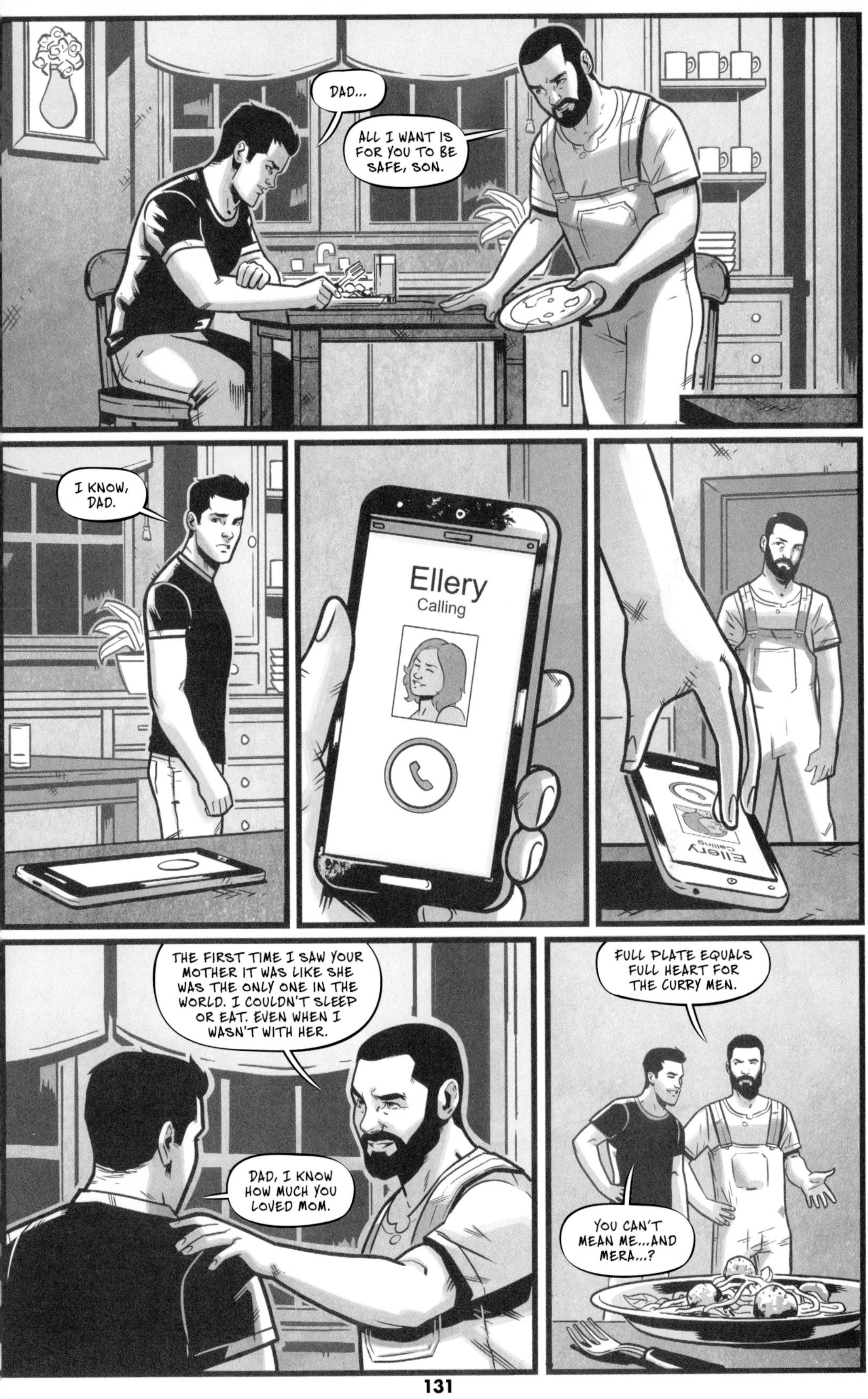
DAD...
ALL I WANT IS FOR YOU TO BE SAFE, SON.
I KNOW, DAD.
Ellery
Calling
Ellery
Calling
THE FIRST TIME I SAW YOUR MOTHER IT WAS LIKE SHE WAS THE ONLY ONE IN THE WORLD. I COULDN'T SLEEP OR EAT. EVEN WHEN I WASN'T WITH HER.
DAD, I KNOW HOW MUCH YOU LOVED MOM.
FULL PLATE EQUALS FULL HEART FOR THE CURRY MEN.
YOU CAN'T MEAN ME...AND MERA...?

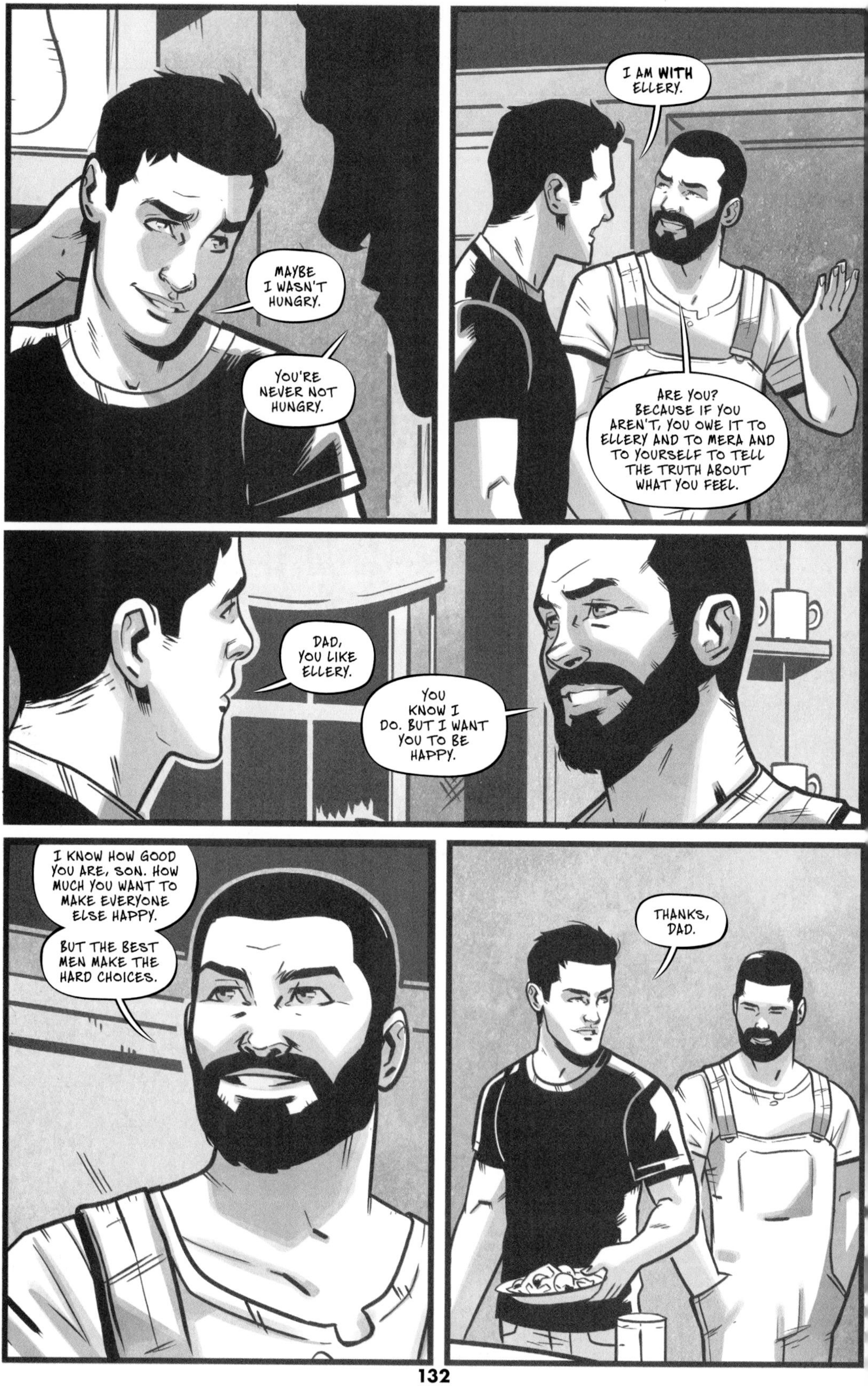

MAYBE I WASN'T HUNGRY.
YOU'RE NEVER NOT HUNGRY.
I AM WITH ELLERY.
ARE YOU? BECAUSE IF YOU AREN'T, YOU OWE IT TO ELLERY AND TO MERA AND TO YOURSELF TO TELL THE TRUTH ABOUT WHAT YOU FEEL.
DAD, YOU LIKE ELLERY.
YOU KNOW I DO. BUT I WANT YOU TO BE HAPPY.
I KNOW HOW GOOD YOU ARE, SON. HOW MUCH YOU WANT TO MAKE EVERYONE ELSE HAPPY.
BUT THE BEST MEN MAKE THE HARD CHOICES.
THANKS, DAD.

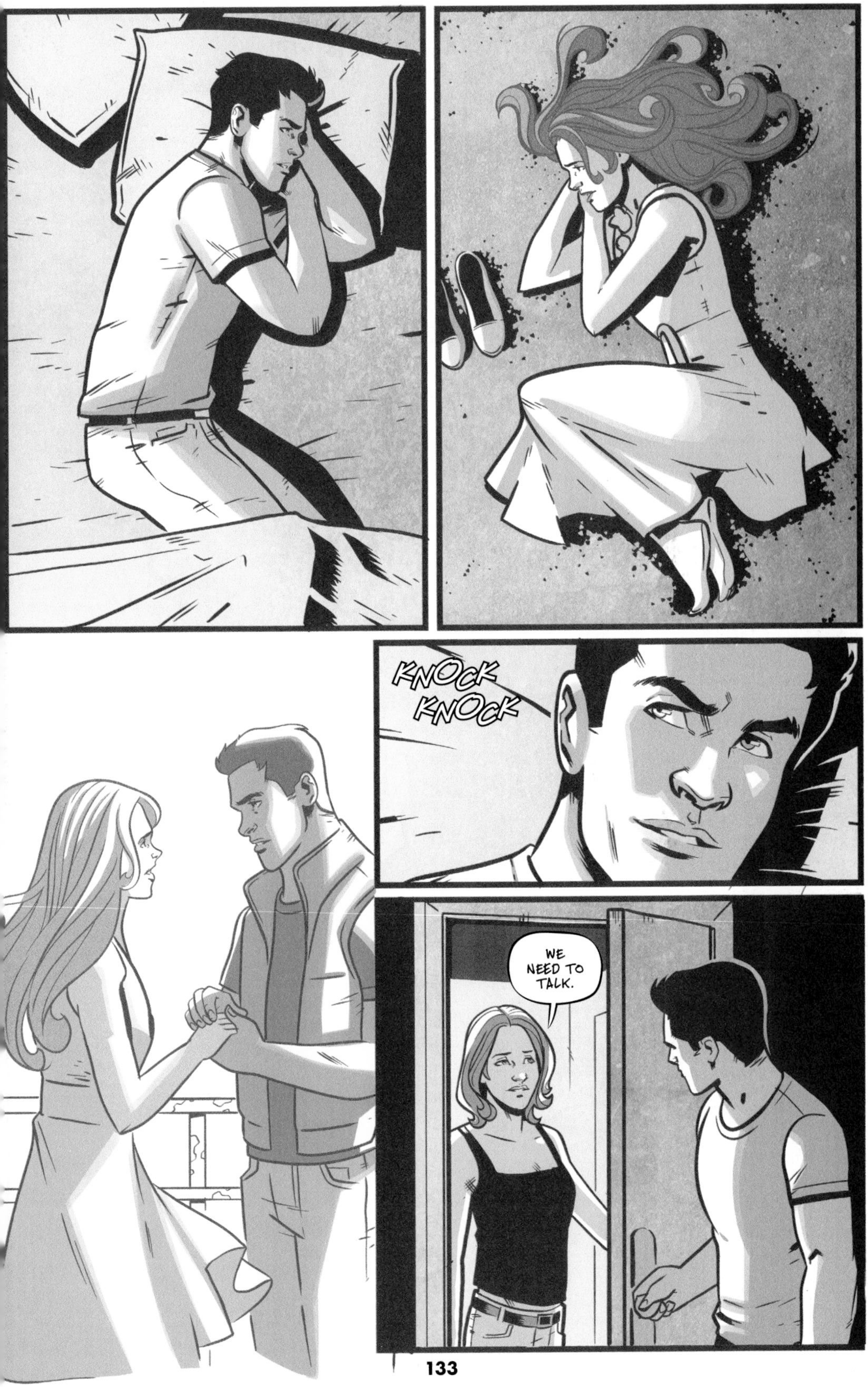
KNOCK
KNOCK
WE NEED TO TALK.

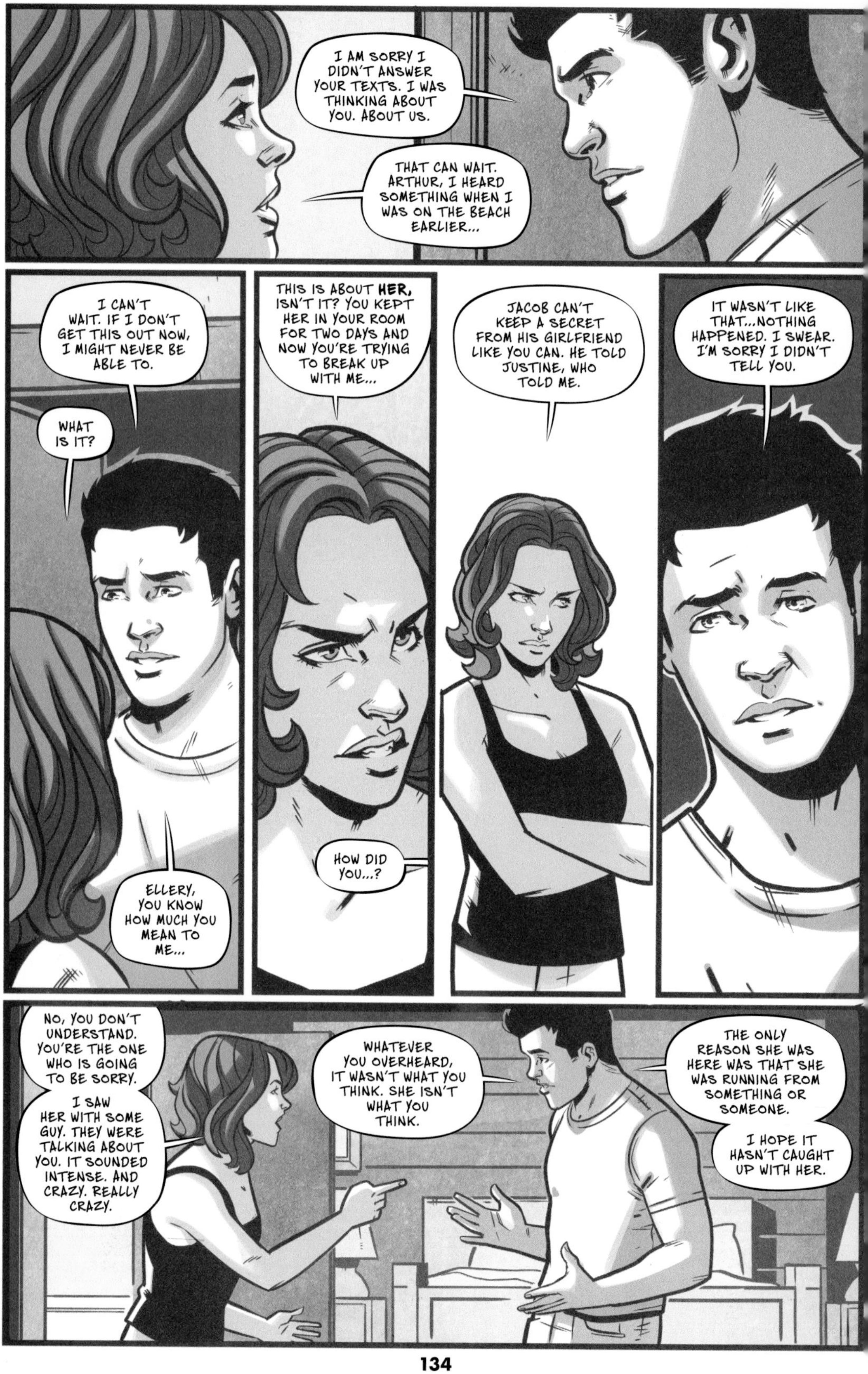

I AM SORRY I DIDN'T ANSWER YOUR TEXTS. I WAS THINKING ABOUT YOU. ABOUT US.
THAT CAN WAIT. ARTHUR, I HEARD SOMETHING WHEN I WAS ON THE BEACH EARLIER...
I CAN'T WAIT. IF I DON'T GET THIS OUT NOW, I MIGHT NEVER BE ABLE TO.
WHAT IS IT?
ELLERY, YOU KNOW HOW MUCH YOU MEAN TO ME...
THIS IS ABOUT **HER,** ISN'T IT? YOU KEPT HER IN YOUR ROOM FOR TWO DAYS AND NOW YOU'RE TRYING TO BREAK UP WITH ME...
HOW DID YOU...?
JACOB CAN'T KEEP A SECRET FROM HIS GIRLFRIEND LIKE YOU CAN. HE TOLD JUSTINE, WHO TOLD ME.
IT WASN'T LIKE THAT...NOTHING HAPPENED. I SWEAR. I'M SORRY I DIDN'T TELL YOU.
NO, YOU DON'T UNDERSTAND. YOU'RE THE ONE WHO IS GOING TO BE SORRY.
I SAW HER WITH SOME GUY. THEY WERE TALKING ABOUT YOU. IT SOUNDED INTENSE. AND CRAZY. REALLY CRAZY.
WHATEVER YOU OVERHEARD, IT WASN'T WHAT YOU THINK. SHE ISN'T WHAT YOU THINK.
THE ONLY REASON SHE WAS HERE WAS THAT SHE WAS RUNNING FROM SOMETHING OR SOMEONE.
I HOPE IT HASN'T CAUGHT UP WITH HER.

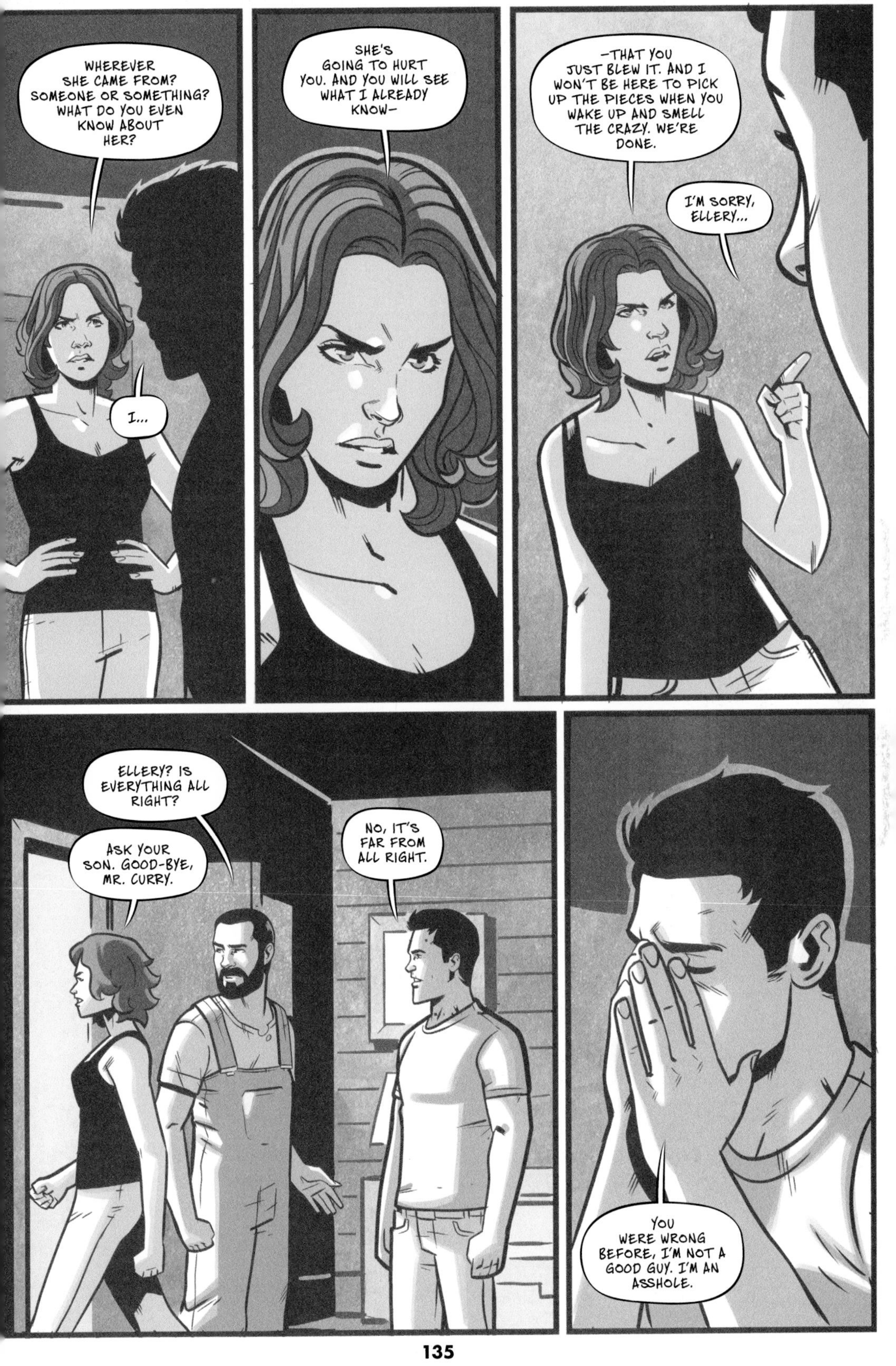
WHEREVER SHE CAME FROM? SOMEONE OR SOMETHING? WHAT DO YOU EVEN KNOW ABOUT HER?
I...
SHE'S GOING TO HURT YOU. AND YOU WILL SEE WHAT I ALREADY KNOW—
—THAT YOU JUST BLEW IT. AND I WON'T BE HERE TO PICK UP THE PIECES WHEN YOU WAKE UP AND SMELL THE CRAZY. WE'RE DONE.
I'M SORRY, ELLERY...
ELLERY? IS EVERYTHING ALL RIGHT?
ASK YOUR SON. GOOD-BYE, MR. CURRY.
NO, IT'S FAR FROM ALL RIGHT.
YOU WERE WRONG BEFORE, I'M NOT A GOOD GUY. I'M AN ASSHOLE.

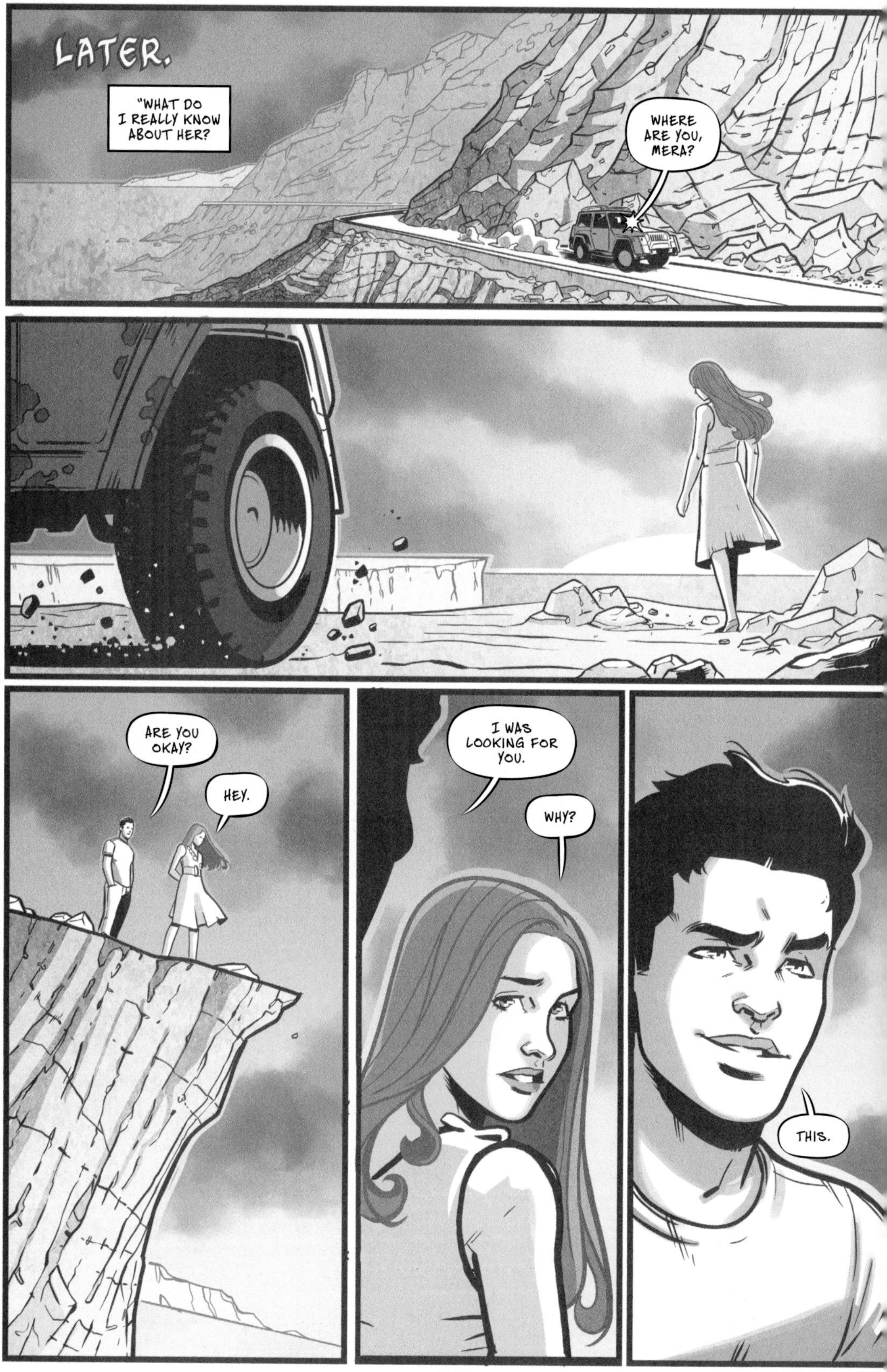
LATER.
"WHAT DO I REALLY KNOW ABOUT HER?
WHERE ARE YOU, MERA?
ARE YOU OKAY?
HEY.
I WAS LOOKING FOR YOU.
WHY?
THIS.

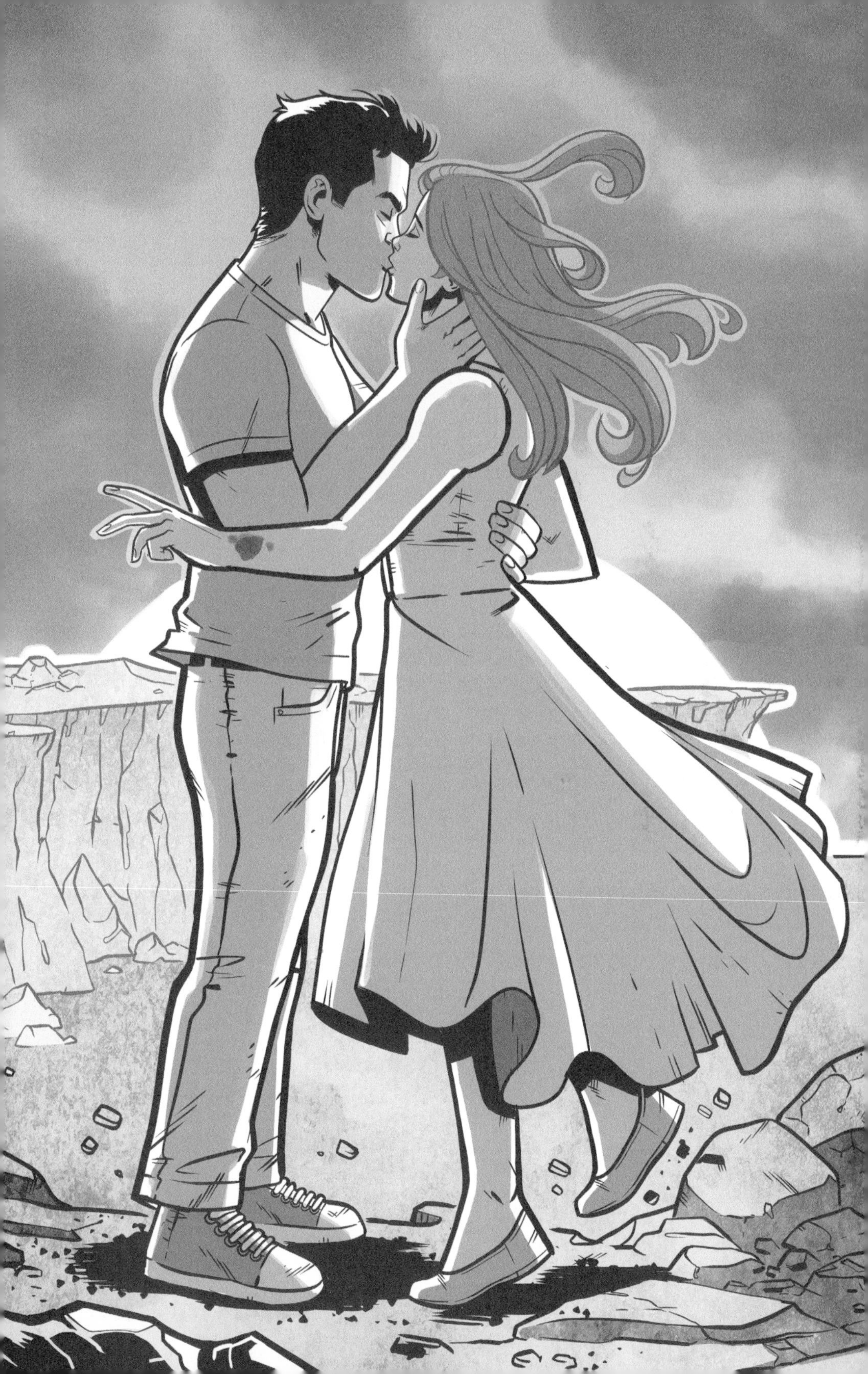

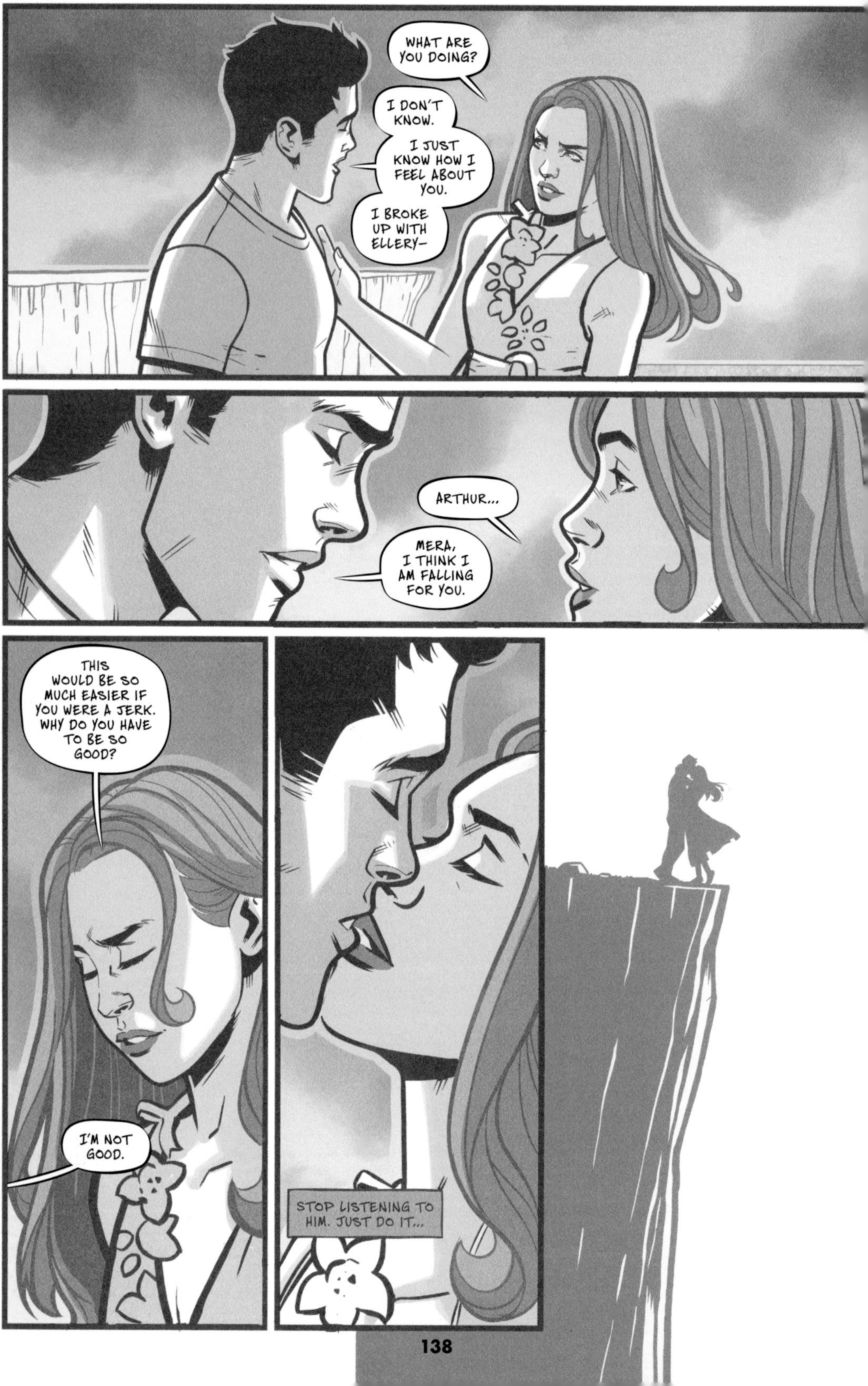
WHAT ARE YOU DOING?
I DON'T KNOW.
I JUST KNOW HOW I FEEL ABOUT YOU.
I BROKE UP WITH ELLERY—
ARTHUR...
MERA, I THINK I AM FALLING FOR YOU.
THIS WOULD BE SO MUCH EASIER IF YOU WERE A JERK. WHY DO YOU HAVE TO BE SO GOOD?
I'M NOT GOOD.
STOP LISTENING TO HIM. JUST DO IT...

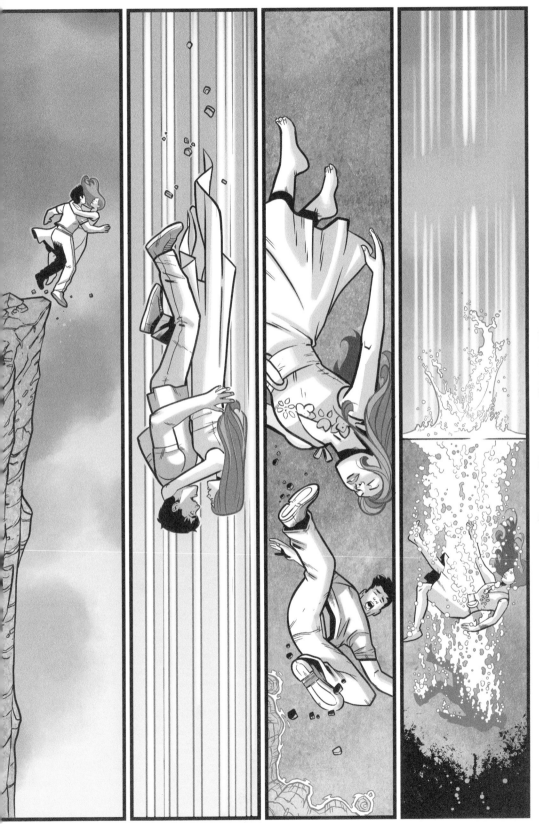

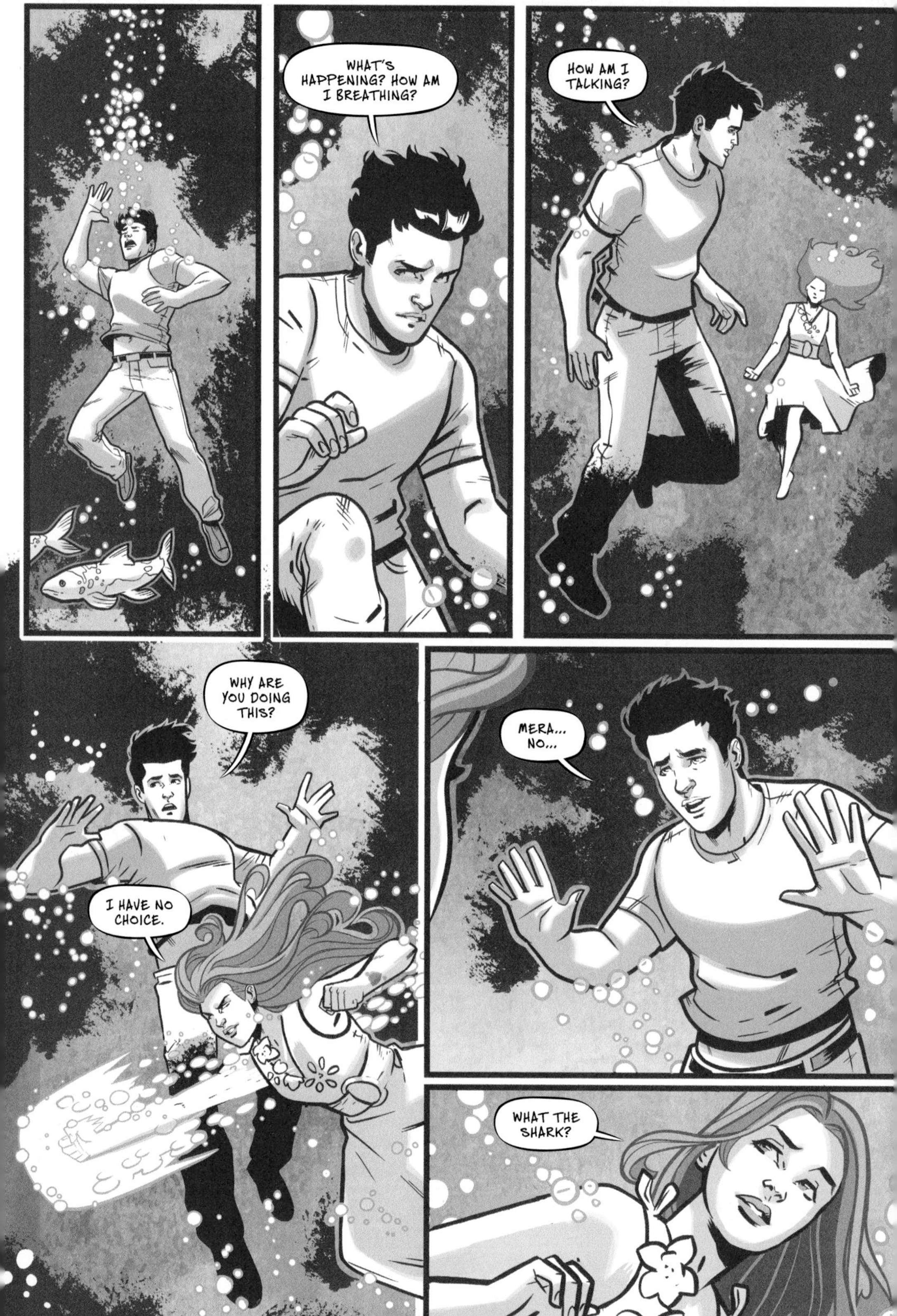
WHAT'S HAPPENING? HOW AM I BREATHING?
HOW AM I TALKING?
WHY ARE YOU DOING THIS?
I HAVE NO CHOICE.
MERA... NO...
WHAT THE SHARK?

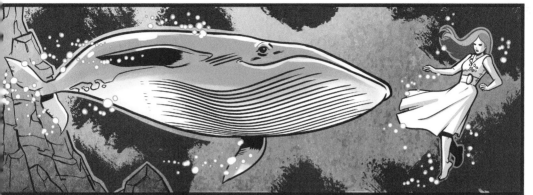

I REALLY AM SORRY, ARTHUR.

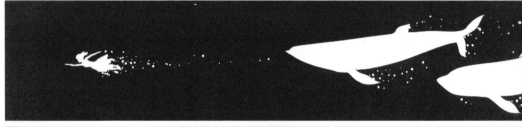

IT...
CAN'T BE.

HELLO, OLD
FRIEND.

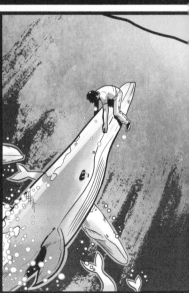

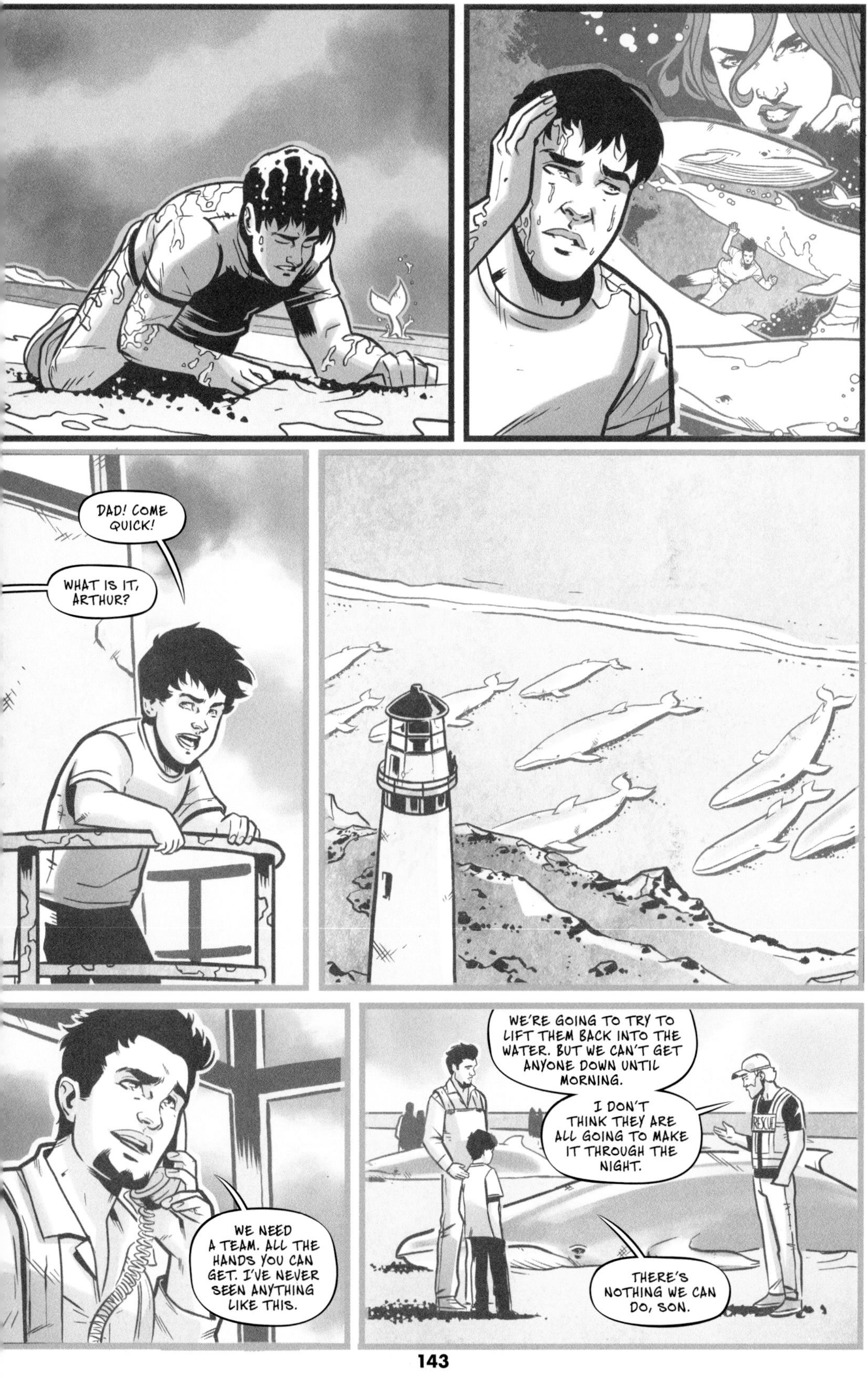
DAD! COME QUICK!
WHAT IS IT, ARTHUR?
WE NEED A TEAM. ALL THE HANDS YOU CAN GET. I'VE NEVER SEEN ANYTHING LIKE THIS.
WE'RE GOING TO TRY TO LIFT THEM BACK INTO THE WATER. BUT WE CAN'T GET ANYONE DOWN UNTIL MORNING.
I DON'T THINK THEY ARE ALL GOING TO MAKE IT THROUGH THE NIGHT.
THERE'S NOTHING WE CAN DO, SON.
RESCUE

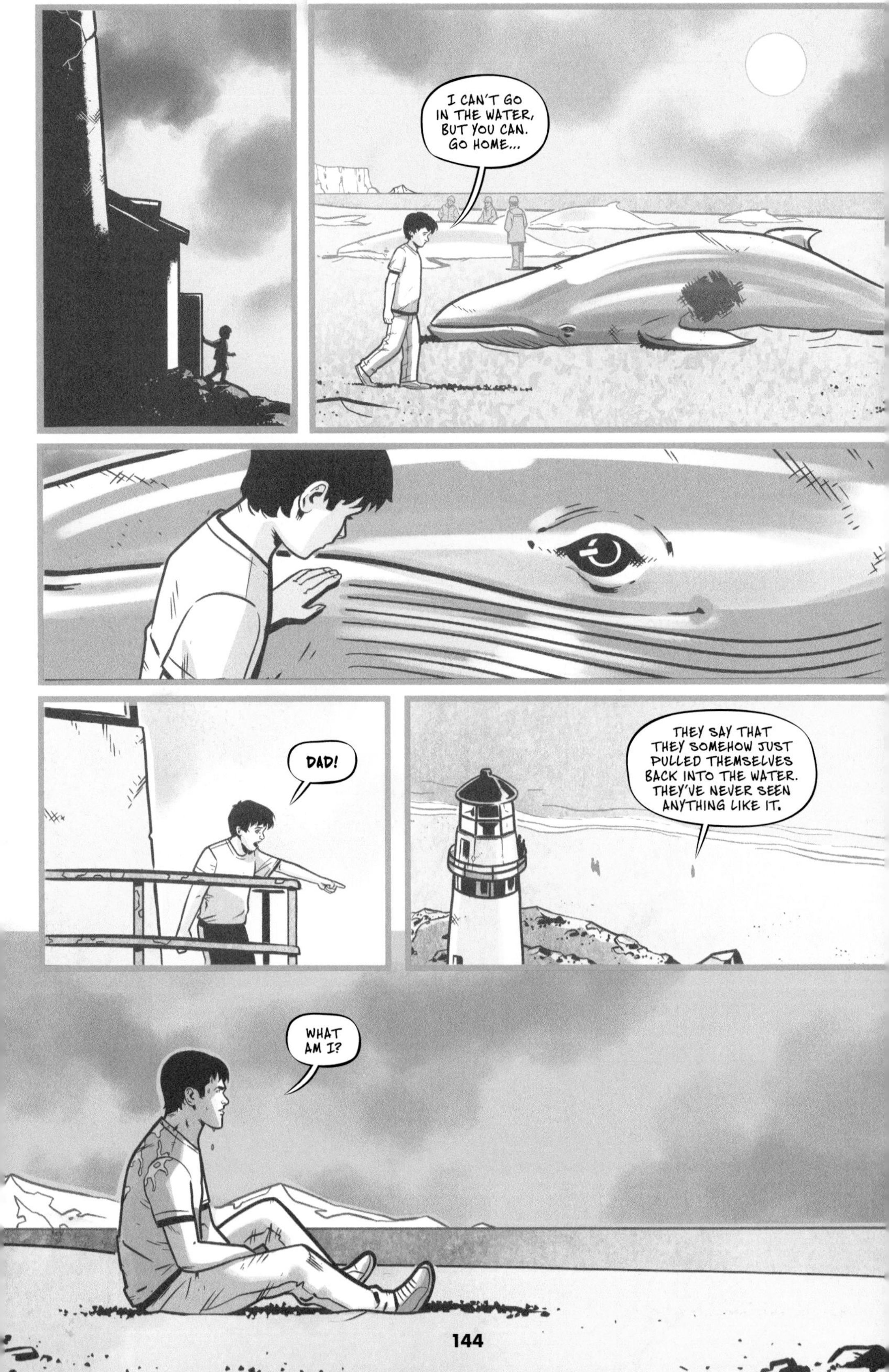
I CAN'T GO IN THE WATER, BUT YOU CAN. GO HOME...
DAD!
THEY SAY THAT THEY SOMEHOW JUST PULLED THEMSELVES BACK INTO THE WATER. THEY'VE NEVER SEEN ANYTHING LIKE IT.
WHAT AM I?

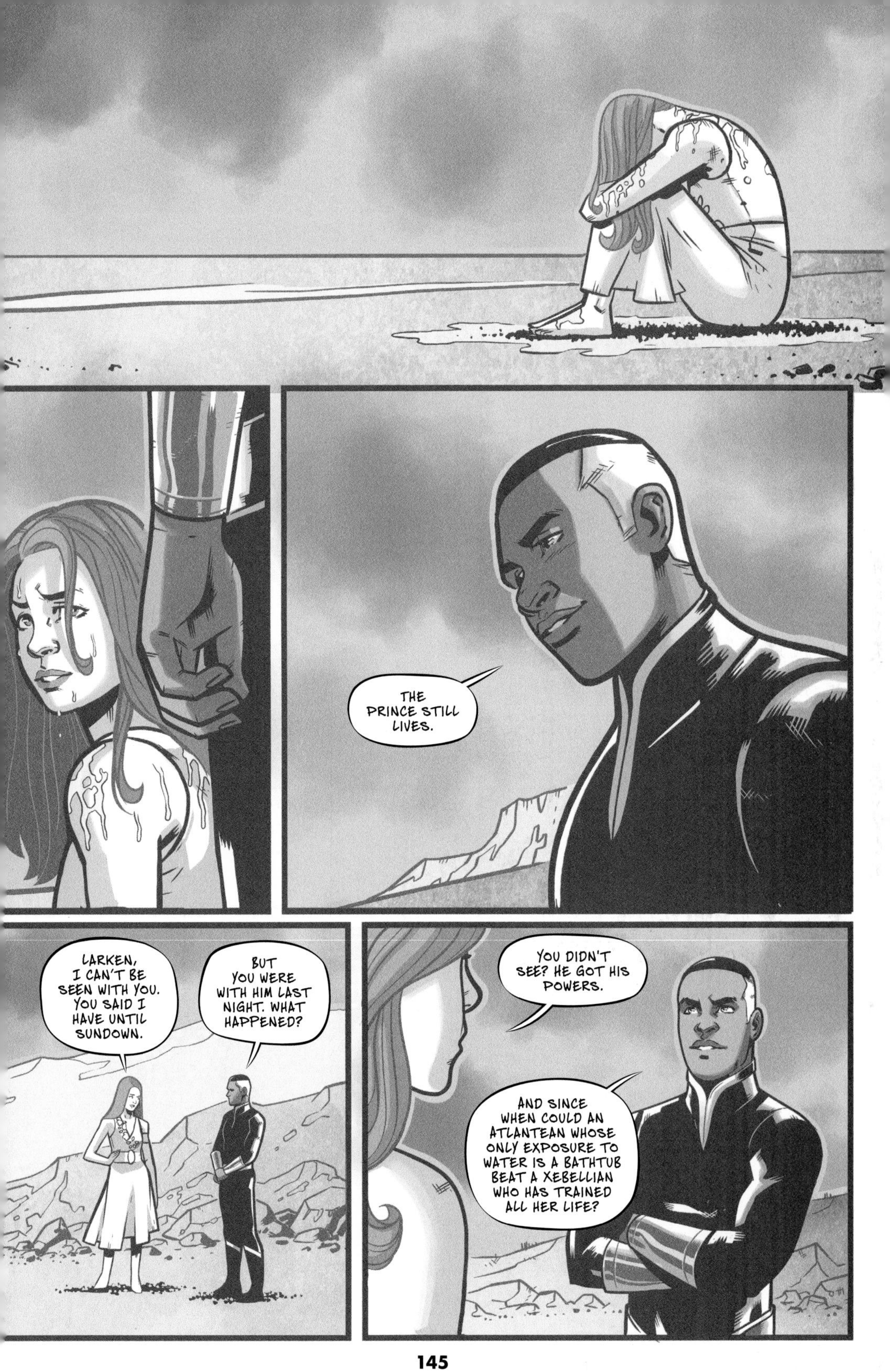
THE PRINCE STILL LIVES.
LARKEN, I CAN'T BE SEEN WITH YOU. YOU SAID I HAVE UNTIL SUNDOWN.
BUT YOU WERE WITH HIM LAST NIGHT. WHAT HAPPENED?
YOU DIDN'T SEE? HE GOT HIS POWERS.
AND SINCE WHEN COULD AN ATLANTEAN WHOSE ONLY EXPOSURE TO WATER IS A BATHTUB BEAT A XEBELLIAN WHO HAS TRAINED ALL HER LIFE?

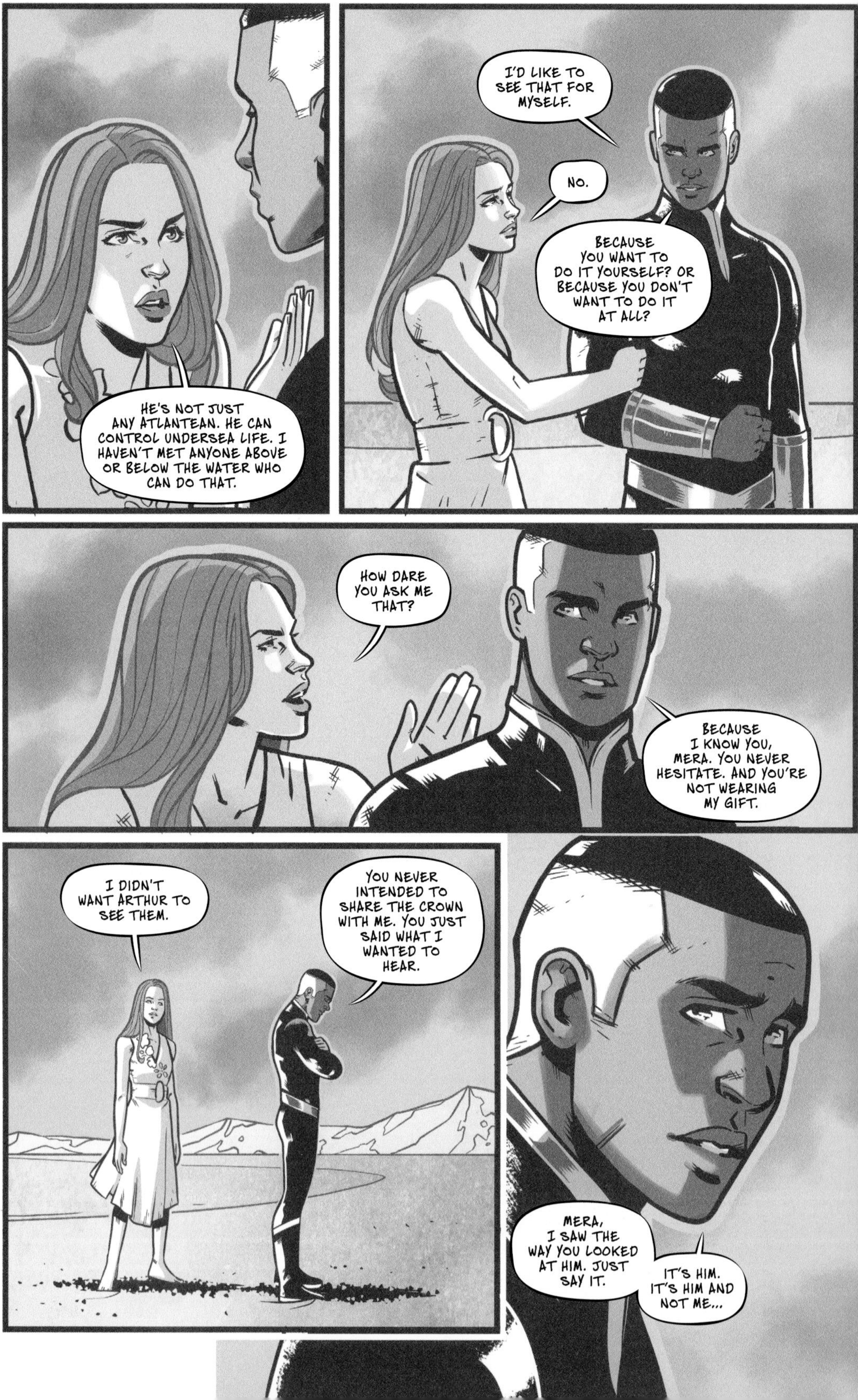
HE'S NOT JUST ANY ATLANTEAN. HE CAN CONTROL UNDERSEA LIFE. I HAVEN'T MET ANYONE ABOVE OR BELOW THE WATER WHO CAN DO THAT.
I'D LIKE TO SEE THAT FOR MYSELF.
NO.
BECAUSE YOU WANT TO DO IT YOURSELF? OR BECAUSE YOU DON'T WANT TO DO IT AT ALL?
HOW DARE YOU ASK ME THAT?
BECAUSE I KNOW YOU, MERA. YOU NEVER HESITATE. AND YOU'RE NOT WEARING MY GIFT.
I DIDN'T WANT ARTHUR TO SEE THEM.
YOU NEVER INTENDED TO SHARE THE CROWN WITH ME. YOU JUST SAID WHAT I WANTED TO HEAR.
MERA, I SAW THE WAY YOU LOOKED AT HIM. JUST SAY IT.
IT'S HIM. IT'S HIM AND NOT ME...

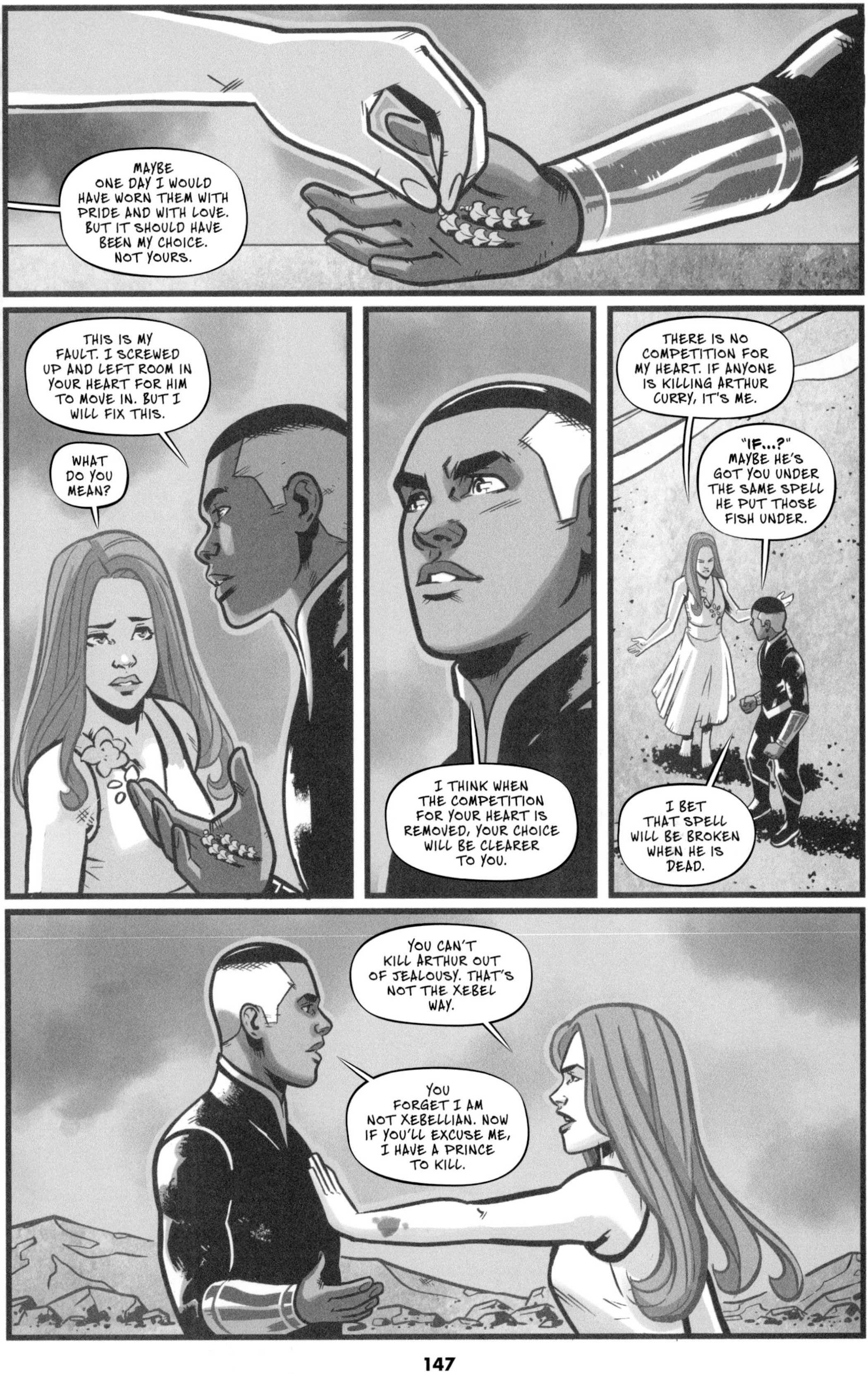

MAYBE ONE DAY I WOULD HAVE WORN THEM WITH PRIDE AND WITH LOVE. BUT IT SHOULD HAVE BEEN MY CHOICE. NOT YOURS.
THIS IS MY FAULT. I SCREWED UP AND LEFT ROOM IN YOUR HEART FOR HIM TO MOVE IN. BUT I WILL FIX THIS.
WHAT DO YOU MEAN?
I THINK WHEN THE COMPETITION FOR YOUR HEART IS REMOVED, YOUR CHOICE WILL BE CLEARER TO YOU.
THERE IS NO COMPETITION FOR MY HEART. IF ANYONE IS KILLING ARTHUR CURRY, IT'S ME.
"IF...?" MAYBE HE'S GOT YOU UNDER THE SAME SPELL HE PUT THOSE FISH UNDER.
I BET THAT SPELL WILL BE BROKEN WHEN HE IS DEAD.
YOU CAN'T KILL ARTHUR OUT OF JEALOUSY. THAT'S NOT THE XEBEL WAY.
YOU FORGET I AM NOT XEBELLIAN. NOW IF YOU'LL EXCUSE ME, I HAVE A PRINCE TO KILL.

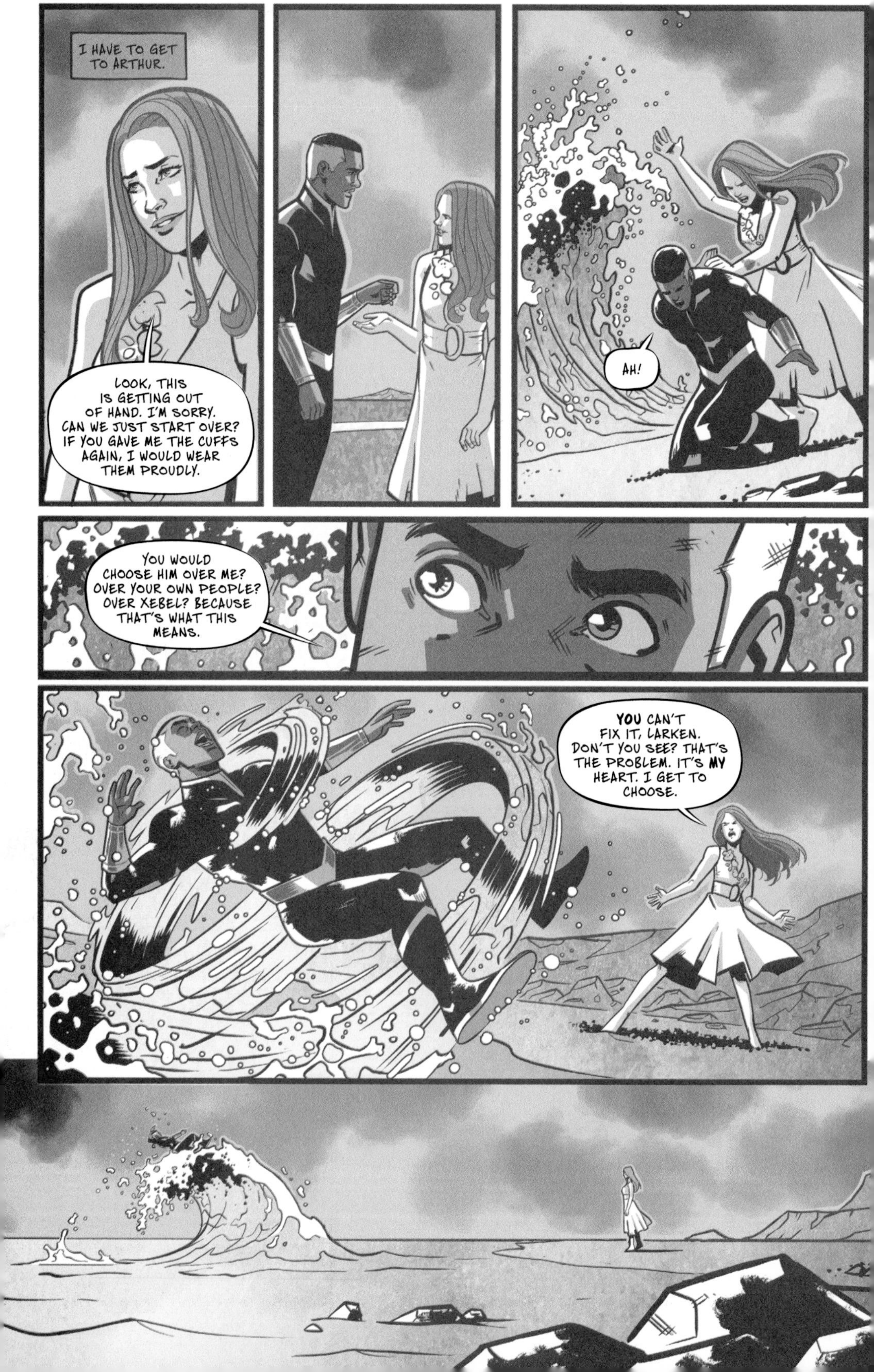
I HAVE TO GET TO ARTHUR.
LOOK, THIS IS GETTING OUT OF HAND. I'M SORRY. CAN WE JUST START OVER? IF YOU GAVE ME THE CUFFS AGAIN, I WOULD WEAR THEM PROUDLY.
AH!
YOU WOULD CHOOSE HIM OVER ME? OVER YOUR OWN PEOPLE? OVER XEBEL? BECAUSE THAT'S WHAT THIS MEANS.
YOU CAN'T FIX IT, LARKEN. DON'T YOU SEE? THAT'S THE PROBLEM. IT'S MY HEART. I GET TO CHOOSE.

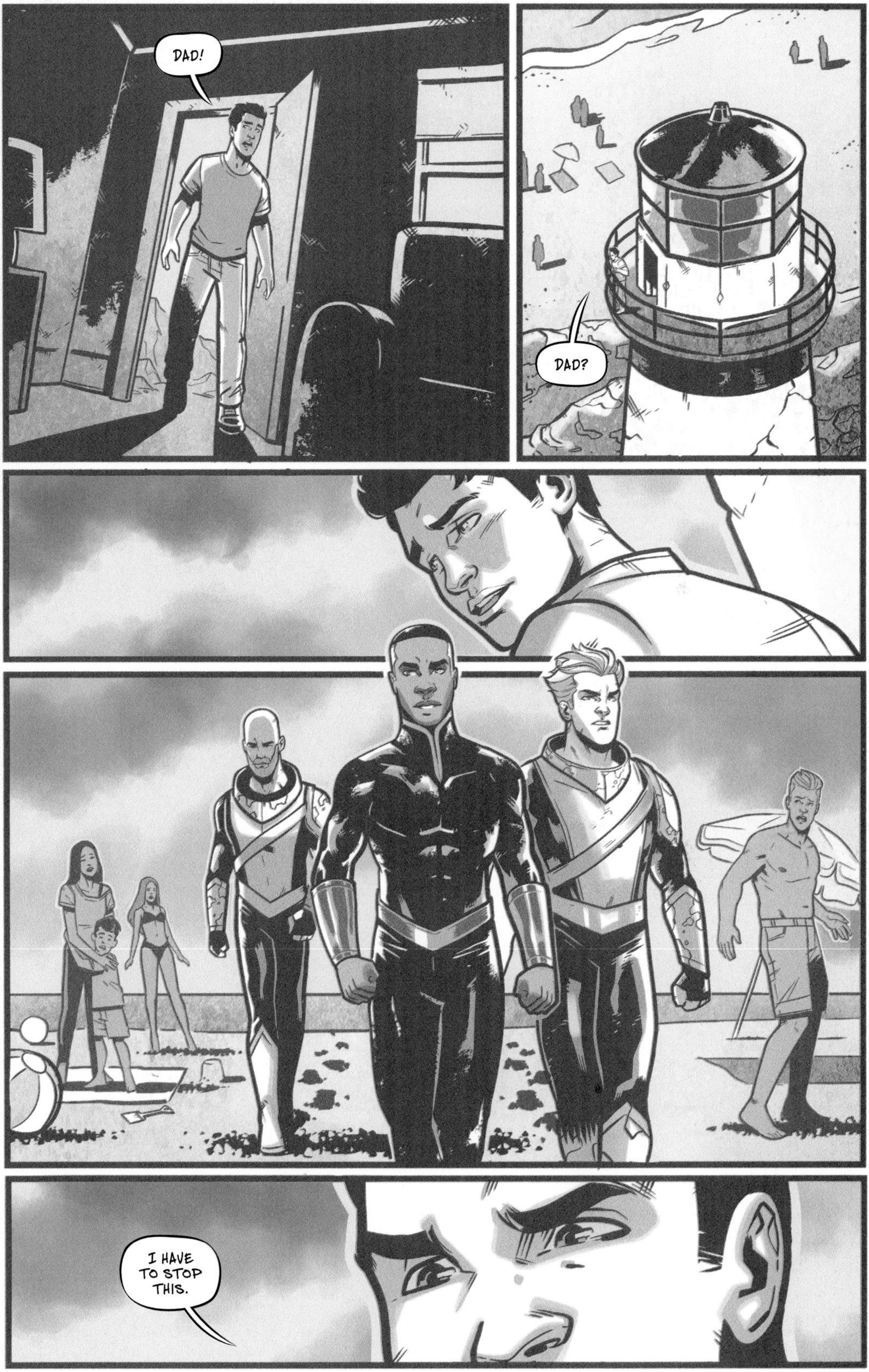
DAD!
DAD?
I HAVE TO STOP THIS.

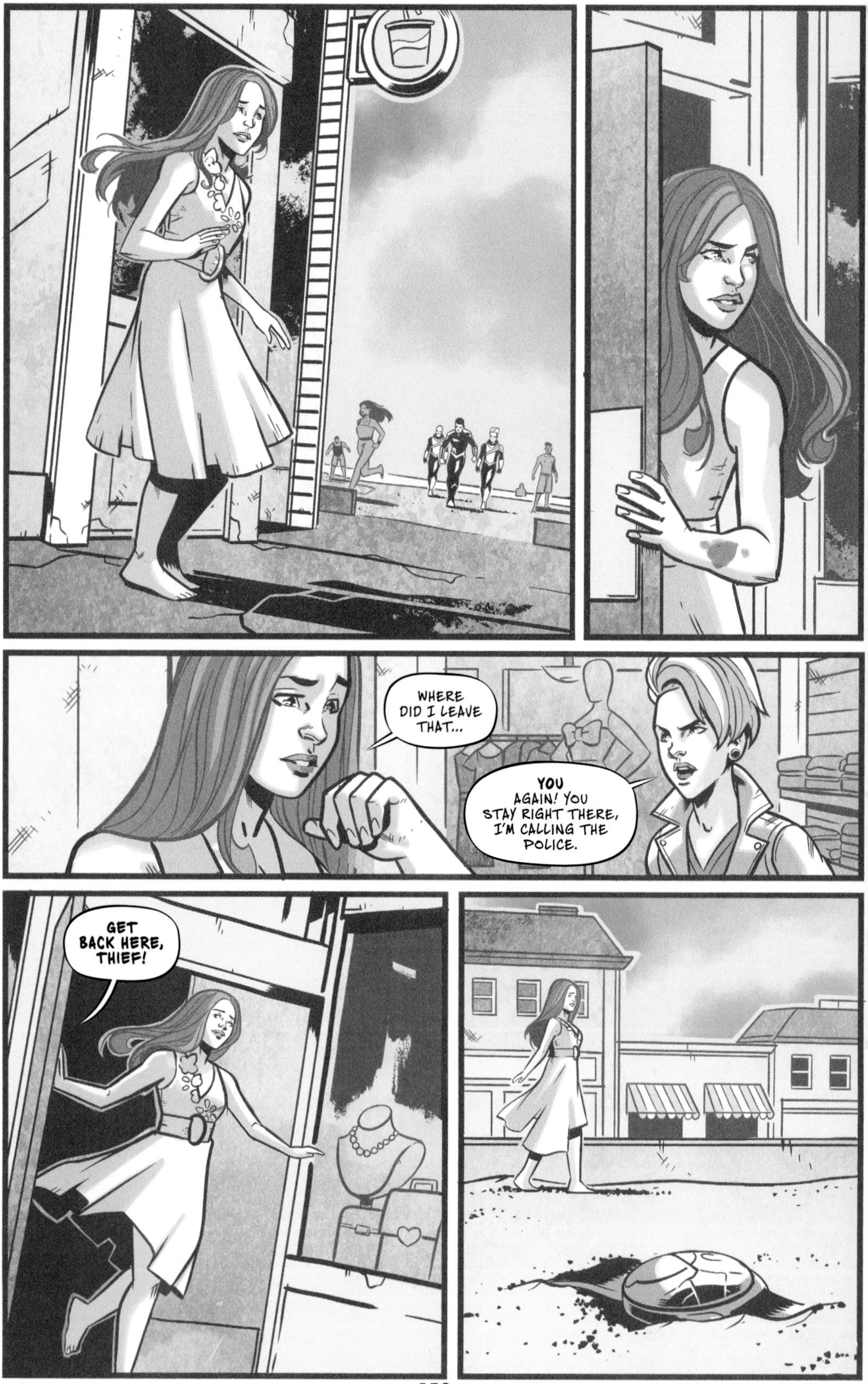
WHERE DID I LEAVE THAT...
YOU AGAIN! YOU STAY RIGHT THERE, I'M CALLING THE POLICE.
GET BACK HERE, THIEF!

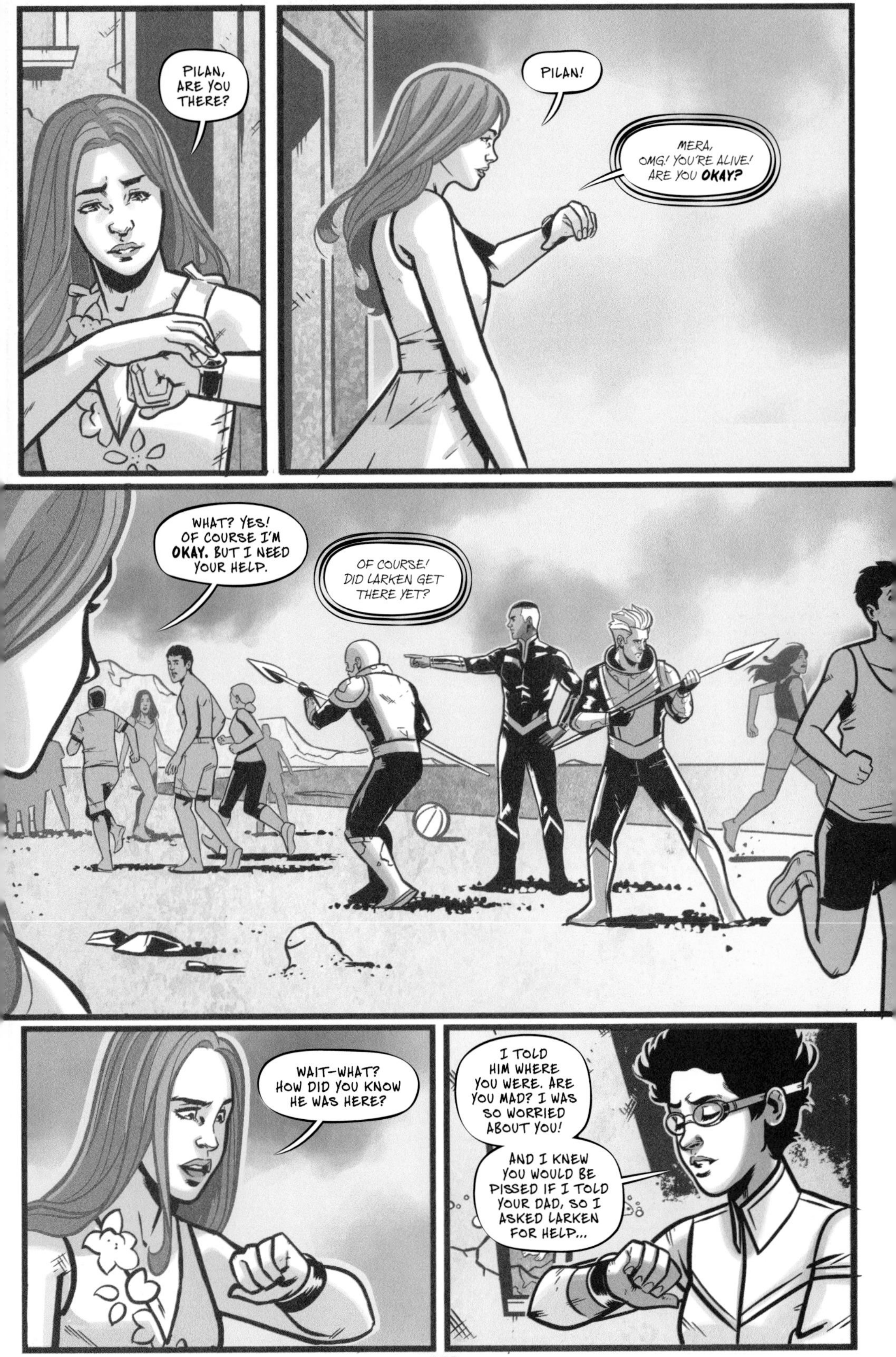
PILAN, ARE YOU THERE?
PILAN!
MERA, OMG! YOU'RE ALIVE! ARE YOU **OKAY?**
WHAT? YES! OF COURSE I'M **OKAY.** BUT I NEED YOUR HELP.
OF COURSE! DID LARKEN GET THERE YET?
WAIT—WHAT? HOW DID YOU KNOW HE WAS HERE?
I TOLD HIM WHERE YOU WERE. ARE YOU MAD? I WAS SO WORRIED ABOUT YOU!
AND I KNEW YOU WOULD BE PISSED IF I TOLD YOUR DAD, SO I ASKED LARKEN FOR HELP...

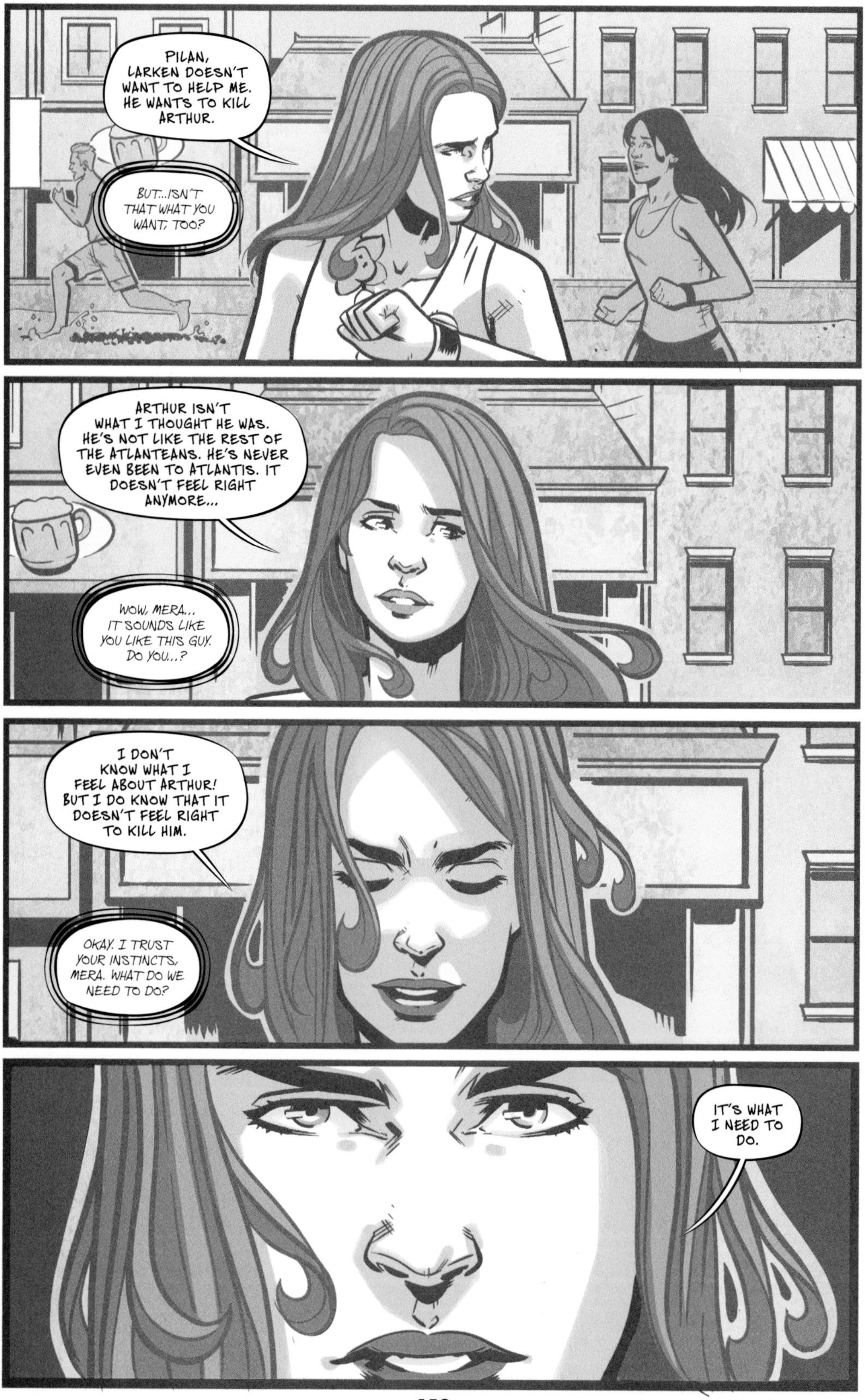
PILAN, LARKEN DOESN'T WANT TO HELP ME. HE WANTS TO KILL ARTHUR.
BUT...ISN'T THAT WHAT YOU WANT, TOO?
ARTHUR ISN'T WHAT I THOUGHT HE WAS. HE'S NOT LIKE THE REST OF THE ATLANTEANS. HE'S NEVER EVEN BEEN TO ATLANTIS. IT DOESN'T FEEL RIGHT ANYMORE...
WOW, MERA... IT SOUNDS LIKE YOU LIKE THIS GUY. DO YOU...?
I DON'T KNOW WHAT I FEEL ABOUT ARTHUR! BUT I DO KNOW THAT IT DOESN'T FEEL RIGHT TO KILL HIM.
OKAY. I TRUST YOUR INSTINCTS, MERA. WHAT DO WE NEED TO DO?
IT'S WHAT I NEED TO DO.

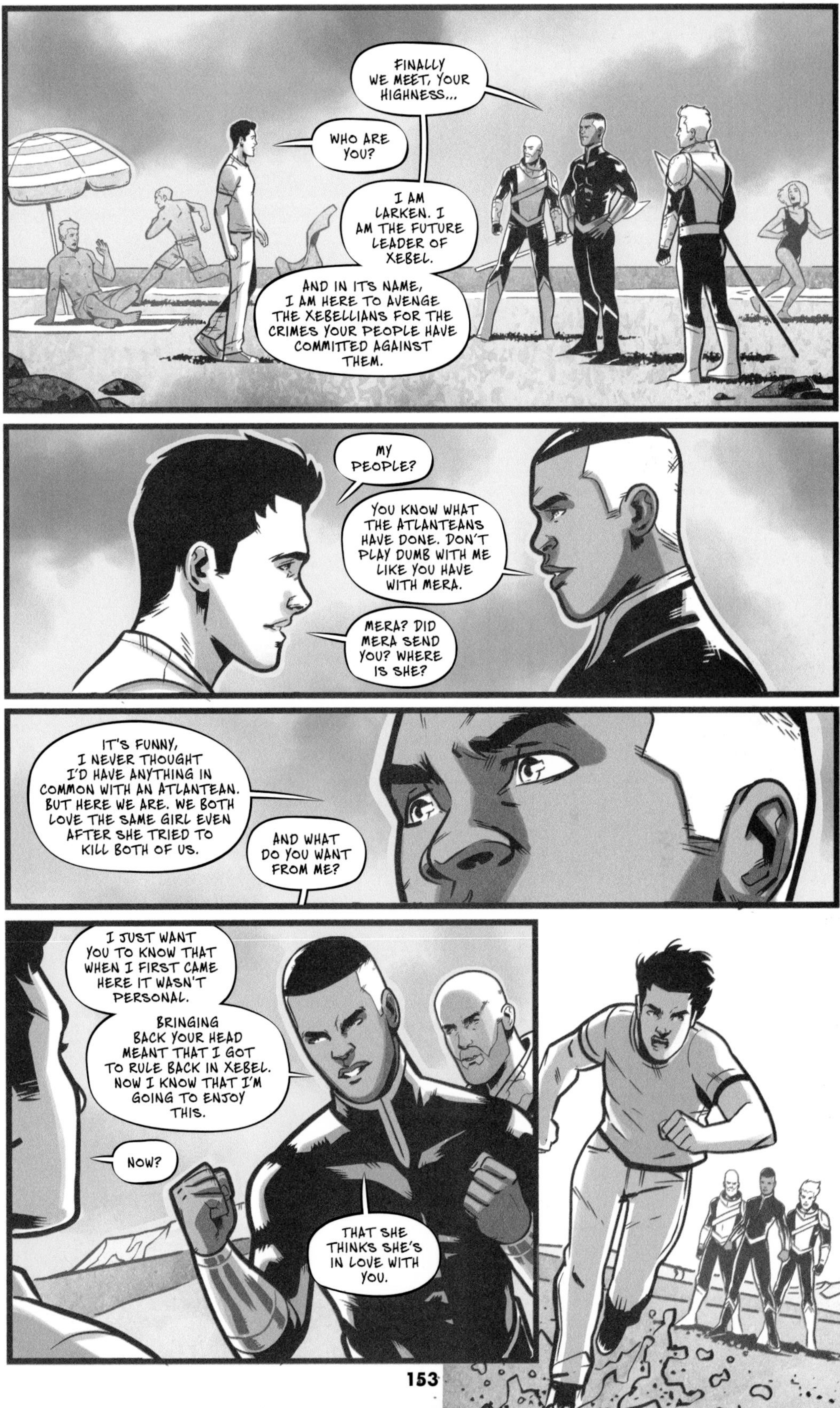
FINALLY WE MEET, YOUR HIGHNESS...
WHO ARE YOU?
I AM LARKEN. I AM THE FUTURE LEADER OF XEBEL.
AND IN ITS NAME, I AM HERE TO AVENGE THE XEBELLIANS FOR THE CRIMES YOUR PEOPLE HAVE COMMITTED AGAINST THEM.
MY PEOPLE?
YOU KNOW WHAT THE ATLANTEANS HAVE DONE. DON'T PLAY DUMB WITH ME LIKE YOU HAVE WITH MERA.
MERA? DID MERA SEND YOU? WHERE IS SHE?
IT'S FUNNY, I NEVER THOUGHT I'D HAVE ANYTHING IN COMMON WITH AN ATLANTEAN. BUT HERE WE ARE. WE BOTH LOVE THE SAME GIRL EVEN AFTER SHE TRIED TO KILL BOTH OF US.
AND WHAT DO YOU WANT FROM ME?
I JUST WANT YOU TO KNOW THAT WHEN I FIRST CAME HERE IT WASN'T PERSONAL.
BRINGING BACK YOUR HEAD MEANT THAT I GOT TO RULE BACK IN XEBEL. NOW I KNOW THAT I'M GOING TO ENJOY THIS.
NOW?
THAT SHE THINKS SHE'S IN LOVE WITH YOU.

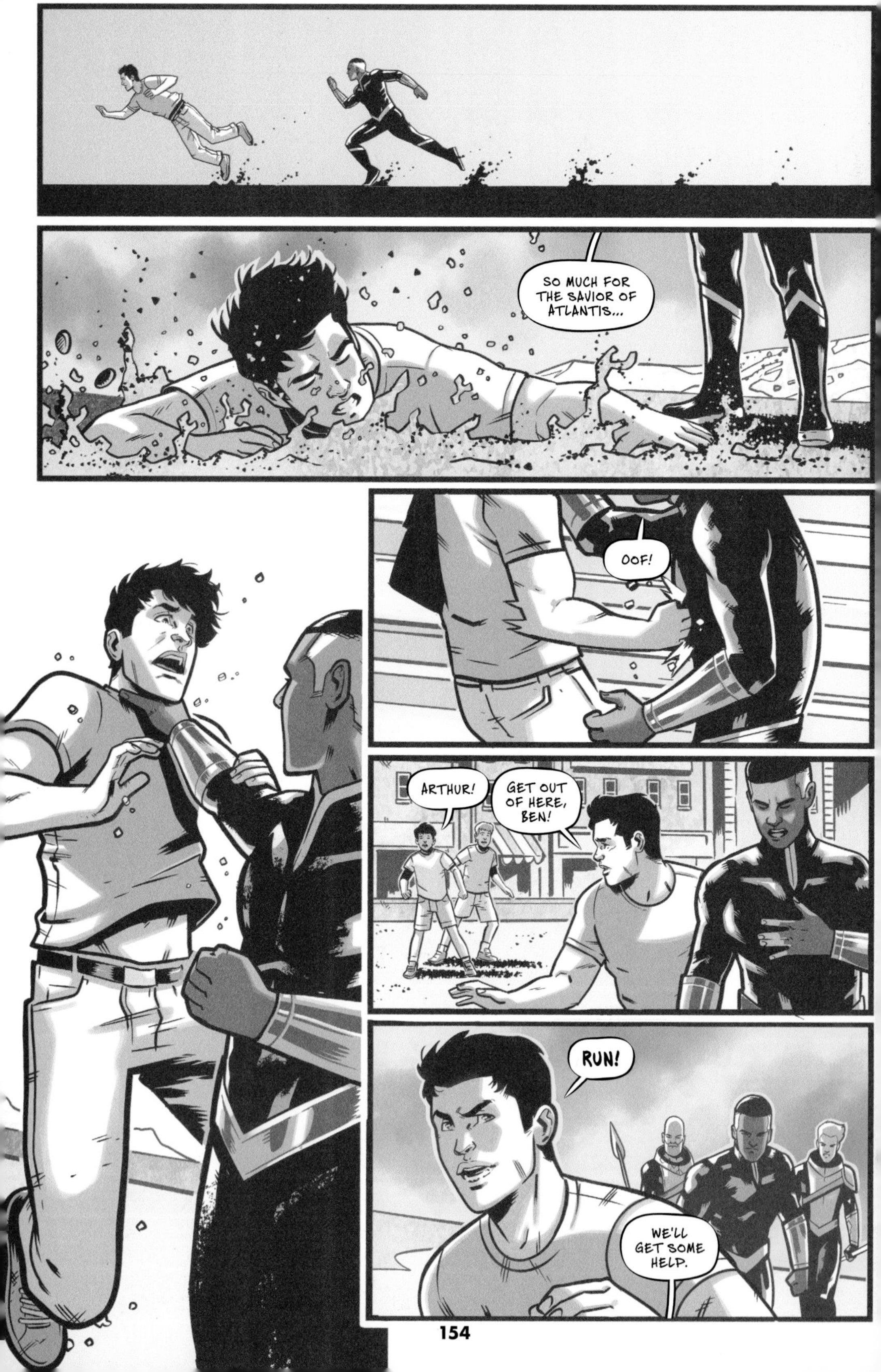
SO MUCH FOR THE SAVIOR OF ATLANTIS...
OOF!
ARTHUR!
GET OUT OF HERE, BEN!
RUN!
WE'LL GET SOME HELP.

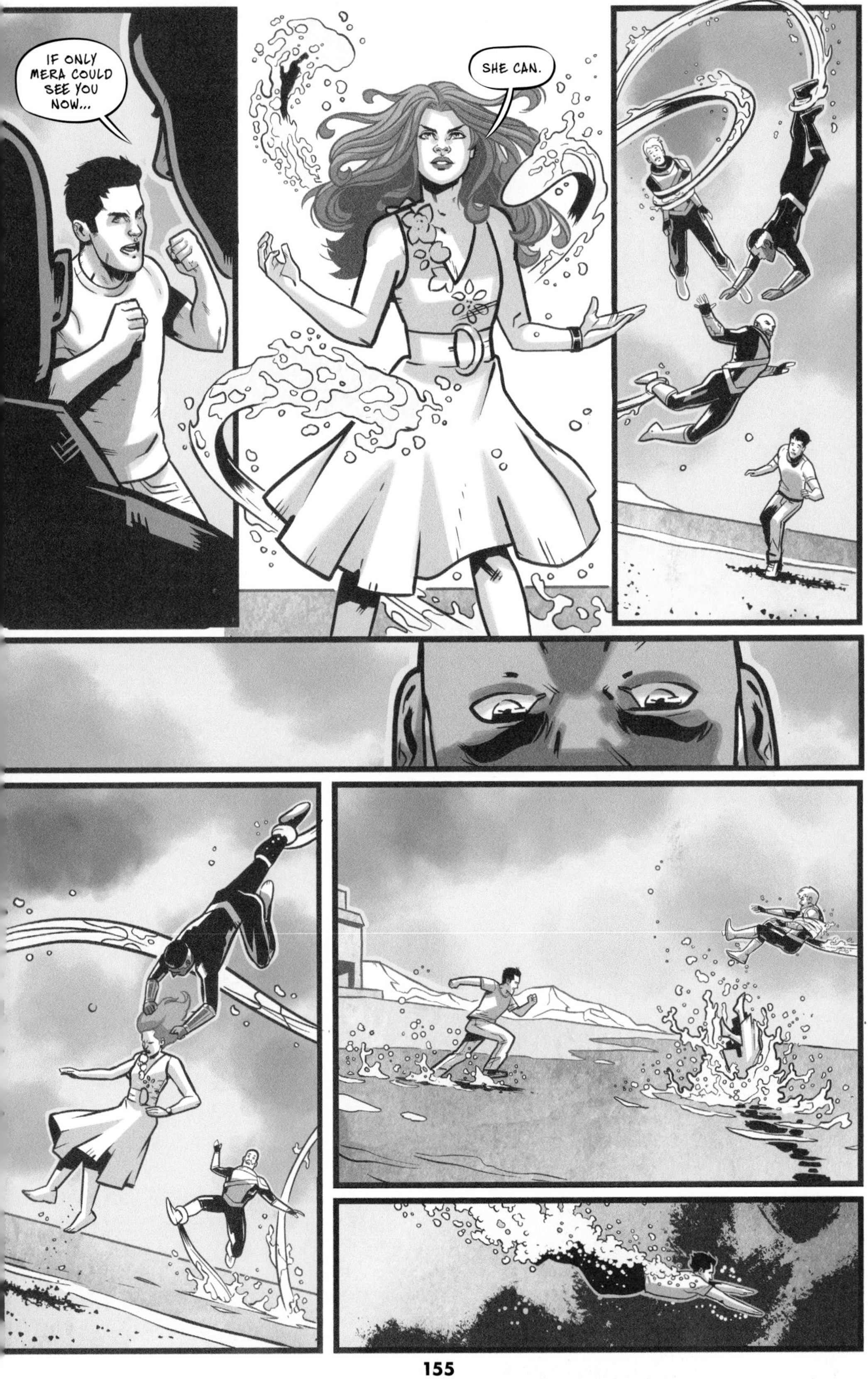
IF ONLY MERA COULD SEE YOU NOW...
SHE CAN.

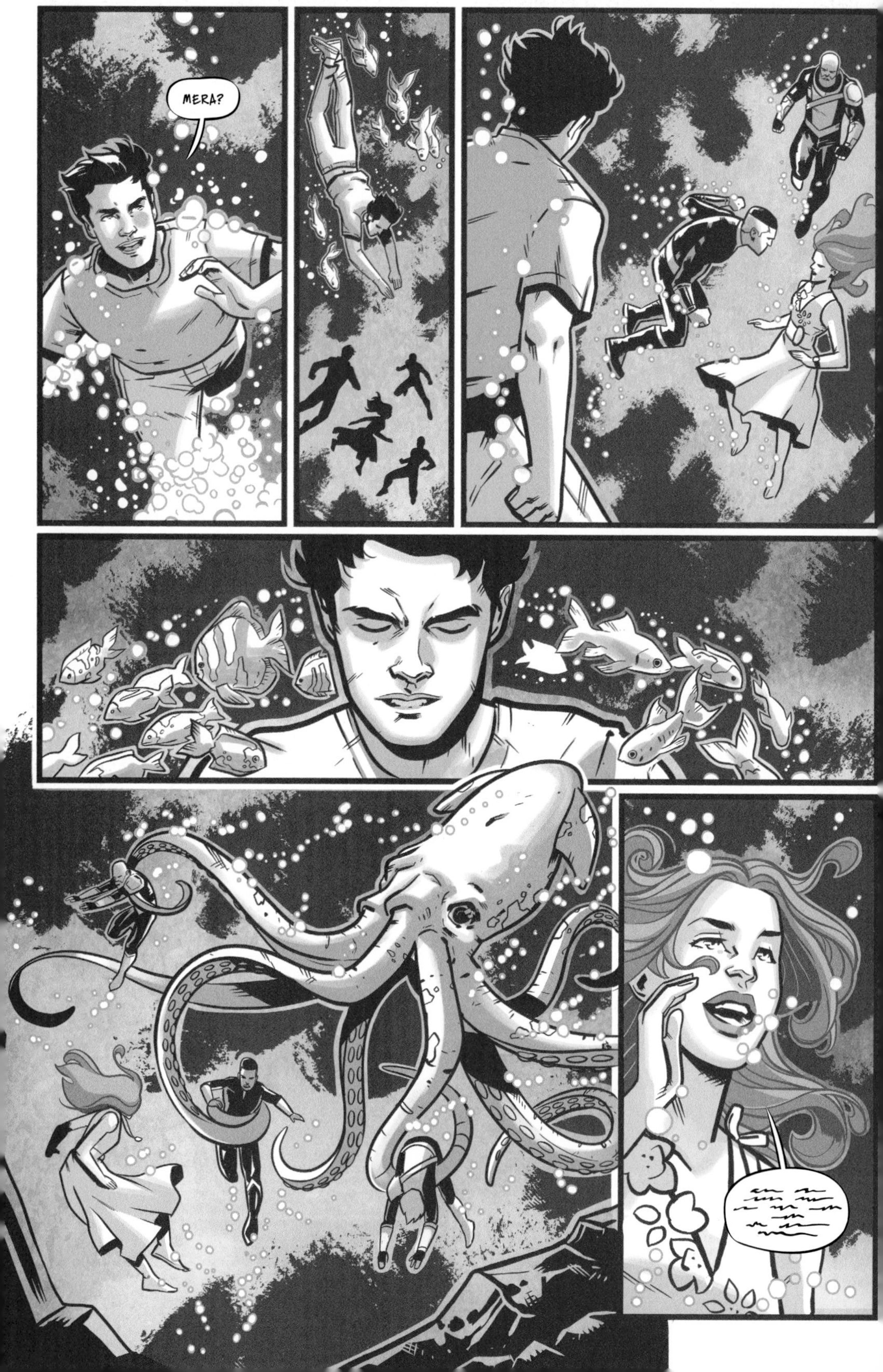
MERA?

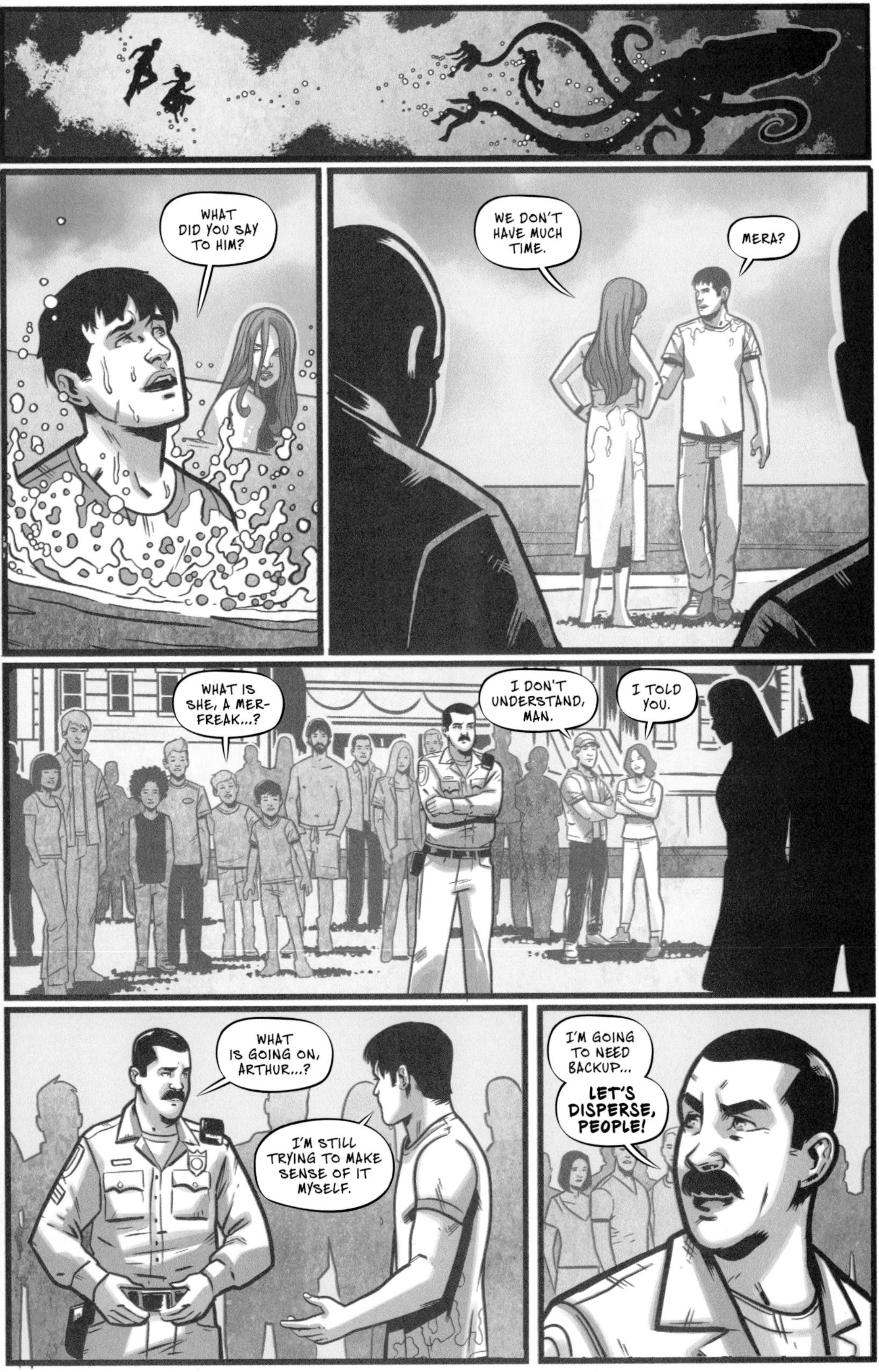
WHAT DID YOU SAY TO HIM?
WE DON'T HAVE MUCH TIME.
MERA?
WHAT IS SHE, A MER-FREAK...?
I DON'T UNDERSTAND, MAN.
I TOLD YOU.
WHAT IS GOING ON, ARTHUR...?
I'M STILL TRYING TO MAKE SENSE OF IT MYSELF.
I'M GOING TO NEED BACKUP...
LET'S DISPERSE, PEOPLE!

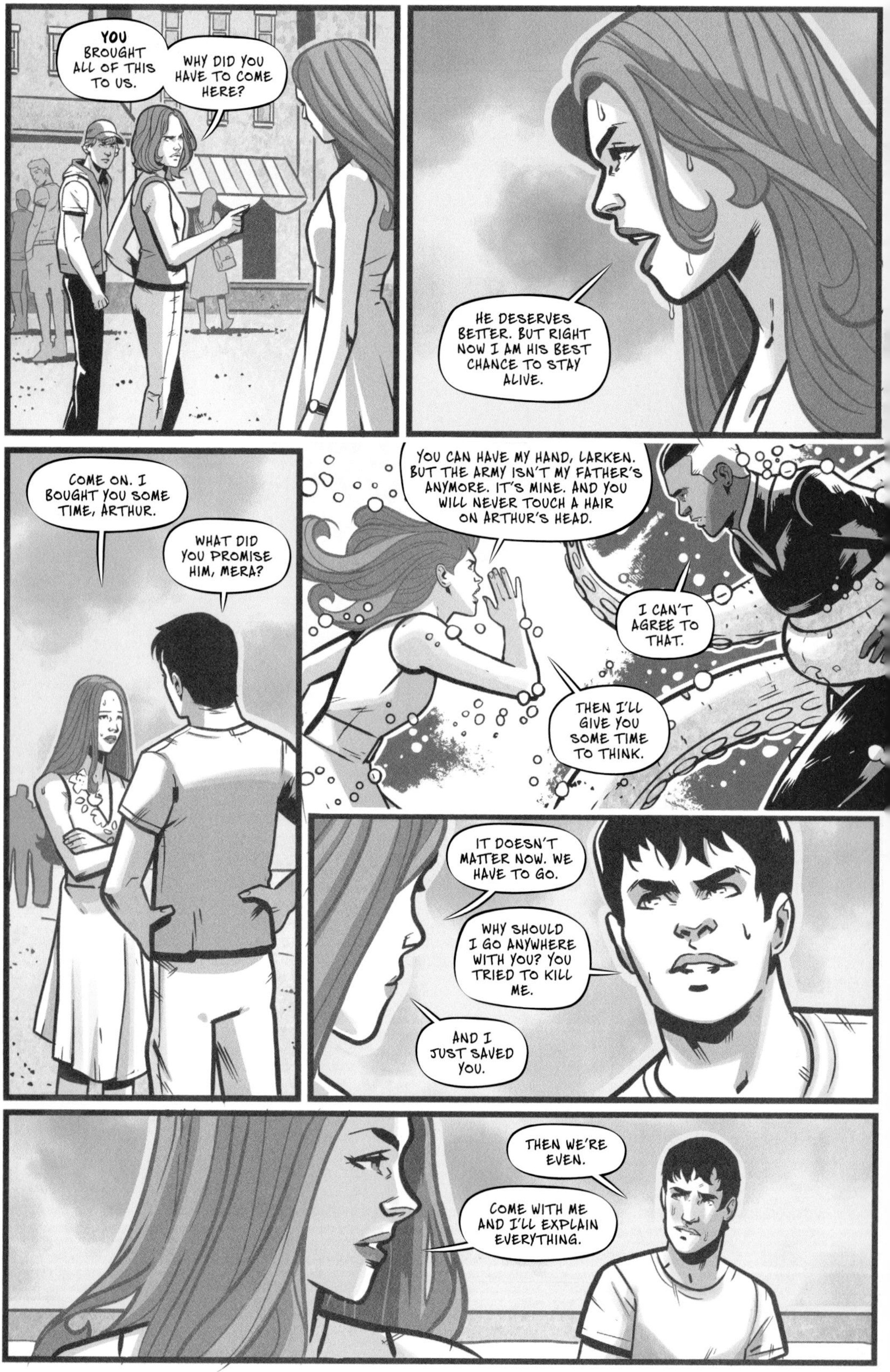
YOU BROUGHT ALL OF THIS TO US.
WHY DID YOU HAVE TO COME HERE?
HE DESERVES BETTER. BUT RIGHT NOW I AM HIS BEST CHANCE TO STAY ALIVE.
COME ON. I BOUGHT YOU SOME TIME, ARTHUR.
WHAT DID YOU PROMISE HIM, MERA?
YOU CAN HAVE MY HAND, LARKEN. BUT THE ARMY ISN'T MY FATHER'S ANYMORE. IT'S MINE. AND YOU WILL NEVER TOUCH A HAIR ON ARTHUR'S HEAD.
I CAN'T AGREE TO THAT.
THEN I'LL GIVE YOU SOME TIME TO THINK.
IT DOESN'T MATTER NOW. WE HAVE TO GO.
WHY SHOULD I GO ANYWHERE WITH YOU? YOU TRIED TO KILL ME.
AND I JUST SAVED YOU.
THEN WE'RE EVEN.
COME WITH ME AND I'LL EXPLAIN EVERYTHING.

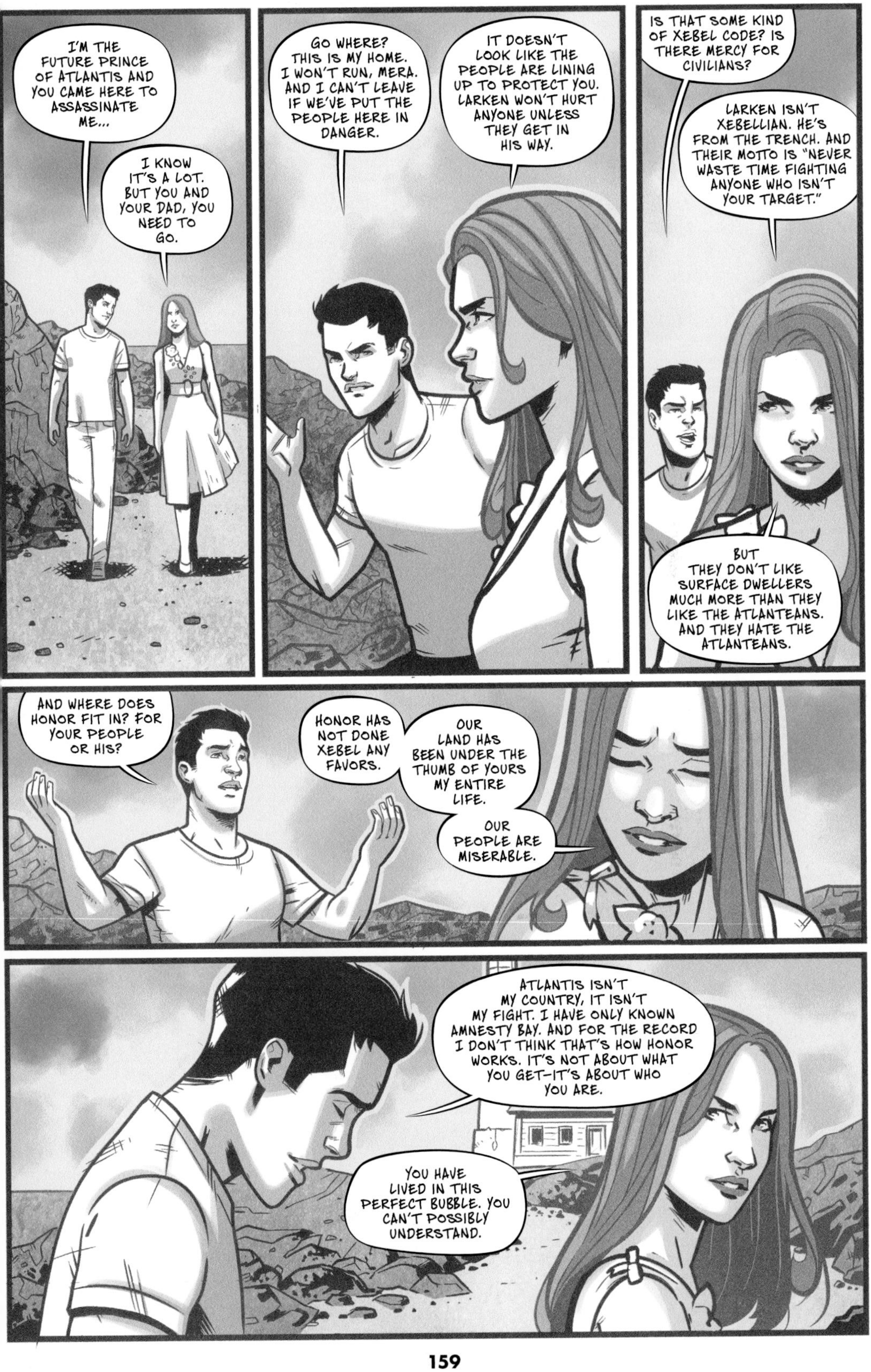
I'M THE FUTURE PRINCE OF ATLANTIS AND YOU CAME HERE TO ASSASSINATE ME...
I KNOW IT'S A LOT. BUT YOU AND YOUR DAD, YOU NEED TO GO.
GO WHERE? THIS IS MY HOME. I WON'T RUN, MERA. AND I CAN'T LEAVE IF WE'VE PUT THE PEOPLE HERE IN DANGER.
IT DOESN'T LOOK LIKE THE PEOPLE ARE LINING UP TO PROTECT YOU. LARKEN WON'T HURT ANYONE UNLESS THEY GET IN HIS WAY.
IS THAT SOME KIND OF XEBEL CODE? IS THERE MERCY FOR CIVILIANS?
LARKEN ISN'T XEBELLIAN. HE'S FROM THE TRENCH. AND THEIR MOTTO IS "NEVER WASTE TIME FIGHTING ANYONE WHO ISN'T YOUR TARGET."
BUT THEY DON'T LIKE SURFACE DWELLERS MUCH MORE THAN THEY LIKE THE ATLANTEANS. AND THEY HATE THE ATLANTEANS.
AND WHERE DOES HONOR FIT IN? FOR YOUR PEOPLE OR HIS?
HONOR HAS NOT DONE XEBEL ANY FAVORS.
OUR LAND HAS BEEN UNDER THE THUMB OF YOURS MY ENTIRE LIFE.
OUR PEOPLE ARE MISERABLE.
ATLANTIS ISN'T MY COUNTRY, IT ISN'T MY FIGHT. I HAVE ONLY KNOWN AMNESTY BAY. AND FOR THE RECORD I DON'T THINK THAT'S HOW HONOR WORKS. IT'S NOT ABOUT WHAT YOU GET-IT'S ABOUT WHO YOU ARE.
YOU HAVE LIVED IN THIS PERFECT BUBBLE. YOU CAN'T POSSIBLY UNDERSTAND.

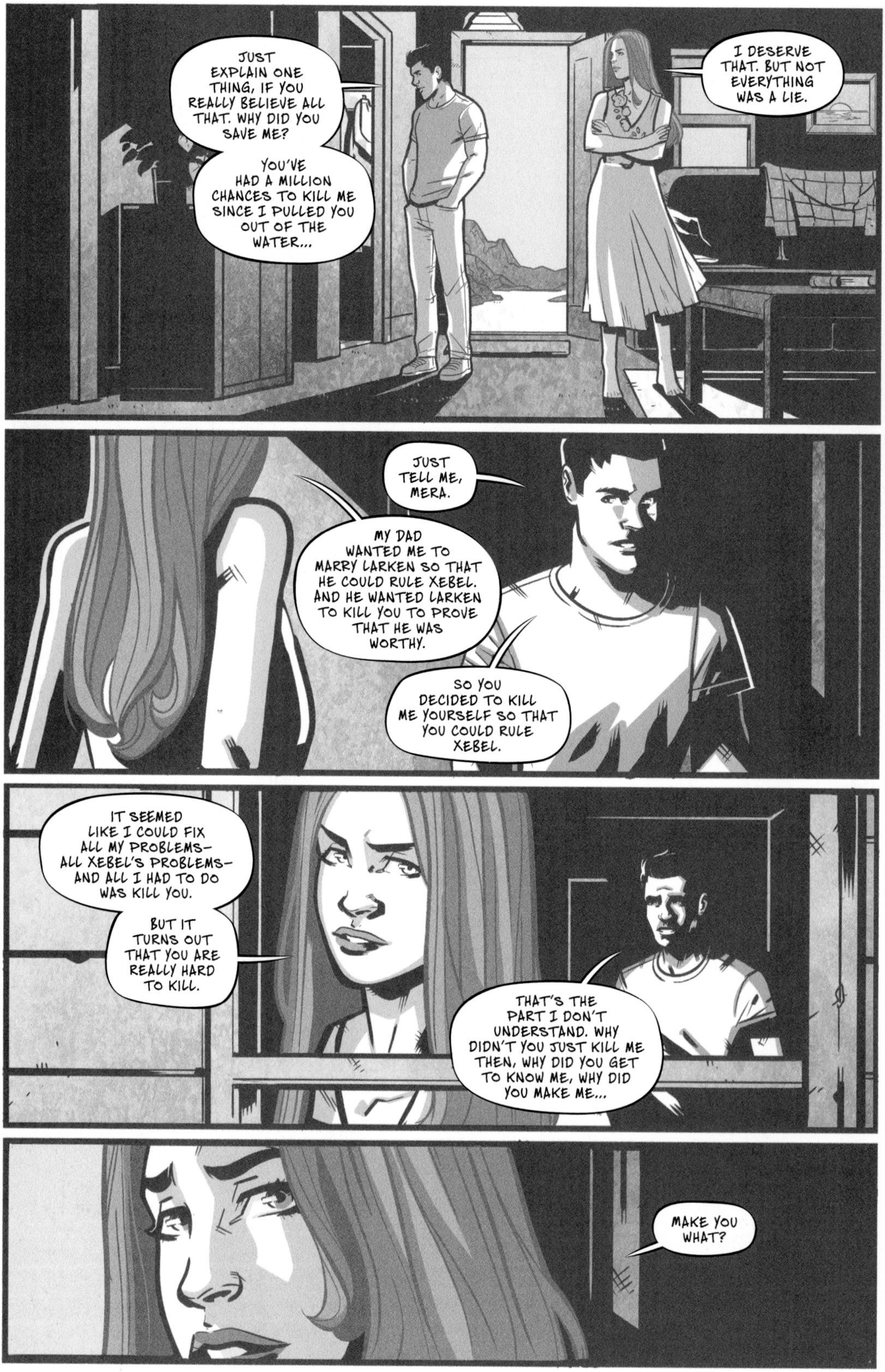
JUST EXPLAIN ONE THING, IF YOU REALLY BELIEVE ALL THAT. WHY DID YOU SAVE ME?
YOU'VE HAD A MILLION CHANCES TO KILL ME SINCE I PULLED YOU OUT OF THE WATER...
I DESERVE THAT. BUT NOT EVERYTHING WAS A LIE.
JUST TELL ME, MERA.
MY DAD WANTED ME TO MARRY LARKEN SO THAT HE COULD RULE XEBEL. AND HE WANTED LARKEN TO KILL YOU TO PROVE THAT HE WAS WORTHY.
SO YOU DECIDED TO KILL ME YOURSELF SO THAT YOU COULD RULE XEBEL.
IT SEEMED LIKE I COULD FIX ALL MY PROBLEMS— ALL XEBEL'S PROBLEMS— AND ALL I HAD TO DO WAS KILL YOU.
BUT IT TURNS OUT THAT YOU ARE REALLY HARD TO KILL.
THAT'S THE PART I DON'T UNDERSTAND. WHY DIDN'T YOU JUST KILL ME THEN, WHY DID YOU GET TO KNOW ME, WHY DID YOU MAKE ME...
MAKE YOU WHAT?

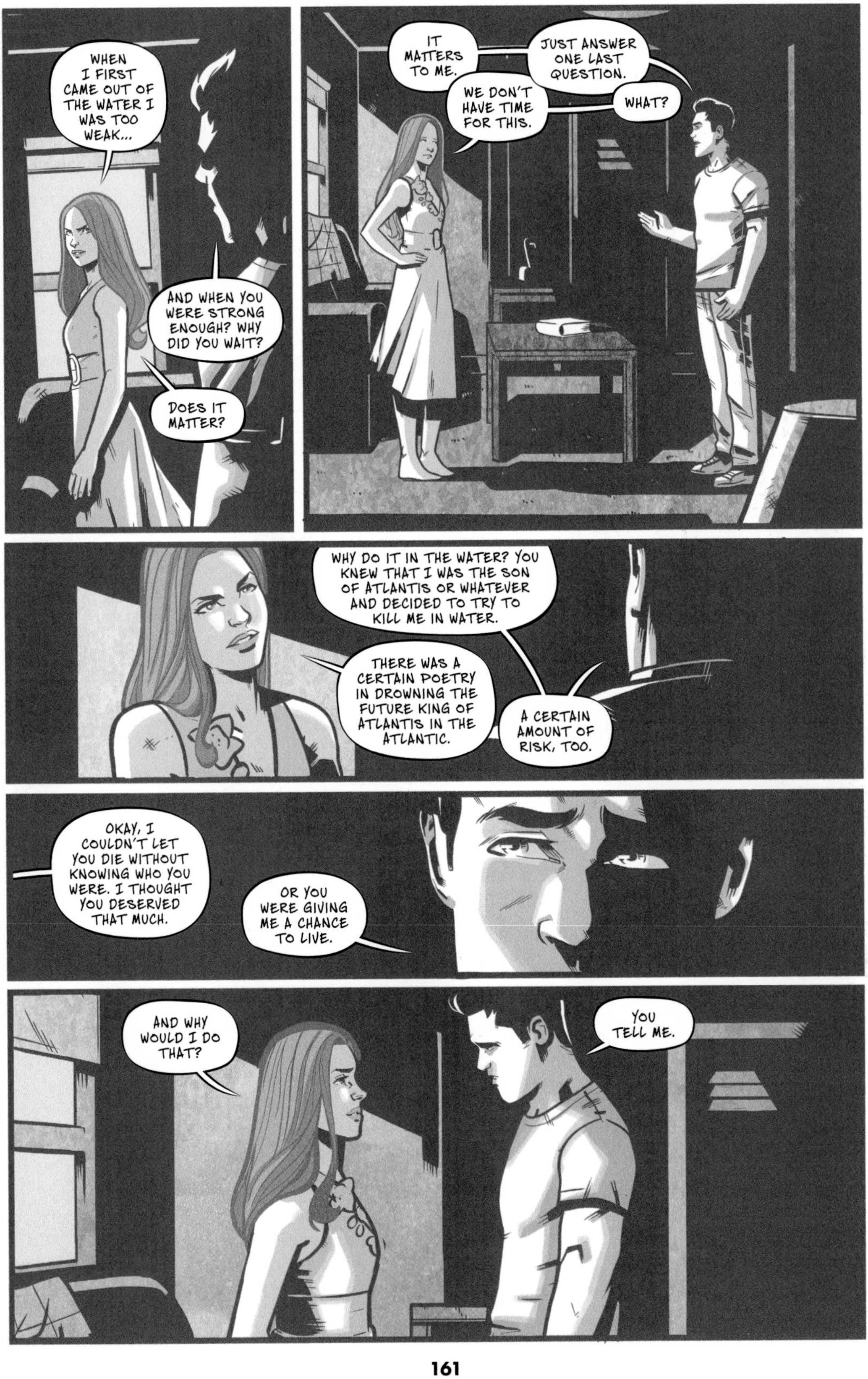
WHEN I FIRST CAME OUT OF THE WATER I WAS TOO WEAK...
AND WHEN YOU WERE STRONG ENOUGH? WHY DID YOU WAIT?
DOES IT MATTER?
IT MATTERS TO ME.
WE DON'T HAVE TIME FOR THIS.
JUST ANSWER ONE LAST QUESTION.
WHAT?
WHY DO IT IN THE WATER? YOU KNEW THAT I WAS THE SON OF ATLANTIS OR WHATEVER AND DECIDED TO TRY TO KILL ME IN WATER.
THERE WAS A CERTAIN POETRY IN DROWNING THE FUTURE KING OF ATLANTIS IN THE ATLANTIC.
A CERTAIN AMOUNT OF RISK, TOO.
OKAY, I COULDN'T LET YOU DIE WITHOUT KNOWING WHO YOU WERE. I THOUGHT YOU DESERVED THAT MUCH.
OR YOU WERE GIVING ME A CHANCE TO LIVE.
AND WHY WOULD I DO THAT?
YOU TELL ME.

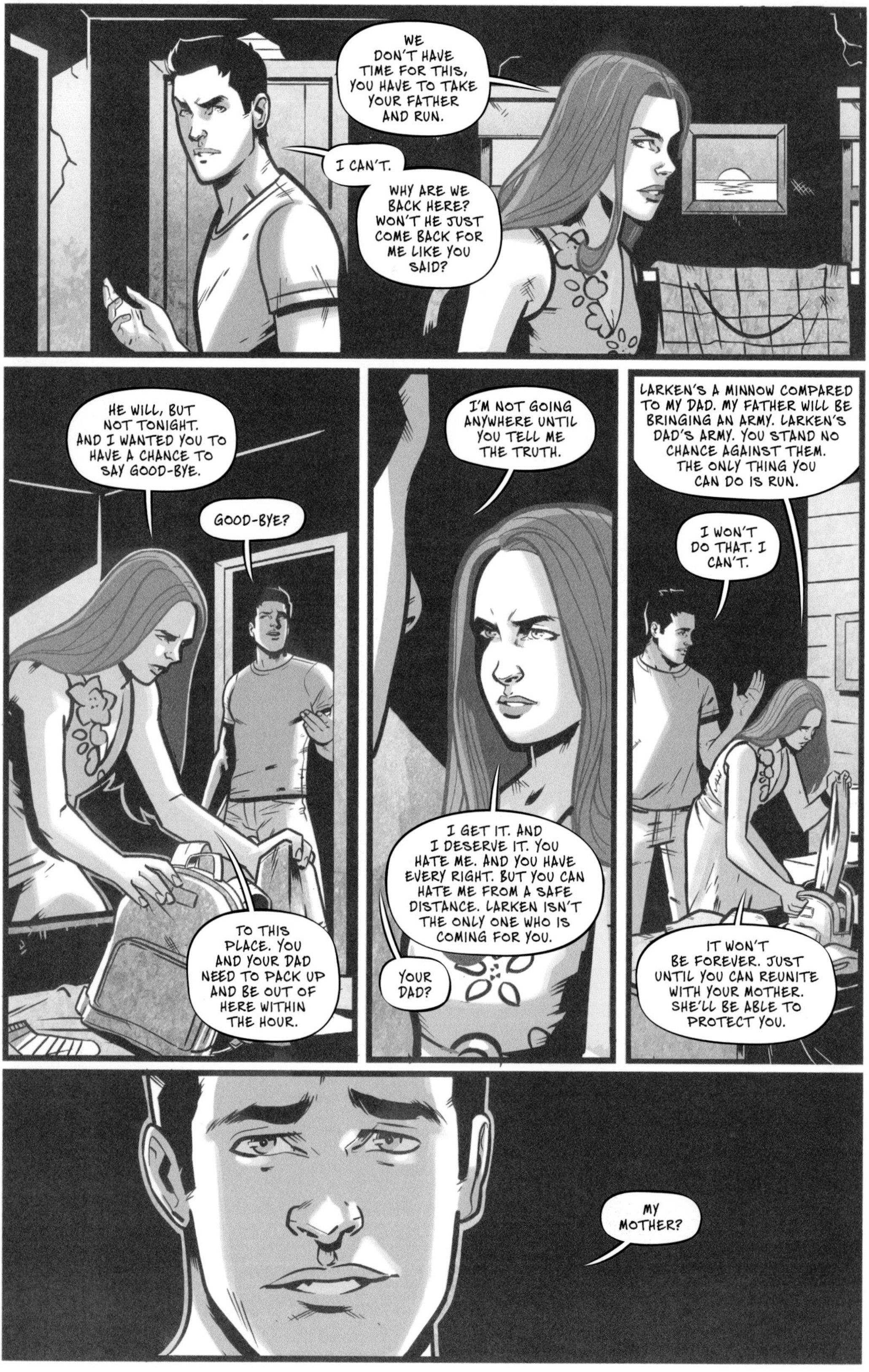
WE DON'T HAVE TIME FOR THIS, YOU HAVE TO TAKE YOUR FATHER AND RUN.
I CAN'T.
WHY ARE WE BACK HERE? WON'T HE JUST COME BACK FOR ME LIKE YOU SAID?
HE WILL, BUT NOT TONIGHT. AND I WANTED YOU TO HAVE A CHANCE TO SAY GOOD-BYE.
GOOD-BYE?
TO THIS PLACE. YOU AND YOUR DAD NEED TO PACK UP AND BE OUT OF HERE WITHIN THE HOUR.
I'M NOT GOING ANYWHERE UNTIL YOU TELL ME THE TRUTH.
I GET IT. AND I DESERVE IT. YOU HATE ME. AND YOU HAVE EVERY RIGHT. BUT YOU CAN HATE ME FROM A SAFE DISTANCE. LARKEN ISN'T THE ONLY ONE WHO IS COMING FOR YOU.
YOUR DAD?
LARKEN'S A MINNOW COMPARED TO MY DAD. MY FATHER WILL BE BRINGING AN ARMY. LARKEN'S DAD'S ARMY. YOU STAND NO CHANCE AGAINST THEM. THE ONLY THING YOU CAN DO IS RUN.
I WON'T DO THAT. I CAN'T.
IT WON'T BE FOREVER. JUST UNTIL YOU CAN REUNITE WITH YOUR MOTHER. SHE'LL BE ABLE TO PROTECT YOU.
MY MOTHER?

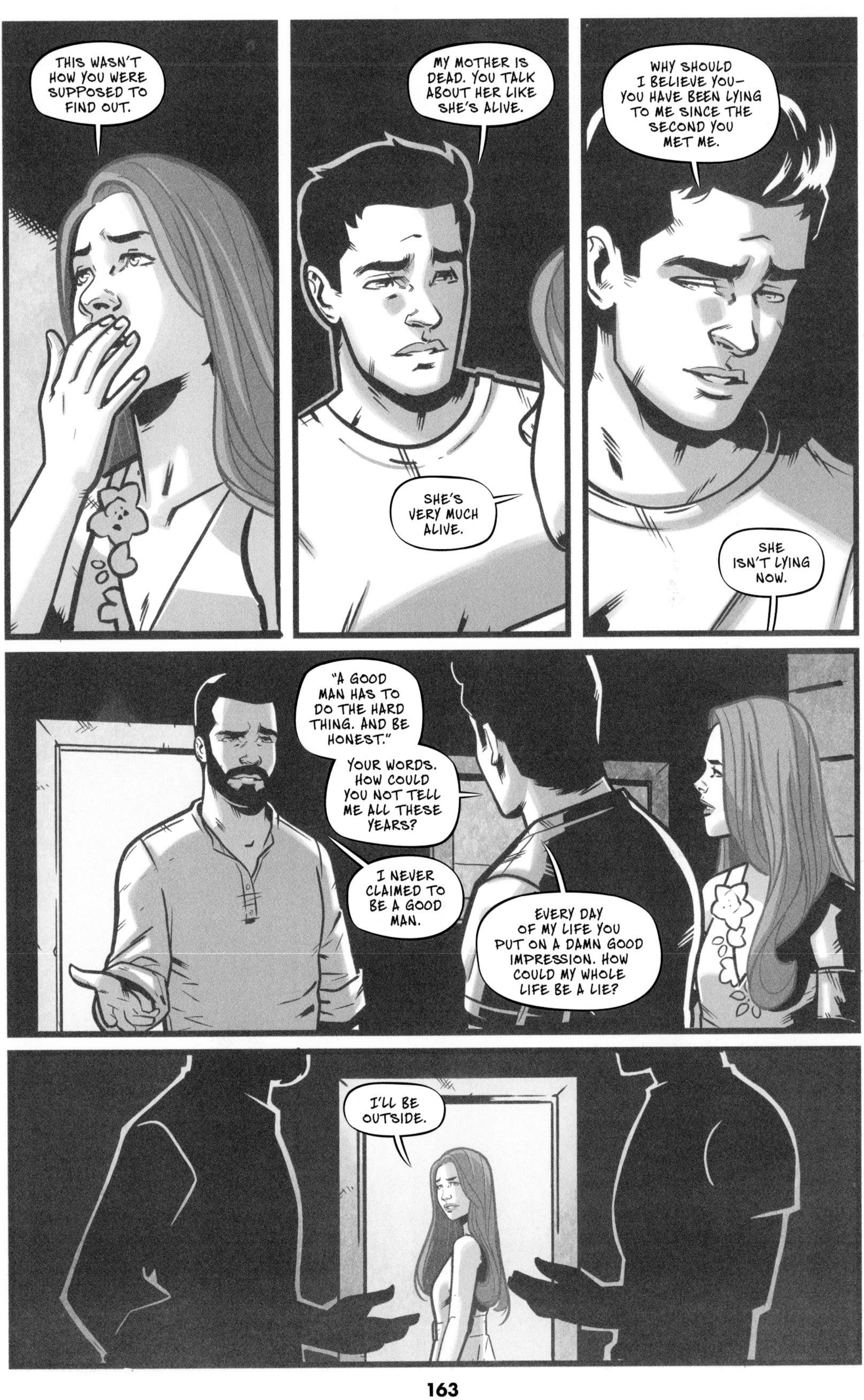
THIS WASN'T HOW YOU WERE SUPPOSED TO FIND OUT.
MY MOTHER IS DEAD. YOU TALK ABOUT HER LIKE SHE'S ALIVE.
SHE'S VERY MUCH ALIVE.
WHY SHOULD I BELIEVE YOU– YOU HAVE BEEN LYING TO ME SINCE THE SECOND YOU MET ME.
SHE ISN'T LYING NOW.
"A GOOD MAN HAS TO DO THE HARD THING. AND BE HONEST."
YOUR WORDS. HOW COULD YOU NOT TELL ME ALL THESE YEARS?
I NEVER CLAIMED TO BE A GOOD MAN.
EVERY DAY OF MY LIFE YOU PUT ON A DAMN GOOD IMPRESSION. HOW COULD MY WHOLE LIFE BE A LIE?
I'LL BE OUTSIDE.

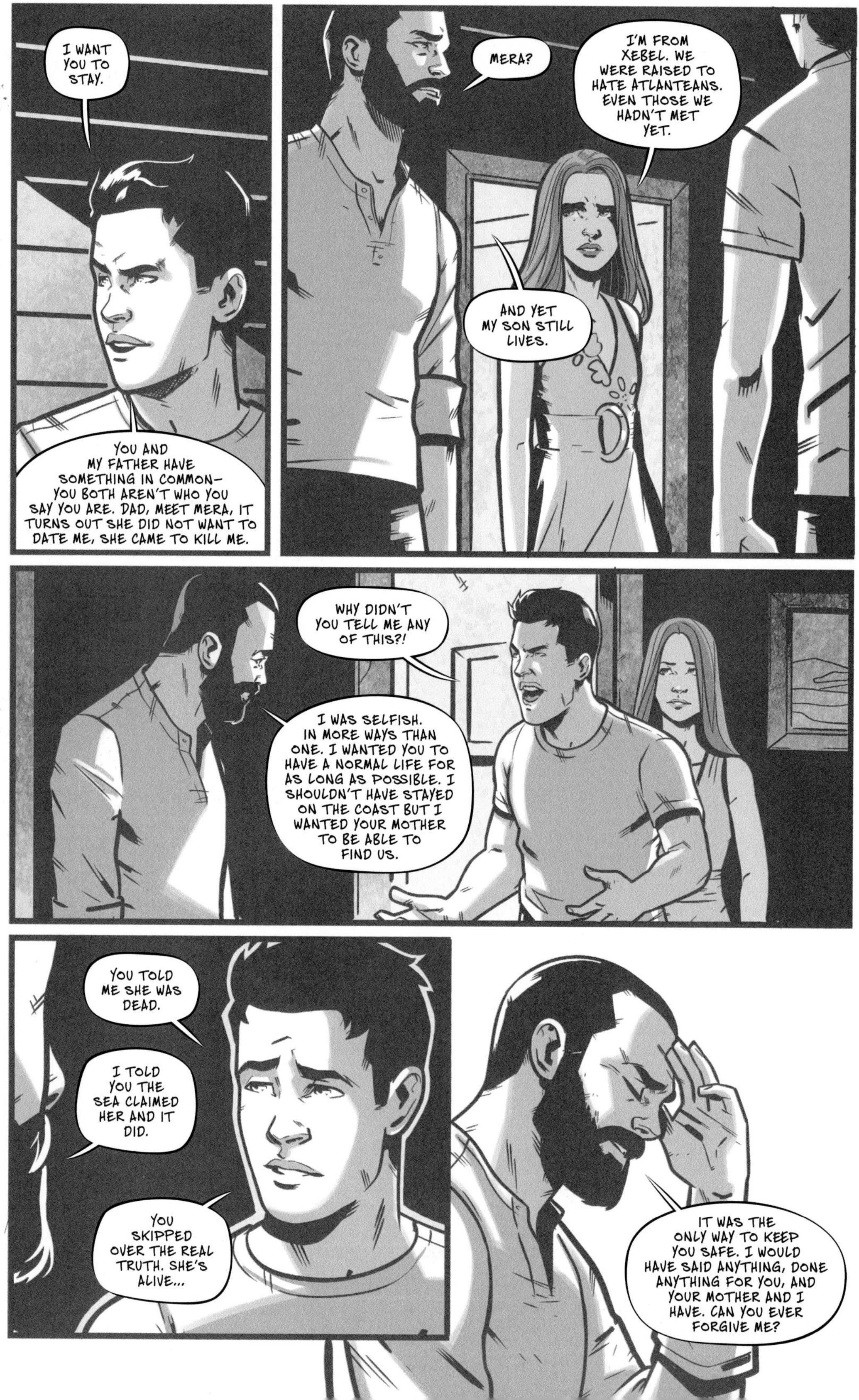
I WANT YOU TO STAY.
YOU AND MY FATHER HAVE SOMETHING IN COMMON— YOU BOTH AREN'T WHO YOU SAY YOU ARE. DAD, MEET MERA, IT TURNS OUT SHE DID NOT WANT TO DATE ME, SHE CAME TO KILL ME.
MERA?
I'M FROM XEBEL. WE WERE RAISED TO HATE ATLANTEANS. EVEN THOSE WE HADN'T MET YET.
AND YET MY SON STILL LIVES.
WHY DIDN'T YOU TELL ME ANY OF THIS?!
I WAS SELFISH. IN MORE WAYS THAN ONE. I WANTED YOU TO HAVE A NORMAL LIFE FOR AS LONG AS POSSIBLE. I SHOULDN'T HAVE STAYED ON THE COAST BUT I WANTED YOUR MOTHER TO BE ABLE TO FIND US.
YOU TOLD ME SHE WAS DEAD.
I TOLD YOU THE SEA CLAIMED HER AND IT DID.
YOU SKIPPED OVER THE REAL TRUTH. SHE'S ALIVE...
IT WAS THE ONLY WAY TO KEEP YOU SAFE. I WOULD HAVE SAID ANYTHING, DONE ANYTHING FOR YOU, AND YOUR MOTHER AND I HAVE. CAN YOU EVER FORGIVE ME?

I COULD HAVE HANDLED IT.

WE WANTED YOU TO HAVE A GOOD LIFE. A SAFE LIFE.

AND YOU THINK I WOULDN'T HAVE TRADED ALL OF THAT FOR HER? FOR A CHANCE TO HAVE A MOM?

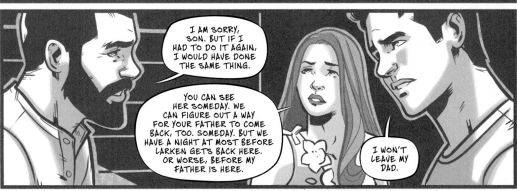

I AM SORRY, SON. BUT IF I HAD TO DO IT AGAIN, I WOULD HAVE DONE THE SAME THING.

YOU CAN SEE HER SOMEDAY. WE CAN FIGURE OUT A WAY FOR YOUR FATHER TO COME BACK, TOO. SOMEDAY. BUT WE HAVE A NIGHT AT MOST BEFORE LARKEN GETS BACK HERE. OR WORSE, BEFORE MY FATHER IS HERE.

I WON'T LEAVE MY DAD.

SON.

AND I WON'T LEAVE OUR TOWN.

SOME OF THOSE PEOPLE OUT THERE TURNED THEIR BACKS ON YOU THE SECOND THEY SAW WHO YOU REALLY WERE.

AND MOST OF THEM I HAVE KNOWN ALL MY LIFE. IT TOOK ME A BEAT TO UNDERSTAND WHAT I AM, I THINK THEY DESERVE THE SAME.

FINE, BUT WE AREN'T EQUIPPED TO FACE THE XEBELLIANS.

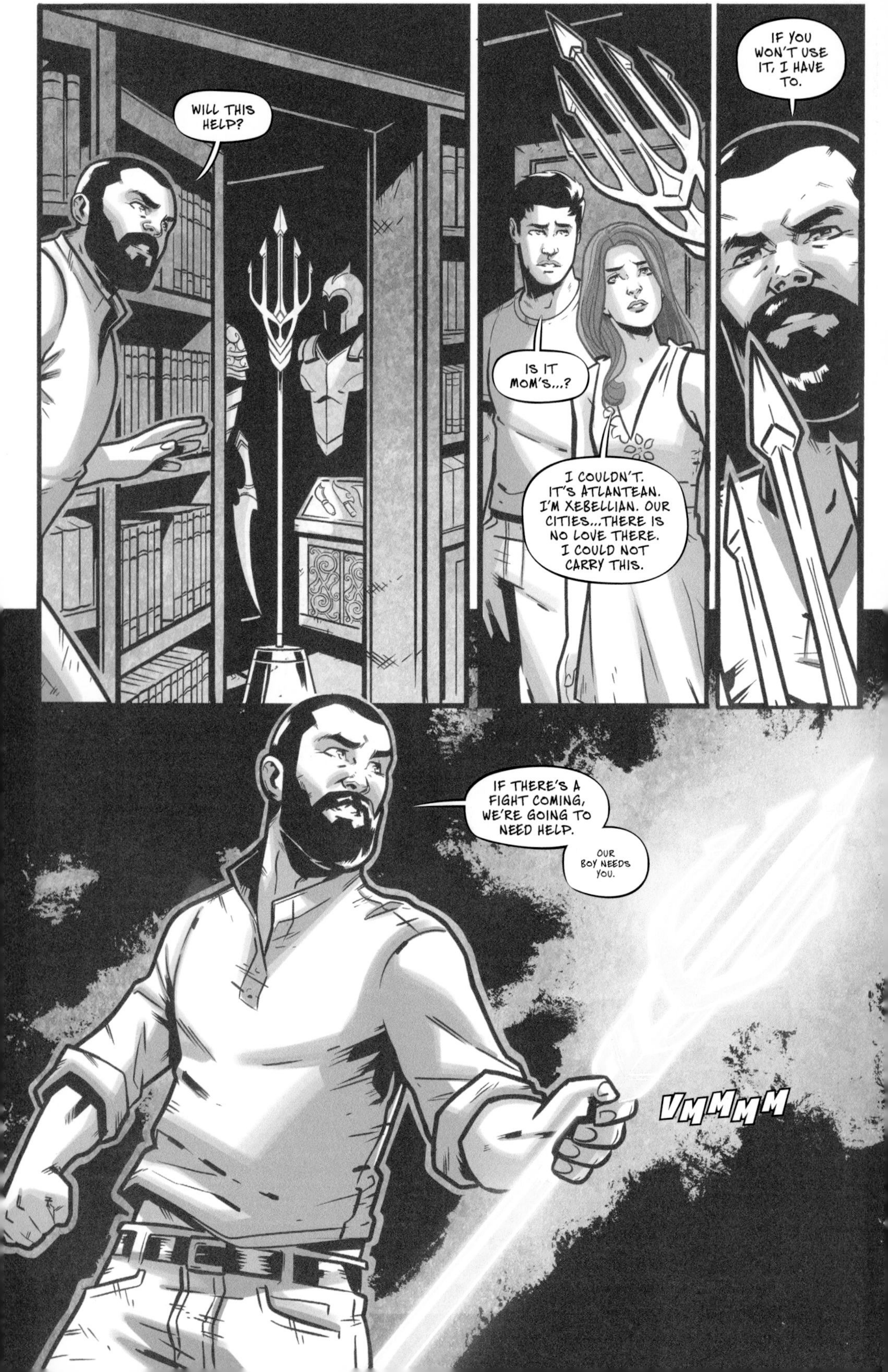
WILL THIS HELP?
IS IT MOM'S...?
I COULDN'T. IT'S ATLANTEAN. I'M XEBELLIAN. OUR CITIES...THERE IS NO LOVE THERE. I COULD NOT CARRY THIS.
IF YOU WON'T USE IT, I HAVE TO.
IF THERE'S A FIGHT COMING, WE'RE GOING TO NEED HELP.
OUR BOY NEEDS YOU.
VMMMMM

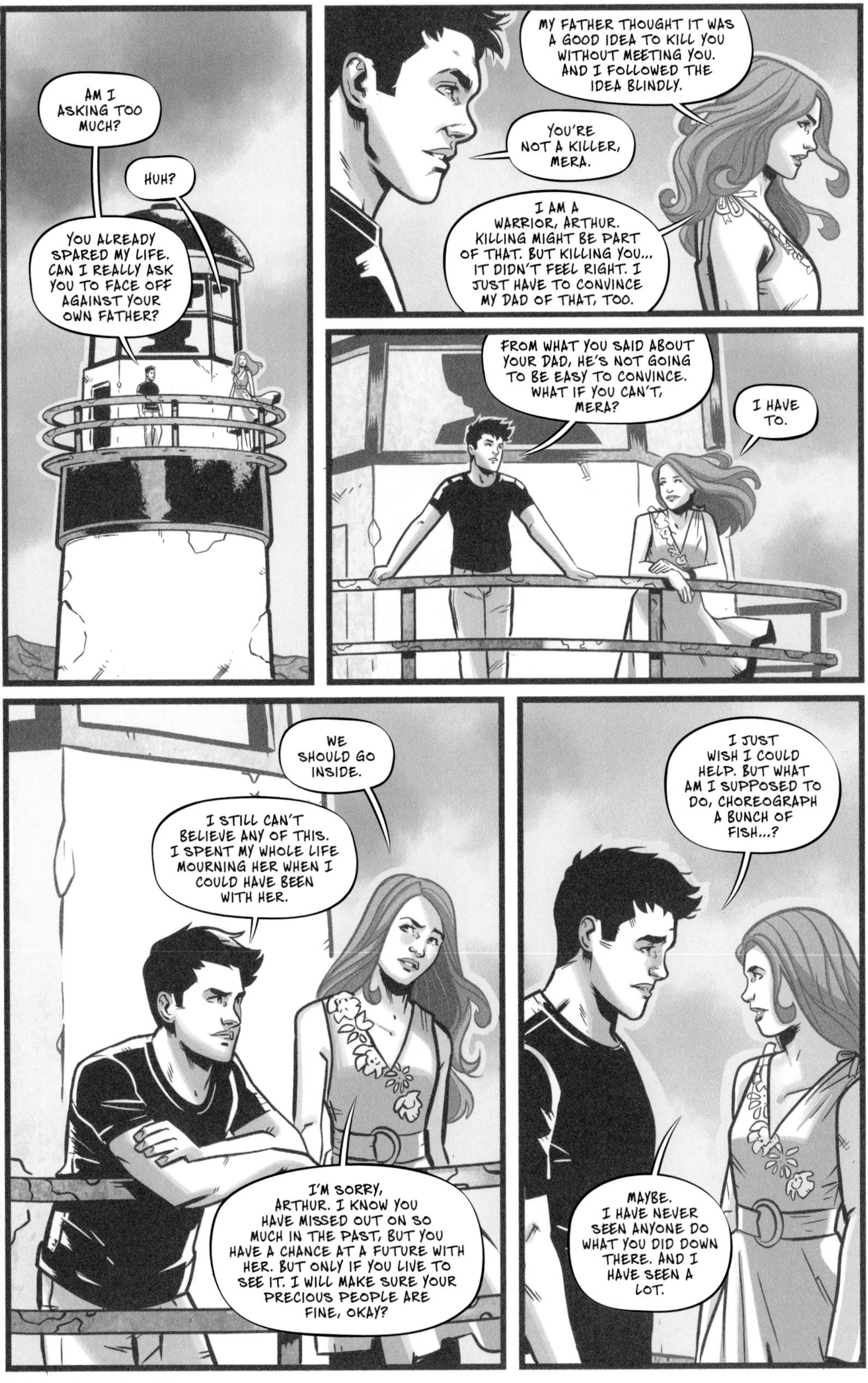

AM I ASKING TOO MUCH?
HUH?
YOU ALREADY SPARED MY LIFE. CAN I REALLY ASK YOU TO FACE OFF AGAINST YOUR OWN FATHER?
MY FATHER THOUGHT IT WAS A GOOD IDEA TO KILL YOU WITHOUT MEETING YOU. AND I FOLLOWED THE IDEA BLINDLY.
YOU'RE NOT A KILLER, MERA.
I AM A WARRIOR, ARTHUR. KILLING MIGHT BE PART OF THAT. BUT KILLING YOU... IT DIDN'T FEEL RIGHT. I JUST HAVE TO CONVINCE MY DAD OF THAT, TOO.
FROM WHAT YOU SAID ABOUT YOUR DAD, HE'S NOT GOING TO BE EASY TO CONVINCE. WHAT IF YOU CAN'T, MERA?
I HAVE TO.
WE SHOULD GO INSIDE.
I STILL CAN'T BELIEVE ANY OF THIS. I SPENT MY WHOLE LIFE MOURNING HER WHEN I COULD HAVE BEEN WITH HER.
I'M SORRY, ARTHUR. I KNOW YOU HAVE MISSED OUT ON SO MUCH IN THE PAST, BUT YOU HAVE A CHANCE AT A FUTURE WITH HER. BUT ONLY IF YOU LIVE TO SEE IT. I WILL MAKE SURE YOUR PRECIOUS PEOPLE ARE FINE, OKAY?
I JUST WISH I COULD HELP. BUT WHAT AM I SUPPOSED TO DO, CHOREOGRAPH A BUNCH OF FISH...?
MAYBE. I HAVE NEVER SEEN ANYONE DO WHAT YOU DID DOWN THERE. AND I HAVE SEEN A LOT.

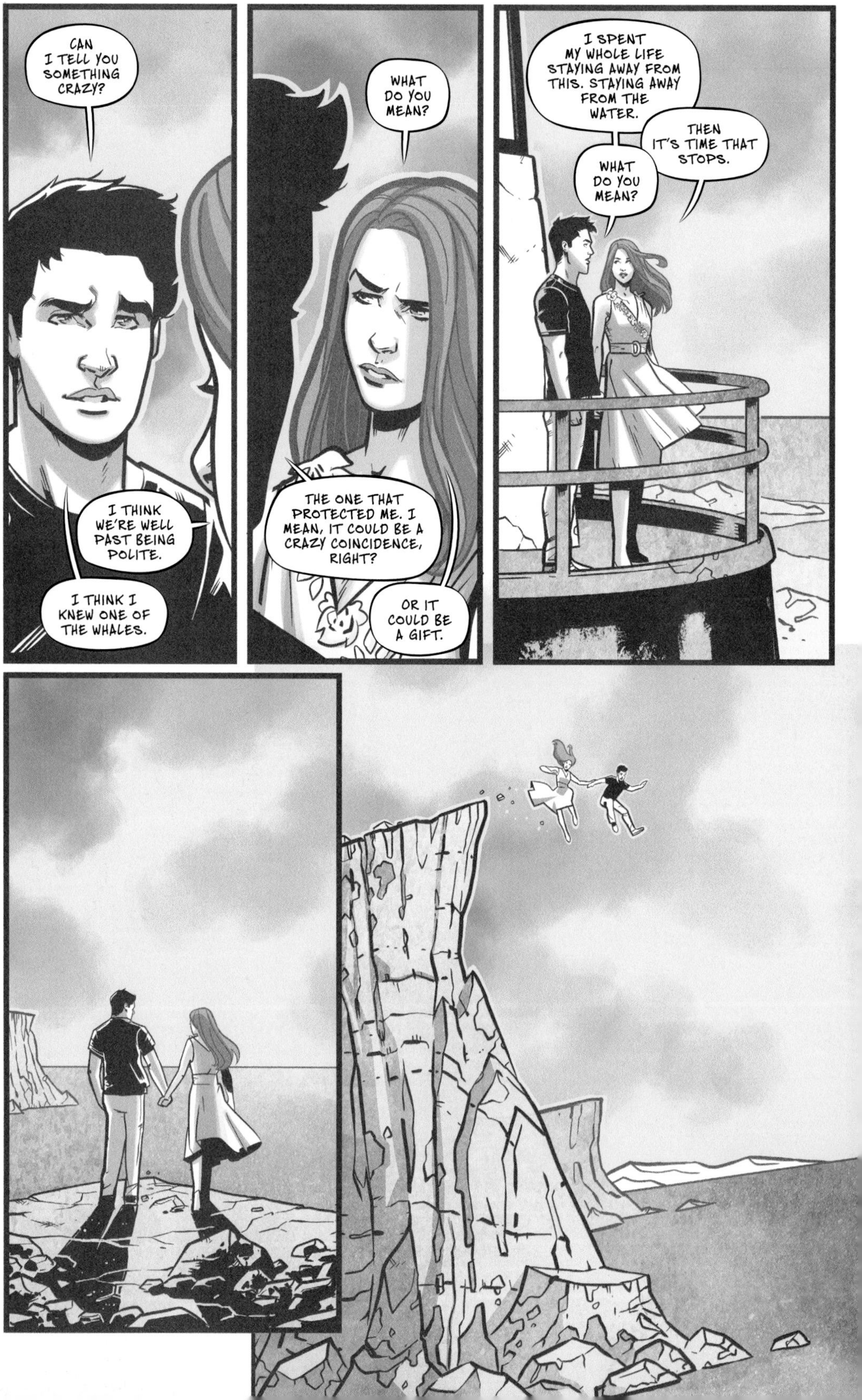
CAN I TELL YOU SOMETHING CRAZY?
I THINK WE'RE WELL PAST BEING POLITE.
I THINK I KNEW ONE OF THE WHALES.
WHAT DO YOU MEAN?
THE ONE THAT PROTECTED ME. I MEAN, IT COULD BE A CRAZY COINCIDENCE, RIGHT?
OR IT COULD BE A GIFT.
I SPENT MY WHOLE LIFE STAYING AWAY FROM THIS. STAYING AWAY FROM THE WATER.
WHAT DO YOU MEAN?
THEN IT'S TIME THAT STOPS.

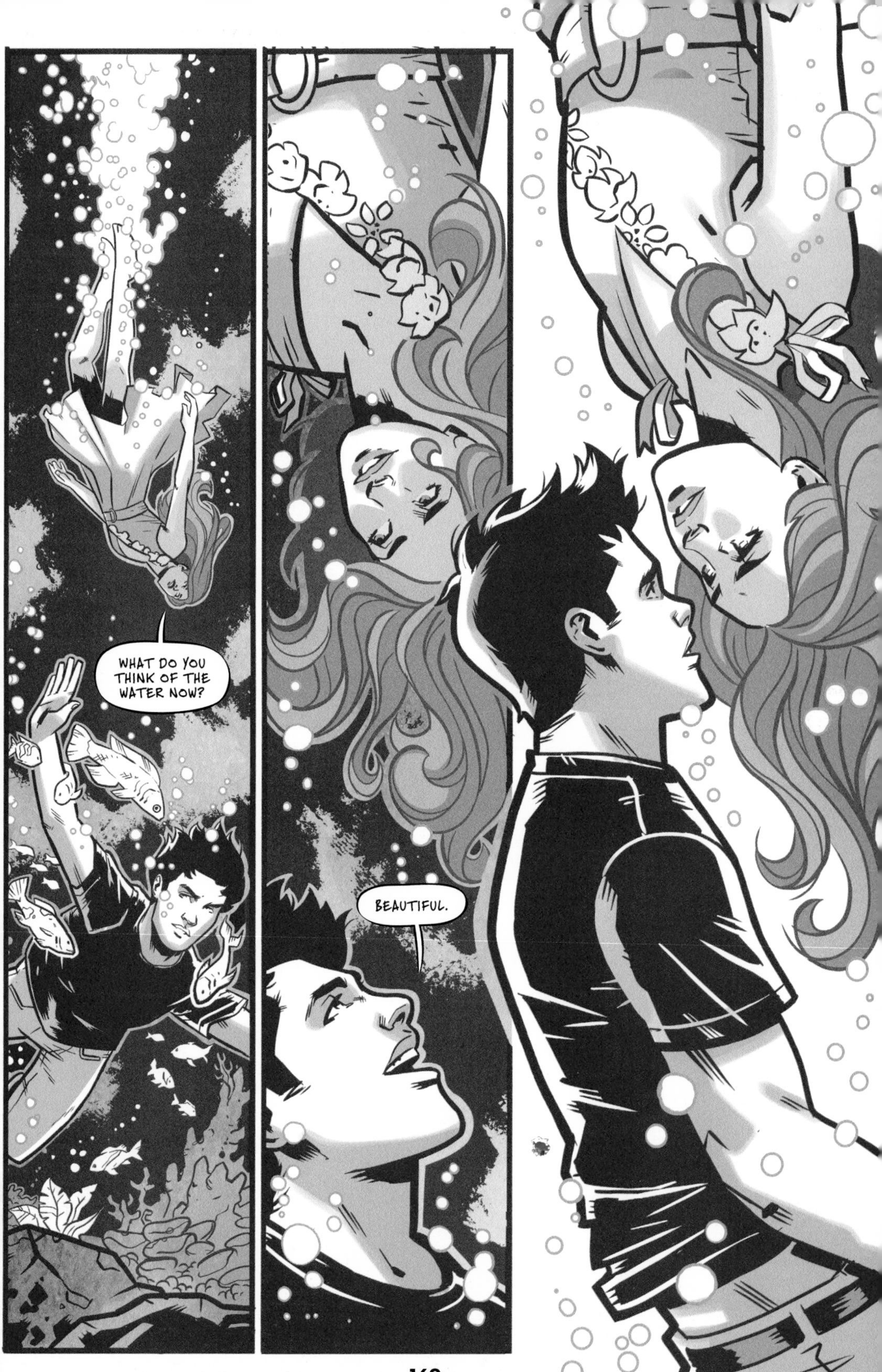
WHAT DO YOU THINK OF THE WATER NOW?
BEAUTIFUL.

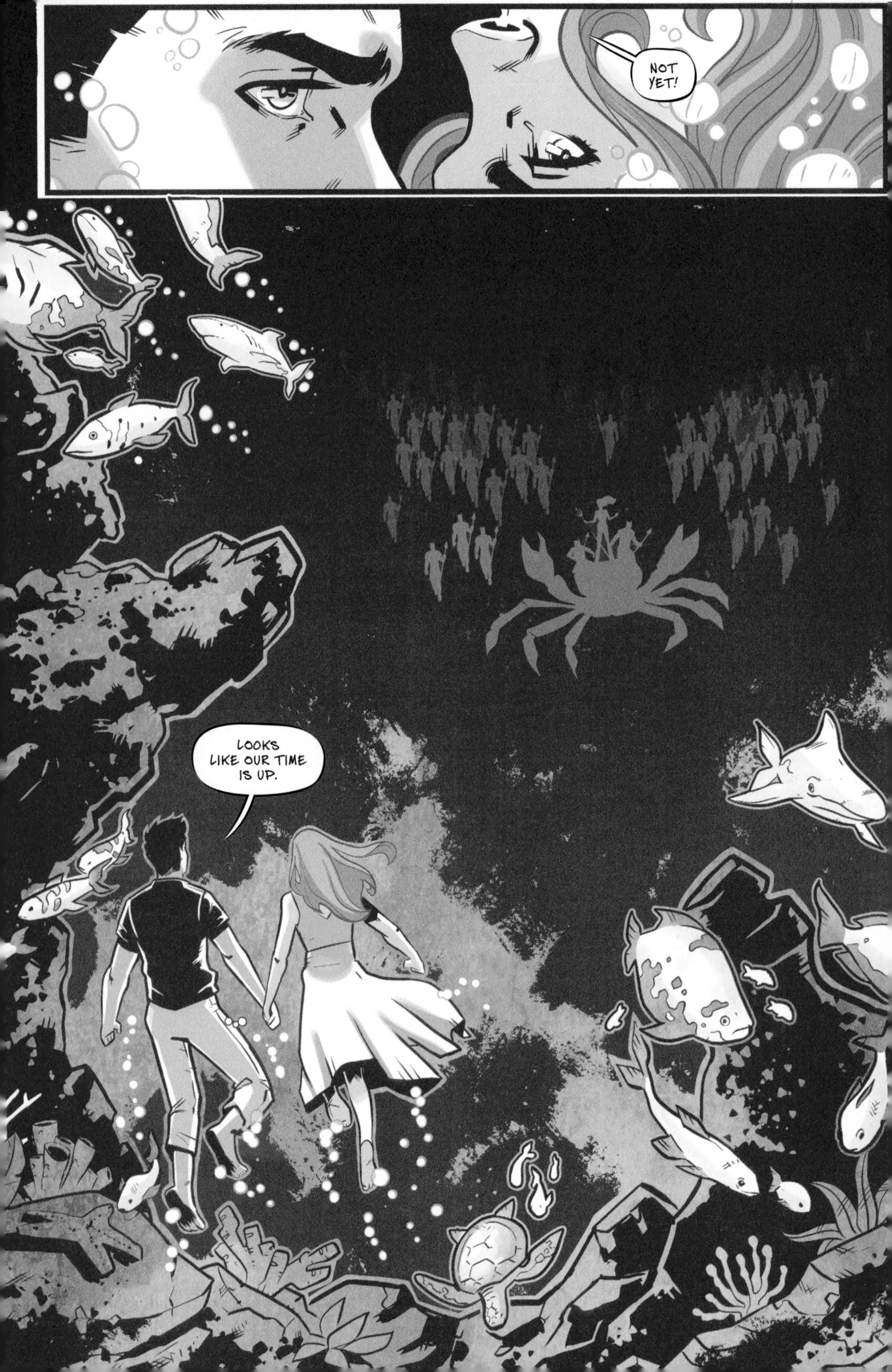
NOT YET!
LOOKS LIKE OUR TIME IS UP.

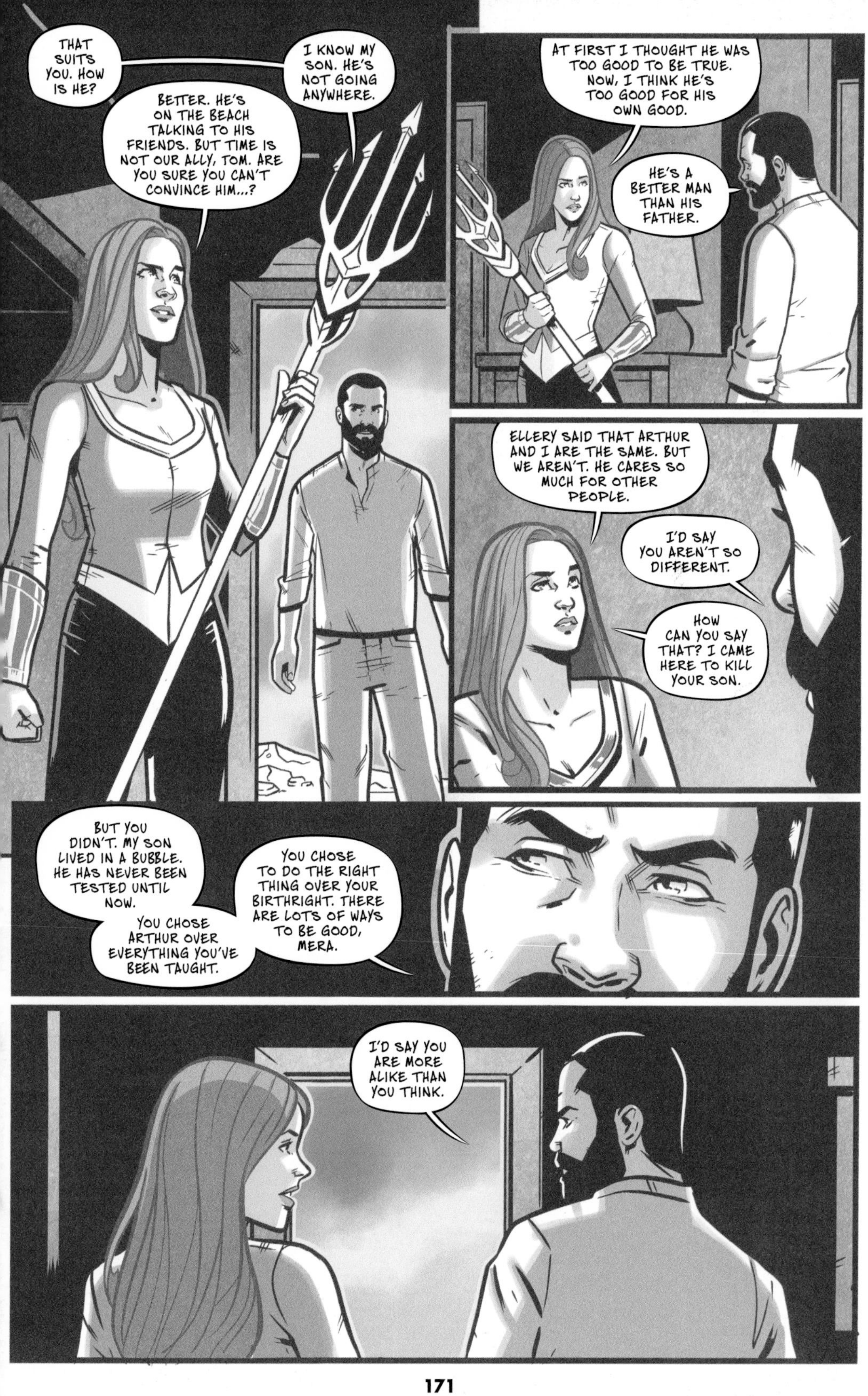
THAT SUITS YOU. HOW IS HE?
I KNOW MY SON. HE'S NOT GOING ANYWHERE.
BETTER. HE'S ON THE BEACH TALKING TO HIS FRIENDS. BUT TIME IS NOT OUR ALLY, TOM. ARE YOU SURE YOU CAN'T CONVINCE HIM...?
AT FIRST I THOUGHT HE WAS TOO GOOD TO BE TRUE. NOW, I THINK HE'S TOO GOOD FOR HIS OWN GOOD.
HE'S A BETTER MAN THAN HIS FATHER.
ELLERY SAID THAT ARTHUR AND I ARE THE SAME. BUT WE AREN'T. HE CARES SO MUCH FOR OTHER PEOPLE.
I'D SAY YOU AREN'T SO DIFFERENT.
HOW CAN YOU SAY THAT? I CAME HERE TO KILL YOUR SON.
BUT YOU DIDN'T. MY SON LIVED IN A BUBBLE. HE HAS NEVER BEEN TESTED UNTIL NOW.
YOU CHOSE ARTHUR OVER EVERYTHING YOU'VE BEEN TAUGHT.
YOU CHOSE TO DO THE RIGHT THING OVER YOUR BIRTHRIGHT. THERE ARE LOTS OF WAYS TO BE GOOD, MERA.
I'D SAY YOU ARE MORE ALIKE THAN YOU THINK.

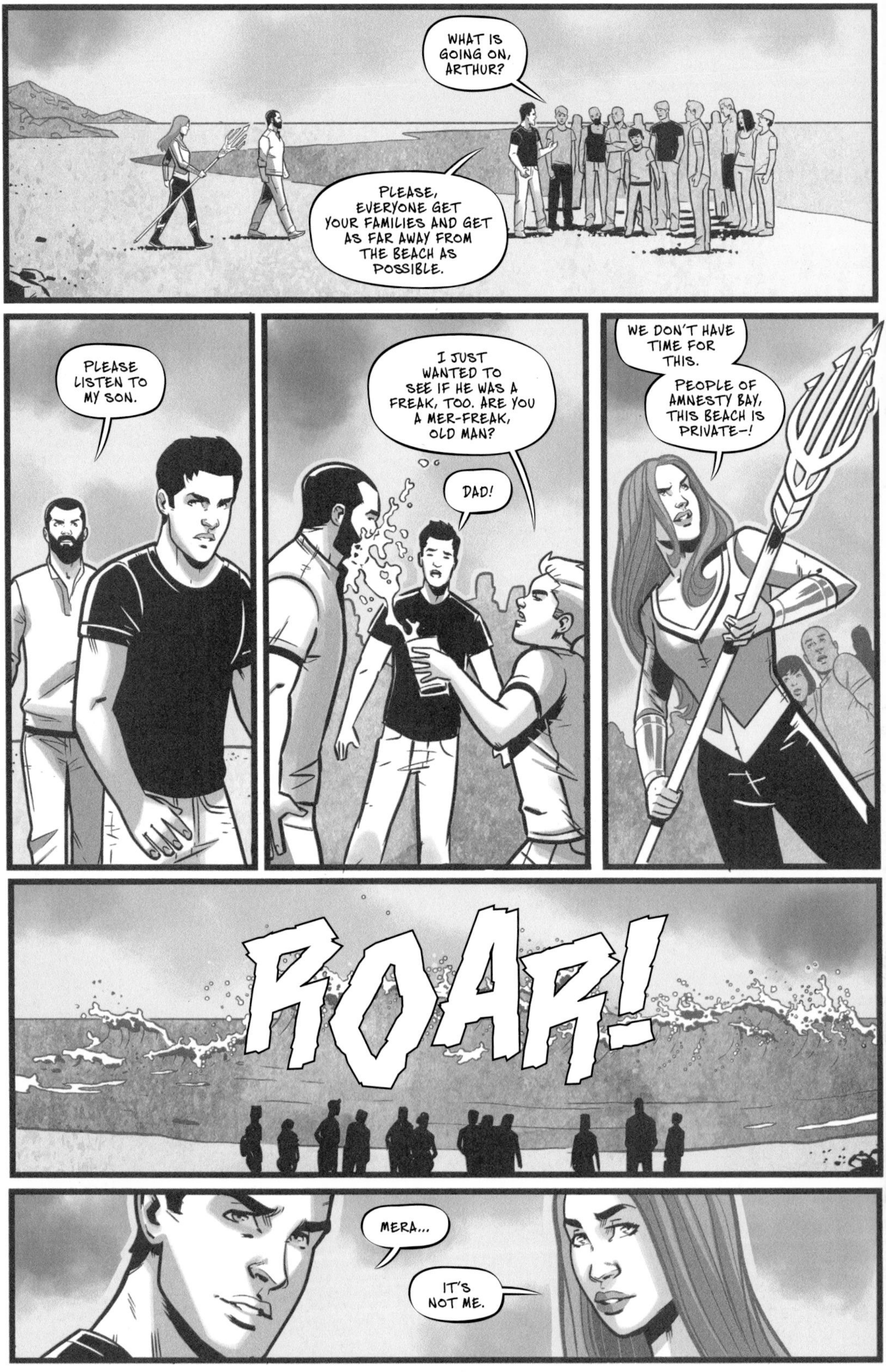
WHAT IS GOING ON, ARTHUR?
PLEASE, EVERYONE GET YOUR FAMILIES AND GET AS FAR AWAY FROM THE BEACH AS POSSIBLE.
PLEASE LISTEN TO MY SON.
I JUST WANTED TO SEE IF HE WAS A FREAK, TOO. ARE YOU A MER-FREAK, OLD MAN?
DAD!
WE DON'T HAVE TIME FOR THIS.
PEOPLE OF AMNESTY BAY, THIS BEACH IS PRIVATE--!
ROAR!
MERA...
IT'S NOT ME.

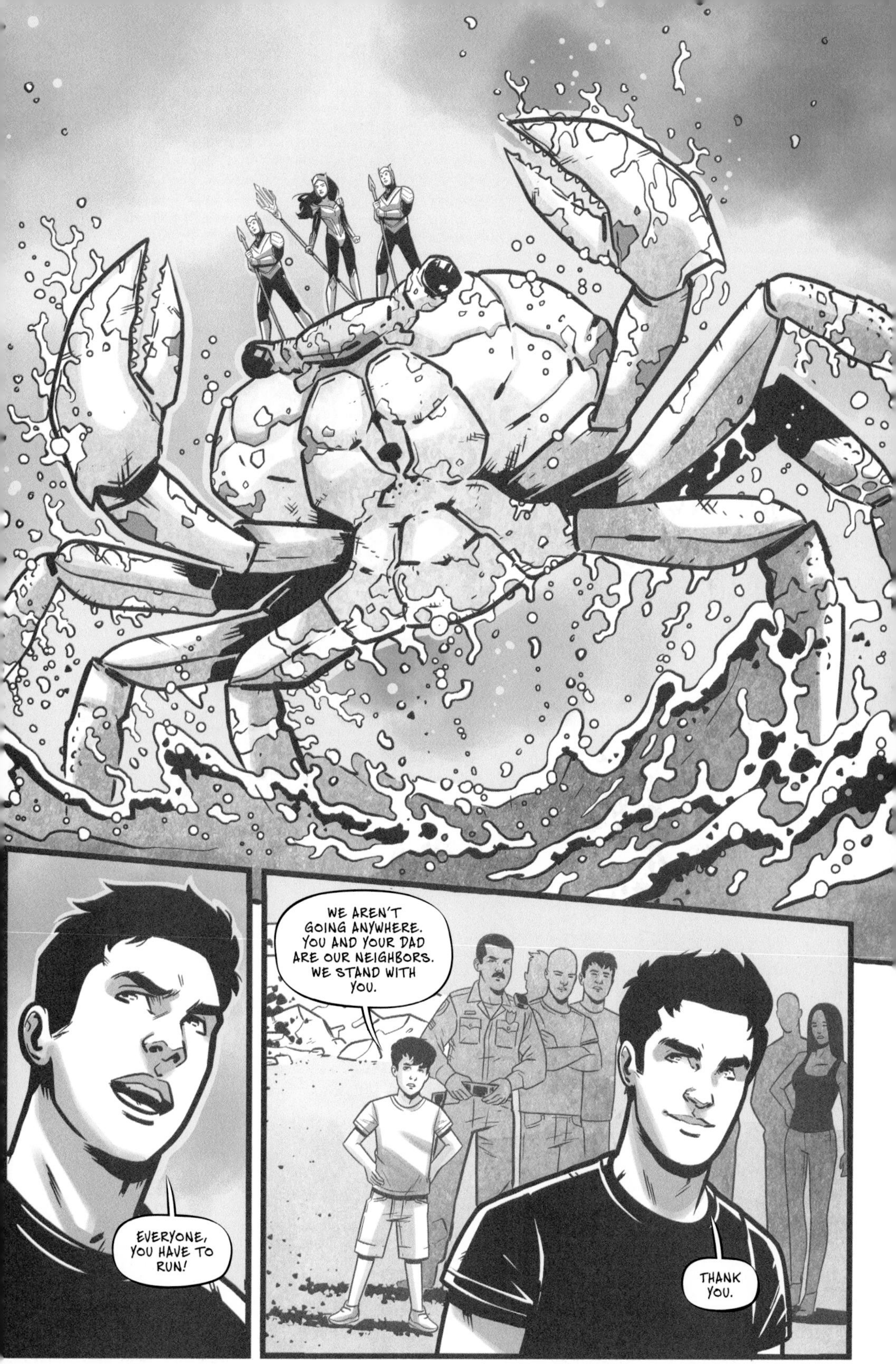
EVERYONE, YOU HAVE TO RUN!
WE AREN'T GOING ANYWHERE. YOU AND YOUR DAD ARE OUR NEIGHBORS. WE STAND WITH YOU.
THANK YOU.

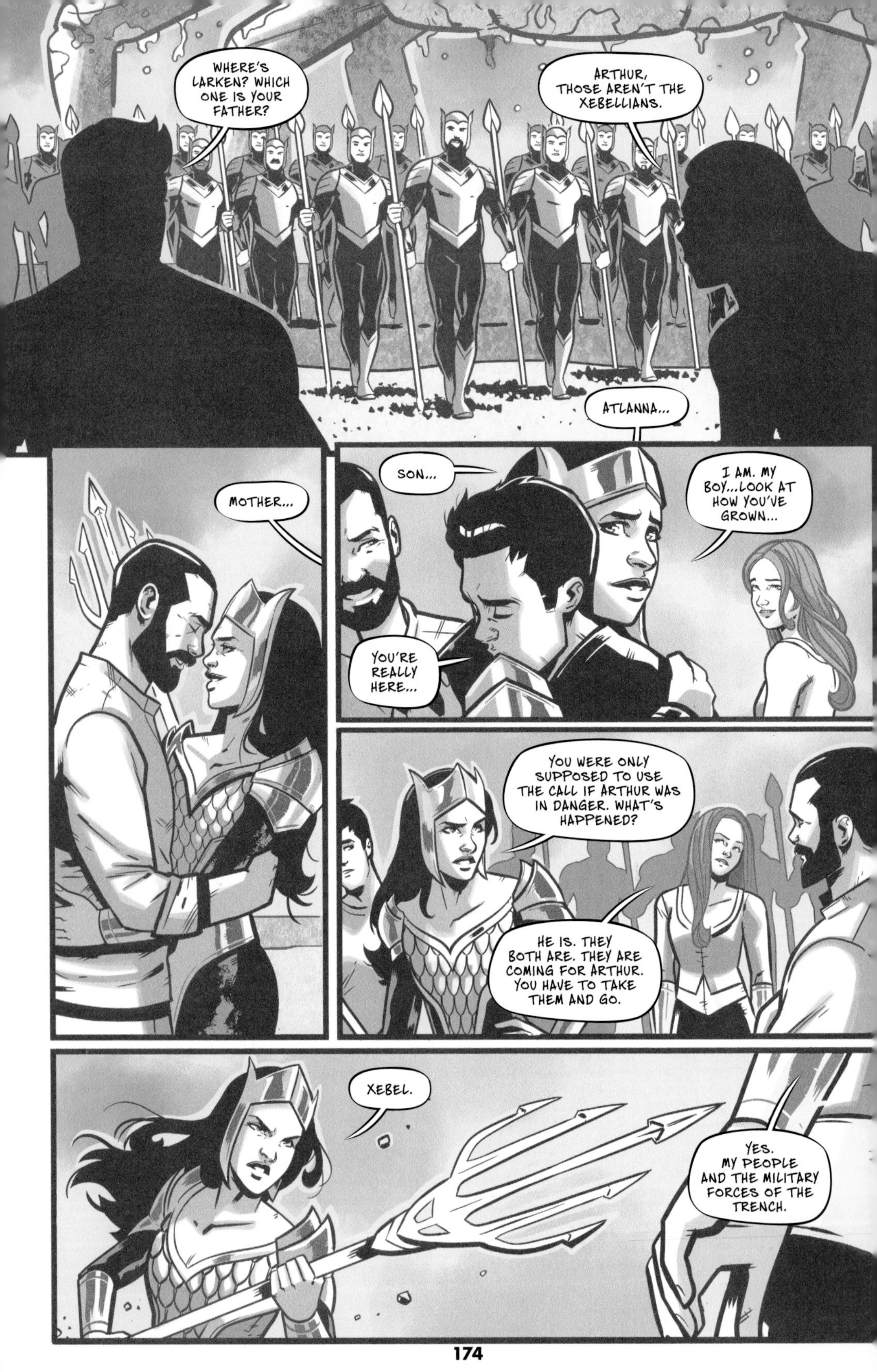
WHERE'S LARKEN? WHICH ONE IS YOUR FATHER?
ARTHUR, THOSE AREN'T THE XEBELLIANS.
ATLANNA...
MOTHER...
SON...
YOU'RE REALLY HERE...
I AM. MY BOY...LOOK AT HOW YOU'VE GROWN...
YOU WERE ONLY SUPPOSED TO USE THE CALL IF ARTHUR WAS IN DANGER. WHAT'S HAPPENED?
HE IS. THEY BOTH ARE. THEY ARE COMING FOR ARTHUR. YOU HAVE TO TAKE THEM AND GO.
XEBEL.
YES. MY PEOPLE AND THE MILITARY FORCES OF THE TRENCH.

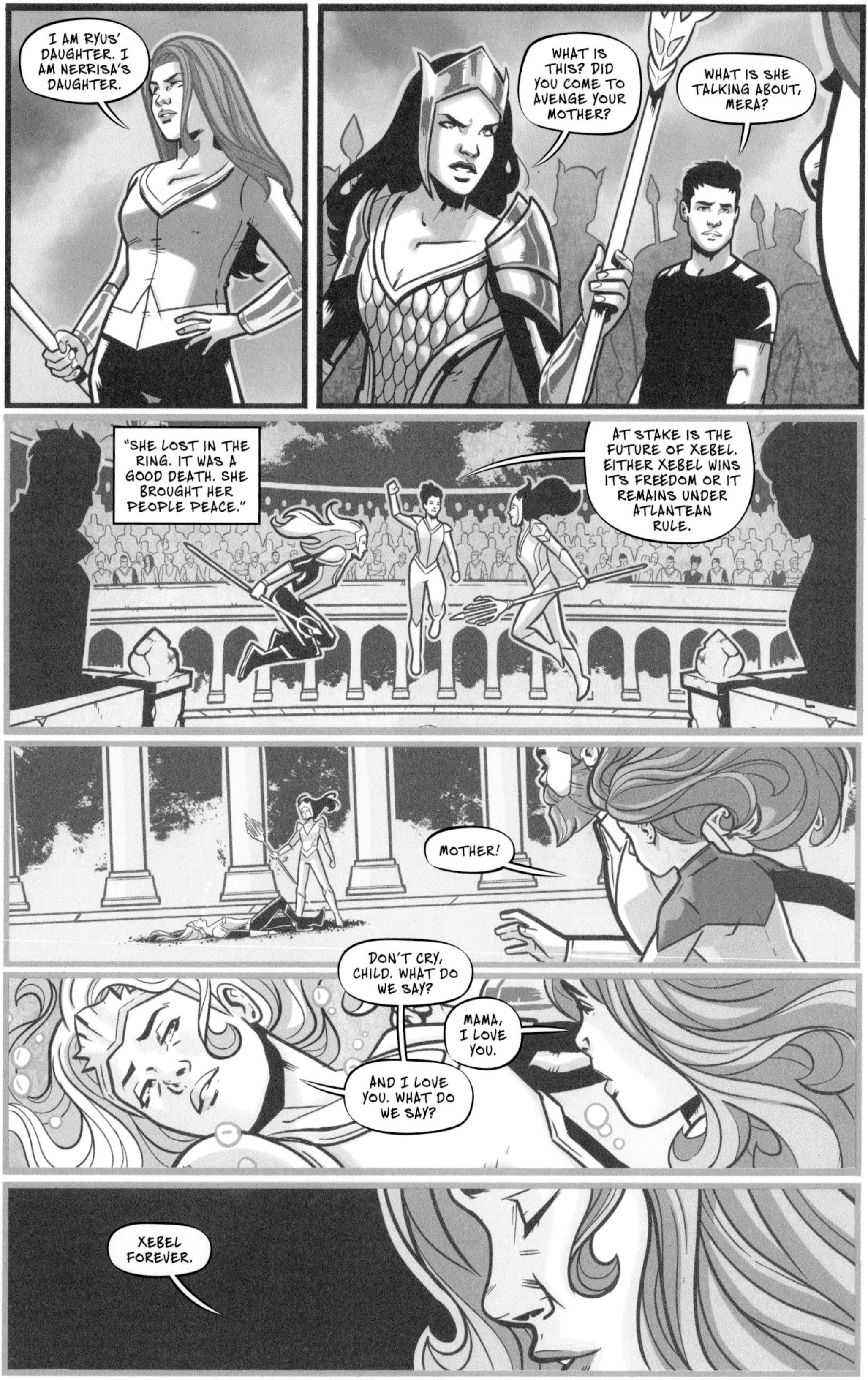
I AM RYUS' DAUGHTER. I AM NERRISA'S DAUGHTER.
WHAT IS THIS? DID YOU COME TO AVENGE YOUR MOTHER?
WHAT IS SHE TALKING ABOUT, MERA?
"SHE LOST IN THE RING. IT WAS A GOOD DEATH. SHE BROUGHT HER PEOPLE PEACE."
AT STAKE IS THE FUTURE OF XEBEL. EITHER XEBEL WINS ITS FREEDOM OR IT REMAINS UNDER ATLANTEAN RULE.
MOTHER!
DON'T CRY, CHILD. WHAT DO WE SAY?
MAMA, I LOVE YOU.
AND I LOVE YOU. WHAT DO WE SAY?
XEBEL FOREVER.

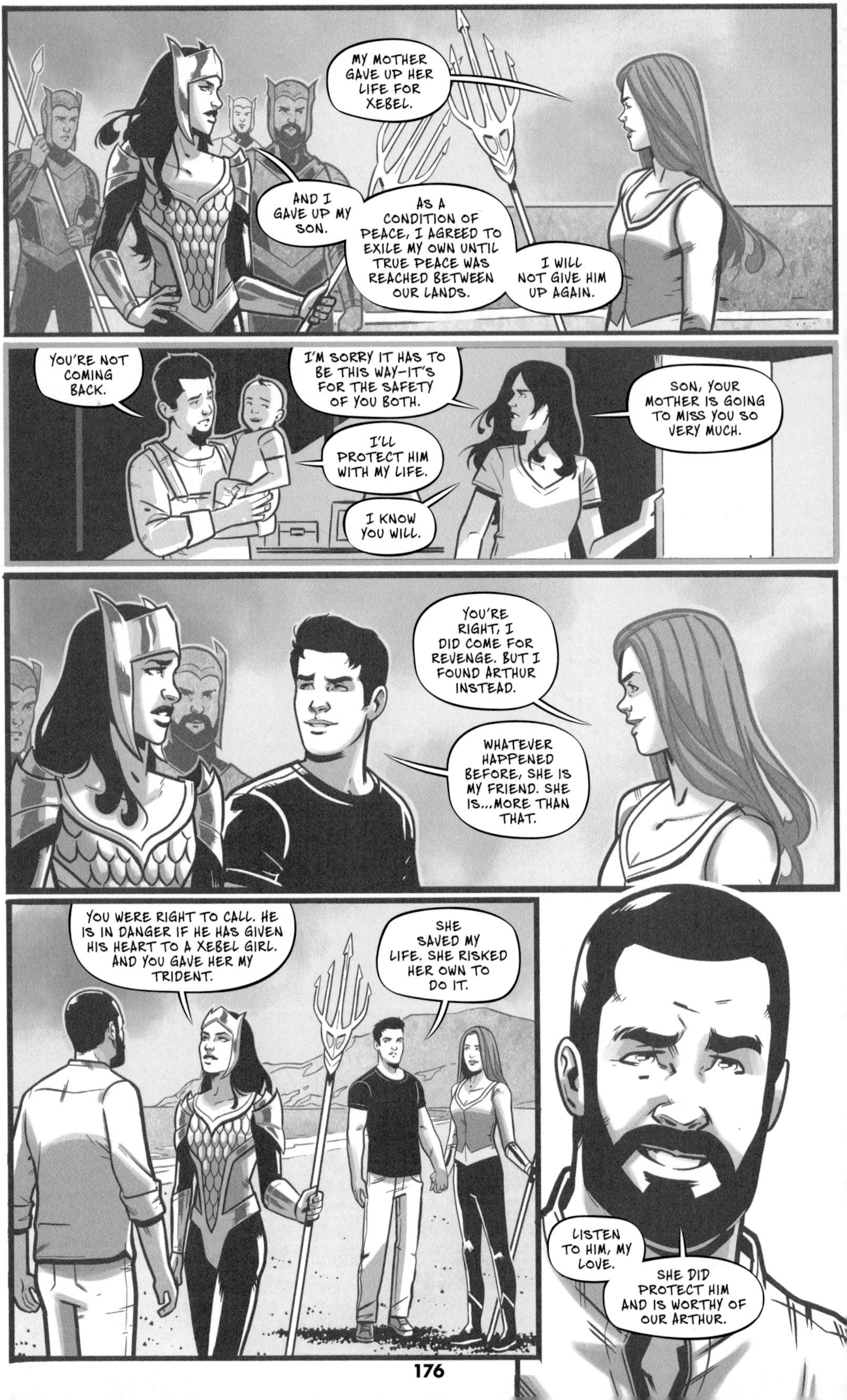
MY MOTHER GAVE UP HER LIFE FOR XEBEL.
AND I GAVE UP MY SON.
AS A CONDITION OF PEACE, I AGREED TO EXILE MY OWN UNTIL TRUE PEACE WAS REACHED BETWEEN OUR LANDS.
I WILL NOT GIVE HIM UP AGAIN.
YOU'RE NOT COMING BACK.
I'M SORRY IT HAS TO BE THIS WAY—IT'S FOR THE SAFETY OF YOU BOTH.
SON, YOUR MOTHER IS GOING TO MISS YOU SO VERY MUCH.
I'LL PROTECT HIM WITH MY LIFE.
I KNOW YOU WILL.
YOU'RE RIGHT, I DID COME FOR REVENGE. BUT I FOUND ARTHUR INSTEAD.
WHATEVER HAPPENED BEFORE, SHE IS MY FRIEND. SHE IS...MORE THAN THAT.
YOU WERE RIGHT TO CALL. HE IS IN DANGER IF HE HAS GIVEN HIS HEART TO A XEBEL GIRL. AND YOU GAVE HER MY TRIDENT.
SHE SAVED MY LIFE. SHE RISKED HER OWN TO DO IT.
LISTEN TO HIM, MY LOVE.
SHE DID PROTECT HIM AND IS WORTHY OF OUR ARTHUR.

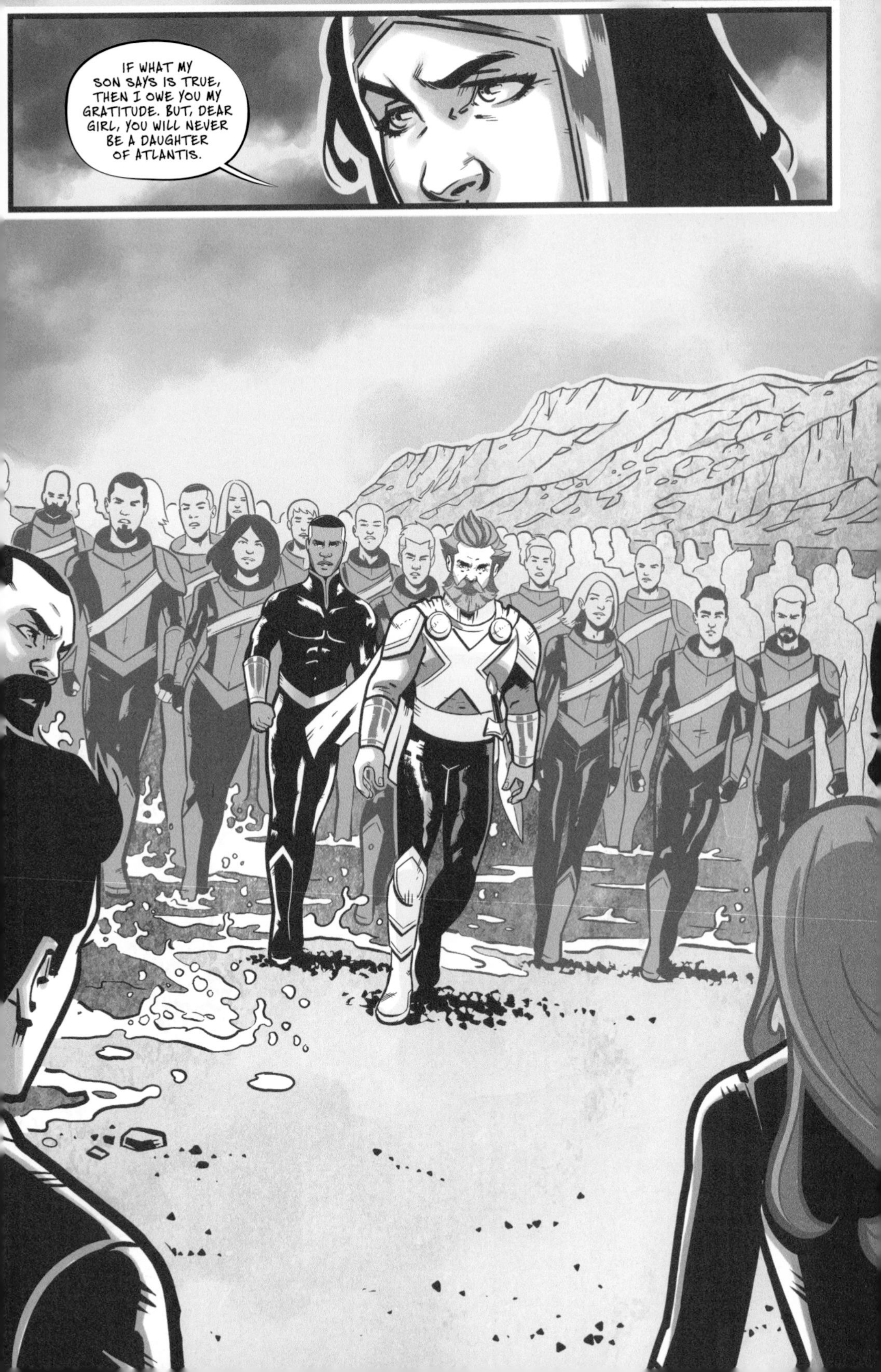
IF WHAT MY SON SAYS IS TRUE, THEN I OWE YOU MY GRATITUDE. BUT, DEAR GIRL, YOU WILL NEVER BE A DAUGHTER OF ATLANTIS.

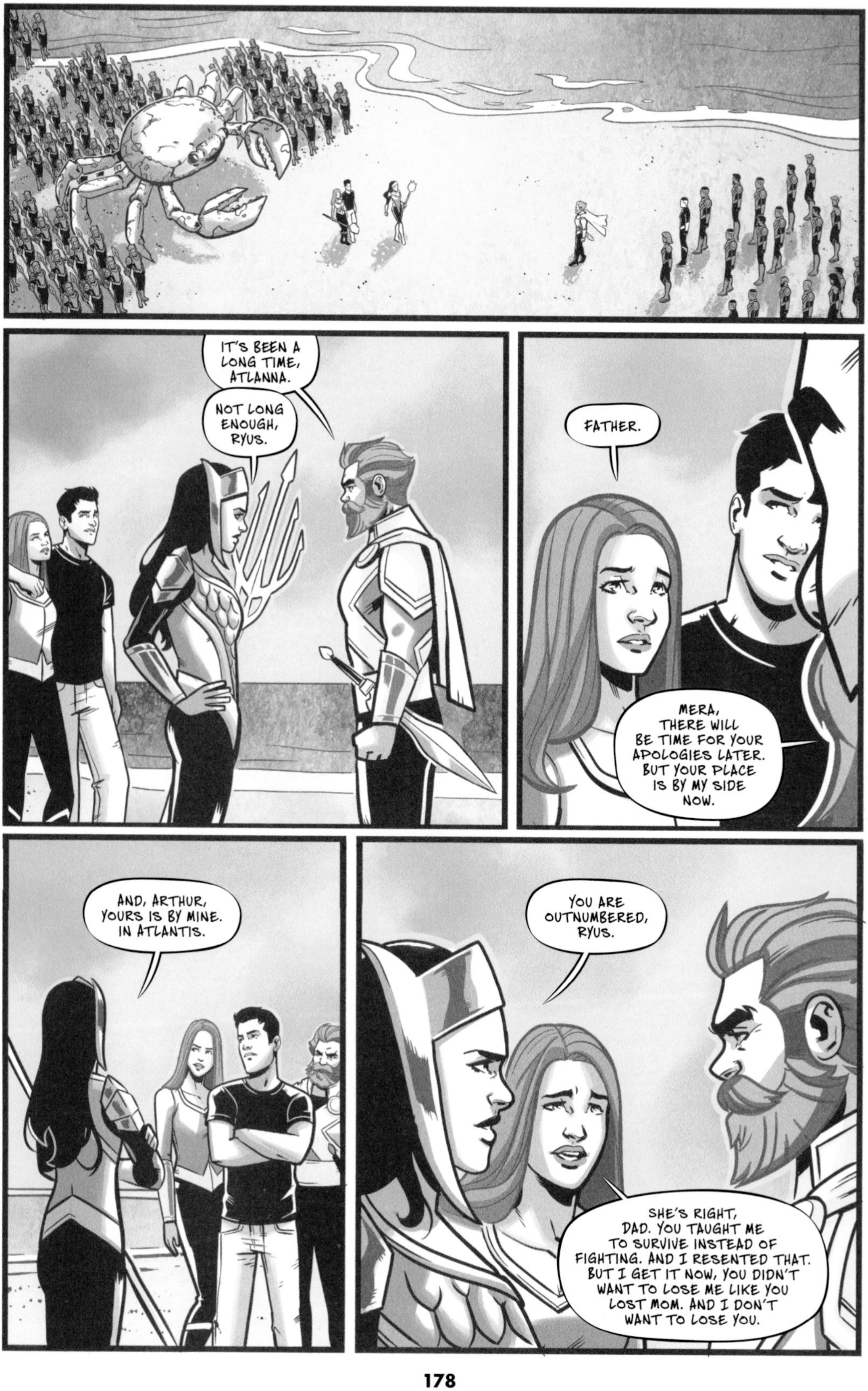
IT'S BEEN A LONG TIME, ATLANNA.
NOT LONG ENOUGH, RYUS.
FATHER.
MERA, THERE WILL BE TIME FOR YOUR APOLOGIES LATER. BUT YOUR PLACE IS BY MY SIDE NOW.
AND, ARTHUR, YOURS IS BY MINE. IN ATLANTIS.
YOU ARE OUTNUMBERED, RYUS.
SHE'S RIGHT, DAD. YOU TAUGHT ME TO SURVIVE INSTEAD OF FIGHTING. AND I RESENTED THAT. BUT I GET IT NOW, YOU DIDN'T WANT TO LOSE ME LIKE YOU LOST MOM. AND I DON'T WANT TO LOSE YOU.

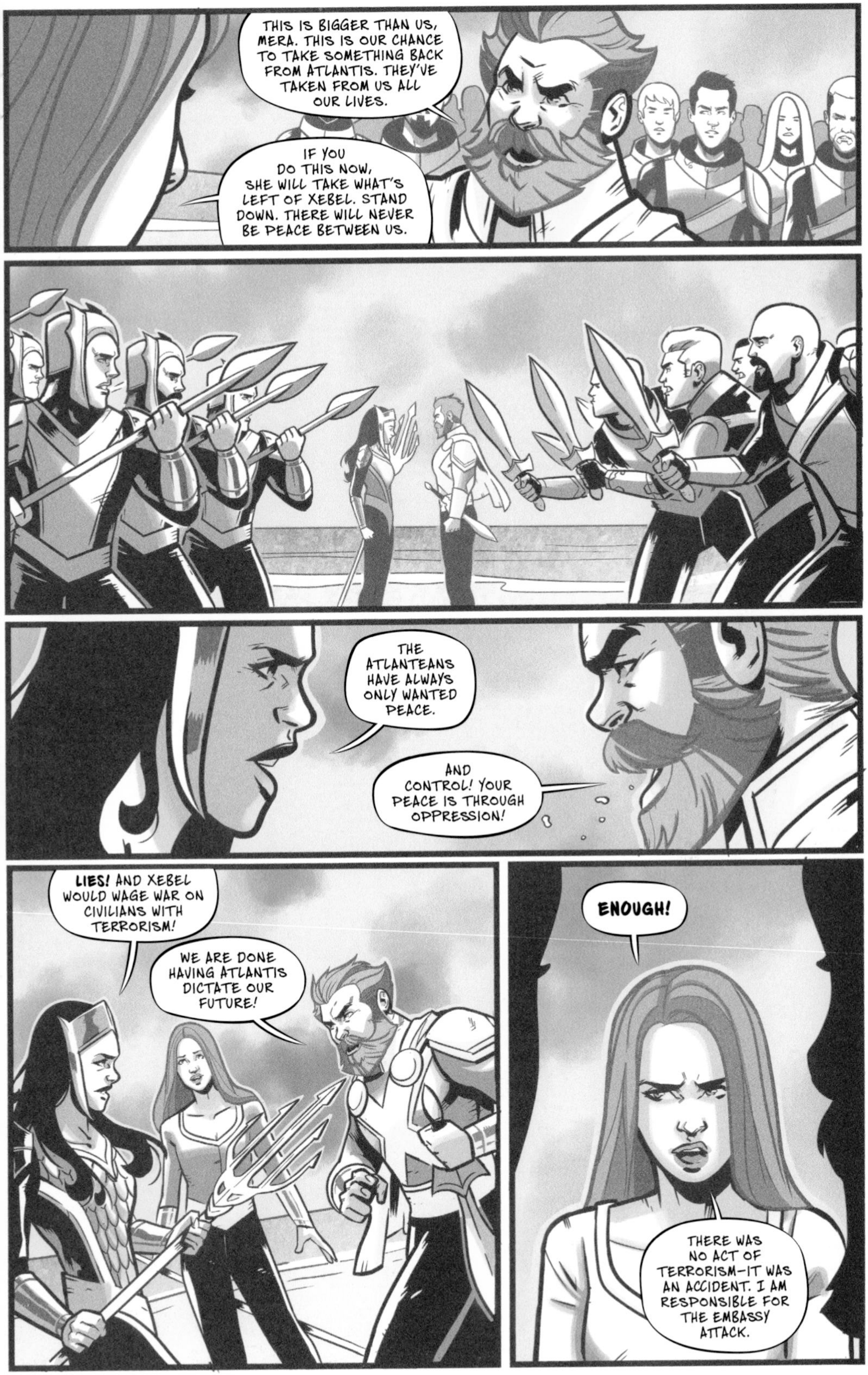
THIS IS BIGGER THAN US, MERA. THIS IS OUR CHANCE TO TAKE SOMETHING BACK FROM ATLANTIS. THEY'VE TAKEN FROM US ALL OUR LIVES.
IF YOU DO THIS NOW, SHE WILL TAKE WHAT'S LEFT OF XEBEL. STAND DOWN. THERE WILL NEVER BE PEACE BETWEEN US.
THE ATLANTEANS HAVE ALWAYS ONLY WANTED PEACE.
AND CONTROL! YOUR PEACE IS THROUGH OPPRESSION!
LIES! AND XEBEL WOULD WAGE WAR ON CIVILIANS WITH TERRORISM!
WE ARE DONE HAVING ATLANTIS DICTATE OUR FUTURE!
ENOUGH!
THERE WAS NO ACT OF TERRORISM—IT WAS AN ACCIDENT. I AM RESPONSIBLE FOR THE EMBASSY ATTACK.

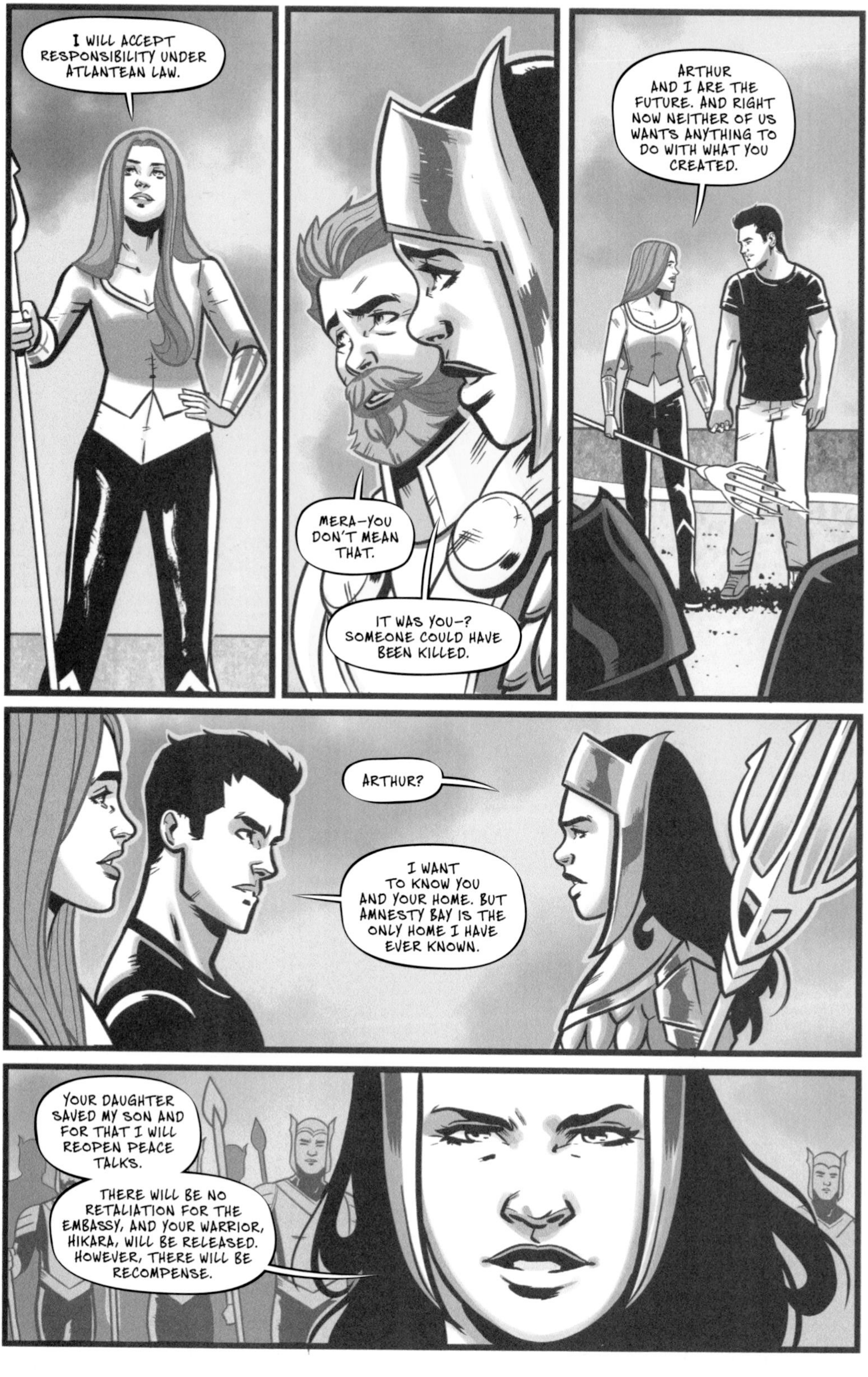
I WILL ACCEPT RESPONSIBILITY UNDER ATLANTEAN LAW.
MERA–YOU DON'T MEAN THAT.
IT WAS YOU–? SOMEONE COULD HAVE BEEN KILLED.
ARTHUR AND I ARE THE FUTURE. AND RIGHT NOW NEITHER OF US WANTS ANYTHING TO DO WITH WHAT YOU CREATED.
ARTHUR?
I WANT TO KNOW YOU AND YOUR HOME. BUT AMNESTY BAY IS THE ONLY HOME I HAVE EVER KNOWN.
YOUR DAUGHTER SAVED MY SON AND FOR THAT I WILL REOPEN PEACE TALKS.
THERE WILL BE NO RETALIATION FOR THE EMBASSY, AND YOUR WARRIOR, HIKARA, WILL BE RELEASED. HOWEVER, THERE WILL BE RECOMPENSE.

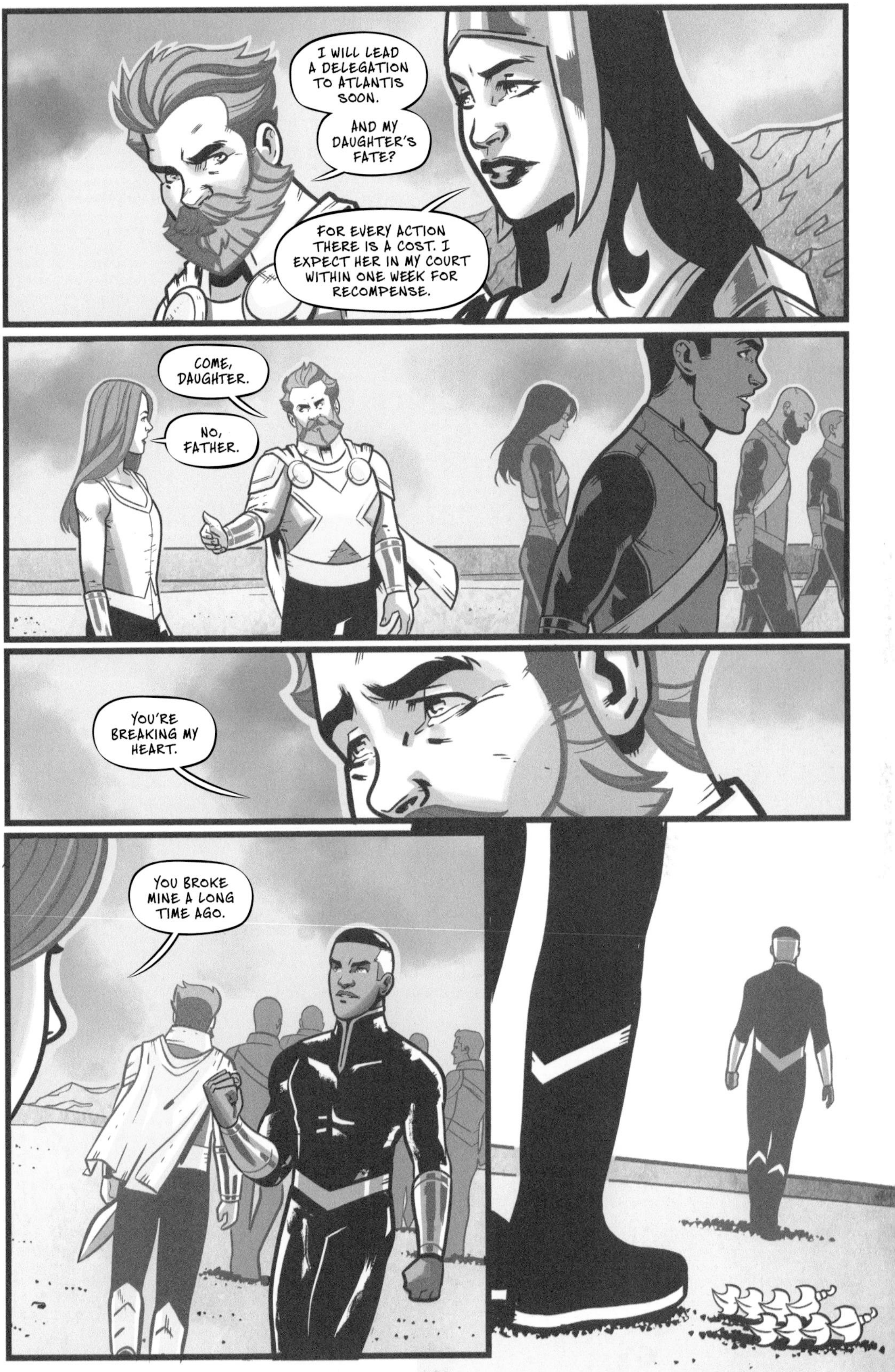
I WILL LEAD A DELEGATION TO ATLANTIS SOON.
AND MY DAUGHTER'S FATE?
FOR EVERY ACTION THERE IS A COST. I EXPECT HER IN MY COURT WITHIN ONE WEEK FOR RECOMPENSE.
COME, DAUGHTER.
NO, FATHER.
YOU'RE BREAKING MY HEART.
YOU BROKE MINE A LONG TIME AGO.

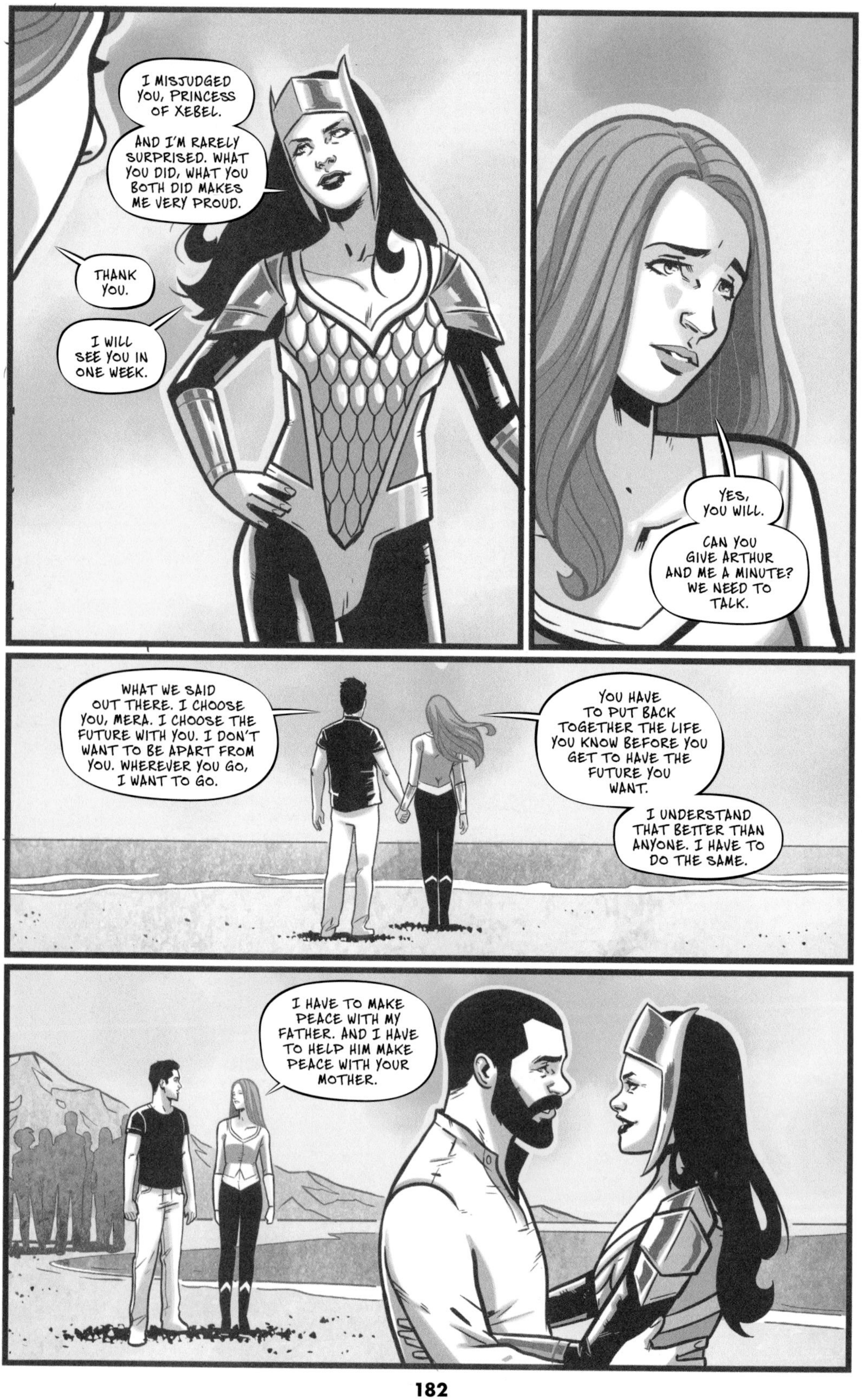
I MISJUDGED YOU, PRINCESS OF XEBEL.
AND I'M RARELY SURPRISED. WHAT YOU DID, WHAT YOU BOTH DID MAKES ME VERY PROUD.
THANK YOU.
I WILL SEE YOU IN ONE WEEK.
YES, YOU WILL.
CAN YOU GIVE ARTHUR AND ME A MINUTE? WE NEED TO TALK.
WHAT WE SAID OUT THERE. I CHOOSE YOU, MERA. I CHOOSE THE FUTURE WITH YOU. I DON'T WANT TO BE APART FROM YOU. WHEREVER YOU GO, I WANT TO GO.
YOU HAVE TO PUT BACK TOGETHER THE LIFE YOU KNOW BEFORE YOU GET TO HAVE THE FUTURE YOU WANT.
I UNDERSTAND THAT BETTER THAN ANYONE. I HAVE TO DO THE SAME.
I HAVE TO MAKE PEACE WITH MY FATHER. AND I HAVE TO HELP HIM MAKE PEACE WITH YOUR MOTHER.

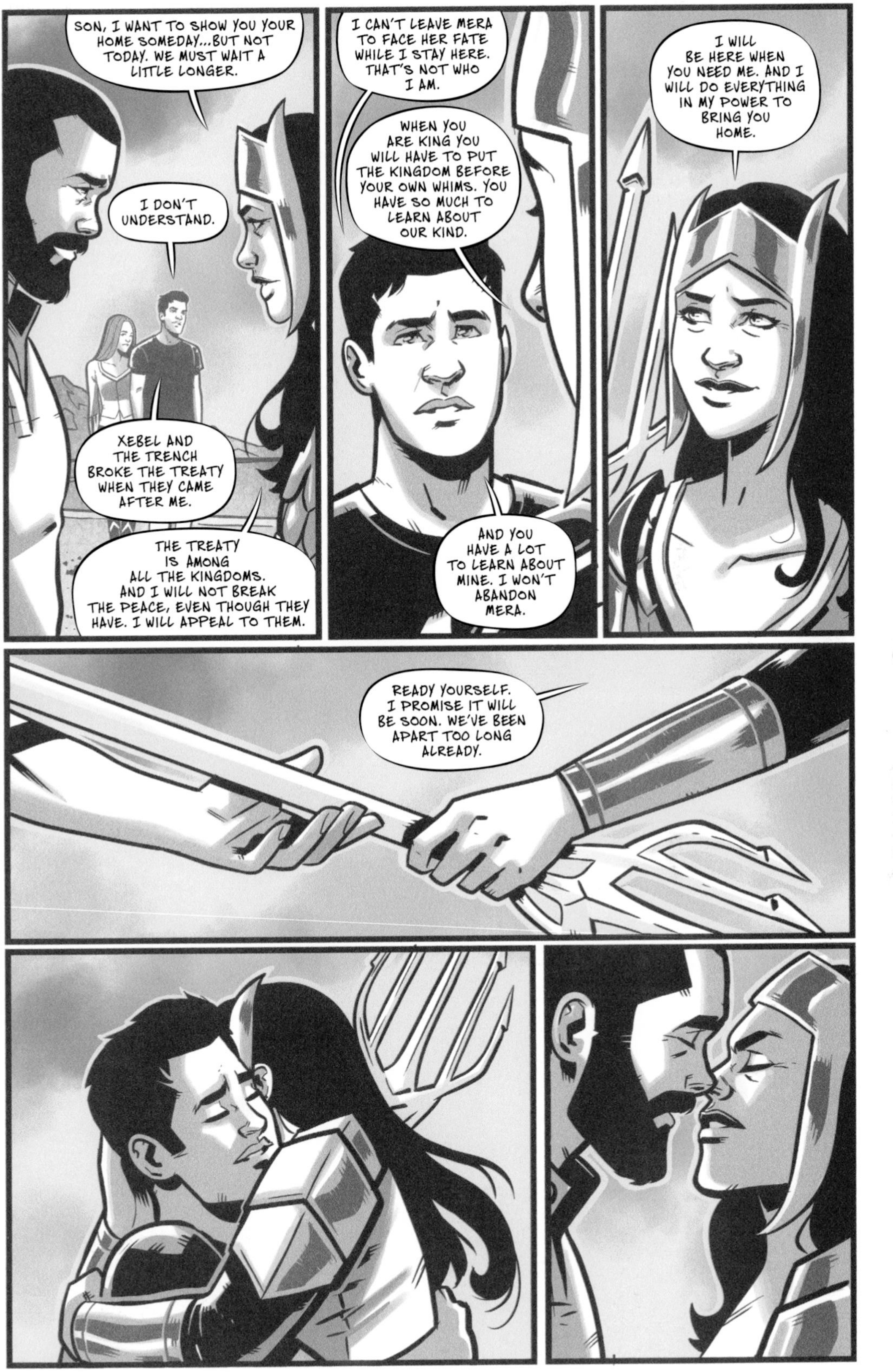
SON, I WANT TO SHOW YOU YOUR HOME SOMEDAY...BUT NOT TODAY. WE MUST WAIT A LITTLE LONGER.
I DON'T UNDERSTAND.
XEBEL AND THE TRENCH BROKE THE TREATY WHEN THEY CAME AFTER ME.
THE TREATY IS AMONG ALL THE KINGDOMS. AND I WILL NOT BREAK THE PEACE, EVEN THOUGH THEY HAVE. I WILL APPEAL TO THEM.
I CAN'T LEAVE MERA TO FACE HER FATE WHILE I STAY HERE. THAT'S NOT WHO I AM.
WHEN YOU ARE KING YOU WILL HAVE TO PUT THE KINGDOM BEFORE YOUR OWN WHIMS. YOU HAVE SO MUCH TO LEARN ABOUT OUR KIND.
AND YOU HAVE A LOT TO LEARN ABOUT MINE. I WON'T ABANDON MERA.
I WILL BE HERE WHEN YOU NEED ME. AND I WILL DO EVERYTHING IN MY POWER TO BRING YOU HOME.
READY YOURSELF. I PROMISE IT WILL BE SOON. WE'VE BEEN APART TOO LONG ALREADY.

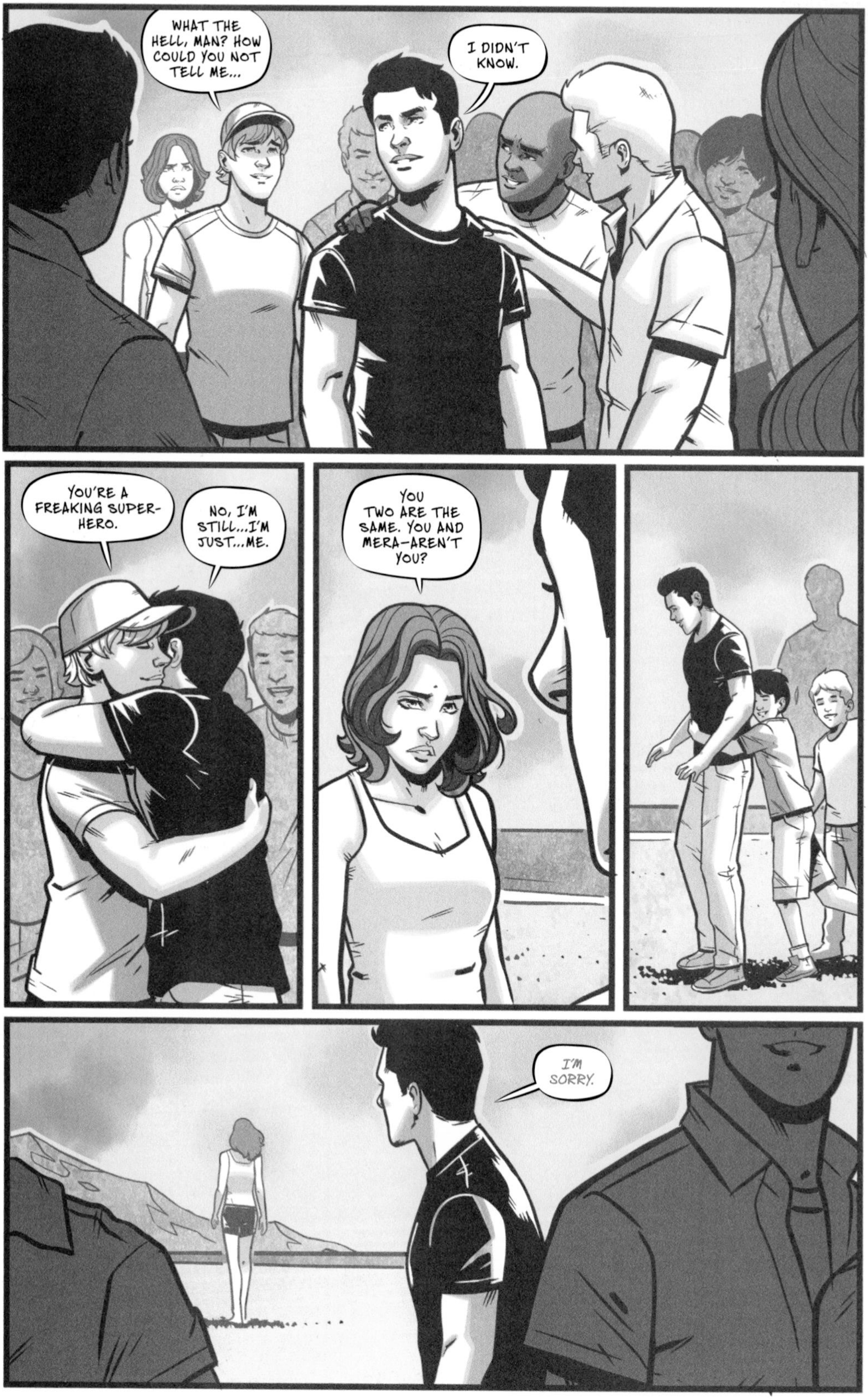
WHAT THE HELL, MAN? HOW COULD YOU NOT TELL ME...
I DIDN'T KNOW.
YOU'RE A FREAKING SUPER-HERO.
NO, I'M STILL...I'M JUST...ME.
YOU TWO ARE THE SAME. YOU AND MERA--AREN'T YOU?
I'M SORRY.

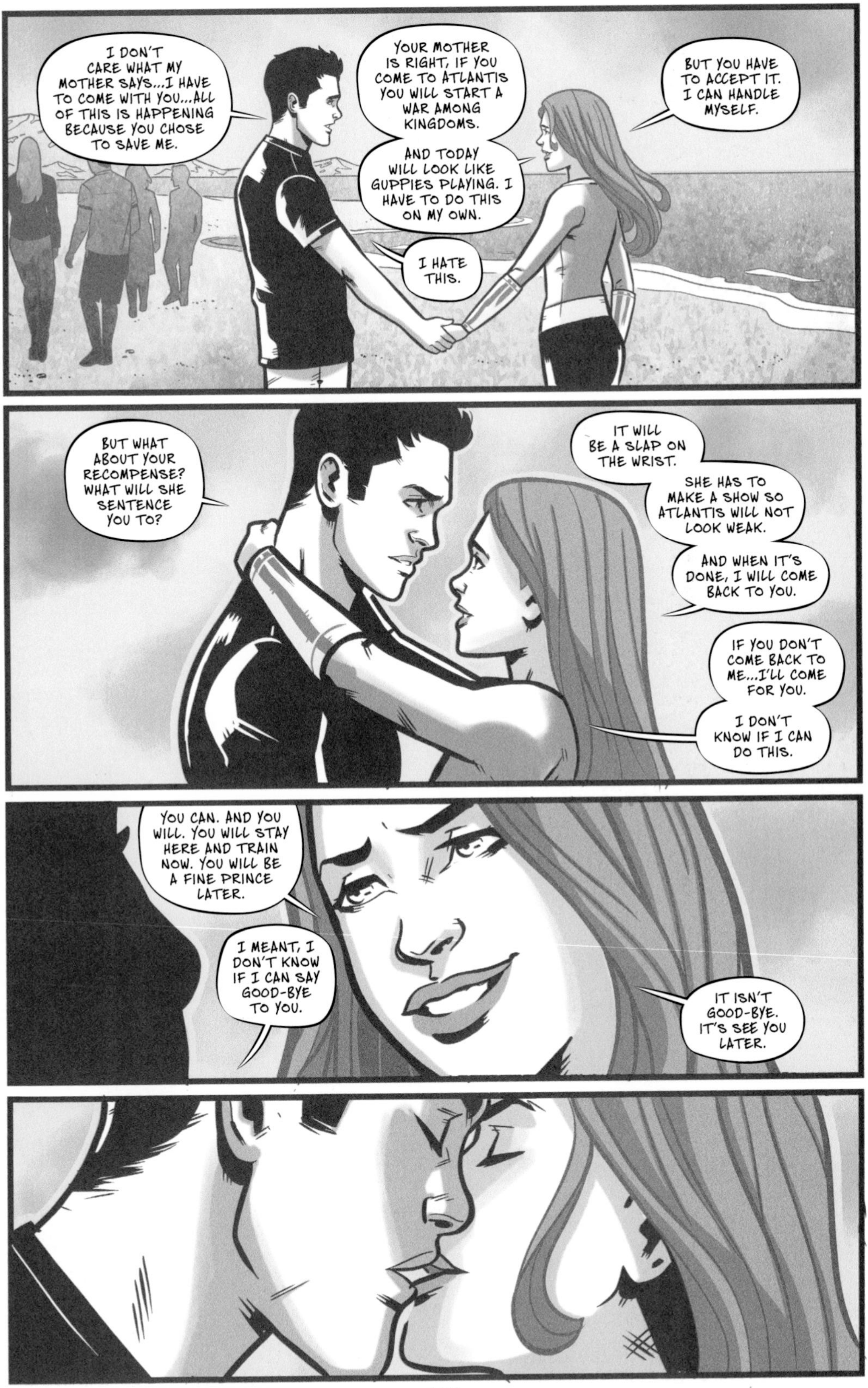
I DON'T CARE WHAT MY MOTHER SAYS...I HAVE TO COME WITH YOU...ALL OF THIS IS HAPPENING BECAUSE YOU CHOSE TO SAVE ME.
YOUR MOTHER IS RIGHT, IF YOU COME TO ATLANTIS YOU WILL START A WAR AMONG KINGDOMS.
AND TODAY WILL LOOK LIKE GUPPIES PLAYING. I HAVE TO DO THIS ON MY OWN.
I HATE THIS.
BUT YOU HAVE TO ACCEPT IT. I CAN HANDLE MYSELF.
BUT WHAT ABOUT YOUR RECOMPENSE? WHAT WILL SHE SENTENCE YOU TO?
IT WILL BE A SLAP ON THE WRIST.
SHE HAS TO MAKE A SHOW SO ATLANTIS WILL NOT LOOK WEAK.
AND WHEN IT'S DONE, I WILL COME BACK TO YOU.
IF YOU DON'T COME BACK TO ME...I'LL COME FOR YOU.
I DON'T KNOW IF I CAN DO THIS.
YOU CAN. AND YOU WILL. YOU WILL STAY HERE AND TRAIN NOW. YOU WILL BE A FINE PRINCE LATER.
I MEANT, I DON'T KNOW IF I CAN SAY GOOD-BYE TO YOU.
IT ISN'T GOOD-BYE. IT'S SEE YOU LATER.

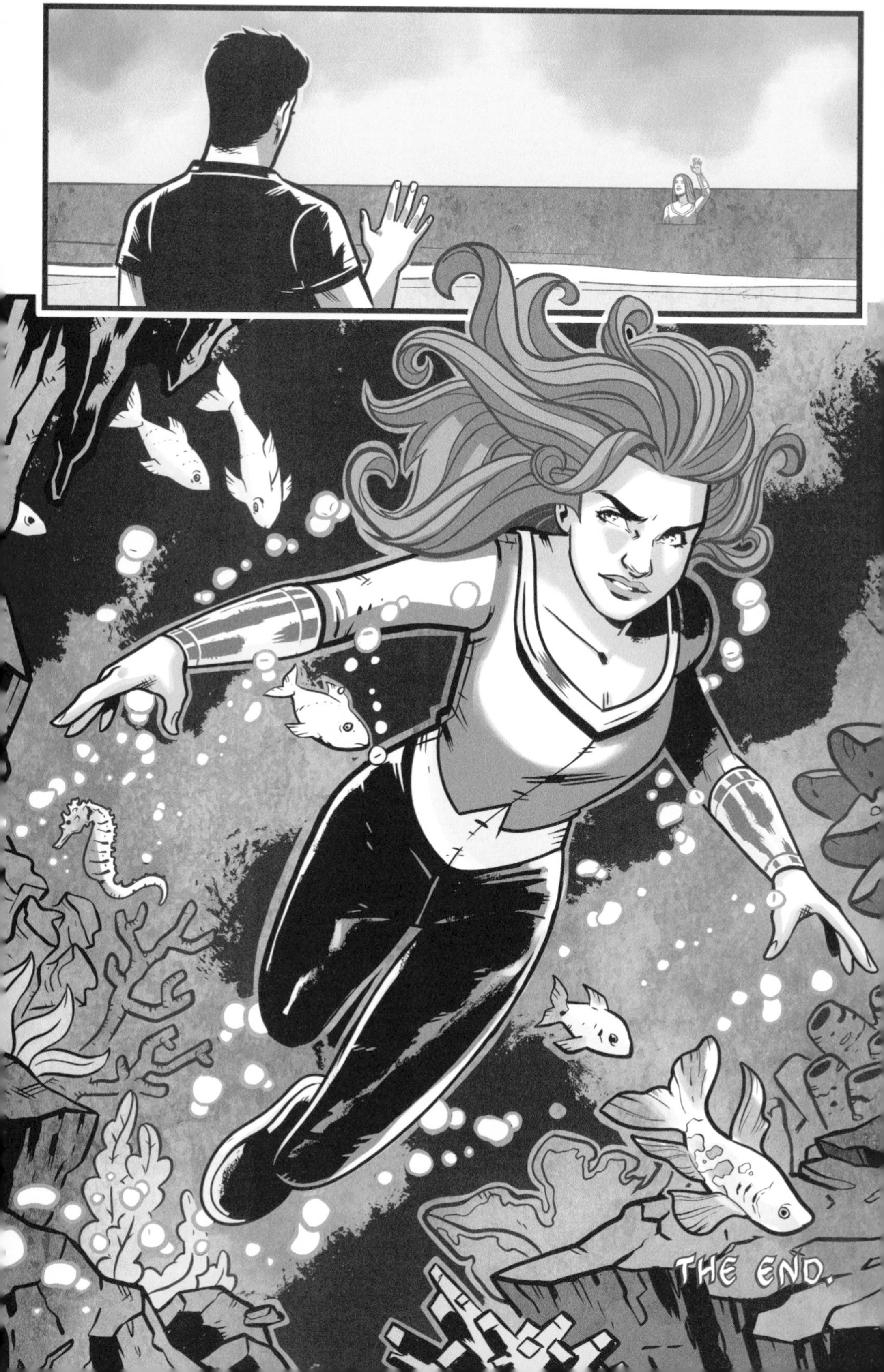
THE END.

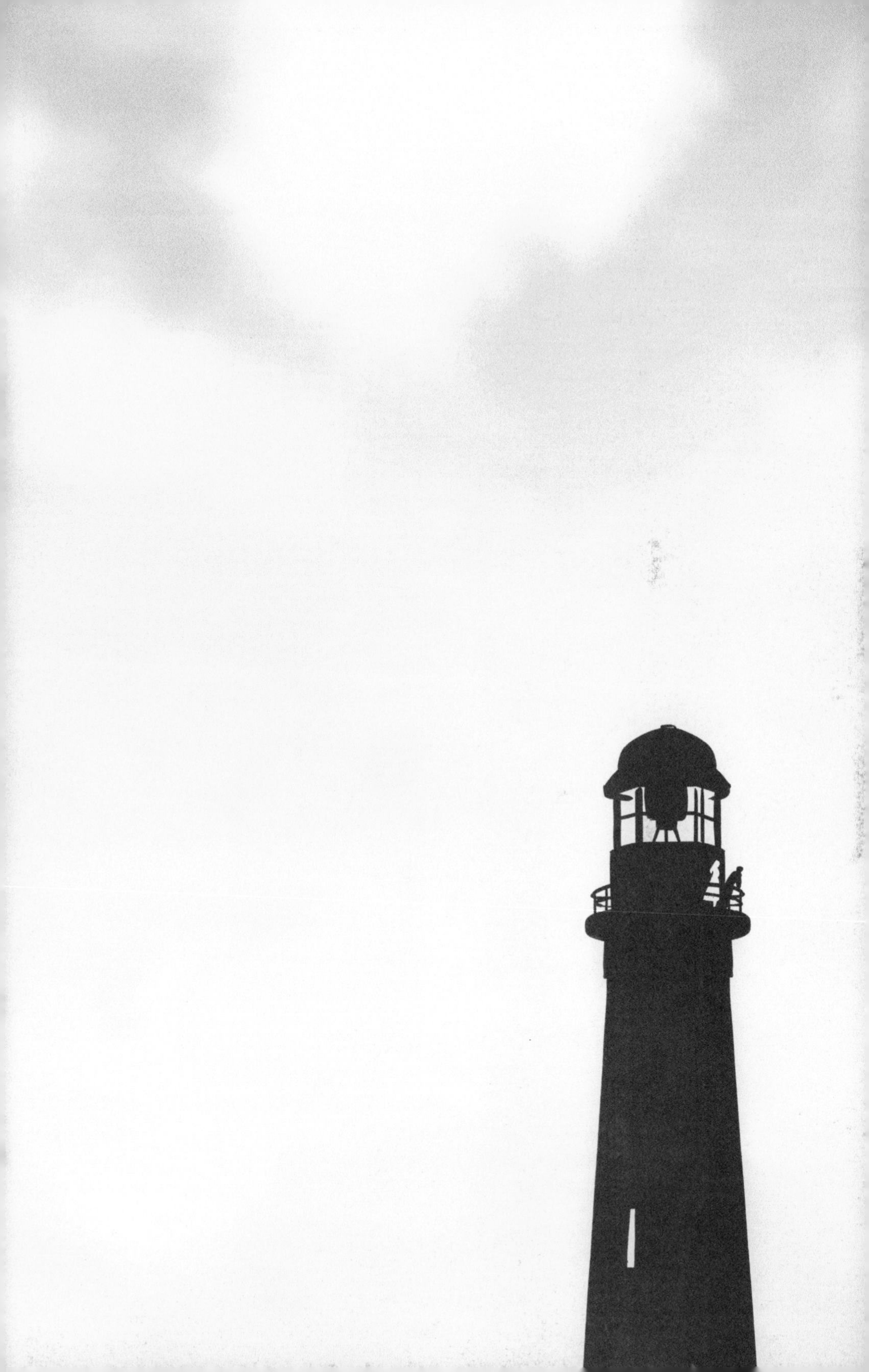

danielle paige

DANIELLE PAIGE *is the* New York Times *bestselling author of the Dorothy Must Die series and the Stealing Snow series. In addition to writing young adult books, she works in the television industry, where she's received a Writers Guild of America Award and was nominated for several Daytime Emmys. She is a graduate of Columbia University and currently lives in New York City.*

stephen byrne

STEPHEN BYRNE *was born in Dublin, Ireland, where he studied at the Irish School of Animation. He has worked in Ireland and the United States in the fields of animation, TV advertising, satirical newspaper cartoons, and video games. He now lives in London, where he works on his true passion, comics.*

MERA: TIDEBREAKER

concept sketches by Stephen Byrne

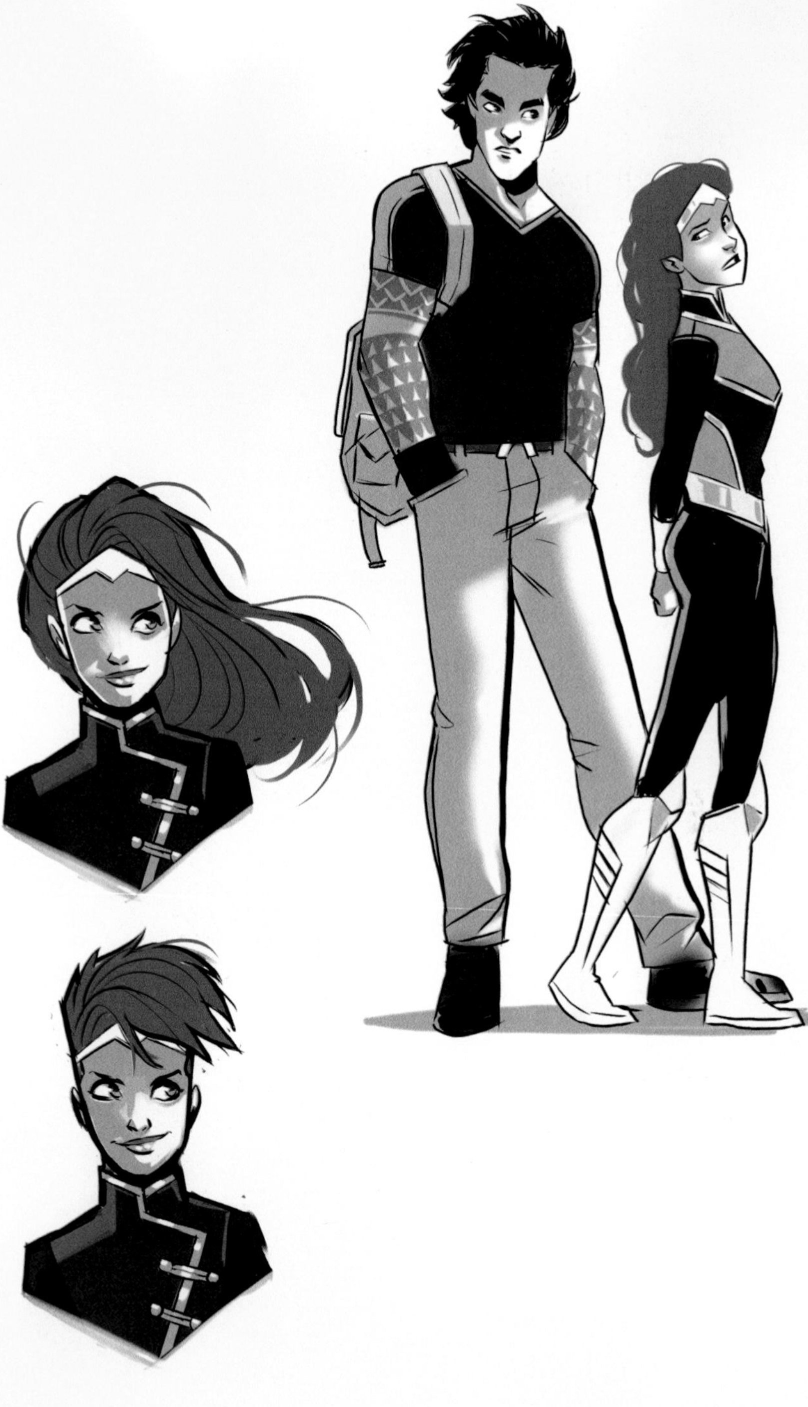

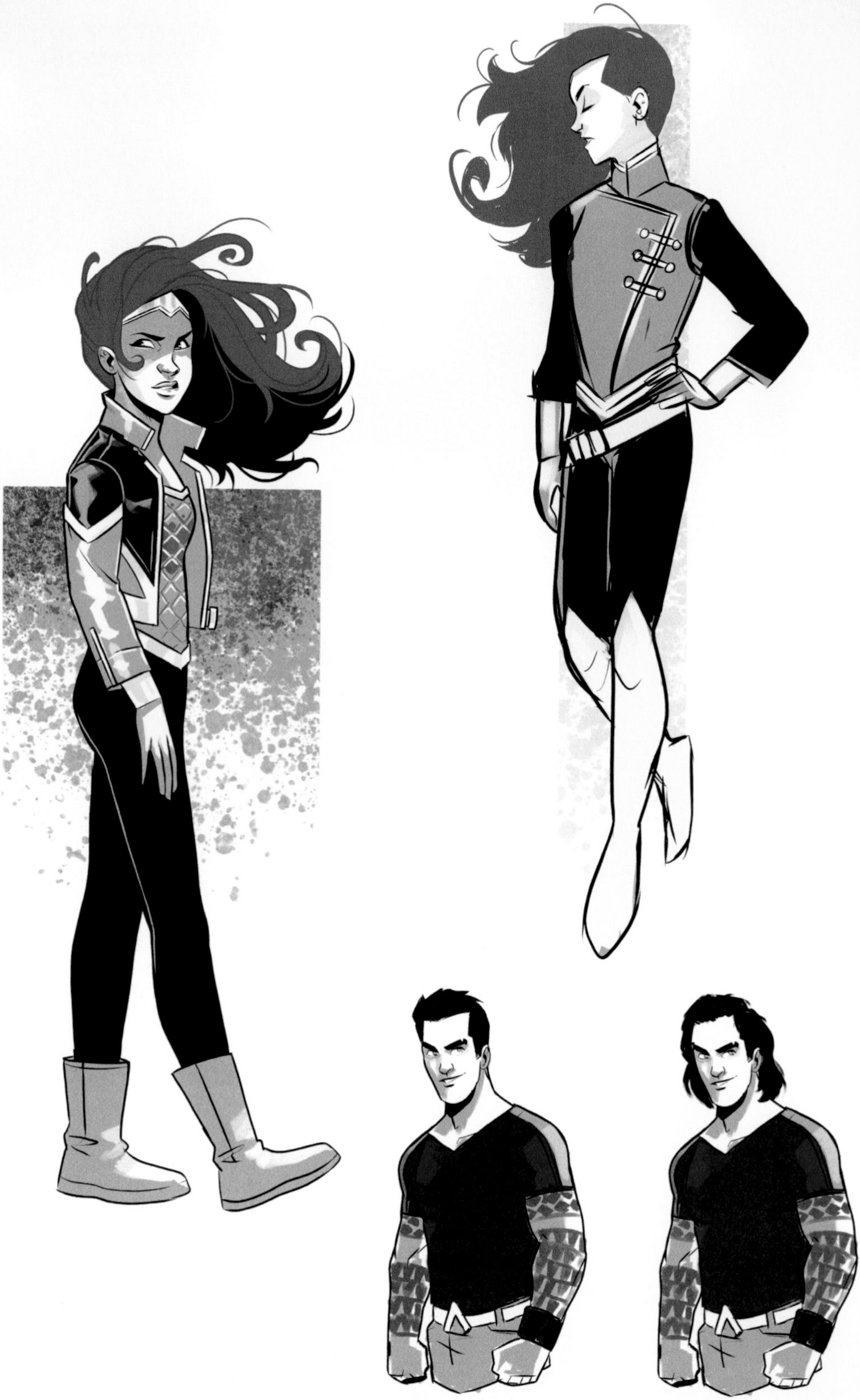

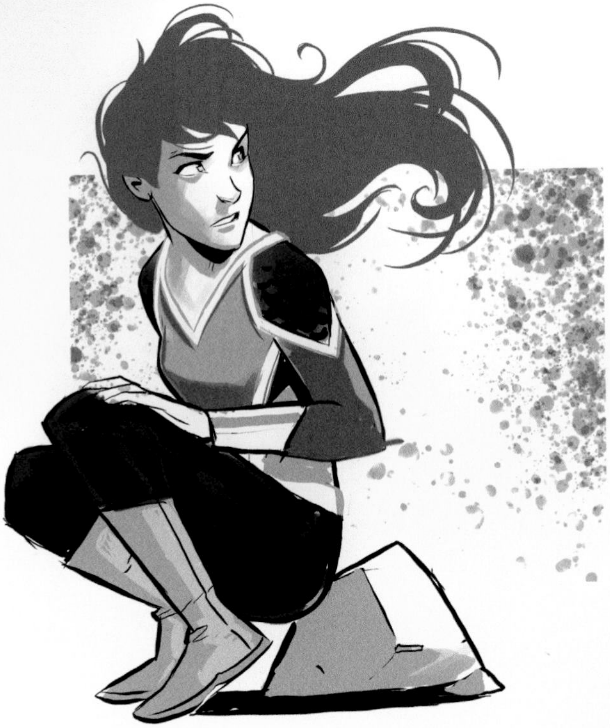

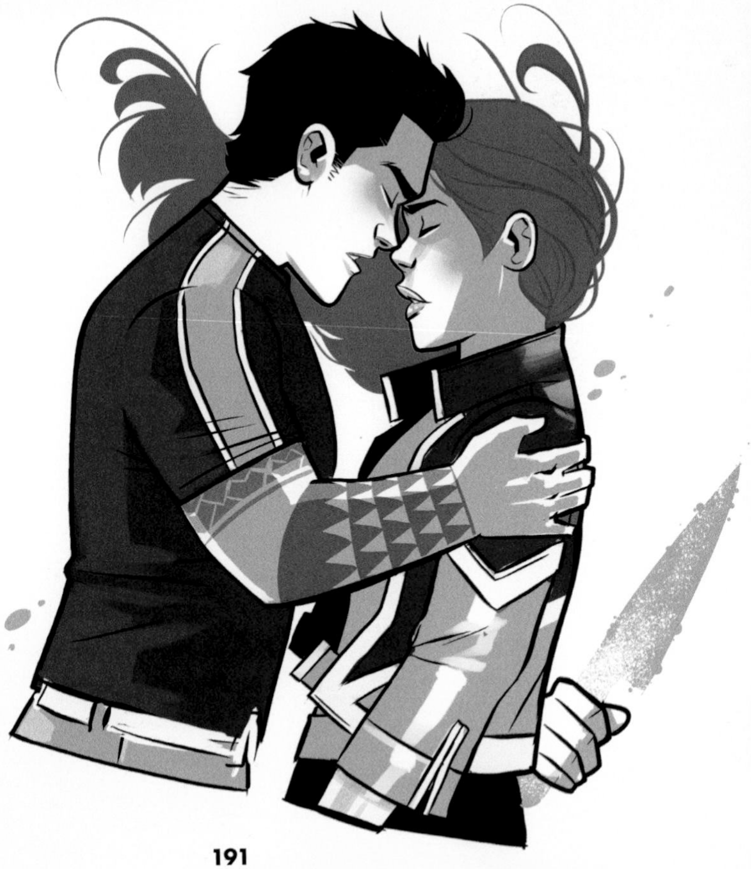

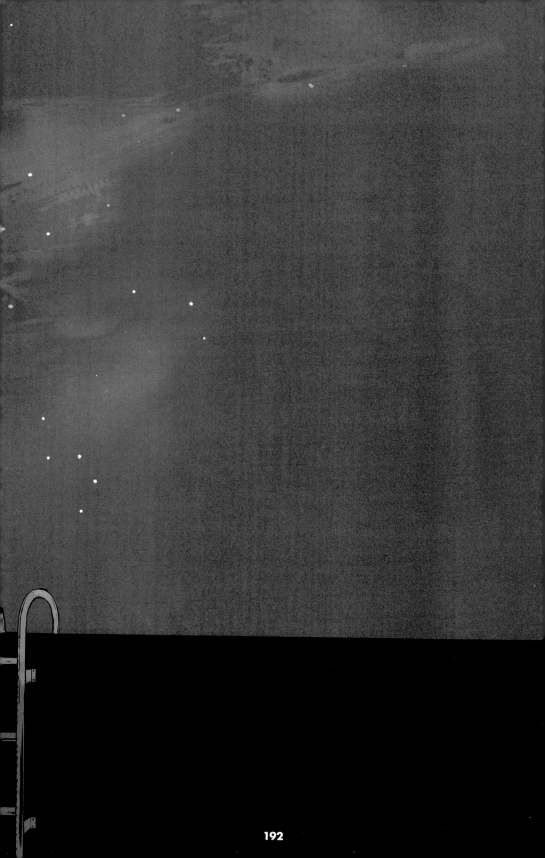

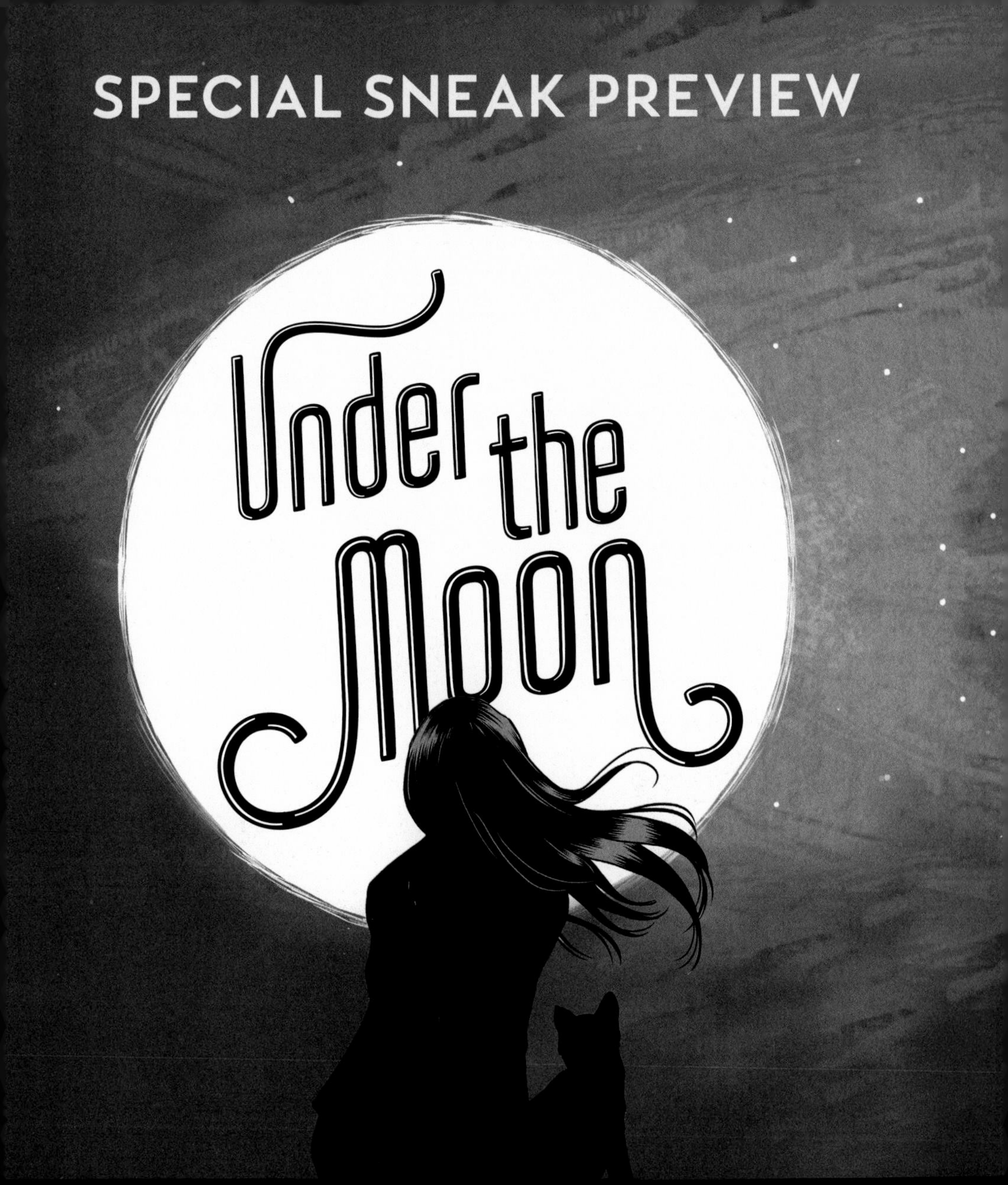
SPECIAL SNEAK PREVIEW
Under the Moon

ONE PURRRFECT MOMENT

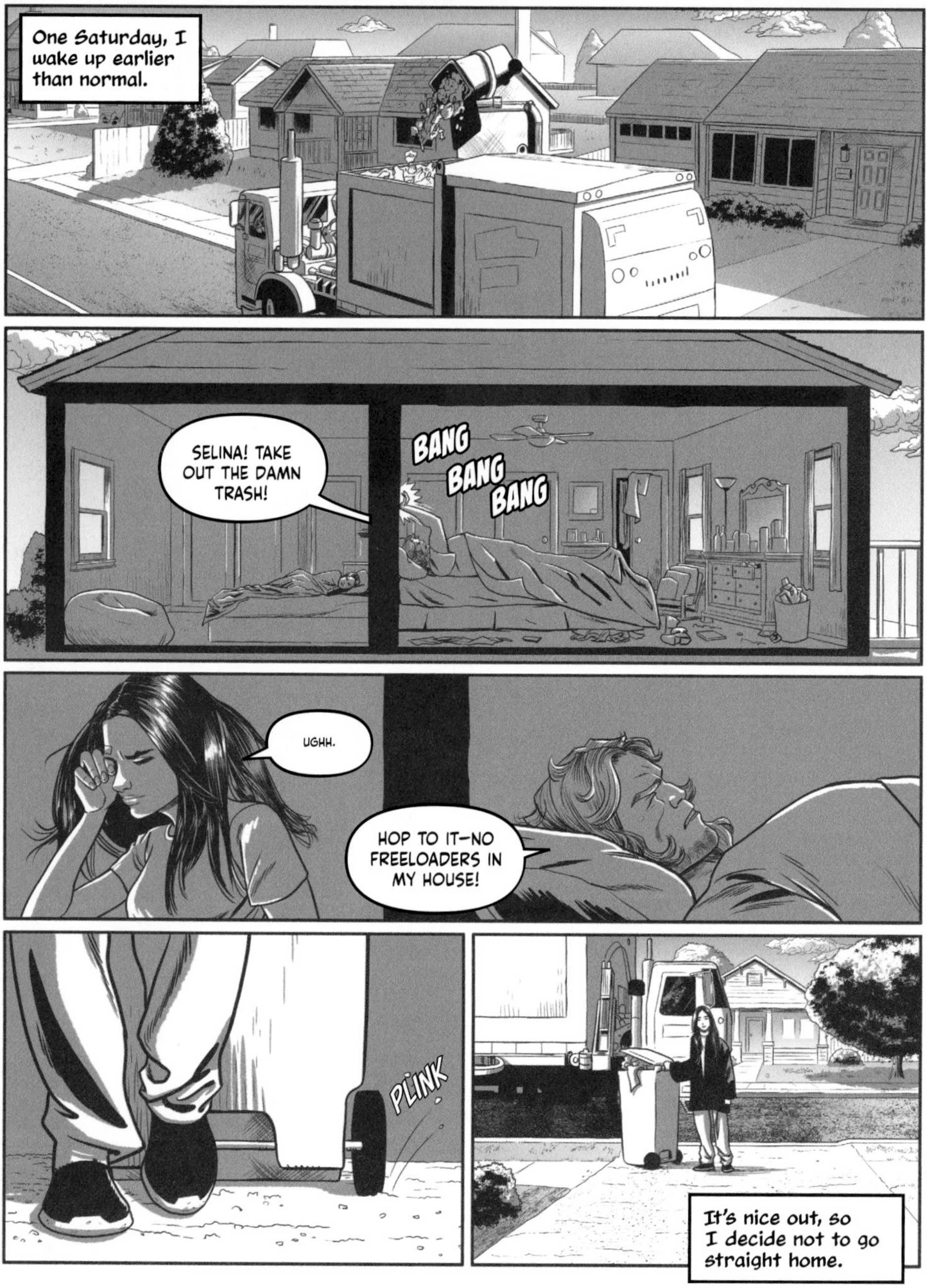
One Saturday, I wake up earlier than normal.
SELINA! TAKE OUT THE DAMN TRASH!
BANG
BANG
BANG
UGHH.
HOP TO IT—NO FREELOADERS IN MY HOUSE!
PLINK
It's nice out, so I decide not to go straight home.

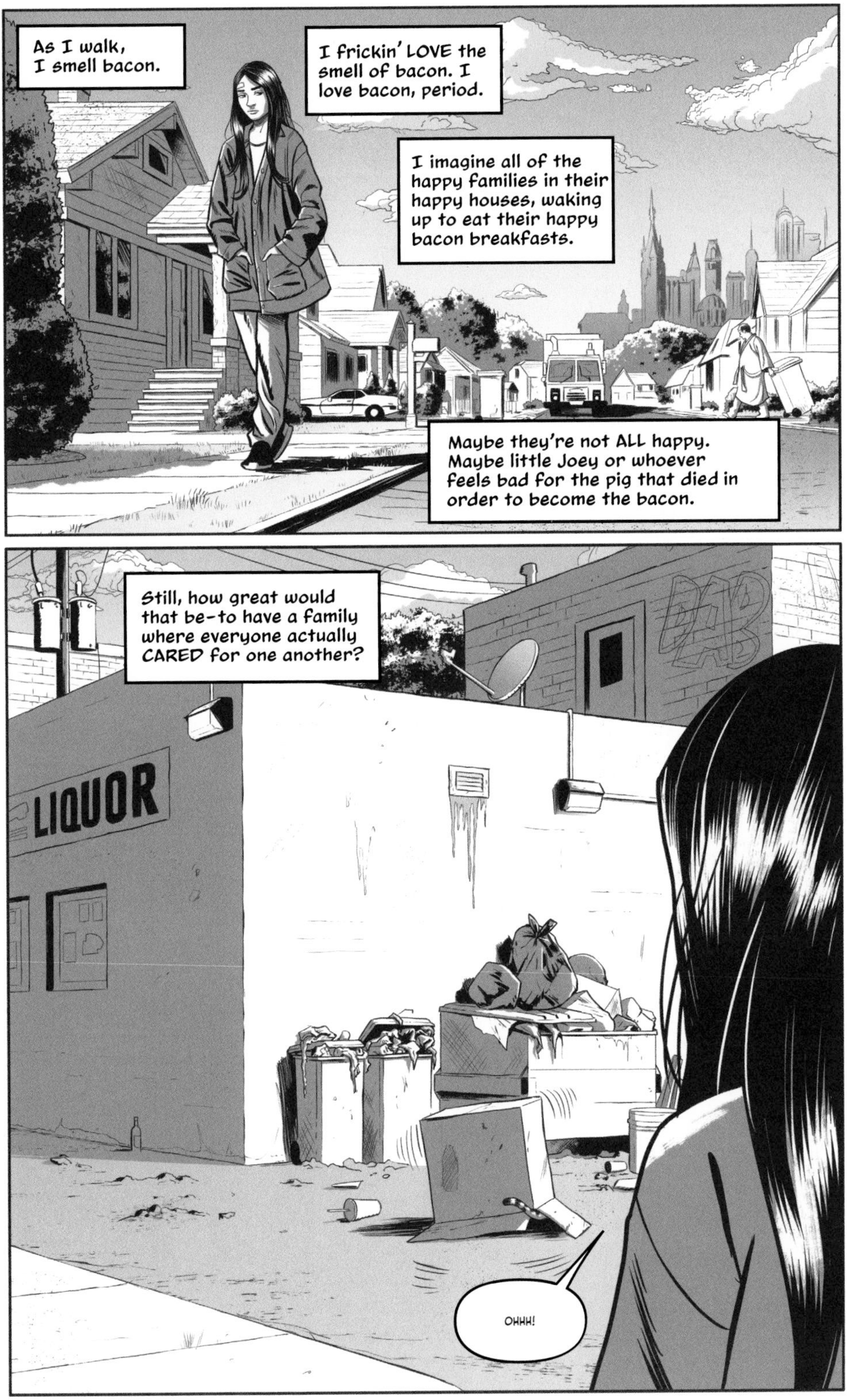
As I walk, I smell bacon.
I frickin' LOVE the smell of bacon. I love bacon, period.
I imagine all of the happy families in their happy houses, waking up to eat their happy bacon breakfasts.
Maybe they're not ALL happy. Maybe little Joey or whoever feels bad for the pig that died in order to become the bacon.
Still, how great would that be–to have a family where everyone actually CARED for one another?
LIQUOR
OHHH!

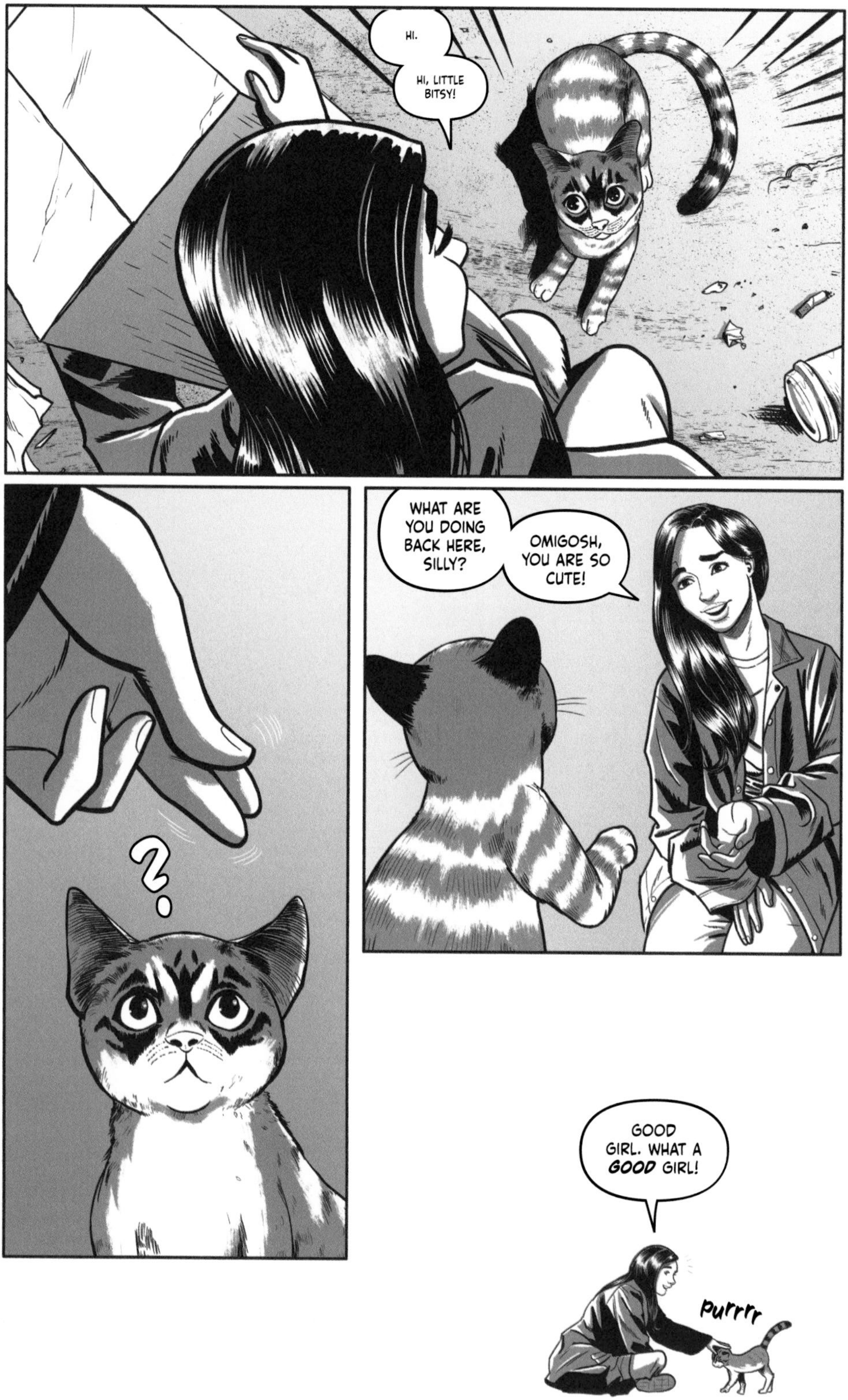
HI.
HI, LITTLE BITSY!
?
WHAT ARE YOU DOING BACK HERE, SILLY?
OMIGOSH, YOU ARE SO CUTE!
GOOD GIRL. WHAT A **GOOD** GIRL!
purrrr

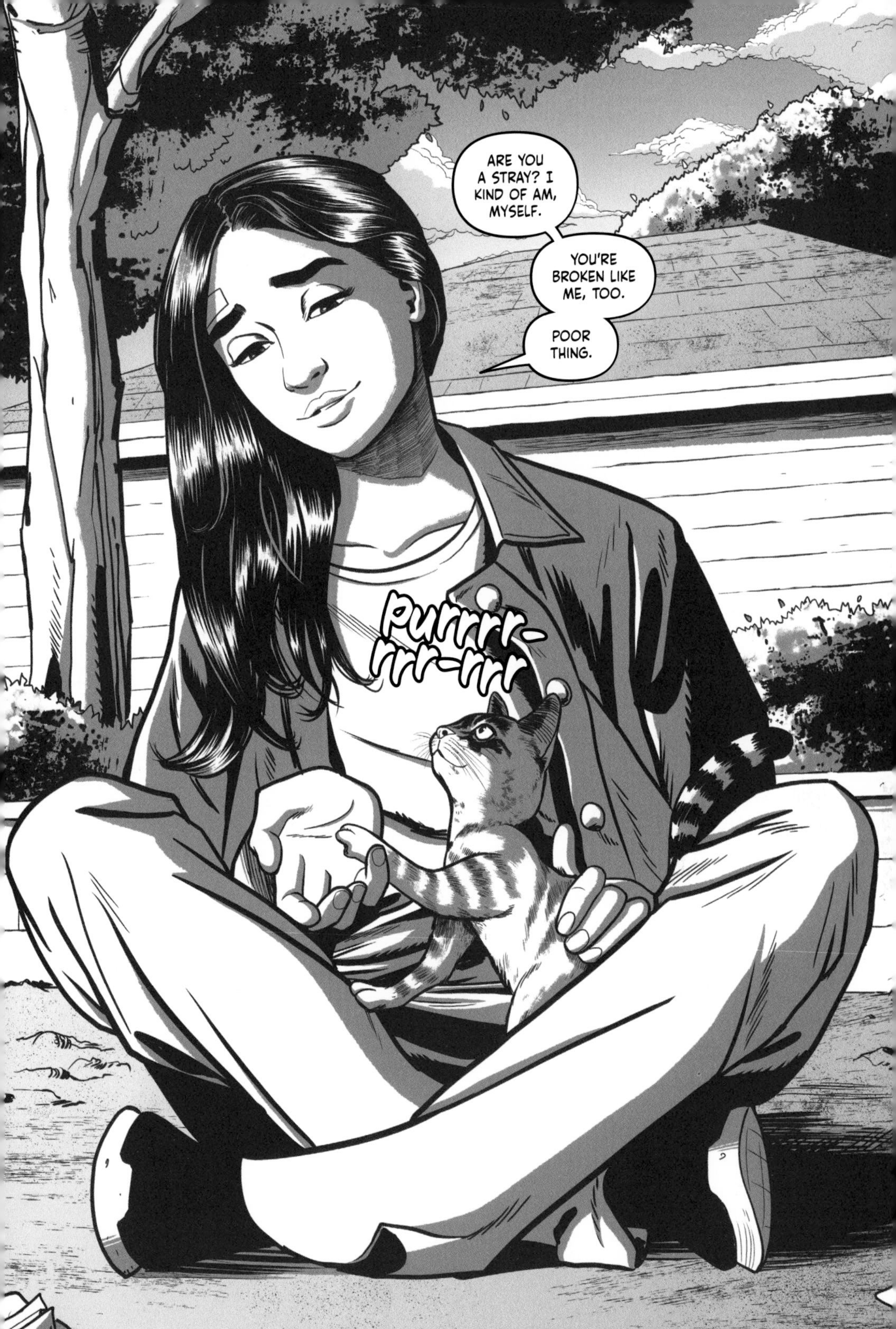
ARE YOU A STRAY? I KIND OF AM, MYSELF.
YOU'RE BROKEN LIKE ME, TOO.
POOR THING.
purrrr-rrr-rrr

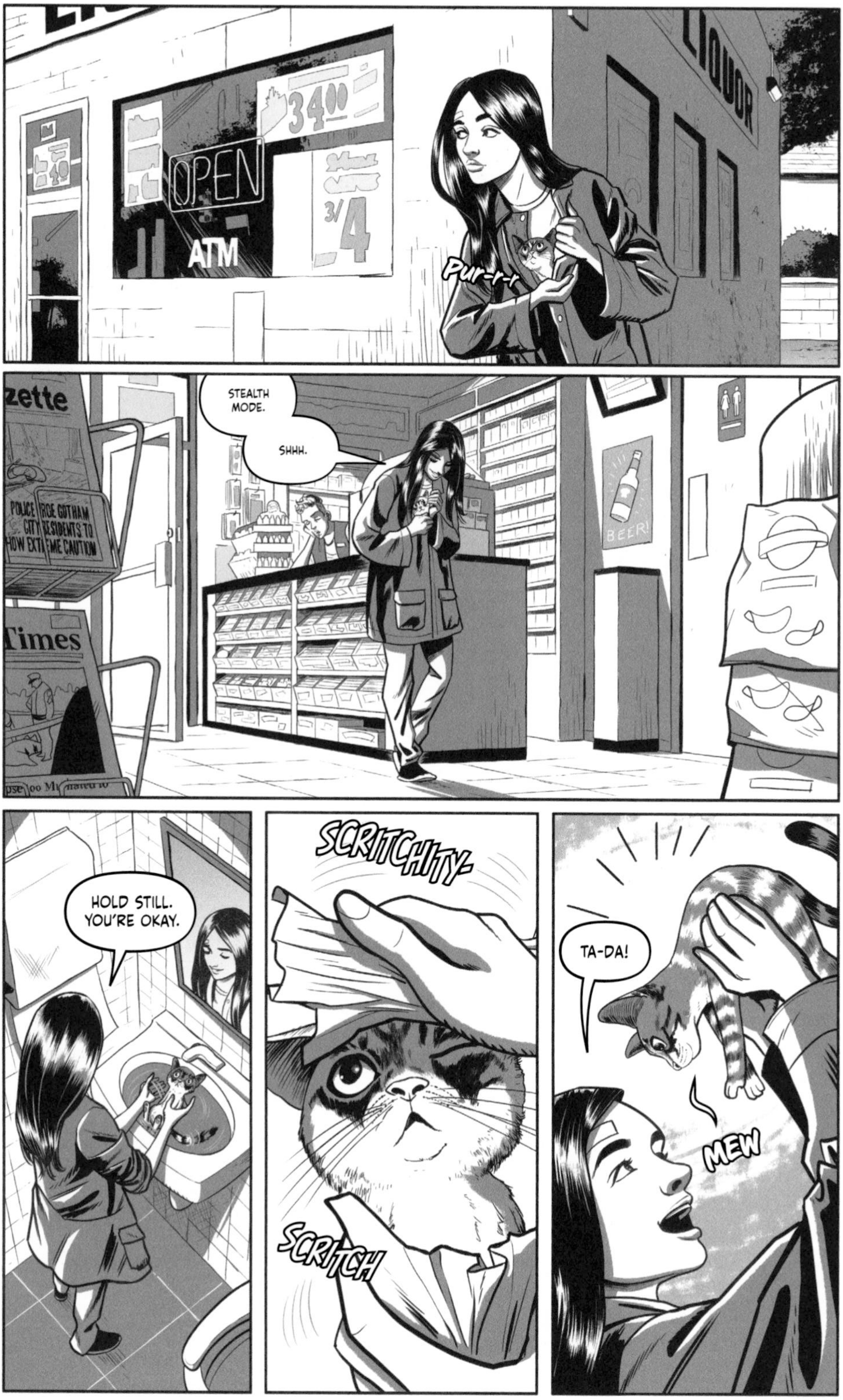
LIQUOR
OPEN
ATM
3/4
Pur-r-r
STEALTH MODE.
SHHH.
Times
BEER!
HOLD STILL. YOU'RE OKAY.
SCRITCHITY-
SCRITCH
TA-DA!
MEW

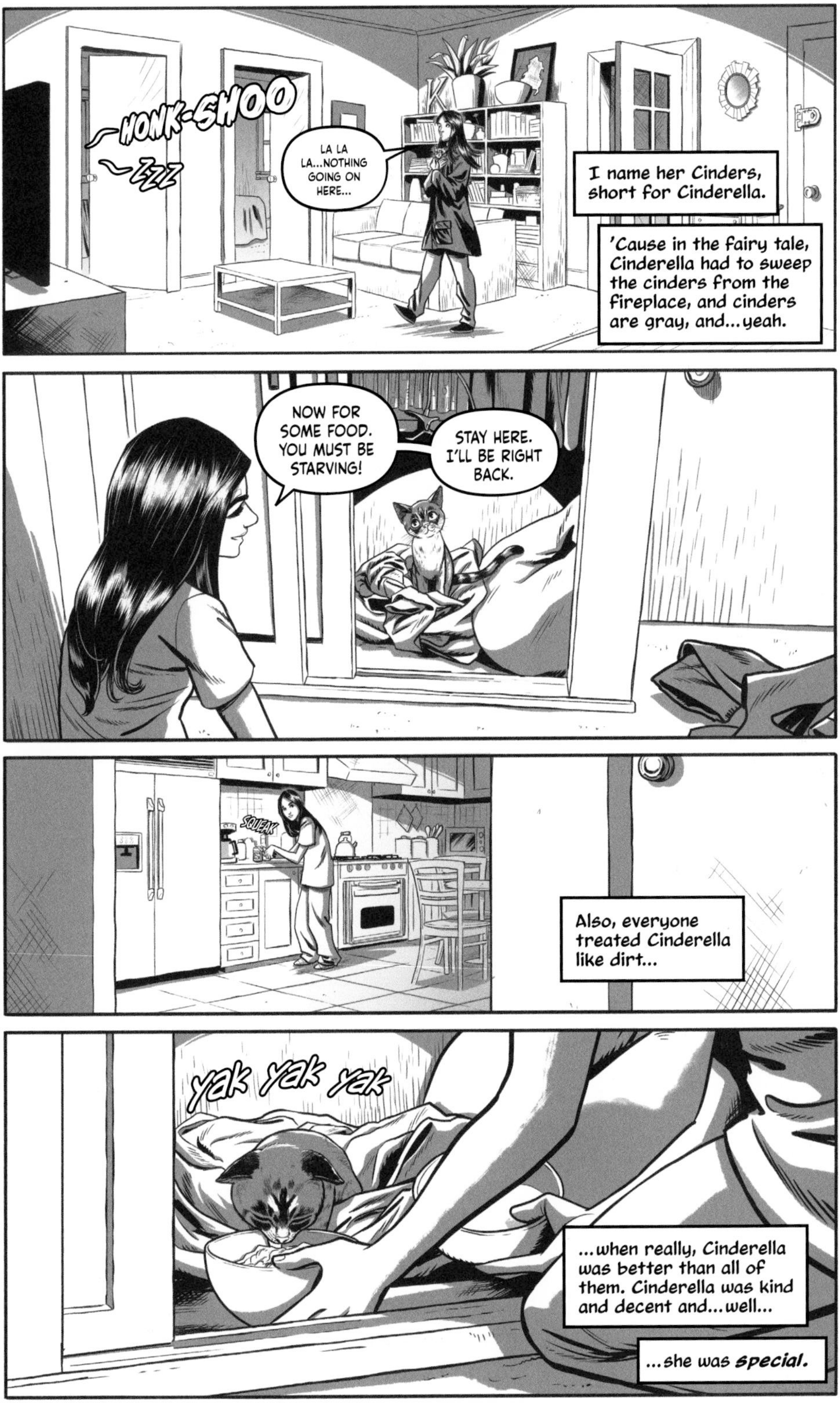
~HONK-SHOO
~ZZZ
LA LA LA...NOTHING GOING ON HERE...
I name her Cinders, short for Cinderella.
'Cause in the fairy tale, Cinderella had to sweep the cinders from the fireplace, and cinders are gray, and...yeah.
NOW FOR SOME FOOD. YOU MUST BE STARVING!
STAY HERE. I'LL BE RIGHT BACK.
SQUEAK
Also, everyone treated Cinderella like dirt...
yak yak yak
...when really, Cinderella was better than all of them. Cinderella was kind and decent and...well...
...she was *special.*

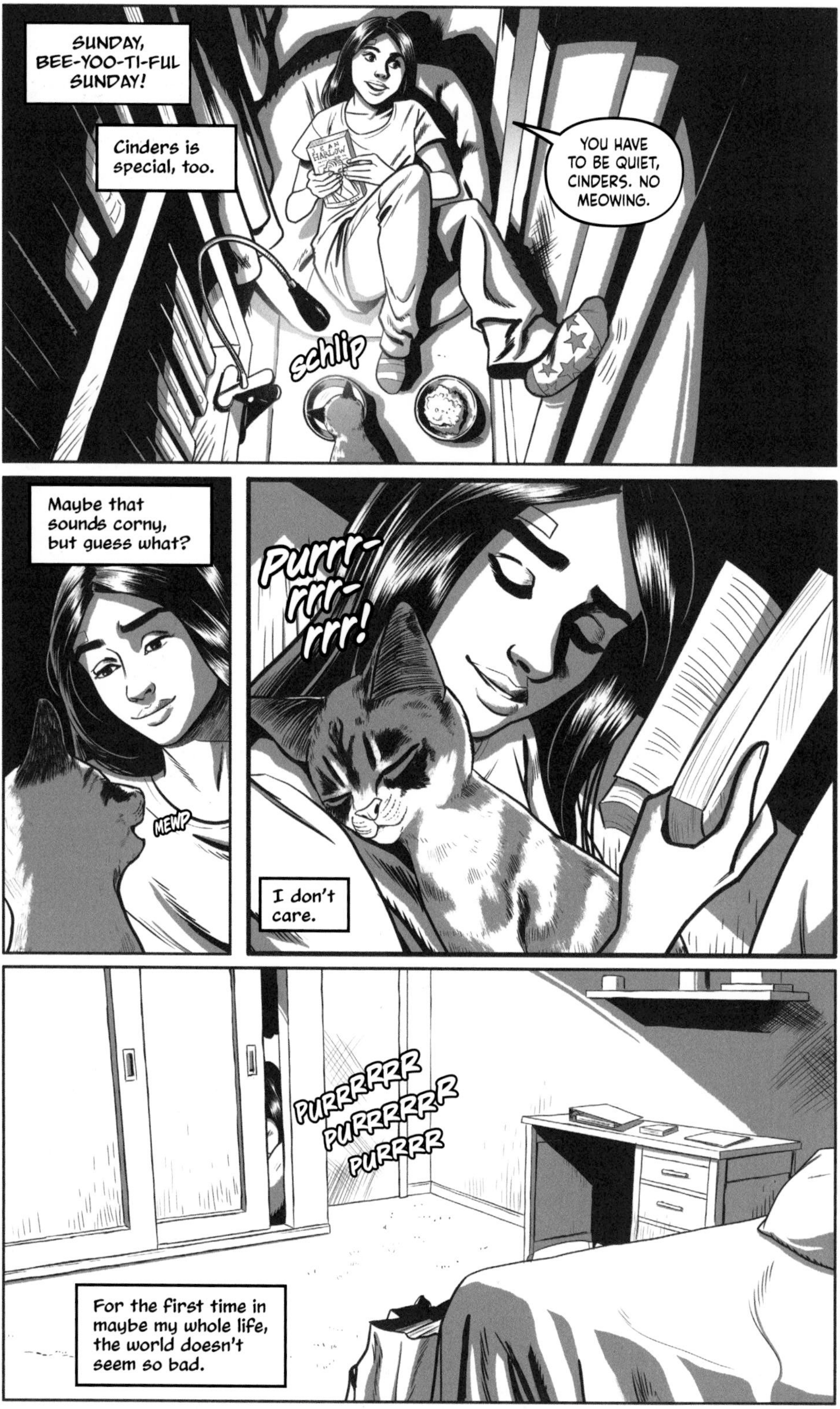
SUNDAY, BEE-YOO-TI-FUL SUNDAY!
Cinders is special, too.
YOU HAVE TO BE QUIET, CINDERS. NO MEOWING.
JEAN HARLOW
schlip
Maybe that sounds corny, but guess what?
MEWP
Purrr-rrr-rrr!
I don't care.
PURRRRRR PURRRRRR PURRRR
For the first time in maybe my whole life, the world doesn't seem so bad.

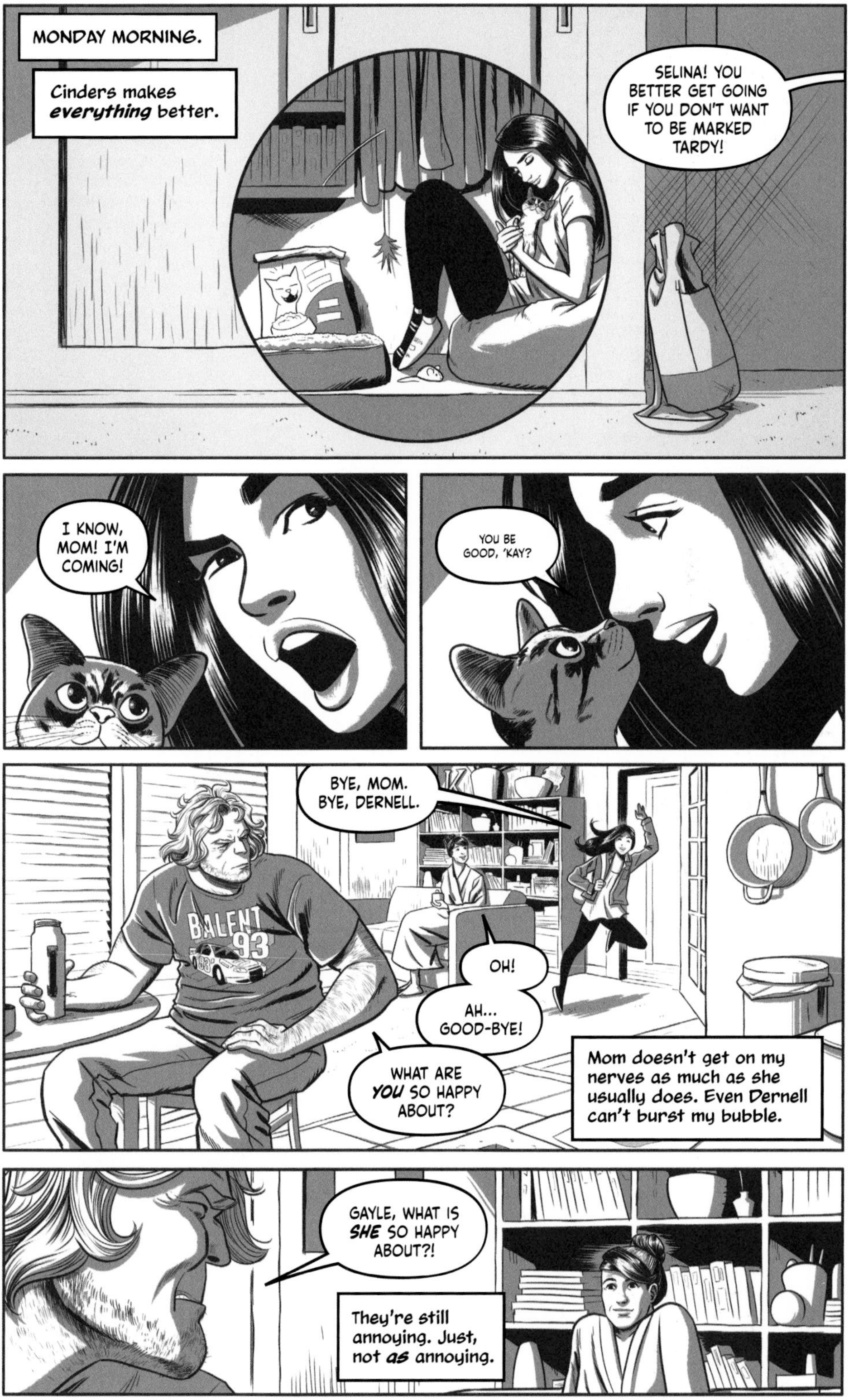
MONDAY MORNING.
Cinders makes *everything* better.
SELINA! YOU BETTER GET GOING IF YOU DON'T WANT TO BE MARKED TARDY!
I KNOW, MOM! I'M COMING!
YOU BE GOOD, 'KAY?
BYE, MOM. BYE, DERNELL.
OH!
AH... GOOD-BYE!
WHAT ARE *YOU* SO HAPPY ABOUT?
Mom doesn't get on my nerves as much as she usually does. Even Dernell can't burst my bubble.
GAYLE, WHAT IS *SHE* SO HAPPY ABOUT?!
They're still annoying. Just, not *as* annoying.

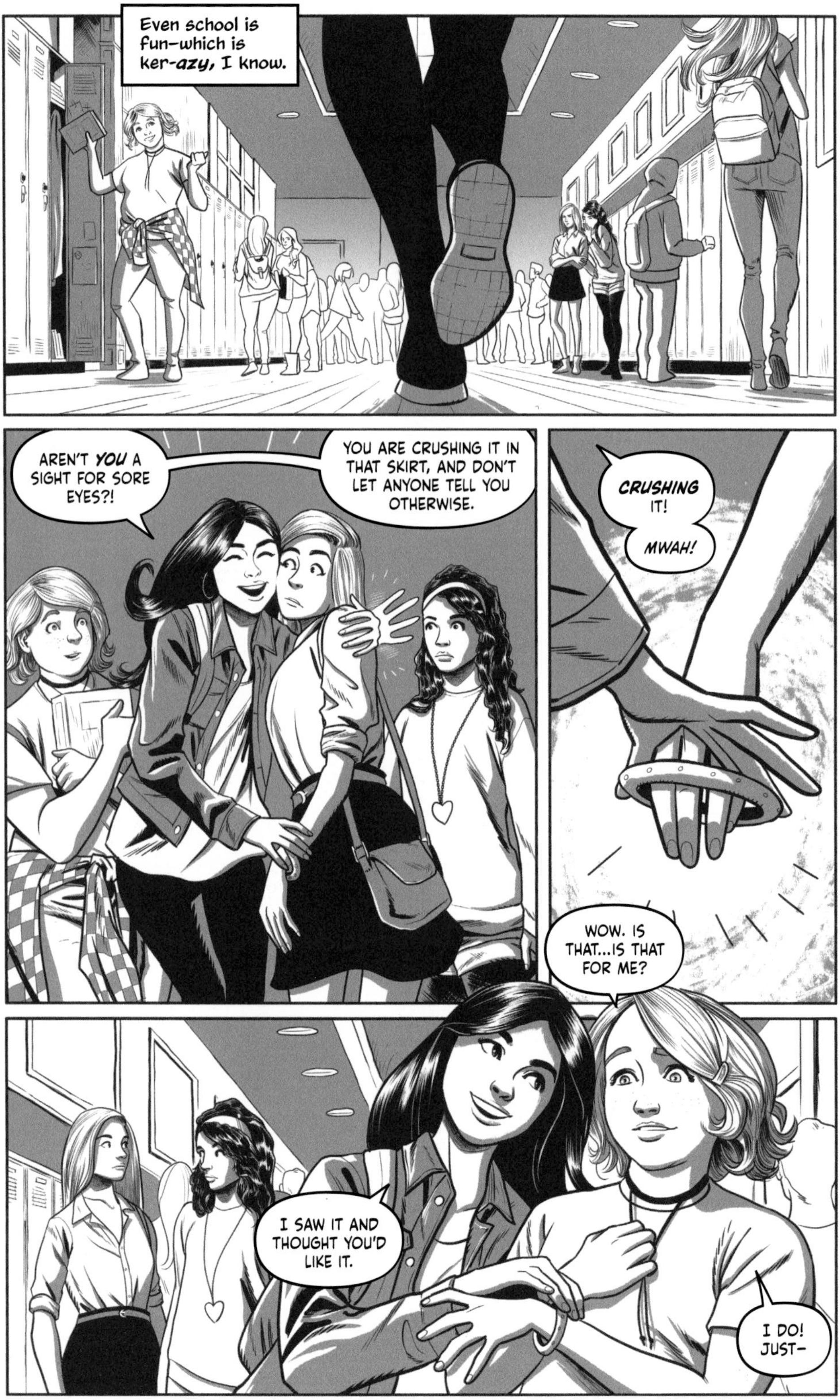

Even school is fun—which is ker-*azy,* I know.
AREN'T *YOU* A SIGHT FOR SORE EYES?!
YOU ARE CRUSHING IT IN THAT SKIRT, AND DON'T LET ANYONE TELL YOU OTHERWISE.
CRUSHING IT!
MWAH!
WOW. IS THAT...IS THAT FOR ME?
I SAW IT AND THOUGHT YOU'D LIKE IT.
I DO! JUST—

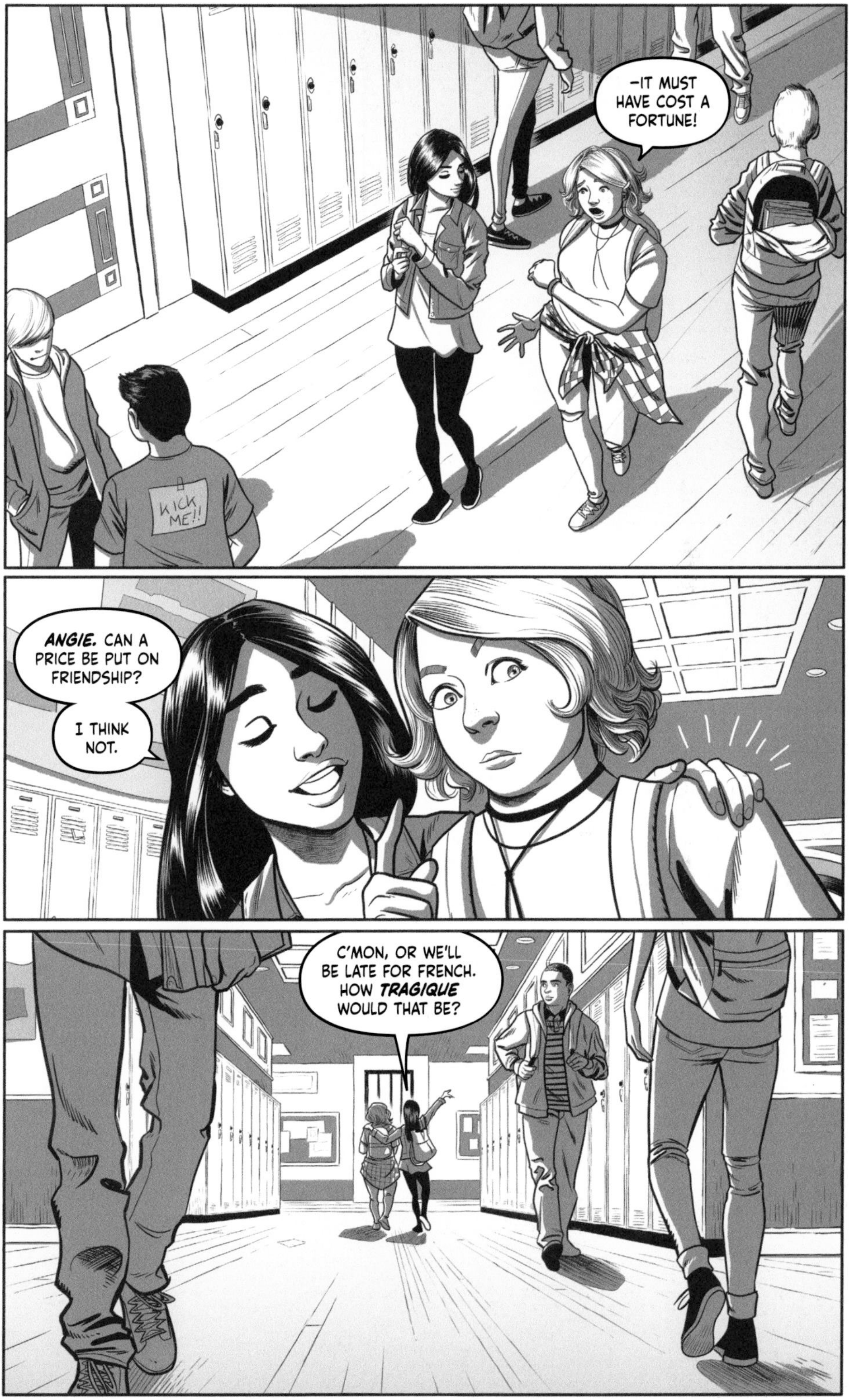
–IT MUST HAVE COST A FORTUNE!
KICK ME!!
ANGIE. CAN A PRICE BE PUT ON FRIENDSHIP?
I THINK NOT.
C'MON, OR WE'LL BE LATE FOR FRENCH. HOW TRAGIQUE WOULD THAT BE?

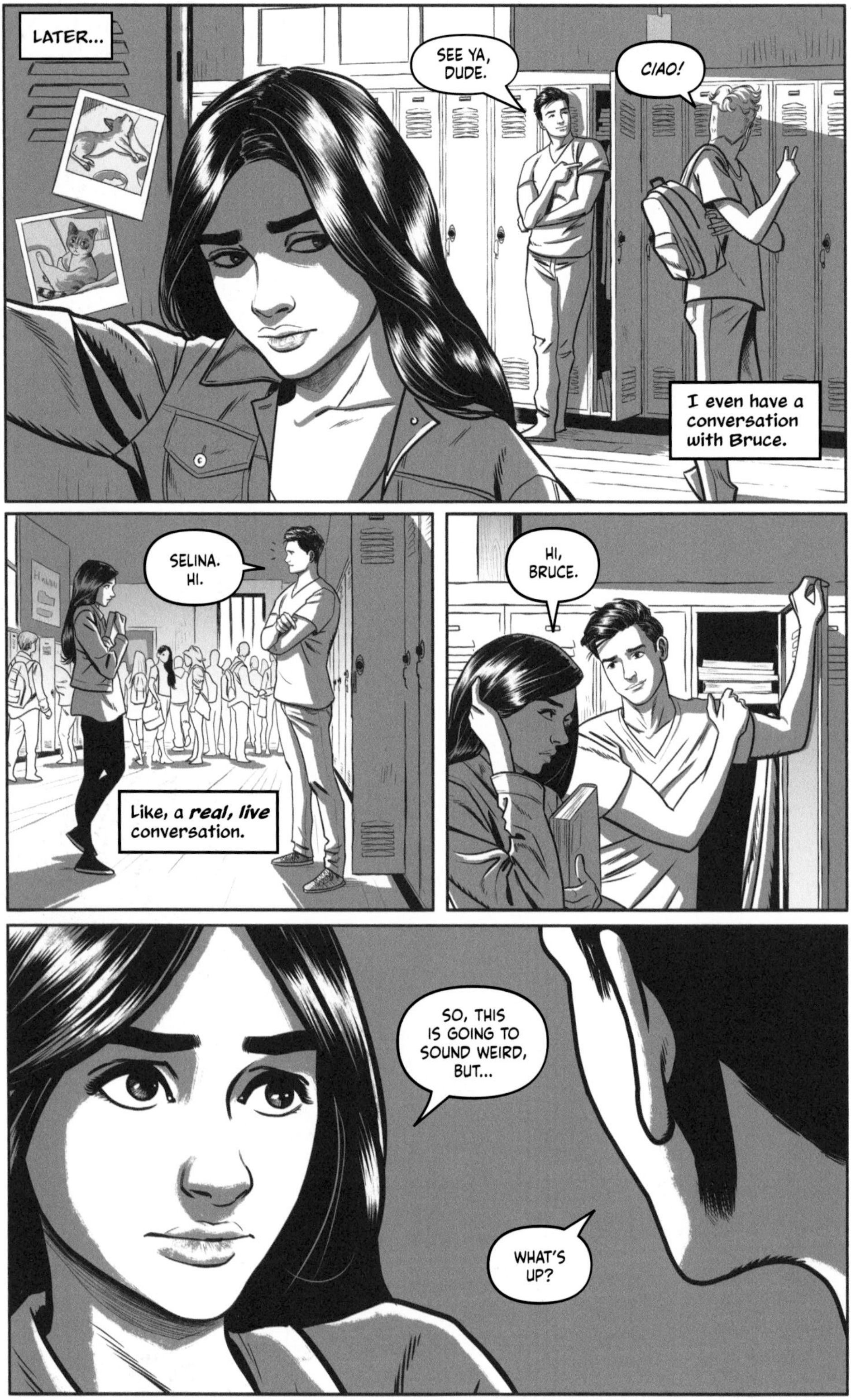
LATER...
SEE YA, DUDE.
CIAO!
I even have a conversation with Bruce.
SELINA. HI.
Like, a real, live conversation.
HI, BRUCE.
SO, THIS IS GOING TO SOUND WEIRD, BUT...
WHAT'S UP?

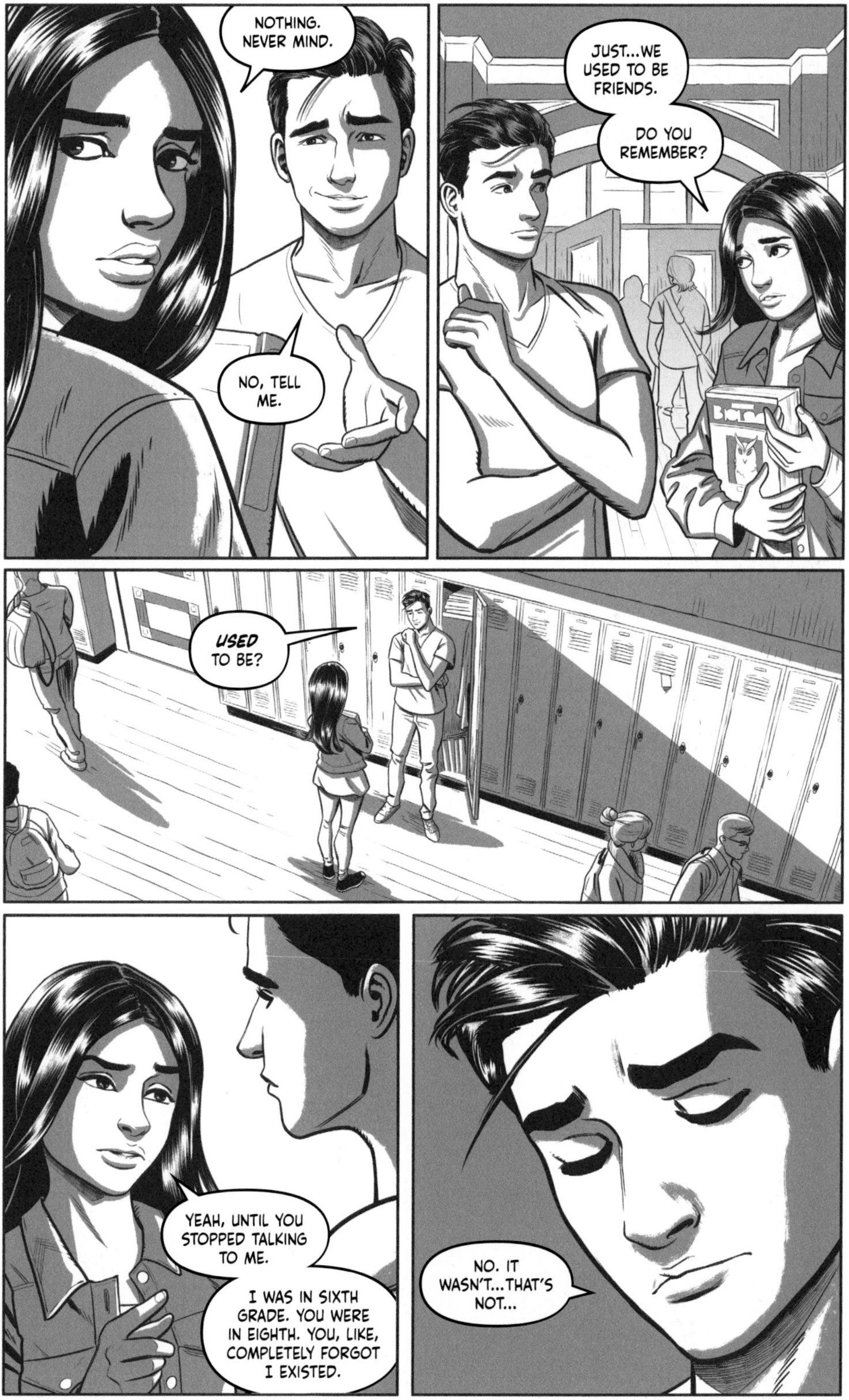
NOTHING. NEVER MIND.
NO, TELL ME.
JUST...WE USED TO BE FRIENDS.
DO YOU REMEMBER?
USED TO BE?
YEAH, UNTIL YOU STOPPED TALKING TO ME.
I WAS IN SIXTH GRADE. YOU WERE IN EIGHTH. YOU, LIKE, COMPLETELY FORGOT I EXISTED.
NO. IT WASN'T...THAT'S NOT...

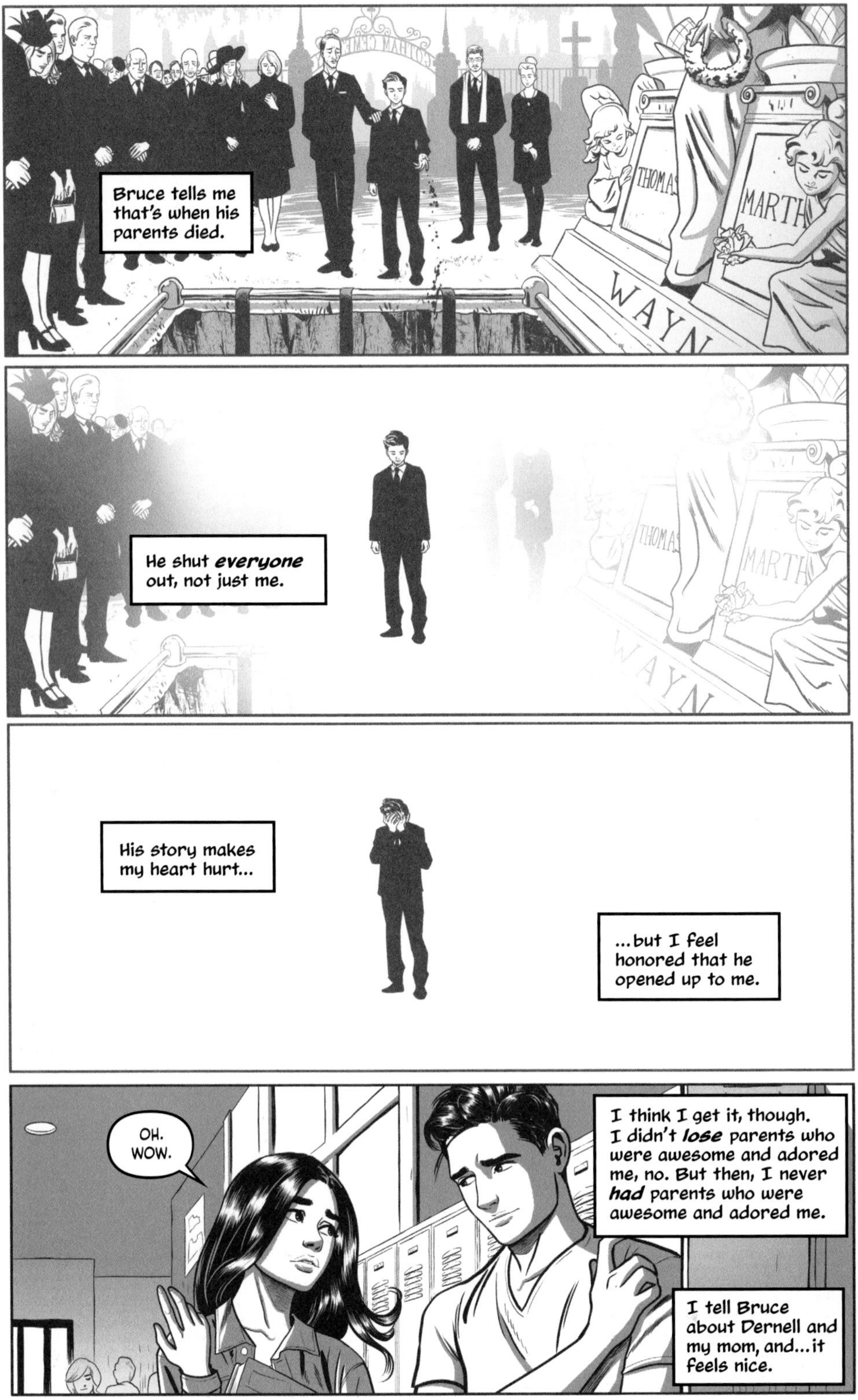
Bruce tells me that's when his parents died.
He shut ***everyone*** out, not just me.
His story makes my heart hurt...
...but I feel honored that he opened up to me.
OH. WOW.
I think I get it, though. I didn't ***lose*** parents who were awesome and adored me, no. But then, I never ***had*** parents who were awesome and adored me.
I tell Bruce about Dernell and my mom, and...it feels nice.

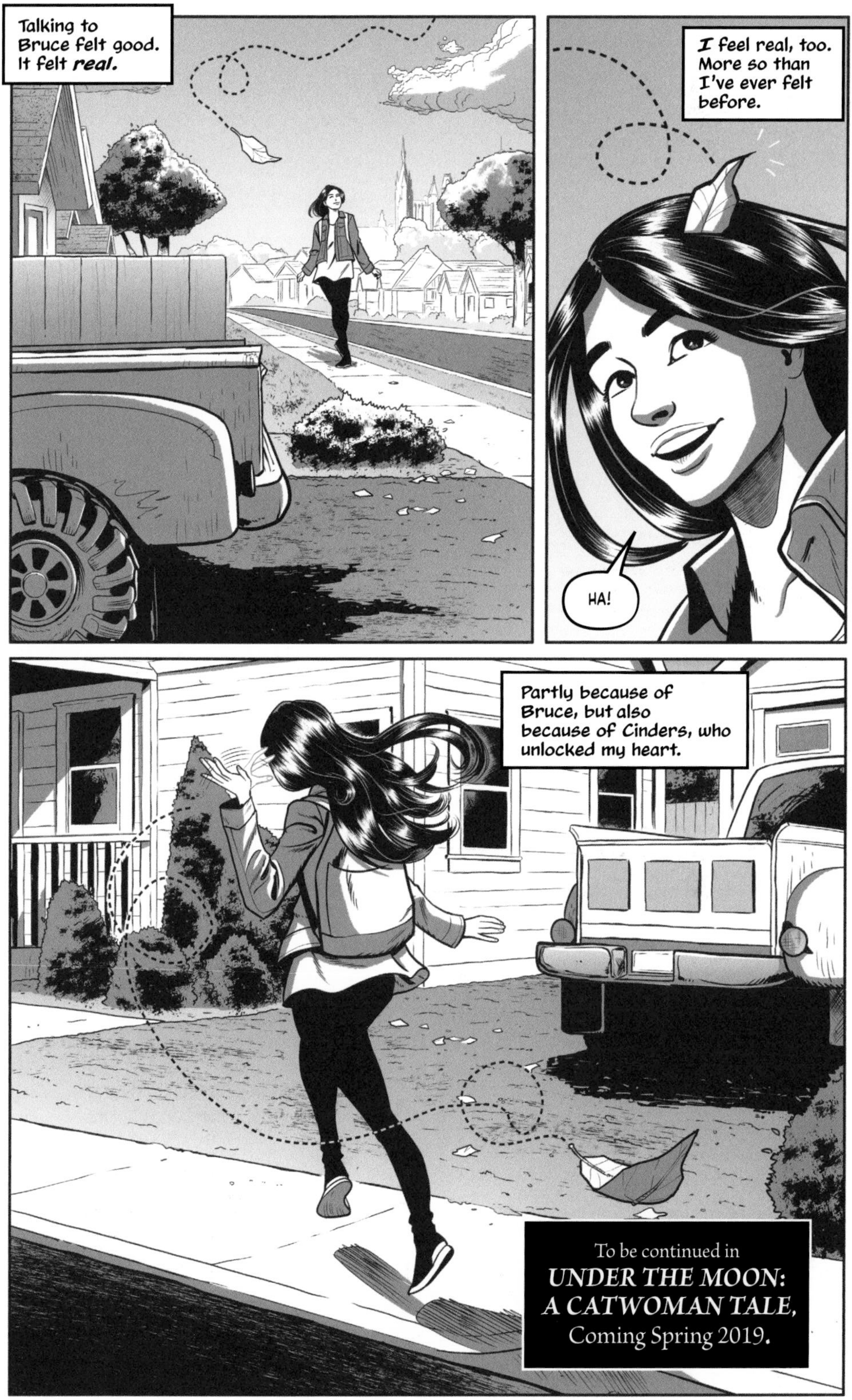
Talking to Bruce felt good. It felt ***real.***
I feel real, too. More so than I've ever felt before.
HA!
Partly because of Bruce, but also because of Cinders, who unlocked my heart.
To be continued in
UNDER THE MOON: A CATWOMAN TALE,
Coming Spring 2019.